# it's in his smile

## A RED RIVER VALLEY NOVEL

# Also by Shelly Alexander

*It's in His Heart*
*It's in His Touch*

# *it's in his* smile

### A RED RIVER VALLEY NOVEL

## SHELLY ALEXANDER

Text copyright © 2016 Shelly Alexander
All rights reserved.

Published by Montlake Romance, Seattle

www.apub.com

Amazon, the Amazon logo, and Montlake Romance are trademarks of Amazon.com, Inc., or its affiliates.

ISBN-13: 9781503936058
ISBN-10: 1503936058

Cover design by Laura Klynstra

Printed in the United States of America

*To my husband, who captured my heart with his smile
the first night we met.*

*To my mom, Frances, and her hilarious sidekick, Clyda.
When you two get to heaven, the angels will belly laugh
at your shenanigans.*

*To my dad, H1. I'll meet you in the back right-hand
corner of heaven someday.*

*To Mozart, a tiny toy poodle who is the newest addition
to our family. I never thought a five-pound pooch could
bring such joy.*

*And to the town of Red River, for being my muse and
my inspiration.*

# Chapter One

Miranda Cruz was sure that getting hot and bothered at a *wake* broke at least one of the unwritten rules of funeral etiquette. Especially since she was the hostess.

Ms. Bea, Miranda's friend and mentor, deserved more respect.

The scent of freshly baked oatmeal and raisin cookies drifted over the bar that separated the kitchen from the dining area, to fill the room and hopefully bring some comfort to the mourners. Miranda pulled the last batch from the oven and dished them onto a plate with a spatula.

The heat climbing up her legs to settle between her thighs was from the oven, right?

Right. Of course it was the oven. Or her black formfitting pants. She probably should've bought the next size up.

It definitely was *not* because of Bea's hot and handsome grandson, Talmadge. His mere presence was absolutely not the cause of her throat turning to chalk dust or her rusty girl parts turning a flip or her need to stay on the other side of the funeral parlor, the other side of the graveside service, and the other side of the room. All damn day. Until she felt like she'd been playing a game of keep-away, and he was it.

No, the heat seeping into every single inch of her five-feet-two-inch body was not because of Red River's prodigal son—a leader in green architecture made famous for his environmentally friendly designs and for bringing hotel chains around the world into the age of energy efficiency—come home to bury his beloved grandmother.

Definitely the oven. She kicked it closed with her black ankle-booted foot. With a toss, her oven mitt landed on the outdated Formica counter.

When she'd bought the small Victorian inn just off Red River's Main Street from Bea Oaks five months ago, she hadn't considered that her first public event would be to mourn the loss of her old friend. She hadn't considered that she'd have to figure out how to run an inn on her own without Bea's experience and advice. She hadn't considered that before opening for business, the renovations would chew up most of her savings from waiting tables since she was fifteen.

Obviously, Miranda needed to spend more time considering.

She waded through the ocean of mourners, offered condolences, sidestepped a few boxes of tile that her contractor still hadn't installed, and placed the fresh plate of cookies on the table of picked-over food.

She arranged a few serving dishes, straightened the stack of napkins, made sure enough clean silverware was available. And then she had no choice but to turn her attention to the roomful of saddened guests who had no idea how much Miranda was really going to miss Beatrice Oaks.

No one except . . .

Miranda's stare settled on Talmadge, who was standing on the far side of the inn's large dining room. His injured arm in a sling under his suit jacket, he chatted with a middle-aged couple.

For the tiniest moment, her heart beat in an odd cadence before it caught the right rhythm again.

She had known Talmadge would come to his grandmother's funeral. Of course he would. But a small part of her had hoped he wouldn't show. Another teensy weensy part of her had hoped he would. *Wouldn't. Would. Wouldn't. Would.*

And then there he had been, his broad shoulders filling the funeral parlor doorway. Eyes rimmed in red for the grandmother who'd raised him.

As they'd done then, her insides were back to doing the jive like she was a contestant on *Dancing with the Stars.* Or a pole dancer at a gentlemen's club. Because Miranda was pretty sure that only a person of questionable habits would have carnal thoughts at a funeral.

Another wave of heat flamed through her. *Gah!*

Sandy hair slicked back, Talmadge's strong jaw moved as he spoke to the middle-aged couple. Midsentence he turned and locked gazes with Miranda like he knew she'd been watching him. His lips stopped moving, and he just stared at her.

The hint of a smile settled onto his lips, and she suddenly found it hard to breathe.

Her gaze flitted away, and she offered a kind word to a guest who walked past, then busied herself with rearranging the food. Maybe the ham should go next to the mashed potatoes? Should her homemade oatmeal cookies really be next to the sauerkraut? And should her obnoxious female pheromones be spewing sexual attraction so close to the deviled eggs?

That might actually be a health department violation, now that she thought about it. *Note to self: no pheromone spewing when the inspectors come to give their stamp of approval.*

Talmadge returned his attention to the couple, shook the man's hand, and headed . . . toward *her.*

Miranda swallowed and looked around for any excuse to avoid speaking to the famous Talmadge Oaks. The man who walked on water—as far as *Architectural Digest* was concerned—and raised out-of-practice girl parts from the dead.

*Aha!*

Ms. Bea's toy poodle huddled in the corner of the dining room and watched the crowd while tremors of fear racked his tiny body. Miranda hustled over to him.

She was being silly, right? So what if she'd crushed on Talmadge since she was in ninth grade. Who cared that he was the only man who made Miranda's insides go all molten and quivering just as much now, at twenty-eight. She was a grown woman! It was time to stop running from him. She'd been avoiding him during his rare visits to Red River for so many years she'd lost count.

Actually, no. No, she hadn't. It had been seven years since she'd decided to never cross paths with Talmadge Oaks again. Seven years, three months, and twelve days, but who was counting?

Talmadge worked his way through the crowd toward her, shaking hands and speaking to the guests as he passed. His stare kept returning to her, and his progress didn't slow. He kept coming. And kept coming. And kept coming.

*Grown woman my ass.* A girl was never too old to play keep-away, and it was time to run before she became "it."

She scooped up the dog and patted the beige mound of fur on top of his little head. "You need to pee, Lloyd," she informed him. She raced down the hall and eased out the back door.

The screen door banged shut behind her, and she nudged the wood swing into motion as she walked across the wraparound porch and descended the stairs. Wheeler Peak was stark white with snow against the blue New Mexico sky, and a few end-of-the-season skiers dotted the slopes. The chairlift creaked as it eased up the face of the powdered mountain, mostly empty because it was the middle of the week.

"Go on, boy." She set Lloyd on the snowy ground and tried to shoo him toward the evergreens that separated the inn from the ski lodge and gave it a quaint air of privacy.

He looked up at her and sniffed as though she'd just asked him to compete in the Iditarod.

Shivering against the mid-April cold, she rubbed the arms of her gray sweater and studied the thawing icicles that hung from the weathered eaves of the porch. Her contractor should've sanded and repainted those already. A prickle of worry shimmied up her spine. Her contractor should also show up for work once in awhile.

Someone inside lifted a window in the dining room. Muffled voices spilled out along with the sound of silverware clinking against plates. Talmadge's deep voice drifted out and coiled and curled around her. A voice so smooth it should be bottled and sold as an aphrodisiac.

She tossed her long black curls over a shoulder and stepped farther away from the window.

A high-pitched squeal from a pair of female skiers riding the chairlift sent Lloyd scurrying under the picnic table that was pushed against the peeling white siding of the inn. Miranda peeked underneath. A small mound of trembling beige fur huddled against the wall.

"It's okay, Lloyd." She patted her knee, but he trembled harder. She eased onto her hands and knees in the snow and scooted under the table, a hand outstretched to coax the dog out. He whimpered and cowered against the wall.

"Let's go, Lloyd." Her tone bloomed into that of a Disney princess. "It's really cold out here, buddy." She smooched for the dog to come.

The dog plastered himself to the wall and shook like a bowl of Jell-O.

Miranda reached for him.

"Dude, I'm putting this on YouTube," a guy said from behind her.

She tossed a look over one shoulder and did a double take. Two stringy-haired teenaged snowboarders held up their phones.

Recording her.

On all fours.

With her ass pointing right at them.

"Hey!" she yelled at Frick and Frack. Gossip in this town already flew at the speed of light. One compromising situation could set tongues wagging for years. "Stop that! You are *not* putting me on YouTube."

Thank God she was wearing pants. Even if they were a little too formfitting. Formfitting was the style. And they showed off her curves, made her feel more confident. Ms. Bea had raved about Miranda's figure when she wore these pants.

She just never thought her ass would end up on YouTube while she was at her friend's wake.

One of the snowboarders snickered.

Miranda's voice softened to a coo. "Lloyd, the show we're putting on is over." She reached for the dog, stretching, stretching . . . *damn these tight pants*. Her fingertips brushed against his curly fur. Just a little farther and she could grab him around the belly.

Her tongue slid between her teeth, and she reached that extra few inches . . .

A loud rip echoed through the entire Red River Valley.

At least it sounded that loud to her. Cold air slid over her silk undies and the bared back of her thighs, the chill biting at her skin.

"Hellfire," Miranda said.

"*Dude!* This one's gonna get a ton of views!" said Frick.

The searing heat of humiliation singed every nerve ending in her body. A feeling she was well acquainted with. A feeling that had shadowed her since she was a kid, sunk its teeth into her, and refused to let go because of a mother who'd been the center of town gossip for years, her colorful past with men the cause of whispers and taunts. Hell, her mother didn't even know who the fathers of her two children were.

Some people in Red River had kept track of her mom's long string of boyfriends, though. Every single one. Until her mother moved to the next town.

"Sweet," Frack joined in. "She's definitely not a dude."

*Oh, for God's sake.* She snagged the dog with one hand and pulled him to her.

"Get lost, boys." Just three words, but Talmadge's voice was firm. Authoritative. The voice of a leader.

*Aaaaand* the singe in her nerve endings turned to a five-alarm fire.

Frick and Frack stumbled over each other, gathered up their boards, and mumbled, "Yes, sir." Miranda could see their legs disappear around the corner, presumably headed for the lift.

"Miranda?" Talmadge asked, but his tone held no doubt as to her identity. He knew the ass greeting him was hers.

Miranda scrambled backward so fast her head connected with the edge of the table. "Ow!" Her free hand flew to the pain that lanced through the top of her head, but her hair caught in a sliver of the rotting wood. "Ah!"

Her eyes clamped shut.

"Stay still." Talmadge bent and managed to free her hair from the headlock the table had her in. Unfortunately, keeping her eyes shut couldn't protect her from the awkwardness of the situation. She straightened. Ignored the incinerating heat that crept up her neck. Focused on the owner of that almost edible voice.

And finally forced her eyes open only to realize she was on her knees, eye-level with Talmadge Oaks's crotch.

Another wave of heat nearly stole her breath. She swallowed, wanting to crawl back under the table.

He offered his good hand. "Let me help."

Miranda's gaze slid up the expensive fabric of his custom-cut suit that fit his tall frame to perfection. A thick, corded neck flexed with power when he spoke, or laughed . . . or just stood there doing nothing except looking like sex on two legs . . .

Miranda lost her train of thought and swallowed again.

With his usual air of confidence, he raised his brows.

Her attention snapped to his outstretched hand. "No! Um, I'm fine."

She tried to stand, but the dog squirmed. Afraid she might drop the fragile little guy, Miranda overcompensated and lost her footing. A powerful arm caught her around the waist and hauled her to her feet. Pressed her against a hard and hot body that towered at least a foot above the top of her head.

She landed against his firm chest and pressed one palm to it.

A brick wall of muscled stealth.

Her stare anchored on the slight dimple in his chin, then moved to his mouth. She lingered there for a second before looking up into silvery-blue eyes, and just like that, she was crushing on him all over again. Just like she had so many years ago in high school while he totally ignored her. Looked straight through her like she was invisible because she was three grades younger than him. The fact that he had been the quarterback of the football team didn't help either. A never-ending entourage of friends—both girls and guys—had followed him everywhere, vying for his attention, while Miranda worked every day after school, waiting tables at Cotton Eyed Joe's to help her irresponsible mother pay the bills.

No, Talmadge hadn't known she existed. Except for that one time seven years, three months, and twelve days ago.

Pressed between them, Lloyd yapped at Talmadge, who loosened his hold on Miranda but didn't let go.

"The dog needed a potty break." Miranda glanced at the trembling dog folded under her arm.

Talmadge's mouth curved just a tad. "That's a dog?"

"Um, yes. He's a poodle."

Surprise flared in Talmadge's expression. "That's a *he?*"

Lloyd's trembling slowed to a quiver. Like her stomach every time she looked at Talmadge Oaks.

A glint of mischief danced in his eyes. "It looks like something you found in a trap nibbling on a piece of cheese."

"He belonged to your grandmother."

Talmadge's brows slid together. His stare flitted to the dog, then back to her.

"His name is Lloyd," Miranda explained. "As in Frank Lloyd Wright."

Talmadge's eyes softened.

Which turned Miranda into a blubbering idiot.

"Because Frank Lloyd Wright's work is what inspired you to become an architect, and Bea said you used to study his projects in a book she gave you, and . . . um, yeah."

*Jesus, Mary, and Joseph.* Miranda almost made the sign of the cross. Instead she pulled her lip between her teeth and bit down to shut herself up.

"I didn't know Bea got a dog." That almost-smile that never quite formed into a full-on grin and always seemed to hold a hint of sadness appeared on his lips, and Talmadge stared at Lloyd like he'd missed an important detail.

The bright blue bows in each of Lloyd's ears trembled in unison with his whimpers. When he pawed at Miranda's arm, his blue nail polish shimmered against the afternoon sun.

"She needed a companion since your grandpa's been gone and you stopped coming home." Miranda bit down on her lip again and nearly drew blood.

The hint of a smile on Talmadge's lips melted away, and something flashed in his eyes, turning them darker. He released her and took a step back.

*Dang.* Apparently some things never changed. Every time she was around Talmadge Oaks, her IQ somehow dropped to the level of a rock, vanishing along with her self-restraint. Good thing she hadn't spent a lot of time with him in the past. And even better that she didn't plan on spending any with him in the future.

———

Miranda Cruz wasn't a bouncy, gum-smacking kid anymore.

That fact had been hard to ignore ever since Talmadge first saw her standing in front of his grandmother's casket, tears flowing and black pants clinging. Every swipe at the wetness on her soft cheeks distracted him from her killer body and made him focus more on the woman she'd become. There for his grandmother when he wasn't. Even hosting the wake to honor Bea's memory and offer support to everyone at the funeral.

Except him.

Miranda Cruz was hard to ignore, period.

Impossible now that he'd walked outside to enjoy a few minutes alone in the frosty mountain air and had been greeted by her black panties and a firm, round bottom that would fit nicely in the palm of his hand.

"I mean it's none of my business that you stopped coming to visit Bea." Miranda plowed on, her unusual gold-brown eyes widening at her own words. "Um, I just meant she loved the dog, and she missed you." Her teeth caressed her bottom lip.

She turned her full attention to the shivering rat-dog, who apparently had belonged to his grandmother. Another detail in Bea's life she'd left out, always so careful not to make him feel guilty about his infrequent visits home. Always so mindful to not seem lonesome, even though she'd obviously been lonely enough to get a dog.

The secure, self-reliant mask Miranda had worn all day evaporated. Her free hand went to the hem of her sweater, and she tried to pull it down in the back.

Talmadge curbed a smile. From what he'd seen, she'd need a knee-length robe to cover the gaping hole in her pants. Not that he minded the view.

"Sure." Talmadge let that one word hang in the air. She looked at him as though she expected more. He just gave her a lazy stare, which made her sink her straight, white teeth deep into that pink lip.

He pointed to Lloyd. "You sure he's not a rat? Bea didn't see all that well the past few years."

"How would you know?" Miranda blurted. "I mean, you haven't been home, so . . ." Her big brown eyes slid shut for a beat.

He didn't care what Miranda Cruz thought of him.

He didn't.

The burning in his stomach was probably indigestion.

"I called Bea every week." Why the hell was he explaining himself? "And I called Uncle Joe to get insider information because Bea always said she was fine." Bea understood how demanding and important Talmadge's environmental projects were. How hard it was for him to come back to Red River and face the memories of his parents. How he needed to give something back to the world. She just never knew exactly why.

Success had a price. Being an international leader in sustainable green architecture didn't leave much time for visits to Red River. Bea never put a guilt trip on him, never made him feel like he'd deserted her. Hell, she was proud of his accomplishments.

Yeah, he'd just keep telling himself that.

Now that Bea was gone, he didn't owe anyone else an explanation. "Calling was the best I could do because of all the building projects I've had going on."

Dammit.

His free hand involuntarily went to the deep, radiating ache in his shoulder and he rubbed.

He cursed his inability to stay off a building site and let the contractors do their jobs. But he had a financial stake in the Trinity Falls project—a big one—and letting others do all the labor wasn't his style. He was a roll-up-your-sleeves-and-get-'er-done kind of guy. The on-site work was the fun part. Watching his designs take shape and come to life, even swinging a hammer once in a while, made his job so much more worthwhile and personal.

The sweat of hard physical labor required to construct his environmental building projects eased the regret of all he'd destroyed in his selfish youth.

Miranda held up a palm. "You don't have to explain."

Damn straight he didn't. "I just thought you should know that I didn't abandon my grandmother." He pinched the bridge of his nose.

Miranda studied the dog as though she didn't know what to say. Well, hell. He didn't know what to say either, now that she had firmly established what a crummy grandson he was.

"Sorry about your arm." She pointed to the sling. "I saw the accident on the news."

Who hadn't? The footage of the ground caving in on him while he directed the heavy earthmoving equipment in the first phase of the Trinity Falls development had been broadcast around the country. Was still airing on most channels in the Pacific Northwest just for shock value.

"You're lucky."

Right. Lucky. That was his middle name. Lucky that the engineering firm he'd hired to assess the feasibility of Trinity Falls had used cheap equipment and missed the existence of ancient tribal ruins before Talmadge had sunk his entire fortune into the project? Lucky that he'd staked his professional reputation on a project that was about to ruin him? Or maybe she thought he was lucky for losing his grandmother during the most difficult time of his professional life.

"I mean, that tractor, crane thingy—"

"Excavator," he said flatly.

She flinched at the harsh edge of his tone. "Um, yeah. That excavator could've killed you. It fell right on top of you." She fidgeted with the bows in the dog's fluffy ears. "At least that's what it looked like on the news."

It *should've* killed him. No *could've* to it. And he didn't really want to talk about it.

"So the rat-dog," he said. "He looks pretty skittish."

A dimple appeared on each cheek when Miranda smiled, and the iciness in Talmadge's heart thawed.

"Maybe we should feed him cheese instead of the expensive dog food Bea usually bought." She gave a small, throaty laugh.

He remembered that laugh. And the dimples. Definitely the dimples. And the way her glossy lips shimmered under the afternoon sun as she spoke made Talmadge go still. They were just so nice and pink. And ripe like a juicy piece of fruit he'd like to taste.

And for a second, time stood still.

She drew in a deep breath of fresh mountain air. Even under the heavy sweater, he couldn't help but notice how her full breasts swelled.

The creaking chairlift passed overhead and the chatter of two skiers drifted down to them.

He gave himself a silent kick in the pants, and Miranda looked away, clearing her throat. He was pretty sure getting turned on at a funeral was inappropriate. Although Bea probably would have cheered him on. She had sung Miranda's angelic praises during every weekly phone call since they'd become such good friends the past few years.

If only Bea had known how well he and Miranda really did know each other.

"Well, I suppose he's your rat now." Miranda pulled at the back hem of her sweater again and closed the space between them to hand him the . . . uh, *dog.*

"Oh, no." Talmadge took a step back and shook his head. No way was he getting stuck with a pet to take care of. "I can't take care of a dog. Can't he stay with you? I have a life." Okay, that might have come out wrong.

Her mouth tightened, and she gave him a glare as sharp as broken glass. "Of course, nothing I have to do in this Podunk town could be important, right?"

Definitely came out wrong. Always had when he was around Miranda.

He drew in a breath. "I won't be in town for long." Now that the biggest and financially riskiest project of his career had ground to a halt, he had to get back to Washington and figure out a solution before all of his investors pulled out. "When I go home, I won't really be *home*. I'll spend most of my time on the jobsite."

The smile she flashed at him matched the defiant look in her eyes about as well as a male dog matched bows and nail polish. Only the lightning-fast pulse that beat where neck met shoulder gave away her nervousness. Her hitched-up chin and proud, level stare hid it well.

"Since you think he looks like a rat, he'll make a great pet for you. A perfect match, if you ask me."

"I didn't ask you." He stared down at her. She was a breath away. Close enough that her sweet and savory scent made blood rush from his head to his groin.

Still holding out the dog to him, her eyes narrowed, and an inexplicable thrill of challenge bolted through him. The same thrill he got every time he was faced with a new environmental building project the experts said couldn't be done.

"Then it's a good thing I don't need your permission to speak," she said.

"Still just as sassy as I remember." His voice dropped to a whisper, and his eyes wandered over her pretty face.

A breeze kicked up, sending a chill all the way to his bones in Red River's high mountain altitude. Miranda shivered against the cold blast of air, and the tiny dog wiggled, trying to escape from her grasp. She lunged forward to catch him just as Talmadge did the same. They collided, his good arm sliding around her waist again to steady her.

Sandwiched between them, Lloyd whimpered. At least he'd helped save the dog from falling even if Miranda was trying to level him with a badass stare.

He should let her go.

But hell no. She felt too right against him. His head dipped, and he inhaled a big dose of the tasty scent of her perfume . . . or soap . . . or shampoo . . . or whatever made her smell so delicious that his mouth watered like a Pavlovian dog.

Not smart.

That had gotten him neutered once before. His balls were probably still mounted on Miranda's wall like a trophy she'd taken down on safari.

But having her so close surprisingly eased the ache of sadness over losing the only mother figure he'd ever really known. And the guilt over having left Bea behind to save the world, one environmentally conscious building at a time.

Miranda pulled out of his embrace, her long, silky hair bouncing around her shoulders. He instantly regretted letting her go. Her warmth drained away from him, replaced by coldness both in his limbs and around his heart. The ache in his chest and his shoulder throbbed even more, or at least it seemed to, without her softness pressed against him.

She clutched for the backside of her split pants, no doubt trying to cover herself. Waste of time, because that part of her very feminine anatomy was forever burned into his memory. Had been long before today. Ever since that one time . . . her first time . . . and the only time for him that was worth remembering.

# Chapter Two

"Lloyd is yours now." Miranda tried to hand Lloyd to Talmadge again, but he took another step back. She splayed a hand across the gaping hole in her pants. Dang, it was cold out.

"No. He's not." Talmadge absently rubbed his shoulder. "I can't take care of a dog."

"He's sweet, but I can't take care of him right now either." The renovations, a contractor who rarely showed up for work, and a dwindling bank account occupied every minute of every day. She was running short on both time and money. If the Closed sign in the window didn't turn to Open soon, she'd end up right back at Joe's waiting tables for the rest of her life.

Fear sliced through her.

More tears of grief threatened.

She beat them back, because as much as she missed Bea, she would not show weakness to anyone in this town again. She'd weathered the fiery looks of condescension and the gossip from a certain group of

Red River's population because of her mother's reputation. She wasn't about to go weak and needy now that she was so close to her dream of independence. Or her dream of becoming a respectable business owner and proving that she was nothing like her mother.

Two skiers slid past and disappeared behind the crop of evergreens, heading toward the lodge. Miranda turned away so they couldn't see her butt. Which meant her butt was pointing toward Talmadge. *Sheee-ut!* She spun back around to face him. Why couldn't he just go away? Leaving hadn't been a problem for him in the past. At the very least, he could go back inside the inn and leave her alone.

She gave him the same wicked smile usually reserved for the occasional drunken tourists who got too fresh when she'd waitressed at Joe's. She'd perfected that look early in life because of the boys who assumed she was easy like her mother. That look said "cross me and die." She closed the short distance between them, grabbed Talmadge's good hand, and placed the toy poodle in the center of his large palm.

His eyes rounded, a horrified expression capturing his perfect features. "But—"

She held up a hand, silencing him.

*Nice.* Surprising too. Seeing Talmadge Oaks look so vulnerable and unsure of himself must be a rare occurrence indeed. And it only took a six-pound poodle with nail polish to do it. Served him right to be stuck with a fluffy, bow-wearing pooch after insinuating that his life was more important than hers. His life might be more high profile, but it certainly wasn't any busier. Or any harder.

"No buts." Mr. Greenpeace had already been allowed one too many butts for today. Hers, to be exact.

He pulled Lloyd into the crook of his arm. The panicked look Talmadge gave the dog said he might as well be holding a baby alien. Talmadge flexed the hand that protruded from the sling, and a deep grimace captured his face.

A pang of guilt stabbed at Miranda's chest. She did love that little dog. And forcing a prissy, high-maintenance poodle on an injured man who probably couldn't zip his own fly right now wouldn't make Bea too proud.

"Can you just take him for a sec so I can adjust this sling?" Talmadge gritted his teeth as he spoke.

With a hand on her hip and the other covering her butt, or trying to, she studied Talmadge. "Okay, fine." She stepped toward him and took Lloyd, cuddling him against her chest. His trembling had spiked when she'd handed him over to Talmadge, and Lloyd buried his nose in the crook of Miranda's arm.

"He'd be better off with you. He's scared of me." Talmadge's hand slipped under his jacket. He adjusted the sling around his shoulder. Another pained scowl flitted across his face, and his eyes dilated until all the blue was gone, and only large, black pupils remained.

An annoying pinch stung Miranda's conscience.

"Why can't you take care of a little dog?" The pain in his expression seeped into his words and turned his voice ragged. He rubbed his shoulder like it was hard to concentrate because of the discomfort.

The heat of rising irritation evaporated most of Miranda's compassion. Obviously, he hadn't gotten the memo that he wasn't the only one with a life. "Shouldn't you be inside getting more slaps on the back for your latest architectural award? And I didn't see you with a date. Where's the requisite hotel heiress?"

A muscle in his jaw flexed and released in a steady cadence. "I wouldn't bring a date to my grandmother's funeral."

No, she supposed he wouldn't. "Ah, that's right. It was a wedding, if I remember correctly." And she definitely remembered correctly, even if it had been seven years, three months, and twelve days ago.

Her hand went to her hip, and she notched her chin up to stare him down with silent 'tude.

He looked away. "I didn't invite her. She just showed up on her own. We . . . forget it."

The familiar weight of disappointment and heartache crushed Miranda's chest just like it had back then. Her gaze shifted to the jagged tops of the Sangre de Cristo Mountains, mostly blanketed in snow this time of year.

"What are you doing out here, Talmadge?" Miranda loved to say his name. Just like him, it was unique. It caressed her lips like warm butterscotch every time she said it, which she'd purposefully kept to a minimum over the years.

Because she adored butterscotch.

Dammit.

"Just getting some fresh air and looking around the place. I did spend a lot of time here with my grandparents when I was growing up." He surveyed the weathered siding of the inn, his eyes traveling up to the roof that was in desperate need of new shingles. "It's really decayed."

She stroked Lloyd's head, but the cold air nipped at her exposed bottom again, and her hand shot around to her backside. "Bea tried her best to keep the inn looking nice, even after your grandfather passed and she had to close it. But the last couple of years she didn't have the same strength she used to. That's why she sold the place to me."

Talmadge flinched, and Miranda wasn't sure if it was because of his injured arm or the truth about his grandmother and the inn.

"Sounds like you did a pretty good job keeping Bea company in my absence. Why is that?" He looked up at the squeaking lift, the muscle in his jaw working again.

Miranda's rhythmic petting of Lloyd's head slowed. "What do you mean?"

Talmadge turned expressionless eyes on her. "I sent money to help Bea out. I'm sure you were well compensated for all the help you gave her."

Miranda's jaw locked down so tight she thought it might come unhinged. "I did not take money from Bea." Miranda may have grown up dirt poor, but she'd never taken a thing she hadn't earned. She certainly wouldn't have taken money from a sweet old woman like Bea, who had taken Miranda under her wing and encouraged her to do more with her life than wait tables and live on tips.

Of course he wouldn't think so highly of Miranda. He had become accustomed to crusading celebrities who poured money into his environmental projects. He was also no stranger to young, beautiful women who had the same last names as hotel chains and were remodeling and trying to "go green." If the celebrity magazines were accurate, he had become well acquainted with a few over the past seven years.

He shrugged with his good shoulder. "But you did let her loan you the money for the inn."

"It's an owner-financed contract." Miranda's voice had gone low and shaky. "And Bea was my friend."

"Don't you have friends your own age?"

"Of course I do." Her teeth ground. "But your grandmother needed someone to schlep things around, and I was it, Talmadge." This time his name didn't roll off her tongue like butterscotch. Her words were more like a steady flow of hisses.

"Was there another reason you spent so much time with my grandma after I moved away?"

"Just what are you suggesting?" And there went another hiss. Miranda slid the tip of her tongue against her teeth just to make sure it hadn't forked.

He lifted a shoulder. "Just gathering information, that's all."

"Bea was like a mother . . ." Miranda's eyes started to fill, and her voice went all croaky. The grief over losing Bea—the best parental role model Miranda had ever had besides Bea's brother, Joe—was finally rising to the surface like a storm churning over the ocean. Finally catching up to her. A tidal wave of tears surged toward her.

"You know what?" She leveled a hot glare at him. "Bea and I signed a contract. I gave her money down. A lot of it, and I haven't missed a payment."

*Yet.*

She hesitated.

"I'll pay you every penny." *Or die trying.* "So if you're implying that I took advantage of Bea somehow, then you're insultingly mistaken."

He studied her, a torn expression on his face. "I wasn't—"

"If you'd been around, she wouldn't have had to depend on me." She stepped up to him, the tips of her high-heeled boots almost grazing the toes of his expensive wingtips. Her stare met his chest, so she had to tilt her head back to look at him.

His eyes went dark and stormy as they caressed down her face to linger on her mouth.

As hard as it was, she tried to ignore the hum of electricity in the air between them. "Bea left what little she had to you. *I* was her witness. So if you're angry that Bea sold the inn to me instead of leaving it to you—"

"I'm not—"

"—then too bad. If it meant that much to you, you should've shown more interest."

His gaze didn't leave her lips. "I did—"

"Legally it's mine unless I default on the payments."

Their eyes locked, and the hum of electricity turned to a high-voltage current that snapped between them. The woodsy scent of his cologne fogged her brain for a second, and she swayed into him.

When Talmadge's muscular neck flexed and his head tilted forward, Miranda let out a tiny, almost inaudible squeak just as his mouth covered hers. To say she was surprised that he kissed her was an understatement.

Like saying that thing Miley Cyrus did with her tongue was only mildly unattractive.

But good God, he *was* kissing her. His lips moved over hers, warm and smooth but patiently in charge at the same time.

She should push him away. She really should.

He must've sensed the tremor of hesitation, because his kiss grew more demanding. She sighed and parted her lips. His warm tongue eased inside to caress hers, and a shudder of desire stormed through her entire body.

This was so not a good idea.

This was *Talmadge Oaks!* The guy she'd longed for and avoided—mostly—for years.

She went rigid from head to curling toes, but his kiss grew deeper, and he slid his free hand around her waist to pull her closer. She followed his lead, allowing her lips and tongue to match his, stroke for stroke.

He just tasted so damn *good.*

The way his commanding mouth was on hers sent searing heat through every nerve ending in her body, and her hesitation ebbed. The rhythmic caress of his lips and tongue against hers soothed her doubt. The cold air turned sizzling hot around them. He sighed against her mouth. The last of her resolve tumbled like an avalanche at the top of Wheeler Peak, and she settled into him.

His freshly shaved jaw flexed as his kiss grew more demanding, his mouth leading and coaxing her into doing his will. She adjusted Lloyd under her arm and relaxed against Talmadge. With a sigh, she slid a hand up his chest, over his neck, and into his soft, straight hair. *Finally.*

Just as she remembered it, that sandy mane was the only soft thing about the man.

When his tongue caressed hers with just enough firmness to let her know he was in charge, a fire ignited down under. He fanned the flames by using the tip of that very clever tongue to trace her bottom lip. Nipped at it, then pulled it between his teeth and suckled.

*Good God.*

Her girl parts went nuclear, and she nearly buckled at the knees. He must've felt her legs go slack, because his good hand sank to her bottom and he caught her. His strong fingers flexed into the bare flesh at the top of her thigh, and his thumb caressed the silk of her panties.

A sigh whispered through her, and she went slack. He steadied her by pulling her tighter against his muscled chest.

Good Lord, what he could do with just one good arm, a tongue, and two lips.

Caught between them, Lloyd yapped. Miranda broke the kiss. As she came back to reality, her eyes fluttered open. Talmadge's hand cupped her ass. Outdoors. For the entire town to see.

*So* not a good idea.

She needed to stop this foolishness before a compromising photo showed up in the *Red River Rag*. As Red River's newest entrepreneur, she absolutely did not need to be the subject of the new Tumblr blog that featured all of the town's juiciest gossip. Whoever the blogger was must work for Homeland Security. They seemed to have hidden cameras all over town, e-mail hacking capability, and they probably had some illegal wiretaps going on, because they knew *everything*!

Bad enough her bared ass might show up on YouTube. At least her face had been blocked by the table.

She looked up into Talmadge's eyes, and they sparkled with confidence.

Arrogance.

She'd tried not to live up to her mother's colorful reputation for so long, she should know better. But after a few stolen moments with Talmadge Oaks . . . She might as well hand him the Sharpie that could permanently mark up her rep for good in this town. He would never smear her name. He wasn't the kiss and tell type. No, he was too much of a crusader for that. Too busy defending the weak. Protecting the innocent. Saving the world. But if anyone saw them . . .

*Gah!* When would she learn that she couldn't trust herself to be alone with Talmadge?

She'd made that mistake seven years, three months, and twelve days ago.

She wasn't going to make it again.

The dirt over Bea's grave probably wouldn't even have time to settle before her grandson left town and returned to his life on the West Coast. If he didn't leave on his own, some silicone hotel heiress who wore dresses so short she'd have to shave up to her eyebrows would waltz in and drag him away. Again.

"Excuse me." Her chin notched up. "Your sense of direction must be off, because your hand seems to have wandered too far south."

"So it seems." He looked down at her from beneath shuttered lids.

She shook off the squeeze of lust that made her want to pull his head down and cradle him against her neck.

The warmth of his expansive palm fell away, and the cold spring breeze returned to bite at the back of her thighs. She cringed and returned a splayed hand to her butt. At the loss of his heated fingers, a swooshing breath of disappointment escaped before she could stop it, and his silver-blue eyes shimmered with amusement.

A knowing gleam danced in his eyes, as if he could tell that she really didn't want him to stop. He looked away and studied the squeaking chairlift. "Sorry, but your fingers running through my hair definitely didn't scream 'let me go.'"

He pulled on the lapel of his jacket and reached under to adjust the sling again. The flash of a grimace coursed across his features for a fleeting moment, then it was gone, and he stood there. Staring at her in complete command of his presence and not the least bit flustered.

"It won't happen again," he assured her.

"Okay. Good," she said with her mouth, but her brain and her quivering girl parts shouted, *Use both hands next time!* She looked away for the briefest of moments, pulling her bottom lip between her teeth.

When she looked back at him his gaze dropped to her mouth, and his eyes went all dark and cloudy.

She had a sudden urge to lick her lips.

*Dammit.*

"Then you have my word I won't touch you again." One side of his strong, lush mouth lifted into a self-assured half-smile. "Unless you ask me to."

Her lips parted at the innuendo. The memory.

As though he'd read her thoughts, amusement flickered in his eyes.

"I assure you I won't be asking." She tried to brush past him but stopped at his side and looked up at him. "About your inheritance—" A twinge of guilt feathered through her when she glanced down at Lloyd. Unfortunately, he had become an innocent pawn in their game of wills.

She gathered her courage and shoved the little football-sized dog into the crook of Talmadge's arm. His arm and hand naturally closed around Lloyd.

This time she did brush past him. Ears burning, hand trying desperately to cover the opening in her pants—thank the angels in heaven she'd worn new panties today—she climbed the wooden stairs. Her boots clicked against the back porch. With a firm push, she sent Bea's old swing into motion again and jerked open the screen door. Time to put on some new pants and tend to her guests before she changed her mind about giving him the dog *and* about asking him to grope her backside again.

Because she'd enjoyed that part much more than she should have.

# Chapter Three

Miranda and her sweet little backside disappeared into the inn.

*Thwack, thwack, thwack.* The thud of the screen door lessened with each bang until it slowed to a stop. Miranda's soft lips against his and her greedy fingers spearing through his hair like she'd been waiting to do that again for years had caused his brain to make the same sound.

Talmadge tried to pull air into his aching lungs. The last time the wind was knocked from his chest he'd fallen through a thin layer of earth and hit the floor of an undiscovered archeological dwelling like a jackhammer hitting solid steel. Watching the excavator fall in right after him with no air left in his lungs to scream was still causing him nightmares. This time, a small, graceful woman who hardly reached chest level had left him breathless by handing him a dog half the size of Talmadge's shoe and telling him his business about his grandmother.

He looked down at Bea's dog, who had erupted into another fit of trembling the second Talmadge's arm closed around him. What the hell was he supposed to do with a poodle?

Talmadge drew in a heavy breath. Who was he kidding? It wasn't just the dog. The truth of Miranda's words—that Talmadge hadn't come home to visit Bea enough—or at all the past few years—had hit him square in the chest and drove the nails of guilt and grief straight through his heart. He'd wanted to double over right there on the snowy ground beside the inn where he'd spent so much time growing up.

Every person at Bea's funeral had made it a point to tell him how proud she was of him and his work. What Bea hadn't known was he'd invested every last dime into the master-planned community of Trinity Falls, Washington, where every building, road, school, park, and home would be environmentally efficient. A project on the cutting edge of green living that had attracted attention from environmental and architectural organizations around the world. And then he'd screwed it up by hiring the wrong engineering firm, which had nearly gotten Talmadge killed.

He didn't even want to think about the damage to his finances and his professional reputation if he didn't find a way around this mess. He'd been too ashamed to share those two details with his grandmother.

Now Bea was gone.

His stomach twisted so tight that pain lanced into his limbs. He studied Bea's dog. "Wow," Talmadge said, taking in Lloyd's bows and nail polish. "Sorry this happened to you." *This* was Bea's surrogate replacement for the grandson she was so proud of? Maybe Bea wasn't as proud of him as he'd thought.

Two skiers slid past, headed toward the lift, and Lloyd let out another high-pitched bark that was more like a squeal. He started to tremble harder.

Talmadge rolled his eyes and lifted his injured hand to give the dog a gentle pat on top of his fluffy head. Perfume wafted out of the cotton ball's hair. Talmadge sniffed and jerked his head back. "Seriously? We need to get your man-card back." Maybe he could drop the dog off at the groomer before leaving Red River. The groomer might even be able to help find Lloyd a new home.

Another stab of guilt sliced through him. He'd obviously abandoned Bea, and now he was doing the same to her dog.

Talmadge cradled Lloyd and walked along the sidewalk that led around to the front door, sidestepping patches of packed snow. Weeds popped up through the cracked sidewalk as proof that spring had converged on the Red River Valley. As he followed the crumbling concrete path along the side of the inn, he assessed the dilapidated condition. The loving attention his grandparents had given the property was gone, and the neat grounds were now in disrepair.

He took the steps up to the front door, pushed it open, and walked through the foyer to the spacious great room to the right. The wake was wrapping up, and several people had filtered out. A few family members lingered to talk in the dining room to the left. Talmadge bent to put the dog down, but Lloyd's quaking resumed.

Really? He had to stand here and babysit a trembling dog? But as small as the perfumed pooch was, someone might step on him. He was pretty easy to miss since he was no bigger than a rat, and Talmadge didn't want to bury both his grandma and her dog in the same day.

He looked around the room that used to serve as a place for the guests to socialize and relax, hoping for a safe place to put Lloyd. Some of the drywall was torn out, exposing the studs. Bea's old antiques and parlor furniture still filled the inn, at least the rooms Talmadge had seen, and were covered with drop cloths. Building materials were stacked around the room in no particular order. Several workbenches were covered with miscellaneous junk, none of which looked like a real project with purpose.

Talmadge gave up, kept holding the dog, and moved across the room to the stone fireplace where a fire blazed. The flames helped kill the chill that hung in the room because the walls were exposed down to the studs, and the insulation was gone. He stroked Lloyd's head with the fingertips of his injured arm. Even that small movement hurt, but the little guy wouldn't stop shaking. When the warmth of the fire started to seep into them, Lloyd's tremors slowed.

Talmadge smiled at the pooch. Funny. Warming himself by the fire had been one of Talmadge's favorite things to do in this room once upon a time. He kept stroking the dog's cotton ball head and stared into the fire.

Uncle Joe, Bea's brother, younger by twelve years, walked over to stand with Talmadge.

"You going to be okay, Uncle Joe?" Talmadge gave his great-uncle a warm smile because the owner of Red River's most popular watering hole—all six feet four inches, two hundred and eighty pounds of him— had cried on and off like a baby since he'd first called Talmadge with the news.

Joe took a handkerchief out of his back pocket and blew his bulbous nose. Loud. "Yeah." He sniffed and nodded, his aging double chin wagging a little. "Bea was like a second mom to me. She darn near raised me, just as much as our mother did."

Talmadge knew exactly what that was like. "She raised both of us, didn't she?"

Another blow and sniff, and Joe put the handkerchief back in his pocket. He propped an arm on the mantle, his tweed sports coat going taut against his enormous girth. "She did. And helped out a whole lot of other folks, too. More than I can count."

Speaking of . . . Without turning his head, Talmadge found the woman Bea never failed to exalt during every single weekly phone call over the past two years. He studied Miranda from the corner of his eye.

In a fresh pair of jeans that fit her rounded bottom like shrink-wrap, she gathered up dirty plates and cups, wadded napkins, and silverware. The sparkly things on her pockets held his attention as she made her way into the kitchen, and then returned to gather up more. She stopped every so often to greet one of the few remaining guests, consoling with a hug or a squeeze of their hand. A fluid smile stayed anchored to her full lips, but it didn't show in her gold-flecked eyes. She clearly missed Bea as much as anyone else, including himself.

Unlike him, though, Miranda had been there for Bea. That fact had driven a rusty nail into his conscience out on the patio a few minutes ago and during most of his weekly calls to Bea. Miranda's deep well of compassion toward his grandmother had brought him comfort as well as pricked his guilt. Which was why he'd interrogated her outside when he really should've been thanking her. Something told him that Miranda wouldn't consider that unexpected kiss he'd laid on her a show of gratitude.

But the grief in her simulated smile made him want to take her in his arms. Kiss her until the hollowness in his chest filled with the same warmth she'd shown Bea and the sadness in her eyes turned to a glimmer of desire. Her eyes shimmering with passion was a beautiful sight. Even if it *had* been seven years since he'd last seen it, it wasn't something he'd ever forget.

Sometimes it occupied his thoughts during lonely nights when he couldn't sleep.

The afternoon sun shining through the windows glinted off her silky black hair as it bounced around her shoulders with each step and movement. Not even the cheap fluorescent lighting made her less attractive.

Even in high school she had always seemed to catch the light. But she'd been too young for him back then. Already three grades behind him, she was still younger than anyone else at Valley High because she'd been moved up a grade.

"Bea mentioned that she sold the place to Miranda several months ago." Still watching her, Talmadge's words were an absent mumble.

Joe hooked a thumb under his lapel. "Miranda's good people. Worked for me since she was a young'un."

Talmadge nodded. "I remember."

"Never had an employee as good as her and probably never will. Your grandma was lucky to have Miranda's help the last few years."

Yes, Miranda's help had been invaluable. Talmadge's throat thickened, and he looked away. He was a shallow prick for being jealous of the bond that had formed between Bea and Miranda because he should've been the one here helping her out.

"Who's doing the remodel?" He tried to get back on point, because he'd much rather talk about Miranda's wayward renovations than about his shitty attempt at being a worthy grandson. And despite all the mess and supplies and torn-out walls, he didn't see any tools. Talmadge didn't just design energy-efficient buildings. He was hands-on throughout the entire construction process and had been doing carpentry work alongside his grandfather since he was twelve. He could spot substandard materials without so much as a backward glance.

Uncle Joe, on the other hand, could cook a mean rib eye, but no one had ever accused him of being handy with a hammer and nails.

Before Uncle Joe could answer the question, two of Talmadge's elderly widowed cousins sidled over and flanked him. Their silver hair turned a bitter shade of blue under the unflattering lighting.

"Clydelle. Francine." Talmadge greeted the elderly sisters with a friendly smile, but Uncle Joe grumbled under his breath.

"There you are. We were trying to find you. Some of the guests wanted to say good-bye," Clydelle said. "Saw the pictures of you in *Time* magazine, Talmadge." Clydelle leaned heavily on her cane. "Nearly sent your grandma to the emergency room with heart palpitations."

Talmadge cringed. It had been hot the day the reporter came to interview him on a job site because he'd been deemed one of the one hundred most influential people of the year. So he'd doused his white

T-shirt with cold water. He never guessed that the thin fabric would become see-through and cling to him like a second skin. He had no idea the hardhat, work gloves, and steel-toed boots would make him look more like one of the Village People than a successful architect who liked to roll up his sleeves and help get the job done.

Francine gazed up at him over the reading glasses perched on the end of her wrinkled nose, one shoulder drooping under the weight of her suitcase-size purse. "Tell me, sonny boy, are the muscles in that picture real or did they Photoshop you?"

"This is Bea's wake," Uncle Joe growled.

At least Francine had the decency to look contrite. Clydelle didn't seem the least bit apologetic. "Next time you're on HGTV, have them hose you down before they start taping."

Talmadge fought off a smile. "I see you two ladies are still keeping Red River on its toes." Not every old lady would invite a twelve-year-old boy to her weekly pinochle game and fleece him of every cent. Talmadge hadn't placed a bet since then.

Unless you count his failing investment in Trinity Falls, which technically wasn't gambling.

"As I was saying before you two old hens interrupted," Uncle Joe grumbled and returned his attention to Talmadge. "There's a new contractor in town who's in charge of the construction. He moved here from Denver last year. Don't know much about him except that he seems to cater to the older folks in town."

*Huh. Why would anyone move here from Denver?* A good contractor would get way more business in a big city. Maybe he'd retired in Red River and took jobs just to stay busy.

"How old is he?" Talmadge took in the rich mahogany crown molding that gave the place so much character. It was dry and faded, but a new coat of varnish would bring it back to life.

"Your age. Early thirties. Maybe a few years older," said Uncle Joe.

Too young to retire. Miranda made another pass through the room, gathering up plates and checking on the guests. Her smooth walk and easy smile lit the room, and no sign of the hardships he knew she'd faced while growing up showing on her beautiful face. She glanced in his direction, and their eyes connected. She seemed to falter, stilled for a second, then turned to speak to one of Bea's distant relatives.

Talmadge tore his gaze from Miranda to survey the amateurish carpentry work.

"What's his name?" Talmadge may need to do some checking.

"His name is . . ." Francine tapped her saggy chin thoughtfully. "Bill . . . no, Brent . . . no—"

"His name is Ben Smith," Clydelle said.

*Smith?* Could be a coincidence, but having such a generic name seemed kind of convenient.

"That nice young man sure has been a lot of help to us widows who don't have a husband around anymore." Clydelle gazed off in the distance, a smile on her face.

"You two just like to watch him work without a shirt on," Joe groused. "He couldn't even provide credentials or references."

Francine piped up, adjusting the weight of her bulging purse to the other shoulder. "He only takes off his shirt when he gets hot."

"It's April," Talmadge deadpanned. "In the Rockies."

"Hard work still makes a man work up a sweat." Clydelle waved her cane at him. "You should know that better than anyone, Talmadge. That picture in *Time* speaks a thousand words."

Eww.

Francine winked up at him.

And eww.

Miranda made her way through the thinning crowd toward them. Talmadge's pulse kicked up a notch, her sweet taste still lingering on his mouth.

As she approached, she laced the fingers that had just been spearing through his hair, and his scalp tingled for her touch. He lifted a hand to run his own fingers through his hair, but Lloyd squeaked.

"Sorry, buddy," Talmadge whispered to the dog. "Didn't mean to try to use you as a brush."

Miranda joined their circle, squeezing her laced fingers. Her thumb furiously scratched against the other. "Can I get you anything else?" Her gaze shifted from Joe to Clydelle and then to Francine. She ignored Talmadge.

"No, dear." Clydelle patted Miranda's arm. "You've done Bea proud today."

Miranda smiled, and Francine pinched one of Miranda's dimpled cheeks.

"Thank you for hosting, hon. I know you've got your hands full with the remodel." Joe looked at Talmadge. "I wanted to hold the wake at my restaurant, but Miranda insisted on doing it here," he said, slinging a burly arm around Miranda's shoulders like she was family.

Talmadge supposed she was, much more so than himself the past few years. Family at least showed up to the party. Talmadge had skipped out of town at eighteen to go to college, visited Red River as little as possible, and then stopped coming home at all after his grandfather passed away. He thought he could leave behind the awful memories of his parents' accident. Instead, his absence had created more guilt and regret. Not only had he not been around for Bea, he never had the guts to tell her that he was to blame for the accident that took her only son and saddled her with the responsibility of raising Talmadge.

"It seems appropriate." Miranda gave Joe a comforting smile and a daughterly hug. "I wouldn't have it any other way." Her gaze fell to the floor. "I'm only sorry that, um, certain people wouldn't come to the wake *because* I'm the host."

"If they'd shown up, I would've thrown them out anyway," Joe assured her.

Ah, her mother's infamous exploits, no doubt. Talmadge remembered the scandal that had caused Miranda so much humiliation in high school that she hadn't come to school for a week. Once upon a time, Ms. Karen Cruz had made enemies out of a few churchgoing families. Apparently, some of the married women in Red River didn't take kindly to their husbands getting hauled in front of the deacon board because of rumors of inappropriate behavior with the disgraceful Ms. Cruz.

Miranda was her mother's daughter in last name only. She shouldn't be blamed for things that were beyond her control. This was Red River, for God's sake. A town that prided itself on down-home, salt-of-the-earth people who were there for each other when it counted. But some old grudges died hard, and a few God-fearing families who had it out for anyone with the last name of Cruz must've skipped church services the day forgiveness was taught.

Francine looked Miranda up and down. "Dear, you've changed pants. The other pair was so darling."

Miranda's hand went to her rear end, and she glanced at Talmadge. He allowed a barely-there smile to glide onto his lips. Her amber eyes flashed, and her mouth pursed. A gesture he was sure she didn't mean to be provocative, but damned if he didn't find it the most attractive thing he'd seen in a long time . . . except for Miranda's black panties, which he'd just had the privilege of seeing up close and personal. And touching. The touching part was even better, because they'd been as soft as the back of her creamy thighs just below her extraordinary ass.

He couldn't help it. She hesitated just long enough for Talmadge to offer up another teasing barb. It was just too easy. And too much fun. But their answers came out at the same time.

"Miranda had a wardrobe malfunction."

"I didn't want to clean up in nice pants."

All three of the older folks volleyed looks between Miranda and Talmadge.

Her cheeks turned light pink, which only highlighted her dark, silky hair and creamy skin. She wouldn't look him in the eye.

He kept his gaze fastened to her.

"Where did you two disappear to?" Clydelle leaned in like she was hoping for a juicy piece of gossip. "You were gone for some time."

"Lloyd just needed a walk!" Miranda's words tumbled out.

Lloyd yapped at his name, and all eyes turned on the quivering dog in Talmadge's arms. Silence fell for a second while the small audience took in Talmadge and his new ward.

He had grown accustomed to being in the spotlight since starting his front-running architectural firm in the Pacific Northwest, where green living was the center of attention. He'd learned to handle the attention from Hollywood celebrities who needed a cause. Holding his thoughts in check, never talking much so his words couldn't be twisted, had become a way of life for him. But somehow holding a prissy dog made him want to pull at his collar and loosen his tie.

"Talmadge, dear." Francine reached up and touched the back of his head. "How did your hair get all messed up? It looks like someone—"

Miranda choked, sputtered, and patted her chest while trying to catch her breath.

"Are you okay, hon?" Joe asked with fatherly affection.

She nodded, still unable to speak, but she glanced at Talmadge.

"Must've been the wind when I stepped outside to get some fresh air." His eyes never left hers.

Miranda's entire face deepened to a nice shade of red, and she looked away.

He didn't miss the look Clydelle and Francine shot each other, and the waggle of Francine's bushy gray eyebrows.

Maybe Miranda deserved a little embarrassment for brushing him off like his kiss had been a nuisance. Okay, she didn't really deserve it. He *had* been a little out of bounds. But she certainly didn't seem to mind by the way she sank into his kiss and molded against him.

Until the dog barked, and she swore she'd never let him touch her again. Kind of like the way she blew him off seven years ago after they'd done a lot more than kiss, chalking it up to a drunken mistake. Still, he liked the color rising up her slender neck and settling in the tip of her dainty ear behind which wavy locks were tucked on one side. Liked it almost as much as her slender fingers anchoring in his hair to muss it up and pull his mouth closer against hers.

*Jesus, this is Bea's wake, not a singles bar.*

Joe cleared his throat. "So, Talmadge was just asking about the remodel."

"Is that so?" Miranda's expression went stony.

"When's it going to be done?" Talmadge asked.

"Why?" Miranda's lips thinned into a hard line.

Talmadge shrugged. "Just curious." *About your contractor.* "I did grow up around the place."

"It's done when it's done." Her head tilted to one side like a challenge.

Her hand went to a curvy hip, and he couldn't help but follow the movement.

"What about you, Mr. Oaks?"

*Mr. Oaks?* Hadn't she just been returning his kiss—with extremely enthusiastic lips—while running her fingers through his hair? "Uh, what about me?"

"How long will you be in town?"

"I'll be—"

"Not more than a few days, I imagine." That sassy fire ignited behind her gold-brown eyes.

"I plan—"

"I would think you have a team of doctors and physical therapists waiting for you back in Washington." She nodded to the sling that cradled his arm.

*True. But—*

"And an entire community of contractors and employees anxious for their fearless leader to return."

Hell, people usually stopped and listened when he spoke, because he was usually the person in charge.

Miranda Cruz didn't.

"And probably a long line of young, hotel-owning heiresses eager for your arrival on the West Coast."

It had been *one* going-green hotel heiress, and Talmadge had never made that mistake again after she'd stalked him for the better part of three months and even showed up in Red River at his best friend's wedding. *Uninvited.* The rumors over his other liaisons were hype to sell gossip magazines. He'd learned to ignore them.

Miranda's eyes narrowed.

Before she could think of another sharp comeback, he launched one in her direction. "I'm here as long as I'm here."

She pressed her lips together and stared at him.

Glared. Glared was a better description.

"Oh, wait!" Miranda tapped her chin with one finger with melodramatic flare. "Maybe Miss January is counting the days until you get home, too." She leveled a flaming stare at him that singed something deep in his chest.

So she'd obviously seen the latest overblown story. The unfortunate incident with Miss January had been a publicity stunt set up by the girl's agent and a damned nervy reporter. Using an important charity event, which Talmadge had organized to spark energy-efficient home construction along the western seaboard, as a stage to grab headlines for a pinup girl had pissed him off. He most certainly had *not* grabbed her ass on purpose! She'd sidled up beside him wearing spiked heels that were six inches too tall and a skirt that was twelve inches too short. When she stumbled and fell against him, his hand had just landed there for a second until she regained her footing. Was he supposed to just let her fall? The media would've crucified him for that. Besides, he'd learned a long time ago that the bad publicity came with the territory, and it was a necessary evil when dealing with celebrities looking for a cause.

Interesting, though, that Miranda's words held a tone of . . . jealousy? Nah. Couldn't be. She seemed to dislike him too much to be jealous. So why in hell was she hammering him over his love life?

"Lately, I seem to attract women who need my assistance with that part of their anatomy." He should probably feel guilty for taunting her.

She searched his eyes, found the hidden meaning, and blanched.

Nope. Not feeling the least bit guilty. Because his hand had not only been on her very nice and round ass just a few minutes ago out on the patio, but she'd needed his assistance in similar form once before. Seven years ago at their mutual friends' wedding.

Her mouth clamped shut, and her plump lips thinned.

At least this time he managed to shut her up without having to kiss her in front of all these people.

Too bad, because he wouldn't have minded that at all.

# Chapter Four

Talmadge's room looked exactly as it did the day he left for college. Bea had been sentimental that way, so she'd left his sports trophies lining the shelves on the wall, a framed picture of him and his parents the year before they were killed sitting on the dresser, and the same dark blue down comforter that used to keep him warm during Red River's frigid winter nights.

Talmadge pulled a fresh change of clothes out of his suitcase and tossed them onto the old quilt that Bea had kept folded at the foot of his bed. Changing out of the suit he had worn to the funeral was no easy task with a third-degree shoulder separation. One-handed it took him about a decade to unbutton his shirt. Just the thought of lifting his shoulder to pull on a fresh T-shirt hurt, so he left the unbuttoned white dress shirt on—the sweet scent of Miranda's perfume still lingering from when she was molded against him just a little while ago. With some effort, he managed to get into a pair of jeans. He fumbled with the button at his waist, gave up, and settled for zipping them. Even that was a struggle.

Just a few more days in this town to get Bea's will out of the way and close up the house. Then he could get back to Washington, start rehabbing his shoulder, work on a solution to Trinity Falls, and leave behind the emotional turmoil that still haunted him in Red River.

He opened the closet, and the scent of cedar and mothballs made him sneeze. Mostly empty hangers hung from the rod. He pulled the string overhead, and the single bulb with no fixture to dull the light stabbed at his eyes. His high school letterman jacket was the only piece of clothing left inside.

He fingered the leather sleeve. There were a lot of memories wrapped up in that jacket. Most of them good, some of them not. But all of them called to him from a different time before his career took off and his life became so complicated.

No. Not true. His life had been complicated since that effed-up day when he was a kid and his defiance obliterated his family and landed him on his grandparents' doorstep.

The dull ache of sadness closed around his heart. Now his grandparents were gone, and he had nothing except his work to fill the void. And even his work was questionable at the moment.

He shook it off and went downstairs to the kitchen to feed Bea's dog. *Bea's dog.* Not his. He could not take care of a dog right now. Especially one with painted nails and a rhinestone collar.

Talmadge shook the dry dog food he'd picked up at the Red River Market into a plastic bowl and set it on the baby-blue linoleum floor that seemed much dingier than his grandma ever would've allowed. "Come and eat, Lloyd." The dog scampered in from the living room. Then Talmadge filled another plastic bowl with fresh water and placed it beside the food.

He stood back. "Bon appétit." Seemed appropriate for a French poodle.

Lloyd sniffed, then sat on his haunches and turned his nose into the air.

"Sorry, buddy, it's all I could find at the market."

Lloyd whined.

Talmadge looked in the pantry for Lloyd's regular dog food one more time but came up with nothing.

He blew out a breath. He had more important things to do than worry about a dog.

"Sorry, buddy. Children are starving in Africa. I'm not driving back to the store tonight just to get different food." And he certainly wasn't going to call Miranda and ask her what Lloyd usually ate.

He'd had enough of Miranda Cruz for one day.

*Hell.*

Actually, no. He hadn't had anywhere near enough of her. That was the problem. He'd kissed her because he'd wanted to ever since the last time. Had never forgotten the time they were together.

And since he'd stepped out onto the inn's back porch and got a nice view of Miranda's panties, he hadn't stopped wanting to see her in nothing *but* those panties. And maybe a pair of boots.

Jesus, he was acting like a horny teenager. Their first kiss—and everything else that had gone along with it—had happened years ago in a moment of weakness. They'd both had a few drinks at a wedding reception. And afterward Miranda told him it had been a huge mistake. A huge, *drunken* mistake.

The throb in his shoulder deepened. It seemed to get worse when he was stressed, and thinking about Miranda Cruz made his blood pressure spike.

Lloyd's disturbing glare hadn't faltered, so Talmadge glared back. In under a minute, Talmadge broke, and grabbed a couple of gallon-sized baggies from the pantry. He started to fill them with ice from the freezer.

"Give me a minute, and I'll see if I can find some human food for you." He looked at Lloyd while scooping ice into the bag.

Lloyd sniffed again.

Talmadge shook his head.

So why had he never been able to completely get Miranda out of his head? He had no idea what possessed him to kiss her today.

Not true.

He just liked the way she was so down-to-earth. So real. So unlike the women who'd tried to latch on to him since he'd become rich and famous. Well, he was still famous. For now. He glanced at his arm, which was cradled against his middle. If his investments and his current building project didn't improve soon, he wouldn't have to fend off shallow women anymore. His market value would plummet like the Dow Jones after an oil spill.

That was probably the only upside to his problems. He had grown tired of the plastic women his career had thrust into his path. Who would've guessed that becoming an architect would turn him into a quasi-celebrity?

He smirked. What a joke. He hadn't dated much the last several years because of it.

He grabbed an ice pick from the drawer and chipped away at the ice cubes that had frozen together in a solid block at the bottom of the ice bag.

Miranda was a breath of fresh mountain air, and she'd obviously cared about his grandmother. And he'd gone and made stupid accusations because his ego had been wounded. Worse, he'd nearly made her cry.

Then he'd kissed the sense out of her until she let out a tiny moan. Which only made him want more.

It seemed to take another hundred years or so to chip and fill the bags, but he finally balanced them over his shoulder. He reached for a rolled-up ACE bandage on the counter and the bags wobbled. The hand on his injured arm shot up instinctively to steady them, and he howled in pain. An ice pack slid off and hit the floor with a thud.

Lloyd skittered into a corner, trembling.

*Shit.* Talmadge threw the other bag into the scarred ceramic sink and gripped the edge of the counter. Opened the ruffled blue plaid curtain and stared out the picture window over the sink that overlooked the twinkling lights of Red River below.

Coming back to Red River for his grandma's funeral had been hard enough. He knew she hadn't been feeling well. Had heard it in her voice during their phone calls. Then it was too late, and she was gone without him saying good-bye. But coming back a failure? An absolute nightmare, even if no one knew he was all but broke.

Kneeling, he gave the dog a scratch and picked him up. "Sorry, buddy. Didn't mean to scare you."

He wandered into the den where he'd spent evenings with his grandparents and every Saturday morning watching cartoons until he was old enough to drive. The worn shag carpet was rough against his bare feet and crunched with each step. The place was tidy, but a thick layer of dust coated the coffee table, and the brown paneling and outdated furniture made the place look dank and dirty.

What had Bea done with the money he'd sent her over the years? She could've remodeled every inch of the place. Better yet, she could've let him tear it down and build a new house. A mansion by Red River standards. But she'd loved this old gingerbread house up on the hill with just enough elevation to look out over the town. His grandfather had built it for her when they first married, and she couldn't part with it.

He eased onto the frayed but comfortable sofa, set the dog in his lap so he could grab the remote, and flicked the channel to ESPN. There. Back to the real world. That should help relax him.

Except it didn't because all he could think about was his floundering project back in Washington that was still headlining the news across the state. He plucked his cell off the coffee table and Googled press coverage on the Trinity Falls accident. He tapped the link for a Seattle-based channel.

Talmadge's chest tightened as the news anchor reported on the accident, the injuries, the ancient ruins, and the unknown future of the Trinity Falls community. A preaching, teaching lecture on the irony of a leading green architect nearly destroying one of the most important archeological finds of the century. Conveniently, the reporter left out the part about how Talmadge himself stopped the project immediately to call in the authorities and every tribal council in the state of Washington.

He stared at the screen as the reporter droned on.

And on.

And on.

He hit the stop button and tossed the phone onto the lace doily in the middle of the coffee table. He let his head fall back to rest on the sofa cushion and rubbed his tired eyes.

A new call dinged on his phone. His office assistant's name popped onto the screen. He touched the green button and answered.

"Hey, Ellen."

"Hey, boss. Sorry to bother you at a time like this. How're you holding up?" Ellen's kids were grown, but she still held that motherly tone.

Probably why he hired her. She reminded him of Bea.

"I'm makin' it. What's up?" Hopefully not Trinity Falls, unless it was good news.

"That crazy reporter called again. The one who writes the gossip column for the local paper. Wanted an update on you and Monica."

That would be Miss January. Talmadge's eyes slid shut.

"I told her you were out of the office for a family emergency. Want me to give her any other message? Like maybe to get lost on a deserted island or something?"

"She'll just get more relentless. Ignore her for now. I'll deal with it when I get back to Seattle. Anything else?"

"I've taken up knitting. It helps pass the time."

He smirked. "Glad to hear business is that good while I'm gone."

"I'll knit you a scarf."

Maybe she could teach him how to knit since he didn't have much work going on at the moment. He let out a hollow laugh. "I'll be back in a few days. Call if anything else comes up."

Fat chance.

He ended the call, and Lloyd nuzzled Talmadge's chest. With his arm wrapped around the pooch, Talmadge used a forefinger to scratch Lloyd's belly.

Someone rapped at the front door, and Lloyd yapped. Langston maybe? At the wake, his high school buddy had threatened to stop by for a beer. A beer or four sounded pretty good right now.

Talmadge drew in a deep breath, left Lloyd on the sofa, and walked into the foyer.

Bea's old house didn't have a peephole, so Talmadge flipped on the porch light and jerked open the door, expecting Langston to be standing there with a six-pack of beer under his arm and a smart-ass smirk on his face. It had become a ritual during Talmadge's rare visits home.

Instead, Miranda's eyes rounded, and she seemed to stop breathing for a beat.

It wasn't the gust of frosty evening air that made his skin tingle. It was her big brown eyes cascading over his chest, bared by the gaping shirt. Despite the frigid April temperatures, heat started to gather below his waist when her gaze fixed to the unbuttoned waistband of his jeans. The copper flecks in her eyes blazed to life.

Still in the clothes she'd had on when he last saw her at the wake, she held a grocery bag in each arm.

But her attention stayed firmly on his . . . crotch.

He couldn't help it. He couldn't. The corners of his mouth curved up.

"Can I help you with something?" Because by the look on her face, she *wanted* help with something.

Her gaze snapped to his, her eyes widening even more.

"*No.*"

Satisfaction bloomed in his chest because even though she'd just said *no* with more defensiveness in her tone than the Seattle Seahawks had in their starting lineup, she nodded involuntarily.

"I, um, brought Lloyd's food. And his dog bowls." She gave one of the bags a jerking boost. "There's some leftover food from the wake in this one. I thought you might get hungry, and the deviled eggs are really good." When she mentioned the deviled eggs her eyes grew bigger and her expression turned to mortification.

Talmadge couldn't imagine why talking about deviled eggs would make her react that way. Deviled eggs *were* good. He liked deviled eggs.

She tried to shove both bags at him at once.

"*Oof.*" The bags jammed against his chest, and his good arm closed around one of them. "I can't hold the other one. Would you mind bringing it in for me?"

She blinked at him.

"You've been inside Bea's house, right?" He knew for certain she had.

Two more blinks.

He raised both eyebrows at her and angled his head to prompt her to speak.

"You're half-naked," she blurted, keeping her eyes steadily on his. The sheer willpower she exerted to *not* look at him from the neck down showed in her stiff expression.

A muscle next to her eye ticked.

He fought off a chuckle. "Come on, Miranda. I'm not naked. I had a hard time changing because of my shoulder." He paused. A tiny pang of guilt gathered in his chest for wanting to tease her. But hell no, he couldn't resist. "Besides, we've seen each other naked before."

———

Like Miranda could ever forget being skin to skin with Talmadge Oaks. Especially since it had been her first and her only time to ever be skin to skin with . . . anyone.

She narrowed her eyes at him and tried to ignore his perfectly sculpted abs.

She really did try.

But then he adjusted the bag against his hip and the hard muscles of his chest rippled and jumped.

Her mouth turned to chalk dust.

"I can't come in." Surely that croaking sound wasn't her voice? "I'll just leave it here on the porch." Yes, she definitely sounded like a frog. Time to go before she leaped all over him or her tongue shot out to lick him or something even more embarrassing. Hadn't she just blurted something about deviled eggs? The very ones that that were laced with her pesky pheromones.

*Holy Jeez.* She started to set the bag down.

"My shoulder's acting up, Miranda. Can you help me out?" He shrugged. "Since you're here and all."

She really shouldn't. She hadn't always exercised good judgment around Talmadge, especially on the rare occasions she'd found herself alone with him. Besides, the way people in this town idolized him because of his notoriety, even jumped when he snapped his fingers, irritated her.

"Please." His voice and his look were a little helpless and a whole lotta cute.

Her insides turned to mush.

Without a word she took a step toward him, and he angled his body so she could cross the threshold. When she brushed past him, the rich scent of his soap sent her pulse racing. He kicked the door closed with a bare foot and headed toward the kitchen.

"In here." He tossed his head in the general direction of the kitchen. With long strides, he walked ahead of her, his shirttails flapping to each side, Levi's draping perfectly over a firm butt and muscled thighs.

Miranda squeezed her eyes shut for a second and nearly bumped into the wall.

Talmadge stopped and frowned over his shoulder. "You okay?"

"Um, yeah. Just tired from putting on the wake."

As soon as he turned to stroll into the kitchen, Miranda mouthed a curse and followed him She set the bag on the counter and stared at the bowls on the floor.

"He'll never eat out of that."

Talmadge's brows pulled together.

She took the bag from his arm and set it on the counter. Digging inside, she produced a small can of expensive gourmet dog food and held it up for him to see. Then she dug into the bag again and pulled out two of Bea's bowls. "He'll only eat this brand of dog food, which isn't available in Red River." Miranda set the can on the blue kitchen counter. "And he'll only eat out of these bowls." She separated the two pieces of fine china and popped the lid off the can.

"That's Bea's good china," Talmadge murmured.

"Yep." Miranda pulled open Bea's flatware drawer and grabbed a spoon. "He's spoiled."

She spooned the mushy dog food into the bowl and called Lloyd's name. She placed the bowl on the floor next to the other two. He pranced into the kitchen and buried his thin snout in the food, lapping it up like it was his first meal of the day.

"That's amazing." Talmadge watched Lloyd eat. "Bea never let me use those dishes, because she didn't want any pieces to get broken."

"What did you need help with?" Miranda wiped her hands on a dishtowel.

He turned those silvery eyes on her and stared at her for a second like he was still trying to wrap his head around a dog eating out of his grandmother's coveted china. "Oh," he finally said. "Can you help me wrap up my shoulder? I can't do it one-handed, and it needs to be iced several times a day."

Simple enough. She could do that.

He tugged one sleeve down over his arm, and that side of his dress shirt fell away, exposing more of his chest.

Miranda's vision went all fuzzy for a second.

"I'll show you how to do it," he said.

Those words made his ripped torso snap back into perfect focus. Once—seven years, three months, and twelve days ago—he'd shown her how to do other things. Very nice things. Things she missed right about now.

"Miranda?" He fished the ice packs out of the sink.

She shook her head to clear her muddled brain. "*Yes.*" She nearly yelled. "Sure thing."

"Can you grab one of the bandages?" He nodded to the two long strips of rolled elastic bandages and set the bags of ice on the counter. "I'm going to hold one bag in the front and the other in the back so they overlap just a little."

She scurried over and snatched up the bandage. Then she sidestepped around him to work from behind. No way was she going to stand face-to-face with him so close that his breath would wash over her cheeks, down her neck, and prickle her skin all the way to her—

"Wrap the bandage over my shoulder."

She jumped. Then reached up to follow his instructions.

The heat of his skin and the cold ice mingled together as her fingers brushed across his chest to stretch the bandage into place, and a shiver ricocheted through her. She swallowed. *Okay. Done.* God, he smelled good.

"Okay, circle it under my arm and back up over the shoulder again."

*What?* She breathed him in. *Oh. Yeah.* She followed his instructions, her hand skimming along the sleek angles of his torso.

"Now diagonal across my back." His tone turned husky.

She smoothed the bandage across his back, and the muscles rippled under her touch.

*Good God.*

"Then all the way around my chest . . ." His voice cracked on the last word and trailed off.

What was that annoying ringing in her ears?

She reached around his torso with the bandage and had to wrap both arms around his middle to catch the bandage roll with the other hand. And oh, sweet baby Jesus, he was so warm and hard. Her breasts pressed against his back, and she really wanted to kiss the bare skin between his shoulder blades, because it was right there just an inch from her lips.

His breath hitched, and she hesitated. Her arms were still wrapped around him like a sensual embrace. He released the ice packs, secured now by the bandage, and placed his hand over hers.

"Miranda?" He said her name, soft and gentle, and this time his tone held a question that entailed far more than just helping wrap his shoulder.

"What?" she snapped, peeved at herself much more than at him. Because, really, how could she let herself react like . . . like one of his hotel-owning groupies? "I just couldn't reach it." She switched the bandage to the other hand and put a few inches between them while she wrapped it over his shoulder again.

His big hand fell away from hers. "I was just going to ask where Bea gets the dog food." His voice went hard, just like his body.

"Oh." She wrapped and diagonaled and circled and wrapped. And tried to shake off the zing of heat pulsing through her veins straight to the spot between her thighs. The spot that only Talmadge had been able to bring to a boil. "She had to drive into Taos for it." She tried to smooth the damned croak in her voice. "I've picked it up for her the past few months because she didn't feel like making the trip."

Finished with the bandage, she secured the end by tucking it into the web she'd woven around him.

He turned to face her. Stared down at her from under shuttered lashes. "Thank you for helping Bea. And thank you for the wake."

Oh. Well. She cleared her throat, and the ringing in her ears got a little louder.

"Is there anything else I can do for you?" She nearly swallowed her tongue. "I mean do you need help with anything else?"

The corners of his strong mouth lifted into that half-smile. And for a moment, she wanted to step into his arms and soothe whatever troubles he'd been carrying inside as long as she'd known him. The sorrow that showed in that almost-smile. The one she'd dreamed about. Owned by the guy she'd wanted since before he went and got all famous and had beautiful, rich women stuck to him like Velcro. The only man on earth who could rip her heart right out of her chest and grind it to a pulp if she let him.

She wasn't going to let him.

She took a step back. "I'm leaving."

His gaze dropped to her mouth. "You don't have to." It was an invitation. "But you probably should."

And *that* was a warning. His lust-laden voice and smoky eyes clouded her senses, circled around her heart and threatened to break it in half. At least he was honest. Always had been. So Miranda gathered what little willpower she had left and walked out. Because the truth was, Talmadge was the one leaving and Miranda never would.

#  Chapter Five

Giving the door to the inn's owner's suite a frustrated slam, Miranda tossed her keys and purse onto the dinette table. She needed a shower. A hot one. Or maybe a cold one would work better after rubbing against Talmadge's bare, muscled back, because she needed something to douse the flames still making parts of her body quiver that had absolutely no business doing so. At least not when anyone else was in the room.

A wavy, black head of messy hair peeked around the corner from the kitchen. Her younger brother, Jamie, waved and pointed to the phone at his ear. His thin build and five feet eight frame made him look more like a high school kid rather than a college sophomore.

"Mom," he mouthed.

Miranda grimaced.

"I've got classes and homework tomorrow, Mom. I can't help your new boyfriend move in." Jamie rolled his eyes at Miranda.

Her grimace turned to a groan. Not another one. The last one was supposedly "for real this time" and was going to marry her mother and take care of her if she'd just let him move in and recover from a back injury. Yeah, he'd lasted about as long as her mother's meager paycheck. Then he borrowed her car to go to the liquor store and never came back.

Jamie shot Miranda an evil grin. "Hold on, Mom. Miranda wants to talk to you." He walked over and shoved the phone at her.

"I hate you." She took the phone, and Jamie laughed.

She flicked on the floor lamp that sat in the corner of the den, and sank onto Bea's old plaid sofa. Talmadge's grandparents had only used the owner's suite to rest during the day when they ran the inn, so the furnishings were sparse. Miranda lived there, and someday she'd redecorate and make it a homey little place all of her own. Right after she figured out how to pay for it. In the meantime, Bea's old sofa was Jamie's bed. It was a whole lot cheaper than a dorm at Highlands University.

With an exhausted breath, Miranda put the phone to her ear. "Hi, Mom."

"How's my little girl?" Her mother's voice, raspy from years of inhaling smoke from menthol cigarettes and seedy biker bars, scratched at her ears like claws against a chalkboard.

Right. Miranda hadn't been a little girl since she was two. She'd been a grown-up practically since birth, trying to fill in the gaps of responsibility in her family just to survive. Once Jamie arrived, Miranda had gone from adult to mother figure. All by the age of six and a half. While Miranda was making sure Jamie was bathed regularly and teaching him to read, her mother's biggest concern was finding another man with a Harley.

"I'm just fine. You?" Why did she even ask?

"You sound tired, sugar."

Oh no. *Sugar* usually meant her mother wanted something. And that something was usually money.

"What is it, Mom?"

"What's that supposed to mean?" Her mother was already defensive.

Definitely wanted something.

Miranda exhaled. "Nothing. I'm just tired. Bea's funeral was today, and I had the wake at the inn."

Her mother sighed. Loudly. "You're a good soul, Mira. Taking care of someone who wasn't even family." She emphasized the last three words.

"Bea did a lot for me. I owed her." For the way Bea had taken an interest in Miranda's life, given her the credit no one else had for raising Jamie when her mother was off doing Lord knew what with God knew whom, sometimes not coming home for days at a time, Miranda owed her a lot more than a wake.

Her heart suddenly squeezed. Her friend was never coming back.

"Listen, sugar."

Here it came.

"Ted is moving in."

Oh, this one's name was Ted.

"Can we borrow your Jeep? All he has is a Harley."

Big surprise.

Well, she wasn't going to chance another one of her mother's boyfriends running off with the only vehicle Miranda owned.

She'd been supporting herself and Jamie since she was eighteen, even moving them into the apartment over Lorenda's garage. Miranda loved her mother, she really did. Who knew why her mother had turned out the way she had? She wouldn't talk about her childhood, but Miranda had figured out a long time ago that it must've been hard and very, very painful. Still, she wasn't going to keep enabling her. "Can't, Mom. I need it to haul supplies for the renovations."

"Maybe the inn was a bad investment, Mira."

Miranda rubbed her eyes with a thumb and index finger. Was it too much to ask that her mother show some support? A little encouragement? Just once? "Look, Mom, I have to go."

Jamie came out of the kitchen, munching on barbecue chips. He picked up one of his textbooks off the table and waved it at Miranda.

"Jamie needs help with his homework."

*Thank you,* she mouthed to her little brother and hung up.

"Okay, I don't hate you quite as much." She kicked off her shoes.

"Good. So . . . I'm getting a job." He shoved another chip into his mouth and chomped.

"What? No, you're not." No he wasn't.

The drive back and forth to college because she couldn't afford a dorm chewed up a lot of his time. Besides, she wasn't about to let Jamie waste precious study time at a dead-end job. Not with his brains. She'd been deprived of a college education even though she'd finished first in her senior class and scored a thirty-one on the ACTs, but she'd see to it that Jamie got one if it bankrupted her.

Which it just might, because her funds were running dangerously low. If she had to choose between paying for Jamie's tuition and paying the mortgage on the inn, she'd have to default on the note and lose her dream of becoming a business owner.

"I want you to focus on school."

"I am focused on school," he argued around a mouthful of chips.

She gave her head an authoritative shake, switching into mother hen mode. "I don't want a nothing job to distract you from studying."

Her phone rang. Good, because she was not having this conversation. She worked too hard to make sure Jamie had a better life. She didn't want him to lose focus now that he was half finished with his degree.

"Hello." She answered the call without even looking at the number.

"Hey, girlfriend," said Lorenda, her BFF since high school.

"Hey yourself. Whatcha doing?"

"I'm packing to jet off to Paris for a romantic weekend with my new rich lover," Lorenda said, all seriousness.

"Okay. Whatcha *really* doing?"

Lorenda laughed. She'd been mostly a single mom since her two kids were born, because her husband hadn't come home from Afghanistan alive. Both boys were still in elementary school, so trips to Paris and romantic weekends weren't on Lorenda's list of priorities. "I'm cleaning the boys' bathroom. They had the stomach flu the last two days."

"Oh dear." Miranda wrinkled her nose.

"Yeah, I'm living the dream." Her tone softened. "Sorry, I missed Bea's funeral."

"Bea would've understood."

"My mom and dad said you did a nice job with the wake. How'd it go?"

The way Miranda saw it, she had two choices. She could tell her best friend the truth about how Talmadge had so thoroughly explored her mouth with his and how he'd done an exceptional job fondling her ass with his big, warm hand. Or she could lie.

"Oh, you know. Just an average wake, I guess." Average wake her ass. Literally.

"Need me to come by tomorrow and help clean up?" Lorenda offered.

"Already done. Besides, it sounds like you've got plenty more to clean than I do."

Lorenda laughed. "Hey, my mom just called. Did you know there was a town meeting tonight?"

"Nope." Between losing Bea and organizing the wake, Miranda hadn't kept up with the weekly events in Red River. "Why?"

Lorenda hesitated.

Never a good sign. "What?"

Jamie wandered into the kitchen and stuck his head in the refrigerator to look for more food.

"You were kind of elected to chair the Hot Rides and Cool Nights Festival this year."

Miranda sat up. "Elected? I didn't put my name in."

"Um, Mom said Clydelle and Francine put it in because no one else volunteered."

"But Mrs. Wilkinson usually chairs it." A flutter settled in the pit of Miranda's stomach, because Mrs. Wilkinson hated Miranda. With a passion. Because Miranda's mother had caught the eye of *Mr.* Wilkinson many moons ago, and that didn't go over so hot at their church since he was a deacon and Mrs. Wilkinson taught Sunday school. Of course, they painted her mother as the aggressor, and Mr. Wilkinson swore nothing physical had happened between them.

To this day, Mrs. Wilkinson's head spun full circle when she saw anyone with the last name of Cruz. That woman had already made Miranda's life uncomfortable by lifting her nose in the air like Miranda was dirt every time they ran into each other. Which was often in a town the size of Red River. "Why didn't she volunteer this year?"

"Apparently, she was late to the meeting. Not a lot of people were there because of Bea's funeral today. Clydelle made a motion to vote on it tonight, Francine seconded the motion. Right before Mrs. Wilkinson walked in claiming someone had sliced one of her tires. Mom said Old Lady Wilkinson didn't exactly take the news with grace. So watch out for her. She's scary."

The woman was way beyond scary. She was one hundred and fifty percent shouldn't-be-allowed-to-operate-heavy-equipment-or-own-a-gun crazy.

And just like that, Miranda was back in the Wilkinsons' crosshairs.

---

"Your ass went viral." Jamie shouted at Miranda over the buzzing of the electric sander in her hands. He sat on a barstool behind the inn's kitchen counter while she tried to keep some forward momentum going with the renovations. She'd lost valuable work time because of hosting the wake yesterday . . . and because her contractor was still AWOL.

"*What?*" She shouted back at him without looking away from the wood beam that ran across the dining room ceiling. Because surely she'd just heard him wrong. He did not just say—

"Your ass," he yelled, "went viral!"

When Miranda jerked her head around to look at him, the old rickety ladder she stood on shook. She went still, regained her balance, and flipped the power switch to off. The handheld sander whirred to a stop, and she glared at her brother through orange safety goggles.

With a toss of his head, Jamie pushed his long, black bangs to one side and turned his laptop so she could see the YouTube video of her on all fours. The recording appeared a little off-color from behind goggles, but it was indeed her ass. Bared for all the world to see on YouTube, except for the thin silk layer of her sheer panties.

She clamped her eyes shut.

"Guess how many views you've gotten just since the wake yesterday?" Little brother sounded way too happy about her butt cheeks showing up on social media.

"I was trying to help Lloyd!"

"No really. Guess."

"Shouldn't you be defending my honor? Hunting down the delinquents who caused my humiliation?"

He smiled. When he leaned forward so he could see the screen, too, his bangs fell across one eye. "I'd rather give them a high five. This is sick stuff. You know how many years I've tried to find something this good to hold over your head?" He answered his own question. "Ever since you practiced cutting my hair because you were thinking of applying to beauty school."

"It didn't turn out that bad." Sort of.

"You had to take me to the barber and have it shaved to the scalp."

True. But on the upside, she'd realized becoming a hairstylist wasn't her thing.

She rubbed her forehead. "Can't you take the YouTube video down?"

Jamie shrugged. "Once it's out there, it's *out* there." He didn't look away from the screen. "Oh, wait. This is the good part." He held up a finger for a second, eyes intent on the screen, then burst into fits of laughter.

"Don't you have college classes to attend? Or do you just like wasting my money?"

He flipped his laptop around again. "Online class today." He pointed to the screen and grabbed a cookie from the bin.

"You eat more than you're worth," she deadpanned. Maybe she'd give him another haircut after she duct-taped him to the barstool.

He tossed his hair to one side again and munched on the cookie. "Precisely why I'm getting a job." He grabbed another cookie, trying to satisfy his voracious metabolism. Damn him. "And I'm going to pay you back all the tuition money one day."

"Every penny." She tried to make it sound like a reprimand but ended up fighting off a smile instead. "*After* you finish your degree. So no job. Not unless it has something to do with a future career."

"You know I love you, sis." Jamie blew her a kiss, and her heart warmed even though she knew he was just sucking up. He was a great kid, and he was there to help her whenever she needed it, just the way Bea had been.

Bea believed Miranda could turn this place into a thriving focal point of the town again. It had been Bea's idea for Miranda to buy it. But now Talmadge had inherited the note. He might consider a grace period on the payments if Miranda needed it.

She chewed the inside of her cheek. *No.* No way would she ask him for help. Not after how close she'd been to tossing her self-control to the wind while helping wrap his shoulder. And especially not after he insinuated that she may or may not have taken advantage of his grandmother, a woman she'd loved like a mother.

She needed to prove her mettle to Talmadge Oaks.

*No. She needed to prove her mettle to herself.* For Jamie's sake, she had to prove once and for all that they didn't have to accept the hand of poverty that had been dealt the Cruz children. Since they'd never gotten any encouragement from their bar-hopping mother, Jamie was worth Miranda's effort.

Even though he enjoyed the humiliation of her ass going viral on YouTube.

She flipped the sander on again, but a loud knock sounded on the back door. Carefully, she leaned to the right and looked down the hall. The door swung open a second later.

Talmadge swaggered in, dressed to the nines. Overkill for Red River, in her opinion. But holy lip-smacking moly, he was the most perfectly formed man she'd ever seen.

She drew in a sharp breath and looked away, only to have his sheer male beauty draw her attention right back. She felt like a bee that had just discovered an ocean of nectar.

He flipped a pair of black aviators to the back of his head as soon as he stepped across the threshold in black tailored dress pants and black driving shoes. A sling still held the injured arm against his midsection, but a black mock turtleneck clung to the hills and valleys of his chest and arms.

He could've done Don Corleone proud dressed like that, except for the tiny poodle under his arm. A mob boss probably would've preferred a pit bull over a bow-wearing toy poodle.

"Morning." His lips seemed to mouth the words as she took him in. She looked down at the buzzing noise and snapped out of the trance. Flipped the switch to off again.

He gave her ladder a long once-over. The muscles in his jaw flexed, and several creases appeared between his eyes.

"Morning." She touched her jaw to make sure it wasn't hanging open, and to her surprise it wasn't. Because the man was drool-worthy.

"Hey, Mr. Oaks, you probably don't remember me, but I'm Miranda's brother." Her little brother's voice shook with admiration.

"Kid brother." Miranda shot him a disgusted look, because Jamie never looked at her with that kind of awe. And she was paying his way through college! "Seven years my junior."

"Six and a half, and you never let me forget it," Jamie mouthed off, but his expression went timid the moment his attention returned to Talmadge.

"Because you should show your elders some respect." Miranda's teeth were starting to hurt from grinding them so hard.

Jamie smiled at her, took an exaggerated bite of a bagel, and plunked his legs up on the counter crossed at the ankles.

"Sure, I remember you. You're just taller now." Talmadge chuckled and notched up his chin at her brother. Miranda thought Jamie would melt right there on the floor from hero-worship.

Really? Talmadge was an architect, not a movie star. She rolled her eyes. But part of her heart cinched tight, and she wondered if Jamie's instant respect for Talmadge had something to do with never having a dad around. Never even *knowing* who his dad was. Of course, Talmadge seemed to command that respect from most people in a room simply by stepping into it.

"Did you forget something, Mr. Oaks?" Miranda turned her attention back to the other annoying male in the room.

Jamie blew out a *humph* like she was the biggest dream crusher in the world and straightened to tap away on his laptop again.

Talmadge gave Lloyd a boost. "I need to leave him here."

Miranda set the sander on the flimsy metal shelf attached to the top of the ladder and grabbed a paint scraper. Furiously, she started to work on a crossbeam directly over her head. "Why would you leave him here? He's your dog."

Talmadge came over and stood next to the ladder. "He whined and yelped all night." The tone of his voice raised a notch like he was kind of desperate.

Involuntarily, her gaze flitted to Lloyd. "Where'd he sleep?" She tried not to look at Talmadge. Tried to focus on the task of stripping an already well-stripped section of the beam. She scraped some more, the speed of her strokes increasing.

"In the laundry room. It was too cold to put him outside. Plus I didn't see a doghouse in Bea's backyard."

Miranda blew out an exasperated breath. *Men could be so dense.*

"He's not an outside dog." As if the bows and nail polish didn't give that away. "He's not used to sleeping alone. Let him in your bed." She swallowed at her own statement.

Talmadge stared at the dog, horror etched across his face. "Beg your pardon?"

"He's used to sleeping with Bea. So, let him sleep with you now."

"This dog is not sleeping in my bed. No one sleeps in my bed."

The tool slipped from Miranda's hand. She grabbed for it, caught it, and steadied herself on the swaying ladder. Right. Not a lot of sleeping went on in Talmadge Oaks's bed when someone besides him was in it. She knew that all too well.

Her insides coiled so tight she thought she might spontaneously combust.

Talmadge set Lloyd down and went to stand at the foot of the ladder. "You're going to kill yourself on this sorry excuse for a ladder." With his good hand, he gave it a small shake. It nearly toppled with her on it.

"Hey!" She grabbed onto a rung. His steadying hand on the small of her back sent heat racing through her.

At least it wasn't on her ass this time.

"I'm not going to let you fall. I just wanted to prove a point." His warm palm molded against her back.

"By killing me?"

"Sorry, but what the *hell* are you doing on this shoddy old thing with tools in your hand? If you don't kill yourself, you could easily lose some fingers, or a limb, or an eye."

She pulled off the safety goggles and propped them on top of her head. "That's what these are for."

His gaze studied her eyes. Looked deep, then dropped to her lips.

The tip of her tongue slipped out to wet them.

"Plastic goggles aren't going to do much good if you fall on top of an electric sander that's going full speed." He took the sander from the top shelf of the ladder and set it aside.

"The remodel is behind schedule. I can do some of the projects myself. I'm not afraid of hard work."

"Shouldn't your contractor be doing the heavy lifting? And if he's a professional, he should have better equipment than this." Talmadge gave the ladder a dismissive wave. "Where is he?"

She hesitated. Good question. Not that it was any of Talmadge's business, but a good question nonetheless. So good, in fact, that she'd been wondering that very thing ever since she handed Ben Smith several thousand dollars for roofing supplies. The next day he'd texted that he was sick with the flu and hadn't shown up for work since.

That was several days ago, and he'd stopped answering his cell. So, where *was* Mr. Smith?

*None. Of. Talmadge's. Business.* All he needed to know was that she was handing him her payments at the end of each month.

Or not.

So why did she feel it necessary to defend her choice to hire Ben Smith? Lots of people in town had used him. All of Red River's silver-haired widows were happy with him. Couldn't stop singing his praises, in fact. So Talmadge's suspicious tone irked Miranda because maybe he was insinuating that she'd made a poor business decision. "Ben needed money to buy roofing materials, and then he got sick." She hoped. She prayed that was true. "When he comes back, he'll bring his equipment. In the meantime, I found these tools in the storage closet."

"In the meantime, get down off that death trap." Talmadge's statement was a demand.

Or rather a command. He was *commanding* her!

She wielded the paint scraper and started on the beam again. "I've got work to do." She *did not* have to do what he said.

"You can't work if you're hurt."

"You should know." She pointed to his sling.

They glared at each other.

Without taking his eyes from hers, he reached for the scraper in her hand, tossed it on top of a pile of materials, and gave the ladder a small but firm shake. She lost her balance on the wobbling ladder and fell right into his arms. Well, *arm*.

He used his good arm to catch her and held her flush against him with her legs dangling in the air. His look was firm, his minty breath caressing her cheeks.

"Put. Me. Down."

He stared down at her with a smoky gaze. "Whatever you say." His words came out more like a murmur, and the tickle of his breath raced down her neck all the way to her toes.

Which curled.

He let her slide down his hardened body, inch by glorious inch. And oh, heavens, if this were a contact sport, she'd trample every woman for miles to join the team. Her feet touched the ground, finally . . . unfortunately . . . and she stepped out of his arm.

"Don't get back on that thing."

This was her place, and she'd been taking care of herself and Jamie since before she hit puberty. She wasn't going to be cowed by a man the way her mother always had. Now that Bea—the closest person to a role model Miranda had ever had—was gone, she'd damn sure help herself instead of relying on a man for anything.

Because men never stayed around.

One of his silky brows arched.

She grabbed at her ponytail and twisted the end around an index finger. Studied the sawdust that she'd left on the entire length of his front, stark against his jet-black clothing. Served him right.

She tried to feign a condescending tone. "Look, *Mr. Oaks*—"

The silver-blue of his irises flared to a dusky purple.

God, she loved purple.

She glanced away for a nanosecond before trying to manufacture more indignation. "I know you're used to commanding your employees, the press, adoring activist fans, and women from all tax brackets—"

A muscle in his squared jaw tensed.

"But I'm not your employee. I'm not an adoring fan." *Liar.* She followed every one of his projects. Had for years. And the last two years, she'd made a weekly date at Bea's to bring her laptop and read articles off the Internet because Bea's vision was deteriorating. "And I'm certainly not a woman who wants . . ." *You.* She had to bite her lip to keep from blurting it. And suddenly her throat went very, very dry. Who turned up the thermostat in here, anyway? She could barely pay her bills as it stood.

She wasn't sure if it was the way he set his freshly shaved jaw, or the way one of his lush brows arched with just enough arrogance to make her teeth grind, but she snapped. This was her dream, not his. His dream had been fulfilled and was still waiting for him back in Washington. Even though he'd caught a tough break with Trinity Falls, his grandparents had made sure he got the education he needed to pursue his career.

So why was he here interfering with the one and only chance she'd ever have to be something more than a waitress? To be in control of her future and take charge of her destiny.

"I'm done taking orders from other people. I'm the boss in this place. The contract I signed says so. So go find someone else to order around."

An almost-smile slid onto his mouth. Without a word, he turned the ladder on its side and stomped on the hinge, which snapped like a twig.

This time Miranda's jaw really did fall open.

He carried the ladder past the counter to the back door.

"Get the door," Talmadge said to Jamie, who scrambled to his feet to do Talmadge's bidding.

Miranda wanted to scream. Talmadge tossed the ladder outside against the trash Dumpster and walked back into the inn. He brushed his hand against his dusty clothes, then Jamie let the door slam shut again.

"Better," Talmadge said. "Now what were you saying, *Ms. Cruz?*"

"That was the only ladder I had!"

"Not saying much. I'll bring you a better one from Bea's. My grandfather's work shed is still filled with equipment."

"But—" Miranda tried to slow her spinning mind. How dare he walk in here and . . . and . . . take charge.

She looked at her brother for some familial support.

Jamie stared at Talmadge, the admiration in her little brother's eyes about as subtle as a neon sign in the middle of a power blackout.

"Dude, that was awesome." Jamie's voice was an awe-inspired whisper. "No guy has ever brought Miranda to her knees." Jamie turned pink and glanced at Miranda. "Uh, pardon the pun, sis." He looked at Talmadge. "Who knew she'd let her new boyfriend boss her around."

Miranda and Talmadge's heads swiveled toward Jamie. *What did he just say?*

"He's not my boyfriend," she blurted at the exact same time Talmadge spoke up.

"I'm not her boyfriend," he said. Not quite as loudly as she did, but the firm authority in his voice was no less effective in conveying his distaste for the thought. Which galled her to the bone.

"Sure you are." Jamie grabbed his laptop and turned the screen to them. A picture of her and Talmadge, lips locked, bodies molded together, his hand groping her ass where her pants had split in two, stared back at them. "This just showed up on the *Red River Rag*."

Miranda's eyes crashed shut. "Oh my God. This can't be happening."

Talmadge's tone turned confused. "What's the *Red River Rag*?"

"It's a Tumblr blog about all of Red River's gossip," said Jamie.

"I thought Tumblr was mostly porn?" Talmadge said. When Miranda shot him her very best disgusted look, he mumbled, "Not that I would know."

Miranda had tried to live clean. Tried not to earn the same bad rep as her mother. And she'd pulled it off spectacularly except for that one tiny indiscretion with Talmadge seven years, three months, and thirteen days ago. Miraculously, she'd been able to keep those few hours they'd spent in the inn's honeymoon suite top secret, but now she was making headlines over an accidental rendezvous that involved her wardrobe malfunction, Talmadge's hand, and both of their lips? At Bea's wake!

*Oh, God.* She was supposed to be building a reputation as Red River's newest respectable proprietor.

Jamie chuckled like it was funny, which it wasn't in the least. "If Tumblr is mostly porn, then you two fit right in." Jamie laughed harder.

So not funny.

"I'm going. Tokillyou," Miranda said through gritted teeth.

"Hey, it's your ass going viral on the Internet, not mine." Jamie held up both hands.

"It will be in the most painful way possible. When you least expect it," Miranda promised.

"It's not my fault you got caught on camera making out with someone famous."

Miranda's jaw locked. "We were not making out," she managed to grind out. Well. Damn. Yes they were. "Were we, Mr. Oaks?"

He just shrugged, one corner of his mouth curling up. "We kinda were."

She pinched the bridge of her nose.

"Sick! My sister's dating Talmadge Oaks. Wait till I put this on Instagram. I'll have girls all over me."

"We're not dating!" Miranda yelled. "And I swear to God if you put that *anywhere* or tell anybody, you will never be able to sire a child to carry on our family name."

She turned on Talmadge. "You have to do something to stop this. People in Red River will listen to you. I can't have people thinking we're . . . we're . . ."

*Gah!*

She pointed to the door, steam virtually swirling from her ears. "Go. Now."

He flexed the hand on his injured arm and looked down at it. "I've got a couple of appointments. Lloyd will stay here while I'm gone."

It wasn't a question. He wasn't politely asking for a favor like normal people would. It was a command. She almost blurted no just to show him she really was the boss, but she did love the little dog.

Talmadge trekked toward her, stopping a breath away. "I'll be back later with a *real* ladder and some tools." He placed the edge of his index finger under her chin and lifted her gaze to meet his. Mockery gleamed in his metallic eyes. "Sweetheart."

# Chapter Six

Talmadge found a parking spot along the curb in the middle of Red River's historic business district and glanced at his watch. He was late for the reading of Bea's will, but he doubted being a few minutes late in Red River would ruffle a lot of legal feathers. He was surprised Red River even had an attorney now.

He picked at the sawdust that Miranda had just left all over him. Dirty clothes were a small price to pay for the feel of her sliding all the way down his body. He'd wanted to hold her there; the contrast of her soft curves against his work-hardened body had ignited a fire down below.

He picked faster.

The sawdust clung to his dress clothes like gum, so he finally gave up and got out of the old Ram truck. The door creaked when he slammed it.

Wheeler Peak was magnificent any time of year, but particularly in the winter and spring when it was still clothed in white all the way to the bottom. He admired it for a second while a few cars tooled by, and then darted across the street to Angelique Barbetta-Holloway's law office, which was above her husband's Main Street medical practice.

He climbed the stairs, rapped a knuckle against the open door, and peeked inside.

"Please come in." Angelique stood and welcomed him.

"Nice to meet you." Talmadge walked in and shook her hand over the desk.

She waved him into a seat in front of her. The tasteful armchair barely fit his large frame, but he was used to it. So he adjusted himself at an angle.

"You as well, Mr. Oaks." Rumor had it she was as smart as she was beautiful and was fiercely in love with her new husband, Dr. Blake Holloway, with whom she was expecting a baby.

And he'd gleaned every bit of that information by scrolling through the *Red River Rag* on his phone since he'd left the inn a few minutes ago. Wow. Anything a person wanted to know about Red River was on that blog. But it was the pictures of him and Miranda that kept drawing his attention. She seemed so perfect in his arms that a spark of pride had swelled in his chest, and a lump had formed in his throat. Something he hadn't experienced when he saw his pictures with beautiful women in the celebrity mags.

"Call me Talmadge." He motioned to the specks of sawdust that covered most of his front. "I was helping a friend with a project."

Angelique shook her head, her black ponytail swishing around her shoulders. She waved toward an open door to his right where several cans of paint sat on the floor along with brushes, rolls of tape, and a few drop cloths. A half-assembled baby bed leaned against the far wall, and miscellaneous parts were strewn across the wood floor. "I totally understand." She laughed. "The words 'It's one baby. How hard can it be?' actually came out of my mouth when I found out I was expecting."

He smiled. Liked her already. "Congratulations, Mrs. Barbetta-Holloway."

"Call me Angelique. I rarely go by my last name, since I chose to hyphenate it. Entire wars can be fought in the time it takes to say the whole thing. Irritates my husband to death." She smiled. "Which is why I did it."

She removed a file from a drawer and set it in front of her. Her silhouette was framed by the large picture window behind her. Talmadge studied the rich design of the classic crown molding that surrounded the window and lined the top of the walls.

Besides running the inn, his grandfather had done carpentry work on the side. Talmadge had helped with some of the repair jobs in these apartments back in the day. Even then he imagined how beautiful the old buildings could be if transformed by someone with a vision for them. The same kind of vision he had for Trinity Falls. Starting an entire green town from scratch had seemed like a brilliant idea until a few weeks ago.

The hand on his injured arm involuntarily clenched and released.

Scaling back to smaller, less ambitious jobs might be forced on him now. So might poverty, if Trinity Falls didn't work out.

"How are you holding up?" Angelique asked, the backdrop of a clear blue sky and a snow-blanketed Wheeler Peak making the situation seem more pleasant than it was.

"I'm okay." He used his fewer-words-are-best method of handling a conversation.

When he didn't elaborate, she got right to the point and opened the folder sitting in front of her.

"I asked you here for the reading of Bea Oaks's last will and testament." Her voice was all professionalism.

Talmadge nodded. *Shouldn't take long.* Although his grandparents hadn't been poor, they also weren't people of significant means. Besides the old gingerbread house where he grew up, there might be a little life insurance money. He'd never asked. He'd been the one to send money home every month since he got his first job right out of college. But Bea gave most of it to charities, saying she had no debt and didn't need more material things at her age. She'd even asked him to stop wiring money into her account at the Red River Community Bank.

He hadn't. How could he not send money home to the grandparents who had taken him in and raised him? What his grandparents chose to do with the money was up to them. If it made Bea happy to help others with it, then Talmadge was good with that. He understood that pull to give back. He'd spent his entire career doing the same. It was the reason he decided on the riskier path into green architecture instead of mainstream designs. It was his attempt to preserve instead of destroy. He'd destroyed too much early in his life.

"You, Talmadge Oaks, are her only living survivor and beneficiary."

Scalding heat bit through his nerves.

Yes, thanks to him, his grandparents had no one else left.

He fought off a scowl and nodded for Angelique to continue.

She proceeded to read the will and all its legalese. Talmadge let her words flow over him as though it was Bea herself speaking.

Bea had updated her will a few months ago. *Somewhat puzzling because Bea didn't have much, but okay.*

She had been of sound mind and body. *Yep. Sharp as a tack until the day she passed.*

Miranda had served as the witness to her last will and testament.

*Miranda.* He shifted to find a more comfortable position. Analyzed the edges of a cottony white cloud that was just starting to come into view over Angelique's head while she spoke.

Bea left all her worldly possessions to Talmadge. *No surprise.*

Angelique read off the list of possessions:

First, the house and everything inside. He had no idea what he'd do with it. His life was back in Washington along with all his screwed-up investments. If he had a chance of recovering his life savings, he had to get back to Washington . . . and figure out how the hell to get his stymied building project moving again.

Next, the Subaru Talmadge had bought her some years ago—which she refused to drive, preferring Grandpa's old Dodge Ram pickup instead. Talmadge couldn't blame her. He preferred the gas-guzzling jalopy too. It felt more familiar. More like home than the new, economical, and environmentally friendly model.

Wouldn't his friends crusading to stop global warming just crucify him for that?

Last, a life insurance policy, the value to revert to her account at the Red River Community Bank totaling . . .

Talmadge sat forward. "Did you just say—?"

Angelique peered at him over sophisticated reading glasses. "Yes, I did. See for yourself." She shifted the papers and leaned across her desk so he could read it.

Holy shit.

That was a hell of a lot of zeros.

"Where'd my grandmother get that kind of money?" It wasn't the Hail Mary he needed to cover his potential losses, but it would go a long, *long* way in keeping his life running until he could figure out a way to preserve the archeological ruins, strike a deal with the tribes in the Trinity Falls area, and the wheels of production could start turning again so his investment could pay off.

Angelique pulled off her reading glasses. "She got a lot of it from you."

Talmadge tried to speak, but no words came out.

"Both of your grandparents had sizeable life insurance policies. Bea donated some of the money you sent her, but she saved most of it for a rainy day. Apparently, she made some very wise investments, too."

Talmadge gave Angelique a blank stare, because his brain couldn't wrap around this news.

"Since I'm fairly new in town, I didn't know your grandmother very well, but Bea seemed like a practical woman." Angelique tapped her glasses against the document. "Bea tried to *give* Miranda the inn, but Miranda refused to accept it. Said she'd pay for it or not have it at all. So I drew up the sale in the form of a contract. You've inherited that contract as well."

Opening the folder, Angelique pulled out another document. "Here it is."

Talmadge reached for the paper, but only scanned it. "I'm aware. Bea told me." He scrubbed his good hand over his jaw. Flexed the injured hand and flinched at the soreness that shot through his shoulder. "I'm not an attorney. I'm just a guy who happens to know how to build things. I'm not even all that smart." *I'm a dumbass when it comes to investments.* "I'm missing your point." He gave the contract a shake. "What does Bea's agreement with Miranda have to do with the rest of my inheritance? Aren't they two separate things?"

Lacing her fingers together, Angelique nodded and leveled keen, intelligent eyes at him. "Normally, that would be true."

Talmadge met her gaze. "But my gut tells me this situation isn't normal."

Angelique smiled, a look of approval spreading across her face like they'd just solved a difficult crossword puzzle together. "And something tells me that you're much smarter than you're willing to admit."

He raked a hand over his jaw again and stared at Miranda and Bea's signatures scrawled at the bottom of the page. Bea's age showed in the shaky lettering. Miranda's smooth, looping strokes flowed graceful and majestic across the page.

Even her handwriting turned him on.

*Hell.*

"Let's hear the *but*," said Talmadge.

Angelique gave him another approving smile. *"But,"* she said with emphasis, "there was a separate codicil that Miranda didn't know about. No one did. Until now."

Something speared at his gut.

Angelique's expression softened like a mother looking at her child. He'd seen it many times in Bea's eyes. Had seen it in his mother's eyes on the rare occasions that she wasn't worrying about how to please his dad so his temper wouldn't turn explosive. "She was very proud of you. Because of how you tried to look out for her financially, she wanted to leave you a legacy in her own way."

That was Bea. Always looking out for him, always showing him unconditional love in everything she did. Wetness welled in his eyes, before he spoke in gravelly, broken words. "She was a good woman."

"The best, I'm told," said Angelique. "But I still haven't fully answered your question about how this relates to Miranda Cruz."

No, she hadn't, and Talmadge wasn't sure he wanted to hear it.

"She also knew that Miranda would have a hard time on her own financially. Apparently, Miranda has been working at Joe's since she was a teenager and used her savings for the down payment on the inn and the remodel."

He waited.

"Your grandmother wanted you to help Miranda get the inn open and running."

He gave his head a hard shake. "Not possible. I have to get back to Washington. I'll hire a new contractor for the inn." A competent one. An honest one.

"Bea was very specific that she wanted *you* to help Miranda with this project. She said your hands-on style would ensure that the renovations would be done right, and it would help Miranda's budget stretch."

It would also ensure his daily involvement.

It wasn't that he didn't want to spend time with Miranda Cruz. She was the first woman in a long while who had sparked an interest in his mind and several other parts of his body. In fact, he'd thought of little else since he walked out onto the back porch of the inn and found her on all fours with her firm, round bottom smiling up at him.

But he *had* to go back to Washington and deal with his problems. Especially now that he had some money to function with.

"Miranda's contractor doesn't seem very competent. I'll find someone else. I can keep in touch with the new guy from Washington. Skype works wonders, so I can look the guy in the eye, and I'll make sure he sends me the receipts. I'll have Miranda's kid brother check the supplies and make sure it all adds up."

That would be helping. So he would still fulfill Bea's last wishes, even if he wasn't onsite. Problem solved.

Except that Angelique's arched brow and sympathetic smile told him that there was definitely still a problem.

Rubbing at his temple—because a migraine the size of a skyscraper was coming on with every second that he sat there—he exhaled. Loudly. "What else?"

Both of her black eyebrows rose. "You are definitely a smart man." Closing the file, she moved it aside and eased back against her burgundy leather chair. "The codicil stipulates that you can't touch the money until the day Miranda's inn opens for business."

His jaw dropped.

"You're joking." The money in Bea's account was the only way he could afford to pay a contractor to finish the renovations on the inn. Had his grandma gone senile, and he'd just missed it? Because including such a ridiculous demand in her will defied logic. "Bea knew it would be next to impossible for me to stay in Red River that long."

Angelique shrugged. "Apparently 'impossible' and 'next to impossible' were two very different things to your grandmother." Angelique folded her hands in her lap. "Bea was certain that even if you offered Miranda help with money, Miranda still wouldn't accept it."

Right. He didn't have much money anymore. His eyes slid shut, blocking out the impossibility of the situation. When he opened them, Angelique gave him a kindhearted look.

"Miranda's not big on taking things she hasn't earned. It's one of the reasons your grandmother loved her. So Bea thought the best way to ensure Miranda's success would be for you to offer your time and skills. She hoped Miranda would be less likely to turn that sort of help down."

He rested an index finger against his chin, staring down at the document in his lap. "What happens if I don't stay and help Miranda?"

Angelique picked up the folder and handed it to Talmadge. "It's laid out in the codicil. This is your copy."

He opened the file and scanned it. "The money goes to the city of Red River. All of it." Talmadge tried to disguise the disbelief in his voice. He hadn't minded Bea giving every cent to charity until five minutes ago when he thought her frugal ways and thoughtfulness had saved his sorry ass. But now? Hot anger rushed through his veins and gathered in his chest. There hadn't been strings attached to any of the money he gave her, so why would she do this to him?

"That's the legacy she intended. If you didn't need or want the money, she figured you'd want it to go toward a building project that benefits others. It will be used to build an after-school sports and recreation facility for kids in Red River," said Angelique.

And the heat lightened to lukewarm. He couldn't help but smile at Bea's motive. She'd always been willing to help any stray kid who came along, including him. And Miranda, too. He ran his thumb over the page where Bea had signed her name. His grandmother was one sharp cookie.

"There's one more thing." Angelique waved to the paper in his hand. "Look at the last paragraph."

He did and didn't like it one damned bit. "Why can't I tell Miranda about the money or about what's in Bea's codicil?"

Angelique's sigh said she understood what a tough spot he was in. "Apparently, Miranda has a thing about not depending on men."

*Already figured that out.* Staying in control seemed to be her mission in life. "How am I supposed to get Miranda to accept my help without telling her my inheritance is tied to the opening of her inn?"

"Bea felt sure you'd figure something out. She saw how you're able to convince celebrities and wealthy business magnates into pouring millions into your charitable environmental projects. You can tell Miranda every detail after the inn opens. Not before." Angelique pointed to the paper. "Your grandmother was very specific."

And the strings attached to the money were to keep him here. But for what purpose?

Inhaling deep, he looked up at Angelique. "Guess I'll be in town for a while."

Talmadge thanked Angelique, even though he wasn't feeling too damn thankful at that moment, and left her office. He stepped out into the sunshine and breathed the crisp air into his lungs.

What the hell had Bea been thinking?

He walked around the building and into the alley to find some privacy while he called his second in command back in Washington. "Hey," Talmadge said as soon as Larry Jameson answered. "I've run into a snag here. I'll have to stay a little longer than I planned."

Tension flowed through the line. "How long? Our investors are antsy, and the subcontractors aren't going to wait forever. They're already mumbling about moving on to their next jobsites."

Talmadge kicked at a lump of dirty snow in the alley. "Any news from the tribal councils?"

"Not yet, but they're meeting in a few days. Rumors are flying up here that they're going to want us to tear down the entire building site and restore the landscape around the ruins. You know what that means."

Hell yes, he knew what it meant. It meant he'd lose everything. Not only would it cost millions to raze the infrastructure of an entire town he'd already started laying, but it would take even more millions to start the eco-restoration process. And even then, it would be decades before the landscape would regain the natural vibrant flora and fauna.

It meant an epic professional failure that would dismantle every effort he'd made in the world of green, sustainable architecture. It meant he'd let Bea down again. Even if she wasn't around to see it, he'd still know the truth about himself. He always had.

---

Fuming, Miranda traipsed down Main Street toward Lorenda Lawson's real estate office after showering off the sawdust and changing into fresh clothes. She needed to vent to her BFF and figure out how to undo the damage caused by the *Red River Rag* and YouTube. A firestorm of gossip had probably burned through the entire county by now because of those pictures. Pictures of her and Talmadge posted on the Internet for the world to see. What people might think was going on in the pictures . . . And he'd broken her ladder!

Well, she wouldn't stand for any of it.

She wouldn't.

No one in Red River would take her seriously as a business owner if she didn't stop the rumor mill from churning. And Talmadge had to help stop it somehow. Except that his response to the pictures on the *Red River Rag* was to call her *sweetheart*.

Her own brother had gotten the wrong impression and thought the pictures were racy. Of course, he also thought they were funny without fully understanding the implications to her reputation.

Miranda crammed her hands into her red wool coat and continued her march down Main Street, bracing herself against the cold wind.

At least Talmadge had been a gentleman about the one time she'd given in to her desire and asked him to satisfy her burgeoning curiosity. It had been time. She'd turned twenty-one, and with few prospects in Red River, she didn't want to be a virgin forever.

When Lorenda's high school sweetheart, Cameron Lawson, came home from the military so they could get married, Talmadge came back for the wedding. He looked so damn hot and worldly in his tuxedo compared to her, whose grand travels had included not more than a few hours in any direction. *And* he was leaving to go back to Washington, so no one would ever know except him and her.

Talmadge had seemed like the perfect choice. She had been inexperienced, but he was gentle when he figured out it was her first time. Taking his time to soothe her nerves, making sure she enjoyed it. A lot. It had been all she'd imagined it would be. And so, so, so much more.

But then they had walked back into Joe's to catch the end of the reception, only to have a tall blonde throw herself into Talmadge's arms and assault him with her pouty lips. The sight of Talmadge's arms instinctively wrapping around the beautiful, not to mention famous, hotel-owning reality star was a sight Miranda never forgot. He'd just been doing the same thing to *her*. Seeing Talmadge with Momma Long Legs—who was wearing a flashy dress that probably cost more than Miranda's tips for a whole year—had crushed her pounding heart, which had still been thrumming from his exquisite lovemaking.

The four-poster bed in the inn's honeymoon suite where Talmadge had taken her that night was still there. Always would be. He'd made love to her in that bed like she was a precious object.

The one thing Miranda had learned that night was weddings and tuxedos and sexual curiosity were a dangerous combination. Okay, maybe she'd learned two or three more things. Very, very intimate things.

She waved absently as a car meandered down the street and beeped its horn.

Talmadge had never told a soul, as far as she knew. And she'd never let her self-restraint crumble again.

But that self-restraint may have been for nothing, thanks to her and Talmadge's glorious wandering hands and persuasive lips showing up on the Internet. The way gossip flowed in this town, the rumors wouldn't stop until a juicier story came along.

*If* a juicier story came along.

Fear pinged around the inside of her chest.

Miranda stopped at the intersection where one of the side streets crossed Main and waited for an old Ford to pass. She crossed the street, and two ladies walked toward her on the sidewalk. Friends of Mrs. Wilkinson.

"Hi, Miranda," the dyed redhead said. "Nice catch." Her voice was sultry, knowing.

Catty.

The other was heavyset with jet-black hair piled on top of her head. "Figures," she said under her breath.

"We weren't—" Miranda tried to say as they brushed past her.

One of them whispered, "At his grandmother's wake no less. Glad I didn't go."

The other one harrumphed. "No wonder she wanted to host it."

Miranda groaned.

In front of the heavy glass door labeled Brooks Real Estate, she came to a stop and threw the door open with a shove.

Lorenda sat behind her rustic log desk, nails clicking against a computer keyboard, blonde hair pulled back into a knot. She looked up and smiled before adjusting the stylish scarf around her neck, then kept typing. "I'd ask what's wrong, but most of the town's already talking about it."

Miranda threw herself into a chair and slid down with her head leaning back and an arm over her face.

"That bad, huh? Funny you didn't mention it last night when I called."

Miranda nodded under her arm. "Last night I didn't know I'd end up on YouTube or that stinking blog. I'm ashamed of what Bea would think."

"Bea would still love you no matter what. Maybe even more."

Miranda peeked from under her arm, giving her BFF a quizzical stare. Lorenda was a few years older than her, but they'd been like sisters since they were kids.

Lorenda shrugged while clicking away on the keyboard. "My mom thinks Bea wanted you and Talmadge to get together."

"How does your mom know that?"

Lorenda shook her head. "No idea, but you know how the older women in this town get together and talk."

"News flash. It's not just the Red Hats who gossip." Miranda sat up, still glum.

"True." Lorenda punched a few more keys and shut down her computer. "The kids' school principal insisted on walking me to my car after a parent-teacher conference, and we were supposedly engaged by the next morning." Lorenda straightened some papers on her desk. "And there were no adults over the age of forty around the elementary school that day, trust me."

"What am I going to do?" Miranda rested her elbows on the desk and plopped her head in both hands.

"Ignore it." Lorenda gave Miranda's arm a sisterly squeeze.

When Miranda looked up, Lorenda's look was earnest.

"Even if it's true, ignore it." One side of her mouth lifted into a sympathetic smile. "*Are* you and Talmadge . . . you know?"

"No, we're not." *We did once. A very long time ago . . . at your wedding reception.* Heat flooded through Miranda, and she studied the bank of snow that lined Main Street through the large office window. Not even Lorenda knew about Miranda's long ago tryst with Talmadge, and she wasn't about to give out that 4-1-1 now. Not after so many years.

Why bring up the humiliating past with Lorenda now, when those stupid pictures were already capable of sinking her reputation and possibly her respectability as a business owner before she even opened?

"'Cause I gotta say, girlfriend, you two were going at it pretty good in that photo."

"It was an accident!" Miranda blustered.

*Good Lord.*

Lorenda's brows rose. "How exactly was *that* an accident?"

When Miranda glared at her, Lorenda said, "I'm not judging. Lord, I'm as green with envy as a Teenage Mutant Ninja Turtle." Lorenda laughed. "See how pathetic I am? My vocabulary has graduated from Kermit the Frog to Donatello, and that's all I have to look forward to with two adolescent boys."

With that, Miranda softened her tone. Lorenda had been a single mom since her husband was killed in action when their two boys were both still in diapers. She'd sacrificed any attempt to meet a nice guy and devoted herself to raising her kids.

"Well, we're *not*." Not that Miranda hadn't thought about it. Dreamed of it. Fantasized about Talmadge for the past twenty-four hours straight. But some things were just that—fantasies. Never meant to become reality. They lived different lives. Had different dreams. And their lives and dreams were half a continent apart, which made any chance of her and Talmadge getting together impossible unless it was a temporary fling.

If Miranda ever trusted a man enough to give up even a smidgen of her independence, it would have to be forever. With a ring, and a license, and witnesses. And maybe a law passed by the US Supreme Court stating that he would be Miranda's equal, her partner for life—not just until her money ran out or a better piece of tail came along like one of her mother's notorious boyfriends.

"He owes me a ladder." Miranda huffed. *And an apology for ordering me around in my own inn.*

"What?" Lorenda gave her a confused look.

Miranda shook her head. "Never mind."

Lorenda drew in a motherly breath, slow and methodical, then let it out. "Want to get some lunch?" Lorenda came around to Miranda's side of the desk and propped her butt on the edge. "My treat to cheer you up."

Miranda stood, and Lorenda gave her a hug. "Do you have a paper bag I can wear over my head? Because everyone in this town now thinks I'm sleeping with Talmadge Oaks."

# Chapter Seven

After Talmadge's meeting with Angelique, he crossed Main Street and climbed the front stairs at Cotton Eyed Joe's, where he and Langston planned to meet for lunch. Maybe he could enlist his buddy's help with the inn. Talmadge sure as hell was going to need it now that Miranda's renovations had become his primary building project instead of Trinity Falls. He was going to have to double-time it to finish the inn so he could get back to Washington.

A wave of panic skated over him.

He needed that money in Bea's account, but would staying here for the next several weeks doom Trinity Falls completely? Miranda also had to agree to him taking charge of the renovations. *Without* him telling her about his inheritance. If her attitude toward him this morning was any indication, he doubted she'd be willing to follow his lead. And why did the prospect of working side by side with Miranda make his panic shift to anticipation?

The large room at Joe's that tripled as a dining room, bar, and dance hall bustled with lunchtime patrons, but his eyes locked onto Miranda.

Sitting in one of Joe's red leather booths at the back of the restaurant with Langston's sister, Lorenda, Miranda laughed. Threw her head back and laughed like a carefree kid. Her profile was perfect. The slight upturn of her nose right at the tip was elegant. She was so natural. So beautiful. Miranda's long silky curls bounced around her shoulders, a wisp falling over a smooth cheek.

From a booth along the right wall, Langston lifted a hand and waved Talmadge over. The familiar red-checkered tablecloths and the crunch of discarded peanut shells sent an odd feeling of comfort coursing through him like he was home.

*Home.*

He slid into the seat opposite Langston.

"I took the liberty." Langston pointed to the mugs of beer on the table. He grabbed menus and tossed one across the table. Aviators were pushed up into Langston's wavy brown hair, his face was bronzed from extreme skiing, and he still sported the same boyish grin from their teenage years when he'd blocked for Talmadge on the football team.

Talmadge took a pull from the frosty mug and glanced at Miranda.

She and Lorenda both stared in his direction. Lorenda gave a friendly wave, so he waved back. Miranda didn't appear as happy to see him. Her dimples disappeared, and a frown replaced the hearty smile that had been on her face.

"I haven't seen your sister since I've been in town. How are she and the kids?" Talmadge knew the entire town still felt the hole left when her husband was killed in action. Talmadge and Langston felt it too, because they'd all been high school friends.

"The boys are growing up fast. Lorenda's still bossy. I tried to sit by her, and she kicked me out of the booth so they could talk girl stuff." Langston shuddered. "So are you going to give your old buddy a huge discount on a vacation condo in your swanky new green town when it's finished?" Langston gave him a boyish grin. "'Cause the only way I could afford it is if it's close to free."

Talmadge's chest went cold. "Sure."

Langston eyed him over the menu. "Is the new town still going to happen? Trinity Falls has to be the most innovative idea of the century."

*Not so much.*

A heavy sigh flowed out of Talmadge. "I'm working on it." That was the best answer he could give because his ability to manage the crisis in Washington had become infinitely more difficult a few minutes ago in Angelique Barbetta-Holloway's office.

Langston gave him an I-know-bullshit-when-I-hear-it look. "What's the plan to get it going again?"

"Like I said, I'm working on it." He tried to keep the pessimism out of his tone, but Langston's raised brow told him he hadn't been the least bit convincing.

Langston leaned in and dropped his voice. "Are things that bad? I know the project has kind of gone to shit, but it hasn't been flushed completely down the toilet, has it?"

Talmadge shrugged. "It's circling the bowl."

Langston sat back. "Don't give up on it yet. The idea was great."

Right. So great it was about to ruin Talmadge financially and professionally. If he left a town half built and uninhabitable, he'd lose the confidence of the entire architectural industry and the environmental community, all in one swoop. If he had to tear it down, it would ruin him and most of his financial backers. If that happened, he doubted he could find investors to build out-houses in the future.

When Talmadge didn't respond, Langston got the hint and dropped it. "How's the arm?"

"Hurts like hell." Talmadge rolled his slinged shoulder and fought a grimace. "How's the new job as a helicopter EMT?"

"Flight paramedic," Langston corrected. "Different than being in an ambulance, but good. I like it a lot."

"Here's to career changes." Talmadge raised his mug.

Their mugs clinked together, and they both took a long drink. Langston gave him a curious look. "Is there a hidden meaning in that statement?"

Without thinking, Talmadge shrugged the wrong shoulder and winced, reaching to massage out the pain. "Looks like I might be here longer than I expected." He glanced in Miranda's direction. She tossed that silky hair over a shoulder and leaned in to say something to Lorenda. "Some things have . . . come up."

"Uh-huh. I saw the *Red River Rag*." Langston eyed him. "Would one of those things be sitting across from my sister?"

Talmadge's eyes darted in Miranda's direction again.

"Maybe." He twisted the frosty mug in a circle. "It has something to do with Bea's last wishes. I have to jump through a few hoops before I can go back to Washington." How could he not do what Bea asked, after all she'd done for him? *Plus, I need the money that's waiting in the Red River bank.*

Guilt washed through him. What would Bea have thought if she knew how much he needed that money? She'd have finally figured out what an awful person he was—the thing he'd been trying to hide since his parents' accident.

He took another long swallow of cold beer. Maybe the alcohol would numb his whirring brain for a few minutes so he could relax, because he wasn't sure Miranda would let him take over the renovations no matter how much she needed his skills and expertise. "It's complicated." And a bad idea, because every time he stepped into a room with her all reason went sailing out the window and plunged over a cliff. "But Miranda is sort of one of the hoops."

She glanced in his direction like she knew he was talking about her. Her gaze flicked away immediately, but she was watching him. His pulse revved to a low thrum.

"If you're going to be in town for awhile, our new chiropractor can probably help with your shoulder."

Talmadge rubbed his chin thoughtfully. "Not a bad idea. Wow, Red River is really growing. Lots of new professionals have moved here since I came home last."

"All the new casinos and movie studios going up around the state created a demand and lots of new jobs." Langston grabbed some peanuts out of the tin bucket at the end of the table and cracked open the shells. He popped a few in his mouth and munched. "They'll all want to vacation in Red River, so I expect new vacation cabins to start springing up."

Talmadge's gaze eased back to Miranda, her silky hair, pretty face, and perfectly proportioned body drawing his attention like a beautifully designed piece of architecture would.

Langston jerked his chin over one shoulder toward Miranda. "She's a good catch. Lots of guys in this town have tried to date her. They've all crashed and burned."

The waitress came over and took their order, then scurried over to the bar.

"At the funeral, your mom made it a point to mention you still weren't married." Talmadge gave Langston an evil grin. "Why don't *you* date Miranda?"

"I tried. She wasn't interested. Said I wasn't grown up enough." Langston shrugged, a noncommittal way of admitting it was true. "Besides, she's like a little sister. She spent as much time around my house growing up as I did. But if the photo on the *Rag* is any indication, I'd say she's plenty interested in you."

Talmadge shook his head. "Not gonna happen. I've got enough to worry about right now." As much as Miranda made his brain go soft and his groin go hard, he shouldn't start something with her that he couldn't finish. "That would just complicate my life even more."

"Women always do. I still can't even figure out my sister," Langston said on a groan. "And don't get me started on my mother."

Lorenda and Miranda stood to leave, tossing their purses onto their shoulders.

"Listen, Bea wanted me to make sure the inn opened as planned. Apparently the remodel isn't going well for the new owner."

As the girls headed toward the front of Joe's, Lorenda detoured toward their table. Miranda let out a muffled protest, but Lorenda must not have heard her, because she kept coming their way. Miranda hesitated. Looked to the front door, then at Talmadge. Reluctantly, she followed Lorenda.

"Think you can help me out with that?" Talmadge asked him before the girls were within hearing range.

"Anything for you and Bea." Langston chugged his beer. "And Miranda."

Talmadge could never repay the network of friends and family who had checked on Bea since he'd moved away, and Langston was at the top of the list along with Miranda. His gaze darted to her.

She and Lorenda walked up behind Langston at the precise moment that the big lout said, "So back to the photo of you feeling up Miranda."

Talmadge's mouth went dry, and he shook his head as a signal for Langston to shut it. It seemed a little more discreet than yelling at his buddy to shut the hell up in a public place. Unfortunately, it didn't work, because Langston kept on talking.

"She looked pretty into it. I gotta say, buddy, I was surprised, because Miranda Cruz doesn't sleep around."

Talmadge exhaled. Should've yelled at him. Or smacked him upside the head.

"Hello, boys." Lorenda's voice was chastising like she was talking to one of her kids, and she glared at her brother. Langston jumped at

Lorenda's voice. His head swiveled around to find her standing at his back, and he blanched.

Miranda's eyes rounded, then narrowed. A deep red burned up her neck and then settled in her cheeks, her lips thinning into a frown.

"Uh," was all Talmadge could manage. He had nothing else.

"I see the two of you are just as mature as ever." Lorenda turned her sharp glare on Talmadge.

"We were just—" Talmadge stumbled over the words until Miranda folded both arms under her full breasts. His gaze slid over the sapphire-blue sweater that accentuated her figure, the sight grinding his brain functions to a complete halt.

"I know exactly what you were doing." Miranda elbowed Lorenda aside so she could lean over the table and speak in an angry whisper. "No, Langston Brooks, I . . ." Red seeped all the way to the tips of her ears, and her eyes shifted to Talmadge before returning to Langston. Like she was remembering. "I *do not* sleep around, for all the good it's done me. Everyone in Red River thinks that I do now . . . thinks that I've slept . . . with . . ." Her gaze slid to Talmadge again, and flecks of fire danced in the brown of her eyes. "I can't build a business if no one in this town respects me. So stay away from me and the inn. I can't afford any more gossip."

He opened his mouth to say he was sorry for offending her, but instead, "You're wrong. My presence would attract business and help your reputation," came out. "I could renovate the inn better than anyone else. It'll be completely energy efficient if I do it."

Wait. Did he really just say that? Because that wasn't even close to what he'd intended.

Langston coughed something that sounded like "oh shit" behind his hand.

Miranda's flame-throwing glare told Talmadge that he'd just screwed up big time.

"Have you forgotten that you don't live in Red River, *Mr. Oaks*? And even if you did, what makes you so sure I'd give you the job?"

"Because I'm the best, and you need me," he blurted. Both true, but shit. Could he have sounded more like an arrogant asshole if he'd tried?

Langston coughed again.

She handed Lorenda her purse and took a step toward Talmadge. "Oh, really?" Both hands went to her curvy hips, and Talmadge wanted to lick his lips. "Then try this on for size."

Plastering on a sad puppy-dog look, she raised her voice for the crowd to hear. "Oh, *Talmadge*," she said dramatically.

Both of his eyes went wide. *What in the hell was she doing?*

"I know I'm not good enough for you, but to hear you say it . . . *hurts!*" She emphasized the last word so much it reminded him of the time he had to watch *Gone with the Wind* with Bea. "And to say you can't stand Bea's ugly dog is almost . . . *cruel.*"

Gasps zinged around Joe's, and several women tried to incinerate him with dirty looks.

Talmadge closed his eyes for a second, only to open them and find Miranda tearing up. She was good. Her mother should've named her Scarlet.

Miranda sucked in a deep breath and let loose again. "You've broken my heart and Lloyd's too, but I can forgive you. I just want one last kiss before you leave us for good."

Before Talmadge knew what was happening, Miranda sank both hands into his hair and laid the sweetest, sexiest, deepest kiss on him. The softness of her lips pulled him into a dream world, and his arm threaded around her waist.

A female voice rang out. "That's it, honey! Show him what he's lost!"

She deepened the kiss.

Her warm breaths whispered across his stubbled jaw, and her honeyed taste made him want more of her. One hand kneaded up her spine, flexing and rubbing the softness of her sweater against her toned back.

"Uh-huh," another female voice hollered. "Make him sorry!"

And just as quick as Miranda had advanced on him, she broke the kiss and backed away. Her absence left him cold, unsatisfied, wanting her back against him. Already lonely for her.

"There," she whispered. "That should give them something to talk about."

Several women clapped in support of the damsel in distress. Talmadge thought he heard the word *schmuck* echo through the room, but he couldn't be sure, because his brain had fogged over.

Taking her purse from Lorenda, Miranda pulled large sunglasses from her bag and perched them on the end of her nose with slow, exaggerated movements.

"Have a good day, boys," she said so only the four of them could hear. She pushed the sunglasses up the length of her nose with an index finger. "I'd call you gentlemen, but the term doesn't seem deserved."

And with that, Miranda Cruz sashayed out of Joe's like a rock star.

---

As soon as Miranda reached the pavement outside of Joe's, she bent, put both hands on a knee, and gasped for air. Had she really just put on a show for the entire town?

"Wow." Lorenda charged through the door, trying to catch up. "That was awesome."

"Served him right." Miranda straightened, her breaths still uneven. She buttoned her wool coat against the bitter wind that was blowing in a late-season storm. "Can you believe what he said?" Her voice rose a notch with each word. "Of all the arrogant, self-important . . ."

"Egotistical." Lorenda zipped her down vest.

"Yes! Thank you," Miranda fumed. They started back toward Lorenda's office. "Well, the gossip was already flowing. At least now no one will think there's something going on between me and Talmadge."

"Quite brilliant, actually. I'm proud to be your friend." Lorenda pulled on leather gloves.

"Mission accomplished." With as little damage to her rep as possible, thank you very much. "The pictures on YouTube and the *Red River Rag* shouldn't be a problem anymore."

Except she couldn't think of anything else except the taste of his lips and the way his big, rough hands flexed into her flesh with just enough pressure to drive her insane. Or how he invaded her sleep all night. Made sweet, passionate love to her in her dreams until she woke up sweating and on the brink of an orgasm.

Yes, that was somewhat problematic.

They stopped at the intersection to cross Main Street, and a muddy car with snow tires beeped as it passed. She and Lorenda both waved.

Whatever. Talmadge would be leaving in a matter of days, and then she could get her focus back. Maybe she could hunt down her contractor and get the renovations jump-started again.

She studied the slushy asphalt as they crossed the street and stepped onto the sidewalk.

So why did the thought of Talmadge leaving Red River make her feel so empty?

She shook it off. Didn't matter. She'd just turned the flow of gossip in her favor for once.

"Uh-oh." Lorenda put a hand on Miranda's forearm and squeezed.

Miranda followed her friend's gaze to the door of Lorenda's office.

Mrs. Wilkinson stood there glaring—face pinching, cross dangling—waiting. For Miranda.

"I hope you know I'm calling another town meeting and demanding a revote," Mrs. Wilkinson barked as soon as Miranda and Lorenda got within hearing distance. "The Hot Rides and Cool Nights Festival and Parade kicks off our summer tourist season. People come from all over the Southwest to show off their cars. There are different divisions, different categories, food vendors to organize, and the *parade* . . ." She poked a finger in Miranda's direction. "It's just six weeks away, and with your lack of experience, it would fail." The older woman's condescending tone snagged on Miranda's already strained nerves. "*You* are not going to be in charge of the most important event of the year."

Clydelle and Francine lumbered up behind Mrs. Wilkinson.

"I thought the most important event of the year was the annual firefighters' dance?" Clydelle leaned on her cane.

Francine adjusted the gigantic purse on her arm. "No." She shook her head thoughtfully. "It's the annual firefighters' marathon to raise money for the department. They get all sweaty and some even take their shirts off."

Mrs. Wilkinson's face pinched even more. "No wonder people are talking . . ." Her lips thinned into an artificial smile, her eyes flashed venom, and Miranda knew Old Lady Wilkinson had heard about the embarrassing pictures. "As if your mother wasn't bad enough, now you've teamed up with these old loons."

Miranda drew in a sharp breath at the insult.

Francine lifted her purse. "Watch it, sister. This purse is a lethal weapon, and I'm not responsible for my actions when my blood sugar drops. I haven't had lunch yet."

"My cane's been known to accidentally slip from my grasp and do some serious damage too." Clydelle waved it in the air.

Mrs. Wilkinson let out an indignant gasp. She eased back against the door of Brooks Real Estate. "This year's chairperson and planning committee are also responsible for organizing the construction of the new town gazebo. I've already taken the liberty of having plans drawn up, so a revote will most certainly swing in my favor."

"There's not going to be a revote if we can help it," said Clydelle. "It's your own fault for not attending the town meeting."

Mrs. Wilkinson sniffed. "And I'm sure you two know nothing about how my tire got slashed?"

Francine drew her purse behind her back like she was trying to hide it. "Nothing at all."

Mrs. Wilkinson turned her prickly gaze back on Miranda. "And whatever you did to win that vote won't work."

"I didn't even put my name in for the nomination," Miranda said. "I wasn't at the meeting."

Mrs. Wilkinson looked Miranda up and down. "I'm sure a woman of your . . . character has other means of gaining favor."

Miranda took a step toward her, her fists clenched, but Lorenda held her back.

"Miranda's sharp. She'll be a great chairperson for the festival. Maybe it's time for a change," Lorenda said.

"She can't even keep a contractor around. Word has it he's left town." Mrs. Wilkinson gave Miranda another evil smile. "Interesting that you were his last client."

Miranda growled.

So did Lorenda.

"He's sick, not gone," Miranda said with so little conviction that she didn't even convince herself.

Mrs. Wilkinson raised her nose in the air and leveled a deliberate stare at each person in the circle. "That gazebo is the biggest civic project in years. *She*"—Mrs. Wilkinson gave Miranda a dismissive wave—"knows nothing about building anything. That inn is already turning into a disaster. I won't let her ruin a new landmark in our city too. The townspeople have no choice but to call for a revote, and they'll appoint me."

Miranda had had enough. "What makes you so sure? Maybe the people in this town are tired of your dominating ways and you trying to control everything."

Mrs. Wilkinson gave a pretentious sigh. "Oh, they'll vote for me. Because if they don't, I'll pull all of my support from the festival and make sure none of my friends offer their help or support either."

Hellfire. That would split the town in half, because people would feel forced to choose sides. Maybe Miranda should resign before a modern-day rendition of the Hatfields and McCoys started right here in Red River.

She felt Talmadge's warmth before she heard his voice. It spiraled around her like protective armor as he stepped up behind her so close that his breath whispered through her hair.

"Turns out I happen to be free the next several weeks." Everyone fell silent the moment Talmadge spoke. People had a habit of doing that. His solid, steady voice commanded respect. "I'll be in town longer than I thought. I can design and build the gazebo for Red River." He glanced down at her, his eyes raking over her face. "With Madam Chairperson's approval, of course. She's one of the smartest people in Red River, so I have no problem working for her."

She turned to look at him. "You won't be in town *that* long. I don't see how it would work."

"I'll be in town long enough." He gave her a reassuring smile that was a little brighter than his usual.

"She might make a good madam, but she'll never be chairperson. Not as long as I have anything to say about it," Mrs. Wilkinson said.

Everyone ignored her.

"I really couldn't ask you to do that," Miranda said to Talmadge. He was perfect for the job, but the point of her obnoxious public display a few minutes ago was to get rid of the man. She could *not* work with him for the next several weeks on a project. He was supposed to be leaving town, so her stupid pheromones would stop spewing all over him, and so she wouldn't be tempted by his hair that felt like heaven between her fingers.

"You're not asking me." His eyes latched on to her lips and wouldn't let go. Traitorously, they parted. And sweet baby Jesus, she wanted to give him another kiss for coming to her rescue. Gah! "I owe you." His famous half-smile appeared. "For Bea. And for giving you the wrong impression about . . . my respect for you." His voice rose a notch, like he wanted to be sure no one missed his point. "And for insulting Bea's dog. This will be my way of repaying you and contributing something to Red River in Bea's memory."

Well. What could she say to that?

He didn't wait for her to say anything. He flashed a heart-stopping smile at Mrs. Wilkinson and said, "It's settled then. No need for a revote. Miranda's got it under control, and I'll report to her."

Masterfully handled, even if it did put Miranda in an awkward position. Mrs. Wilkinson might be able to sway public opinion about Miranda, but no way could she influence Red River to oust one of America's most sought after architects, especially since he was a hometown boy willing to donate his services for free.

Clydelle and Francine cheered. Lorenda volunteered to be on the planning committee. Mrs. Wilkinson looked as though she might commit a violent crime.

Talmadge stared down at Miranda with his usual confident air.

"I'm heading back to Bea's to start some preliminary sketches. I'll pick Lloyd up tomorrow when I bring over the drawings for you to look at."

Before Miranda could answer, Talmadge stepped off the curb and strolled over to his grandfather's old truck. Tall, proud, confident.

His tailored black pants cupping the nicest ass this side of the Rio Grande.

Miranda's heart sank to her snow boots, because she'd never be able to resist him if they spent too much time together. So he'd be in town for a while. So they'd work on the gazebo together. How much time could that take? He'd show her drawings, give her updates. A few minutes a week tops.

She'd just have to make sure the minutes didn't stretch into hours. If she had to spend hours with Talmadge Oaks, she'd be so screwed. Literally. And the problem with that was, she already knew she'd like it.

# Chapter Eight

Late-morning rays of sun cascaded through the aluminum blinds of Miranda's bedroom and heated her cheeks. The warmth on her face roused her from sleep. She yawned and looked at the clock on her bedside table. Her head fell back on the pillow, and she rubbed her eyes.

Yesterday she'd tried to deal with two pesky problems—getting rid of Talmadge Oaks and stifling the gossip about them—only to find herself in deeper with both. Today she had to deal with another roadblock as big as Wheeler Peak—either find her contractor or hire a new one with what little money she had left. This was exactly the kind of problem she would've taken to Bea, asking for guidance. Sound advice and wisdom. Now she had no one to turn to.

She threw an arm over her eyes and pulled the worn quilt up to her chin. She'd rather lie in bed and pretend her dream of owning a thriving business wasn't about to splinter into a million pieces. Extra sleep wouldn't hurt, because she was exhausted after a long night of fitful sleep. Well, not actual *sleep*. More like lying in bed with Lloyd curled at her feet, thinking of Talmadge's arm circling her waist when she kissed him yesterday at Joe's. His hand wandering and massaging up her spine.

Dammit.

She lifted her arm and peeked at Lloyd.

He whined like he knew she was thinking about him.

"All right. Let's go outside." Miranda threw back the heavy covers, exposing her flannel Tweety Bird pajama pants and yellow tank top. With a push, she got out of bed and the old brass frame creaked. She went to the closet to find a pair of flip-flops.

She rummaged through the antique dresser in search of her favorite sweatshirt.

How was she going to work with Talmadge on the gazebo for weeks and not run her fingers through his luxurious hair? No, the festival and the gazebo would seal her reputation as a solid, responsible pillar in the community. She had to stay professional. Distant. Unattached. Unfortunately, Talmadge didn't inspire any of those things. In fact, a new side of her came out when he was around. A sensuous side she didn't know existed.

Sort of like having an evil twin.

Lloyd yapped, and Miranda shut the drawer without finding her comfy Sylvester the Cat sweatshirt. She smooched at Lloyd, and he jumped off the bed to follow her down the hall.

The comforting, protective look in Talmadge's eyes when he deflected Mrs. Wilkinson's personal attack against Miranda had made her heart thump for hours. This morning her girl parts were quivering all over again just thinking about it. Even as she showered before bed last night, she couldn't think of much else. Imagined his warm hands on her back, caressing and kneading up her spine. Willing them to find her aching breasts.

Imagine her lack of fulfillment when the hot water ran out and she had to turn off the pulsing shower massager.

Her inability to curb her wandering thoughts and curiosity every time she was with Talmadge was becoming a serious problem.

She shuffled outside through the private entrance of her suite, and Lloyd promptly hiked his tiny leg on a paper cup someone had tossed to the ground. The sky was overcast, and a blast of cold wind reminded her she was wearing a thin tank top. Shivering with her arms wrapped around herself, she smooched at Lloyd. "Come on, boy. Let's go in where it's warm and get some breakfast."

She reached for the doorknob but it didn't budge. She jiggled it. When it didn't open, she shook it violently.

Crap. It must've locked when it slammed shut.

Wait. Bea kept a key hidden in a planter on the front porch. She called for Lloyd to follow and went around to the front of the inn.

When she rounded the corner, she stopped cold. Bea's old Dodge and Langston's classic convertible Mustang sat out front.

Miranda hesitated, but another cold blast of wind made her trot up the steps and reach for the front door. It opened.

Lloyd ambled alongside her, and they entered the foyer and walked through the great room.

Miranda stopped.

New sheets of drywall leaned against one side of the room along with rolls of insulation. A sturdy ladder and tools were laid out on one of the workbenches that had been draped with a cloth yesterday.

A stream of male voices reached her from the dining room, and she rounded the corner to find her little brother sitting on a stool at the counter that separated the kitchen from the dining area. His laptop was open, and Talmadge and Langston—a virtual wall of all things male, especially ego—surrounded Jamie.

Talmadge's sling was gone, and his arms were crossed over his firm chest. The flexed muscles of his biceps strained against a gray thermal shirt, and faded Levi's hung low on slender hips, weighed down by a tool belt.

*Tool belt?* She rounded on the supplies behind her in the great room, then turned back to stare at the interlopers.

"Dude, no way is Superman more powerful than Batman's gadgets," Jamie, the techie geek, said.

Miranda rolled her eyes.

"You're wrong," Langston said. "Superman is the most powerful superhero. Period."

Talmadge spoke up, all seriousness. "You're both wrong. Thor is the most powerful superhero in the universe."

Jamie shook his head. "Thor isn't from this universe. Plus, there's nothing cool about a hammer."

"Depends on the size of the hammer." Miranda couldn't see Talmadge's face because his back was angled away from her, but the smart-ass smirk was evident in his tone.

All three men laughed obnoxiously.

"Dude," Jamie said. "It would have to be a *really big* hammer."

*Oh for God's sake.* Miranda cleared her throat, and all heads swiveled in her direction. Hands on hips, she stared at them as Lloyd ran over to Talmadge and whined up at him.

"He wants to be part of the conversation." Jamie clicked his tongue at the dog, but Lloyd pawed at Talmadge's foot.

"That dog is too intelligent for this conversation." Miranda leveled a firm stare at Talmadge. "What are you two doing here?"

Langston walked behind the counter and poured more coffee into his travel mug. "I'm here for the free coffee." He didn't look at her. "The rest is between you two."

Talmadge scooped Lloyd up into the palm of one hand. "I came for my dog, for one." His not-quite smile was back, but then his stare dropped to her braless bust that had just been outside in single-digit temperatures. His gaze went smoky.

Her arms flew to her chest and she wrapped them around herself. Despite the cold temperatures and the fact that she was wearing a tank, scalding heat scored her insides and raced over her.

"Nice pants." Amusement threaded through his words.

"Did you bring gazebo sketches?" She ignored his smart-ass comment.

"Yes, but I came to help with the inn, too. Looks like you need it."

Before she could tell him "Hell no," even though she did need help, Jamie started clicking away on his laptop. "Oh, wow." He stopped and stared at the screen. Something flickered in her little brother's eyes as they darted from her to Talmadge.

And the heat at her core turned to a block of ice in her chest.

She did not want to know. Really, she didn't.

"What?" She blew out a heavy sigh.

"Um." Jamie gave her a wide-eyed look, then glanced at Talmadge again. Her little brother's cheeks turned a subtle shade of pink. "I think I've got a text." He pulled a phone from his pocket and tapped at the screen.

Talmadge turned the laptop toward him and Langston. Talmadge slid a slow, lazy look at her while Langston let out a low whistle.

No. *No, no, no.* Something told her the day was about to go south, and she hadn't even brushed out her bedhead yet.

"I was sitting right there yesterday, but that kiss looks even hotter online." Langston angled his head toward one shoulder. "And look. They misspelled *tongue.*"

She forced her legs into motion and joined the fray of onlookers.

There it was emblazoned across the screen, the title of today's post on the *Red River Rag*: *Heartbreaker or Hero? Can Red River's architectural icon redeem himself? Can the wounded Miss Cruz and her new pup, Lloyd, give Mr. Oaks another chance? That steamy kiss with all that tonggue has us rooting for them to work it out. Looks like Red River's favorite young lovers have their work cut out for them, and we'll be watching. So stay tuned!*

Oh. My. God. Her clever plan to get rid of Talmadge couldn't have backfired. Now Red River wanted them to work it out?

A picture of Miranda all over Talmadge like she was an octopus on his face glared back at her, his hands on her as though he knew his way around her body well. Had done the same thing before.

Actually, they had. Once. No, wait. Twice.

*Dammit.*

Was the author of that smut rag an undercover operative? Because they had cameras everywhere! *Damn Patriot Act.*

"Nice." Langston grabbed a screwdriver from his belt and absently tapped it against the counter while he stared at screen.

Miranda turned a searing glare on him.

He glanced at her and did a double take. "Um. The sweater you were wearing. Nice . . . ensemble."

Right. Guys like Langston Brooks didn't use words like *ensemble*.

Miranda thought she might actually spontaneously combust.

"I mean . . . those jeans really compliment your—*oof*." Langston said when Miranda's elbow connected with his ribs. She snatched the screwdriver out of his hand.

One arm still trying to cover her chest, she pointed the tool at Jamie and Langston. "Out."

When they scurried toward the door, Talmadge tried to follow. Miranda's hand shot out and anchored flat against his chest. "Not you."

He stopped cold. Surprising, because he was two hundred pounds of lean muscle and towered over her like one of his buildings would dwarf a hut. When he stared down at her through hooded eyes, his heat coiled around her like a cloak. Wound around her girl parts and squeezed like a closing vise.

Her mind blanked.

Wait. What was she going to say again?

When she didn't speak, an almost-smile appeared, lifting one corner of his mouth.

God, that was *hawt*. Her stare sank to those divine lips. Really, how could she not stare at them? She knew how good they tasted.

The vise cinched tighter, setting off a barrage of quivers somewhere below her belly button.

"We should get to work," he said. "There's a lot to do around here."

Work? *Yes!* That's what she had been about to say. His presence distracted her from her work.

"There's a reason I asked you to stay away yesterday. I appreciate what you did with Mrs. Wilkinson and helping with the gazebo, but—" She waved the screwdriver in the air to make a drama-queen point. "I can't have people getting the wrong impression about us."

One of his golden brows lifted.

"Getting the wrong impression *again*. I don't want any more pictures of us showing up online."

Talmadge's eyes anchored to her mouth. She sucked in her bottom lip in response. Then those baby blues traveled down her neck to her shoulder and all the way along the length of her arm to her hand still resting flat against his solid chest.

She tore it away and immediately missed his warmth. "I already have a contractor."

Talmadge looked around. "He's doing a stellar job."

Okay, so the guy hadn't been the most reliable. And she was behind schedule because of his lax work hours. And she may very well run out of money before the renovations were done and she could open for business. But was that really the point?

Well. That kind of was the point. But Talmadge would only complicate her situation even more, and she could figure this out on her own. Maybe.

"He's doing a *fine* job." Sort of. "He's just having some personal problems."

"He's fired," Talmadge deadpanned.

Miranda sputtered. "He is not." There'd be no firing around here unless she decided to do it. "That's not your call." Her voice started to shake with uncertainty, and she bit her tongue to stay focused.

Did absolutely no good. She was still ready to cave like an igloo in an avalanche. Because of the way the male scent of his freshly showered body washed over her. Because of the way his still-damp hair was slicked back behind both ears, and a little chunk fell forward across his forehead. Because of the way he looked at her with such confident assurance that it made her want to believe that his mere presence would make every one of her problems go away and set her world right. Or turn it completely upside down.

She drew in a ragged breath.

He was just so freaking *tall*. And muscular. And gorgeous.

She mustered her very best bitchy stare. Which was so totally not believable, because his mouth curved into a boyish smile.

Dammit. She really needed to work on upping her bitch-factor. It just didn't come natural.

"I hold the note and the deed to this place," he informed her as though she weren't already aware. "The quicker these doors open for business, the sooner I can have some peace of mind that the investment I inherited from Bea is safe, and I can be on my way."

And *theeeere* it was. He couldn't wait to get out of this little town and get back to the prestige of being a celebrity architect. Small-town life was beneath his pay grade.

"I don't need your help." She kinda did. "Nor do I want it." Okay, maybe she wanted it a little. Among other things.

*Good Lord! Snap out of it!* She absolutely did not want . . . no . . . she did not *need* to count on a man the way her mother had. Miranda could do this on her own.

"Doesn't matter, sweetheart." Talmadge's smile was cocky. "You've got my help whether you want it or not."

After his colossal gaffe yesterday at Joe's, the chances of Miranda agreeing to let him take over the renovations were about as good as her contractor giving back her money, even if Talmadge *had* kept Mrs. Wilkinson from sinking her fangs into Miranda.

The way he saw it, he had two options.

One: play the I'm-your-creditor card and take charge of the renovations whether she agreed or not. When it came to any kind of building project, everyone followed his lead. Hell, he'd earned that leadership role in his profession.

Miranda's face glowed red with anger.

Right. Option one wasn't working out so well.

He shifted to option two: make her think she was still in charge.

"Don't be foolish, Miranda. You need help with this place." Talmadge was trying real hard to keep his mind and eyes off the taut nipples showing through her thin shirt. The moment he'd turned and saw her standing in the dining room staring at him with sleepy eyes and messy pillow-hair . . . glaring at them over the absurdity of superheroes while wearing silly cartoon pajamas . . . Well, hell. His throat had closed up, and he'd wanted to toss her over his shoulder and take her back to bed.

"You're calling *me* foolish? How can you help, Talmadge? You can't stay in Red River that long. I'm surprised you're staying at all."

*So am I.* But sure enough, here he was, trying to seize the one chance he had at gaining some capital that would help keep the lights of his firm back in Washington turned on for a little while longer. "I'll be here for as long as necessary. I never leave a job unfinished." Not willingly, anyway.

Her lips parted. Several small creases formed above her brows. "Oh. Well, um . . ." She glanced at his shoulder. "Your shoulder. You can't do this kind of work."

"I'm starting rehabilitation this week," he countered.

"In Red River?" Her tone turned a little desperate and her eyes a little wild.

He nodded. "Doc Holloway and the new chiropractor in town are going to help." Luckily, Langston had given them a call last night, and within an hour, an entire posse of physical therapy assistance was at his service. One of the perks of a small town.

"So? You're still hurt. I need someone who can handle manual labor." She waved her arms around the inn.

*Nice.* Her round, firm breasts bobbed a little and both nipples strained toward him. Disappointment threaded through him when she crossed her arms over her chest again.

"Jamie and Langston have agreed to help with the heavy lifting. I'm going to be the foreman," Talmadge said.

The copper flecks in her irises blazed to life. "*I'm* the foreman. It's my place."

"It won't be if you don't get some help with the remodel." Talmadge leaned a hip against the Formica counter. "Bea's last wishes were for me to help, since you wouldn't let her give you the inn."

A fact Talmadge deeply respected.

"So you know I didn't take advantage of your grandmother."

Talmadge winced. "Yeah, sorry about that. Emotions were running high."

"I was her witness. There was no statement to that effect in her will." She said it like she didn't believe him.

Her exposed skin was goose-bumped, so Talmadge grabbed his jacket off the counter and draped it around her shoulders. She pulled it close around her and snuggled into it.

"Thank you." Her voice softened.

Good. He might be wearing her down. Because she was sure wearing *him* down. He wasn't sure how much longer he could be in her presence without tasting her again. "Uh, she left me a note." He was skating on thin ice here. He hadn't said anything that would violate the terms of the will, but he was getting close.

He hesitated. Helping Miranda would be a win-win for both of them. She would get her business open and running, the inn would be more energy efficient if he did the work, and the pot of money waiting for him at the end of Miranda's renovation rainbow would provide cash flow while he sorted out his derailed project.

Her big, chocolaty eyes stared up at him.

"Uh . . ." Damn, he didn't want to lie to her. "This place meant a lot to her . . ."

Miranda's expression softened, and wetness shimmered around the rims of her eyes.

"She, uh, wanted to see it become a success and thought I could help." Okay, still the truth.

He almost pulled it off without lying. He did.

Until he opened his big, stupid mouth and said, "Her note said she wanted me to stick around until the inn is open again, then she wanted us to use her life insurance to build an after-school rec center for kids here in Red River." *Ah, shit.* A thread of truth ran through that statement, but not enough to keep it from being a lie.

A tear glided down Miranda's smooth cheek, which still had the impression of a sheet mark creased into it. She swiped under her eyes with a finger.

Talmadge's eyes slid shut for a second. *Liar, liar, pants on fire.*

"That's just like Bea." Miranda sniffled. "Always trying to help kids."

"Uh, yeah," was all Talmadge could say without blurting the truth.

The back door cracked and Langston stuck his head in. "What gives, you two? It's cold out here."

"Give us a second," Talmadge said to Langston, who rolled his eyes and shut the door. Talmadge looked at Miranda. "Plus, I owe you big-time for looking out for Bea the last couple of years. Consider my work payback." She pulled that lip between her teeth again, and he wanted to bend down and suckle it. He coughed. "Do we have an agreement?"

"Well . . ." She bit her lip. "I guess when my contractor comes back to work, I could return the supplies he's probably already bought with the money I gave him."

Right. And Trinity Falls was going to build itself overnight.

She chewed that plump lip. "And I'll have to find a way to let him go without hurting his feelings."

Talmadge wanted to sigh. He doubted that so-called contractor would ever step foot inside the county again after the cash payload Miranda had obviously handed him.

"But what about the gossip about us?" Her expression dimmed. "People already think the worst. It'll only get worse with you hanging around here all the time. I mean come on, Talmadge." Her voice turned to a plea. "You're famous. People are not going buy into you hammering nails and reshingling my roof unless . . ." Her cheeks pinked, and her gaze darted away.

He couldn't help but chuckle. "You know I wouldn't do or say anything to hurt your reputation. Didn't I prove that seven years ago? And it's about time someone takes Mrs. Wilkinson's tiara away. She still hasn't realized she's not queen of Red River."

Miranda's eyes closed on a slow blink. "I mean you're stealing my thunder, Talmadge."

His brows scrunched together.

Miranda took a deep breath. "The inn, the gazebo. I appreciate all you're doing, but it'll hurt me as much as it'll help. I needed to do these things on my own to prove myself in this town as a business owner."

The door cracked again, and Jamie stuck his head through. "Seriously, people. My teeth are chattering."

"I think I know a way to work this to your advantage." Talmadge dangled the bait. "I have connections with home remodeling shows.

Let me make some calls." And, shit, again. Because he did not want to call public attention to his prolonged stay in Red River with Trinity Falls sitting stagnant back in Washington. His investors were already squirming. "I can play this off as a project that's for my professional benefit, not yours. Everyone will think you're doing me the favor." She was. She just didn't know it. "We'll make it clear that you're calling the shots. It would mean a lot to Bea if you let me work on the inn." And there went the guilt card.

Her chocolaty eyes clouded with skepticism, and she chewed her lip. Finally she nodded. "Okay. For Bea. But I'm the boss, not you."

"Fair enough." Talmadge smiled down at her. Without looking away, he called to Langston and Jamie. "Come on in, guys. We can start by coming up with a plan and a timeline."

With any luck, he could pull this off and get out of town without anyone getting hurt. Most of all him, because coming to the rescue of Miranda Cruz was becoming a habit. A habit he wasn't sure he wanted to break.

# Chapter Nine

Had Talmadge screwed himself six ways to Sunday?

At 8:00 a.m. sharp four days later, he parked in front of Noah's Bark Grooming before meeting Miranda at McCall's Hardware. With everything on his mind—especially the bossy, beautiful woman—he'd forgotten some necessary supplies. Several times. Because this would be his sixth trip to McCall's Hardware in three days.

He never forgot supplies. Never.

But Miranda, in all of her sassy glory, had him thinking about much more than supplies and renovations and home-improvement shows. He didn't know if he could keep his hands or his mouth off of her lush curves and kissable lips for the next five weeks, which was about how long both the inn and gazebo projects would take if he worked at full-throttle times ten.

But first he had to help Lloyd with the whole man card thing. He scooped a trembling Lloyd from the passenger seat and gave him a pep talk.

"Bart Simpson's mom called. She wants her hair back." Talmadge patted his fluffy head. "You've got this." Maybe a new haircut would make him look like a *he*, instead of a ferret in drag.

Talmadge left Lloyd with a frowning groomer who insisted he looked exactly the way a poodle was supposed to look, regardless of gender, and drove over to McCall's.

He pulled into the parking lot. Miranda's Jeep was the only other vehicle there.

He parked and stared at the front door. Four days ago he'd worked up a renovation plan, hit the ground running with the remodel, showed Miranda his preliminary drawings of the new gazebo, scoped out Brandenburg Park where the gazebo would be built, and put in calls to several home remodel shows to see who could run a segment on the inn's renovations when they were done—all while trying to make Miranda feel like she was in charge.

The glow on her face and the shine in her eyes as she processed and organized everything he said, the gears in her sharp mind snapping and grinding, and the way she rolled up her sleeves and worked harder than anyone he'd ever seen had been worth it. She'd be an exceptional business owner. Hell, she'd probably be an exceptional project manager—as good as any he'd worked with.

He, on the other hand, was lower than dirt for not telling her the whole truth about his reasons for staying in Red River. Sure the inn held a special place in his heart, and he did want to see it finished just as much as Bea had. But he had still twisted the truth, because he didn't want to lose his inheritance. That's what he got for giving an answer on the fly while distracted by her spectacular rack—that had one, been braless, and two, been outside in the cold.

Talmadge got out of the truck. The fresh layer of snow blanketing Red River was the only evidence that a late-season storm had rolled through the area. That was one of the things he missed about Northern New Mexico. The sun came right back out to turn the air crisp and brighten the sky, unlike in the Pacific Northwest where gray clouds hung over the landscape for weeks at a time.

He shoved his hands in his pockets and trekked across the lot toward the entrance. Time to see if he could buy the supplies he needed without getting distracted by lips and tank tops and cold weather.

---

Miranda stood in front of the paint samples, sipping a cup of coffee from the Ostergaards' bakery. She needed a few dozen more cups before starting another day of work with Talmadge. After agreeing to let him help her, she was going to need a lot of strong coffee.

Or Xanax. Either would work. Too bad she didn't drink, actually.

But there seemed to be little she could do. He *did* hold the note and the deed to the inn. And there was no other way to fend off Old Lady Wilkinson and prove that Miranda could manage a major community event. Truth was, Miranda could use Talmadge's help. Since the inn had meant so much to Bea, she hoped he'd put his heart into it for his grandmother's sake, get the job done quickly, and leave.

And the gossip about them . . . well, the plan for her to be in charge had lasted about five minutes. As soon as Talmadge shifted into architect mode, he did nothing but spout orders and step on her toes. Worse, he didn't notice. Sure, he was helping, and that help was invaluable. But he was also snatching away a big part of her independence, something she couldn't give up.

"You need help, Miranda?" Mr. McCall walked over to the paint mixing counter and pulled a set of keys from his red work vest to unlock the register.

"Just browsing for now. Thanks."

He nodded. "Let me know if you need anything." He disappeared down the aisle labeled "Hammers and Nails."

Miranda rolled her eyes. Men and their hammers.

She returned her attention to the colorful display, and her thoughts to Talmadge. Help or not, she was pretty sure if she had to spend several weeks in close quarters with the only man who had ever touched ground zero, she would be toast.

She sipped from the to-go cup and plucked a powder-blue sample from the display. It was so early in the morning, she was the only customer in the store, and the quiet was nice. She could actually think without Talmadge's male scent and her spewing pheromones clouding her mind.

How was she going to get through this? *Gawd*, but he was awful about bossing her around every time he walked into the room. Yeah, he might be good at this kind of construction project. Okay, he was freaking great at it, in an I-can-save-the-planet-all-by-myself kind of way. But Miranda could use her brains to manage the situation. Except she was pretty sure Talmadge would end up managing her right out of her clothes if she wasn't careful, because she couldn't hide her attraction forever.

So maybe she could make him *not* want to get her out of her clothes.

She chuckled. The thrill of anticipation coursed through her as she looked down at the new shirt that had been delivered to her door late last night.

After Talmadge left the inn yesterday, she'd made a small investment that would surely turn him off and keep it all business between them.

She pulled a few more paint samples from the display that would complement the powder-blue and lifted the piping cup to her lips as she smiled. She savored both the rich flavor of the coffee and the clever purchase that was going to drive Talmadge insane. It had taken two hundred dollars that she really couldn't spare to find what she needed at a store in Albuquerque and then have a delivery service drive it all the way to Red River.

She downed a big gulp. Studied the rectangular paper paint swatches in her hand. The blue reminded her of Talmadge's eyes.

Dammit.

The storefront doors slid open and Mr. Blue Eyes himself walked in.

She turned toward him. Ignored him, of course, continuing to study the samples and sip her coffee, but from the corner of her eye she watched him stop and harden his jaw into granite. He stared at her, taking in her *investment* without so much as a blink.

Slowly, like she had all day, she looked up from the color sample. His unmistakable glare slid over her torso, fire spitting from those silvery-blue pools.

Yeah, the powder-blue sample with a hint of gray definitely matched his eyes. Probably why she liked it so much.

"So what do we need?" Miranda kept her tone all sunshine and cheer even with Talmadge's stare shooting poison straight through the black T-shirt that had "Earth First—We'll Strip-Mine the Other Planets Later" screen printed on the front in bold yellow letters. "I brought you a cup of coffee." She laid the samples on the mixing counter and picked up the second cup she'd set there when she first arrived. She tried to hand it to him.

He didn't reach for it. "What the hell are you wearing?" His voice was low and darned near lethal.

He was clearly pissed.

*Booyah!*

"Normally I'd tell a man to get lost if he asked me a question like that."

"It's not a come-on, and you know what I'm talking about."

"Oh, this old thing?" Miranda tugged at the front of her T-shirt. "I pulled it out of the back of my closet."

He took the coffee. "Then why does it still have the price tag dangling from the back?" His free hand slid under his coat and rubbed his shoulder.

Miranda reached for the back of the neckline and found a small rectangle of paper still attached.

Dammit. She yanked it off.

Talmadge blew on his coffee. "Since when are you an anti-environment activist?"

*Since never.* "Don't you have a sense of humor?"

His mouth closed over the rim of the cup, and he drew in a long sip. Long lashes lowered for a second longer than a blink, and Miranda lost her train of thought.

He swallowed, smooth and slow. The muscles in his neck rippled as the liquid traveled downward like floating along a lazy river on an inner tube. "I do when something's actually funny."

She pulled her gaze from his neck and blinked at him. "How about we get to work?"

He nodded to the blue swatches on the counter. "That isn't the best color choice." He let the cup hover at his lips.

"What?" She looked up at the samples. "It's a beautiful shade of blue." He could look in the mirror if he needed proof.

He closed the space between them, the savory scent of coffee on his lips. "I didn't say it wasn't beautiful." His presence unsettled her. His nearness came pretty close to setting her on fire below the waist.

Casually, he leaned his backside against the counter and crossed his legs at the ankles, his boot brushing against hers. Like a magnetic pull, she leaned toward him.

"Just because something's beautiful doesn't mean it's right." His gaze latched on to her lips.

"Um, why isn't it the best choice? I like it." She pulled her bottom lip between her teeth, self-conscious that he was still staring at it. Turning, she wandered down an aisle. Not any particular aisle. Just any old aisle would do with him looking at her like he wanted to drink her in as if she were a mocha latte with double whip.

He pushed off the counter and followed. "Too pale. It's more of an indoor color. What are you going to name the place?"

She turned, surprised at the unexpected question. Actually, she'd thought about it a lot and hadn't been able to come up with a name that felt right. He looked at her from under hooded lids, which had her trying to find another distraction.

Damn that fire down below. Maybe she should find the aisle that displayed portable fire extinguishers, because she needed something to put out those flames.

She grabbed a chisel off the rack. Chisels were handy tools. Surely something around the inn needed to be chiseled. In quick, nervous strides, she darted to the other side of the aisle. She ran her fingers over a few tools with no idea what they were used for. "Maybe I'll name it the Runs Inn and Café." Okay, she was just being contrary now.

He shook his head and reached into his jacket pocket to produce a list. "No way. You're too smart for a name that stupid."

Her hand stilled against a tool that looked something like a wrench. *Mmmkay.* Not what she expected him to say. Everyone in Red River just thought of her as the best damn server in town.

He took another long drink of coffee before setting it on the shelf. He walked toward her. His easy gait shouldn't make her pulse hum. But it did, and the hum grew into a song when he stood in front of her.

"How about naming it the Bea in the Bonnet Inn?" Laughter sparked in his eyes. "The double entendre would pay tribute to your friendship with Bea and your badass boss routine." His glittering gaze never left hers. "Two birds, one stone."

Her eyes fixed to his lips. "Um, Pot, you're black. You dish enough out, maybe you deserve a little bossiness in return." His mouth was like a drug. Not a pansy-assed over-the-counter drug. But the kind pharmacists double-checked your ID for and still gave you the stink-eye as they handed it over.

"For trying to save your ass?" He glanced down to her hips. "Nice as it is."

"Can we get the things we need?" She looked over the top of the paper in his hand and read the items on the list.

"Sure. Just as soon as you give me this." He snatched the chisel from her.

"Hey. We agreed that you're not in charge."

"Okay, boss, what exactly were you going to do with a chisel?"

"Um." She bit her lip.

"That's what I thought." He replaced the chisel on the rack, and metal clattered against metal.

His phone dinged, and he dug it out of his front pocket. "Jamie's driving straight back to Red River after class to help out."

"You're texting my little brother?"

"Yep. Langston's on his way to the inn, too." He tapped on his phone. "I have others lined up, but they'll have to come and go as they have extra time."

"I don't want Jamie neglecting his schoolwork because of the inn." She knew all too well that putting work over studying led to dropping out, which led to fewer choices in life.

"You should stop treating Jamie like a kid. He's a grown man." Talmadge didn't look up from his phone.

"Excuse me?"

Talmadge thumbed the screen of his smartphone, and his eyes went wide. "Holy—" Cutting off the sentence, he glanced up at her. His face cracked into a wide smile. The sweetest, most honest smile she had ever seen on him. He wielded it like a weapon, and it stole her breath for a second. He turned the phone toward her.

"What the . . . ?" She grabbed the phone.

There she was with Talmadge. On the *Red River Rag*. A picture of them standing inside the inn, one hand pressed flat against his chest like she was pushing him away, the other hand brandishing a screwdriver like she was threatening him, and her face crinkled into a scowl. This one had to have been taken through the window.

"Did they take this from the lift? Who carries a telephoto lens on a ski lift?"

"Could've been hiding in the tree line." His smile got even bigger. "But you're the bad guy in this one."

The title of the post read *Miss Cruz resorts to threats! Are such drastic measures necessary, even if she is a woman scorned?*

He tried to take the phone away, but she wouldn't let go.

"I'm not sure you want to see the next one." His tone turned to concern.

"Why?"

He tried to snatch the phone again, but she turned and pulled it out of reach. She scrolled to the next post. Her chest tightened. A picture of a shirtless Ben Smith wearing a sombrero, with full shot glasses lined up on a cabana bar and the ocean cresting on a beach in the background, glared at her. The *Rag's* second post of the morning read, *Looks like Red River's favorite contractor has traded his tools for tequila. But we forgive him as long as he keeps posting shirtless pics to his FB page.*

Her heart dropped like a chunk of lead. When it came to trusting men, her judgment was obviously as bad as her mother's.

Talmadge's expression wasn't smug. It was soft and sympathetic.

"I'm sorry," he said. "I know what it's like to make a professional mistake." He shrugged. "I've trusted the wrong people before." His jaw ticked. "I won't let it happen again."

Neither would she. Miranda flipped to the next post by swiping a finger across the screen.

Talmadge peeked over the top of the phone. "I just left the groomer a few minutes ago. Didn't notice a soul taking pictures. The only other vehicle out this early was the senior center van. Whoever it is, they're damn good."

Her vision blurred from rolling her eyes so far back into her head.

A picture of Talmadge and Lloyd going into the grooming salon was there with the headline, *Town hero redeems himself with his pooch.*

*Can he do the same with the woman by renovating her inn now that her contractor has shucked his work boots for flip-flops? Should Mr. Oaks even try?*

"You've got to be freaking kidding me!" She glared at him.

He held up both hands. "I didn't take those pictures." He pointed to the phone. "That's your fault. You're the one who made a public scene at Joe's and set the whole thing in motion."

"You have to do something. *Anything.* I can't have this. Eventually you're going to be gone—thank the Christ child—and I'm going to be left here with people talking. I can't have that."

"In this town? People are gonna talk, Miranda."

"Well, they can't!" She shoved the phone back at him.

He took a step closer to her. So close that his fresh, soapy scent closed around her and made her heart skip a beat. "They can." He didn't touch her, just crowded in on her so that his height, his broad shoulders, his warmth enveloped her. "And they will. They already are, even more than before because of that kiss at Joe's." Her fingers screamed to touch him, so she locked them to her sides "How do you think I can stop it?"

"Um, kick some photographer ass? You're big enough. You can handle it."

His head dipped a little closer, and she leaned her head back to look into his eyes.

She should push him away. She really should.

His quickened breaths washed over her and set her skin on fire. Definitely checking into that fire extinguisher.

"I'm not planning to hit anyone." His voice had gone husky.

"What then?" *Her* voiced turned to gravel.

"Ignore the talk. You can't stop a gossip rag from gossiping. Trust me, I know." His arm grazed hers, and something in the air around them stirred.

"What will people think? About us? What if they think I'm like my . . . ?" She swallowed, because his beautiful blue eyes caressing over her face made her want to take every bit of her respectability outside and start a bonfire.

Yep. She needed that fire extinguisher.

"Earn their respect." They still didn't touch, but his head tilted forward and his nearness encircled her. Hemmed her in as though his arms were around her. "Put on the best damn festival this town has ever seen." His stare lingered on her lips again, and the hunger in his eyes was so powerful Miranda wanted to throw herself against him and let him taste his fill.

*Aaaand* the rest of her body went up in flames. At that moment, Miranda didn't feel the weight of shame from her mother's sexual exploits. At that moment, Miranda knew what a beautiful thing sex could be. Had been. And she didn't feel at all ashamed of her one time with Talmadge.

That mouth of his curved up again into a soft, sweet smile, like he could read her thoughts.

"You're smart. You're organized. More importantly, you're determined. If you weren't, you wouldn't have been in a position to take this opportunity my grandmother offered you. So use some of that grit of yours and put together a planning committee. A team of people you trust. Like me." His tone was so confident that Miranda felt like she could put on the World's Fair right there in Red River. "And don't ever give money to your employees. You pay the bills, buy the supplies, or whatever. People will do crazy, unpredictable things for money."

For the briefest second, something indiscernible raced across his features. Then it was gone, and that odd look, almost like regret, didn't matter anymore because his blue eyes grazed over her face. So close, so intimate that he might as well kiss her. It turned her insides to a puddle of need.

"I'm not good at asking for help," she whispered. "I don't like being rescued. I can take care of my own responsibilities."

"Letting people help at the right time isn't a weakness, Miranda. It's smart business."

The back of his index finger smoothed across her jawline, and her pulse raced as his lips lingered just a breath from hers. He looked down at her through those heavy lids and thick lashes that probably made every woman in America want to donate money to Save the Whales.

She should step away. Pull out of his magnetic hold and come to her senses.

Instead, her traitorous lips parted, and her eyes slid shut as she waited, anticipated, welcomed his kiss. Lust settled over her like a mist on a cool mountain morning.

A throat cleared behind her. "Uh, sorry." Mr. McCall's voice had her shaking the haze from her head. "You kids need anything?"

"Shit," Talmadge whispered, looking over Miranda's shoulder toward the front of the store.

"*This* is the kind of person Red River is going to trust with the biggest event of the year?" Mrs. Wilkinson's snide tone echoed down the aisle. "You're worse than your mother. At least she didn't carry on in public. Much."

Miranda's breath caught in her chest.

"Just wait until everyone hears about this. They'll be begging me to step in and take over."

Oh. Hell. No. This bitter old woman wasn't going to make Miranda feel worse than she already had.

Miranda turned. Slowly. Methodically. Until she could look Mrs. Wilkinson in the eye. "Go ahead and try."

Talmadge's palm pressed into the small of her back. Giving her strength, encouragement, false bravado. Because *what the hell was she doing taking on Mrs. Wilkinson?*

Miranda drew herself up to stand taller before she chickened out. "*I'm* the chairperson this year." Holy crapoly, she must be crazy talking like this. "And as long as I'm doing my job, there's nothing you can do about it."

Mrs. Wilkinson sniffed. "We'll see about that." Her shoes clicked against the cement floor as she turned and stomped out of the store.

Mr. McCall gave Miranda a nod. "Since you're my first customer of the day, I'll give you a nice discount." He scratched his scruffy gray beard. "And I'll donate any supplies you need for the gazebo."

Talmadge smiled down at her like he was proud. "There you go. Another person for Team Miranda, and it's only eight in the morning. You'll be headed for world domination by dinner tonight."

Miranda tried to smile. "How about we buy stuff to build a bomb shelter?" Because she was sure she'd just started a war.

# Chapter Ten

Talmadge followed Miranda back to the inn to start the day's work. As he motored down a virtually empty Main Street, his phone rang. A Seattle number he'd come to know and dread popped onto the screen, and he declined the call. The reporter who was stalking him wouldn't take a hint. When his voicemail beeped with a new message, he set his cell to speakerphone and listened.

"Mr. Oaks." Her voice grated, even though it was smooth and fluid. "I'm going to run a story about your relationship with Monica Strayer with or without your input." His hands tightened around the steering wheel. There was no relationship. It was a publicity stunt to get the cheesy gossip columnist a raise or maybe a promotion, and more headlines for Miss January, who couldn't seem to keep her career going any other way. "She's given me a quote, and I wanted to give you a chance to do the same." The reporter's voice went silky. Calculating. "And I wondered if you'd care to comment on why you've decided to take a sabbatical during potentially one of the biggest environmental catastrophes in the Pacific Northwest since the *Exxon Valdez*. A catastrophe that your firm is responsible—"

He punched the End button.

He turned onto the inn's driveway and parked next to Miranda as she hopped out of her Jeep and grabbed an armful of supplies from the back. He plunked his elbow against the window and rested his fist against his chin.

The inferior supplies her old contractor bought and Talmadge had thrown out had been rescued from the Dumpster and were organized on the front porch.

It was gonna be a long damn day.

He grabbed two sacks from McCall's out of the backseat and followed Miranda up the walkway. The first hints of spring flowers were starting to peek through the snow-patched dirt along the front of the inn. Bulbs he'd helped Bea plant as a kid.

"There's a reason I threw all this out." He climbed the porch steps and eyed the materials. "The insulation and drywall are the cheapest on the market, the nails will rust, and those two-by-fours don't meet code." He stomped some mud off his feet before walking through the front door. "You'll save money in the long run if you use better materials."

She set her armful of supplies on a workbench and leaned a hip against it. "I'm not used to wasting things. I've always had to make do with what I had. Throwing things out that have never been used gives me hives."

Another thing Talmadge admired about her. She knew how to conserve. That was the cornerstone of his specialized field—conserving energy and resources. Conserving everything except money. Green architecture was expensive. Which was why he'd invested so much of his money . . . okay, all of his money into Trinity Falls. He'd wanted to ante up and show his investors how much confidence he had in the project.

He set his sacks down next to her load and faced her. "How about we compromise and I try to find another use for some of them?"

She crossed her arms under her full breasts. It would've been a sight that inspired dirty thoughts if not for that silly T-shirt.

"Deal. Can at least a few of the supplies be used in a storage closet?" Her eyes lit. "Oh! How about we use the wood and drywall to make cute decorations for the rec center?"

Talmadge froze for a second before he recovered. "That's one option."

"When will we start on the rec center, anyway?" The sincerity in her expression made him want to grab one of the cheap nails off the porch and stick it in his eye.

"Uh." He scrubbed a hand over his jaw. "We have our hands full right now. If you want to outsmart Mrs. Wilkinson, it's not a good idea to spread ourselves too thin." He almost choked. Trinity Falls had spread him so thin he should be transparent by now. "We'll figure out the rec center later."

"Thank you." Her eyes went soft. Her gaze dropped and she picked at a fingernail.

She was thanking him. For a rec center that he never intended to build. Which made him want to stick a *rusty* nail in his eye.

"I'm not very good at accepting help." She picked harder.

He leaned against the bench, too, and bent a knee. Which grazed her thigh, and a sizzle of desire skittered up his leg to his groin. "Really? I wouldn't have guessed that."

Her head bobbed up, eyes rounded. But when she saw his smile, she let out a breath, and the tension in her shoulders eased. "I don't want to be needy, that's all."

Ah, mommy issues. He could relate.

The way she'd pretty much raised herself and still turned out so good, only to let the sound of Mrs. Wilkinson's voice make her entire body go stiff at the hardware store and the soft, vulnerable look on her beautiful face right this minute made him *want* to rescue her whether she needed it or not, the same as he wanted to save the world. Give something back because of what he'd taken away. She'd lost so much of her childhood, but it hadn't been her fault the way his loss had been his. He couldn't help but touch her, even though he shouldn't.

He brushed a finger over her soft, creamy cheek, then put that same finger under her chin and lifted her eyes to meet his. A cloud of lust swirled around them as fierce as a tornado.

"Needing help and being needy are two very different things, Miranda." His hand dropped to her neck, and he caressed it with his thumb. A slow burn started in his fingertips, skated up his arm, and stole the breath from his chest. "You're definitely not needy."

She swallowed. "Thank you for everything." Her voice was almost a whisper. "Only a handful of people have ever had my back like you have."

"Maybe because you haven't let them." Before she could disagree with him, he let his lips graze hers. Just a soft graze, but a rush of excitement jolted through him, and he had to go back for more.

Her mouth opened and he deepened the kiss, slipping his tongue in to find hers. Her lips were like velvet, and she let out a little whimper when he laced his arm around her waist and pulled her into him.

And then some asshole cleared his throat behind them for the second time that morning. "Uh, sorry," said Langston. "Should I come back later?"

Pain lanced through Talmadge's shoulder when Miranda pushed at it to break his hold on her. He winced, but Miranda didn't seem to notice in her frenzy to put distance between them.

Hell yes, he'd rather Langston come back later. Talmadge rubbed his shoulder and shot daggers at Langston with a scowl. Which was totally undeserved because Langston was using his days off to help with the inn. Langston had also just saved him from making a mistake that both Talmadge and Miranda would likely regret.

But damn if her steel-toed boots, which contrasted with her tight jeans with the bling on the pockets, didn't turn him on like a thousand-watt bulb. Completely inefficient but well worth the energy. And it would've been nice to finish that kiss.

"No!" Miranda all but yelled at Langston. "Stay. Please."

Langston's hesitant look darted back and forth between them, probably uncertain where his loyalty should lie.

Talmadge waved him in. "We were just getting started."

"I could see that." Langston raised a brow, his tone smart-alecky.

Miranda shot him a frantic look. "With work. We were just getting started with work."

"Uh-huh." Langston's brow stayed raised, which seemed to irritate Miranda all the more. "Nice shirt, by the way."

"Shut up." Miranda pointed to the bar. "There's bagels if you're hungry." She spoke to Langston in that familiar way siblings usually do, and it warmed Talmadge from the inside out.

If he was being honest with himself, because he sure as hell wasn't being totally honest with Miranda, he was also a little jealous of their familial closeness. The camaraderie, the easy way they exchanged barbs and talked to each other, those things came from a lifetime of living in the same town. It was something Talmadge missed.

"Where should I start, Tal?" Langston asked, shrugging out of his coat.

Talmadge let out a frustrated breath. "Let's finish the upstairs bathroom this week. After lunch we can start installing the new insulation." He turned to Miranda. "That okay with you, boss?"

Miranda gave him an appreciative smile like he'd offered her a priceless gift. "That'll be fine." If him asking her permission over such a trivial thing made her eyes light like stars, damned if he didn't want to offer her the moon, too.

Talmadge tried to focus. "Then let's roll."

Langston hauled some tools and caulking up the stairs.

"What about me? What should I do?" she said.

He wanted to tell her that she could take off that shirt, get in a hot tub with him, and massage the soreness out of his shoulder. Or kiss it with those velvety lips of hers. But that would only make him a bigger prick than he already was.

He pulled on thick work gloves and handed her a steamer and a scraper. "Can you start taking the wallpaper off in the bedrooms?"

She grabbed the tools.

"I got high-quality insulation yesterday. Much better than the stuff on the porch. I'll measure and cut it while you and Langston work." Because his shoulder hurt too much to swing a hammer. He slid a pair of goggles on. "I have an appointment in a little while for my shoulder, but when I get back, I'll need you to help me install it. I can't lift my arm high enough to hold it in place, so you can do that while I staple." He smiled at her. "See? Asking for help isn't hard."

She gave him an insincere smile. "Is that why the muscle in your jaw just tensed into granite?"

No. It tensed into granite to match his dick, because he'd really like to see her in nothing but those steel-toed boots. Thinking of anything else but Miranda Cruz naked and writhing under him while she whispered his name was getting more difficult no matter how much he tried.

"My shoulder hurts. I grit my teeth a lot." His gaze slid from her mouth all the way to her boots. "Ready to work . . . *boss?*"

⸺

Moist heat billowed from the steamer as Miranda worked to remove yet another layer of outdated wallpaper from the honeymoon suite. She reminded herself that Talmadge wasn't in Red River for her. He was there because of Bea. Yes, her intellect understood that. Her body, on the other hand, refused to listen. It was hot and humming for his touch. And her heart, well, she was already losing it to a man who was only helping her out of a sense of duty to his grandmother.

Having a man as sexy as Talmadge Oaks come to her rescue, then touch her and kiss her like he meant it made it really difficult to keep her heart in line. Talmadge's head appeared through the open doorway. "Hey. How's it going?" He leaned against the doorjamb.

"Good." She shut off the steamer and started scraping. "It's like an archeological dig site. I keep peeling back more layers and don't know what I'm going to find next."

His expression darkened, and he stared at the floor. Hellfire, he had to be thinking about Washington. She stopped scraping.

"How is Trinity Falls going?" She'd been so caught up in her own problems she hadn't bothered to ask about his.

He shook his head. "It's not."

"I'm sorry. You really don't have to stay in Red River." She cleaned the sticky bits of paper off the end of the scraper. "I'll figure something out."

His eyes went cloudy, and he looked around the honeymoon suite like he was remembering. "I always liked this room." His eyes found hers and held them.

"It's my favorite room in the house." She pulled her lip between her teeth, and his eyes followed the movement.

They both startled when Langston yelled up the stairs that he was taking a lunch break and would be gone for a few hours.

Why couldn't her body do a tap dance for a guy like Langston instead? He was hot and handsome too. He was available and, most importantly, he would stay around. But *naw*. She wanted the one who was leaving.

Must be genetic. She'd have to ask Doc Holloway about that. Maybe there was medication.

Talmadge straightened. "I'm heading out to my appointment. Jamie will be here later. You can handle things here while I'm gone?"

She raised a brow. "It's a few hours. I'll be fine. I'm not helpless."

He chuckled. "Right. I got that." Without another word, he disappeared, the wood stairs creaking under his boots.

Miranda stared at the empty doorway until she heard him drive away.

*Could she handle things here? Pffst.*

She went downstairs, snagged Jamie's laptop from the bar, and Googled how to install insulation. With southern exposure and Red River's dry climate, the inn wasn't hard to heat during daylight hours, but after the sun set each night, a chill settled into the older buildings so prevalent along Main Street and along the base of the slopes. She appreciated Talmadge helping save on the cost of energy more than he would ever know. Any way she could cut expenses would help until she built up clientele.

Even though she did appreciate his help, she could still help herself, though. And moving the renovations along would only help both of them. She skipped over the first few steps about wearing goggles and such.

Ah. Number five got to the point, and she started fitting Talmadge's neatly cut pieces of insulation in between the studs, making sure there were no gaps. Simple enough. She went back to the laptop. Okay, number six demonstrated how to fluff, so she fluffed. Number seven said to staple, so she climbed Talmadge's industrial-strength ladder to staple.

Jeez, even his ladder reeked of testosterone.

When she was done, she stood back to admire her handiwork. She was quite proud of herself for not being helpless. And dang it, it irritated her that she wanted Talmadge to be proud of her too.

She started on the next piece of insulation. She fitted, fluffed, and stapled.

Fitted. Fluffed. Stapled.

Until a strange, prickly sting started on her neck and arms.

She ignored it and kept working. Hard work was her friend, because there was a payoff when it was done. Her inn would be open, and she could get on with her life.

Alone.

Which made the sting worse, because it spread to her chest and stabbed at her heart.

She ignored that too, but after another forty-five minutes of fitting, fluffing, and stapling a five-alarm fire went off over every inch of her exposed skin. When she couldn't stand it any longer, she ran for the shower.

Almost thirty minutes later, she still stood under the hot streaming water, hoping it wouldn't run cold. She braced both hands against the outdated pink tile on the shower walls, praying the electrifying sting would go away.

*Please, Baby Jesus, make it stop.* The razor-sharp pain bit into her skin as the water flowed over her.

It only seemed to get worse.

All she had to do was let the hot water wash away whatever was setting her skin on fire before Talmadge got back to the inn, and he'd never know that she'd screwed up like a helpless woman.

She reached for the knob labeled with a red H and cranked it up. And groaned and moaned even louder.

"Miranda?" Talmadge's voice reverberated through the thin bathroom door of the owner's suite. "Uh, is everything . . . okay?"

*Good God.*

What did he think she was doing that would cause moaning? Her insides heated from embarrassment as much as the hot water heated her on the outside.

"Nothing! Just taking a shower." She clamped her eyes shut. "What are you doing in my suite?"

"Well, I . . . heard . . . uh . . . noises." His tone in that last word sounded amused.

Hellfire.

"I'll be out in a minute." She grabbed a rag and raked it over her arm. A muffled scream escaped because of the pain that sliced over her skin before she could bite it back.

"Okay. Finished now?" Amusement definitely laced his words.

"Very funny," she yelled around the shower curtain. "Get out of my private quarters, please."

"Yeah, not going away. You're one stubborn-assed woman. I told you to wait until I got back to hang the insulation."

She didn't answer.

"It's the fiberglass."

*Probably shouldn't have skipped the safety instructions.* "I'm fine." She ground her teeth against the fiery pain.

"I hope you're not taking a *hot* shower." He wasn't even trying to hide the laughter in his voice.

And the temperature of her shower was his business because . . . ?

"Hot water makes it worse," he said.

Her eyes clamped shut. Reaching for the knob, she turned the hot water down until it was lukewarm.

"Turn the hot off completely. Just use cold water."

She really hated him right now.

Eyes still closed, her head fell back in defeat. Without looking she reached for the hot water knob and shut it off. Nothing on earth could possibly describe the petrifying jolt of misery that rocketed through every nerve ending in her body when the icy water hit her like an eighteen-wheeler hitting a squirrel.

An involuntary shriek tore from her lips. And a bark of laughter echoed through the door.

*Damn the man.*

"Shut it, Talmadge," she growled around the shower curtain again. "How long do I have to stand here?" Her teeth started to chatter.

"Not long." He bellowed out a full-blown fit of laughter.

*That's it.* Hair up in a clip, she turned off the shower and reached for the towel hanging on an antique brass bar. Dripping wet and mad as a hornet, she wrapped it around her and held the ends closed with one hand.

She jerked the door open, and Talmadge's sputtering laughter died. He was squeezing a small therapeutic ball. The rhythmic squeezes slowed to a stop, and he coughed out the last few chuckles as his gaze traveled her length. His eyes went wide, then darkened to a deep purple that shimmered against the bathroom light. Something sparked in those deep pools of incredible color.

She didn't care.

"You could've told me *why* I needed to wait."

Shoulders filling the old narrow doorway, he put his good hand above his head and grabbed onto the frame. Leaned in until she could feel his heat reaching for her, wrapping around her like a warm blanket on a cold winter night. She bet he would feel much better, much warmer than that damned insulation that was biting into her arms and neck.

Her pebbled skin prickled even more.

"I didn't think you'd start without me." His gaze dropped to her mouth, and it parted under his stare.

Okay, so he had her there. "Well, I wouldn't have if you'd left more detailed instructions." She'd just wanted to do something to help herself. And maybe impress him a little.

"Right. Because you're so agreeable." His voice had gone all husky, and his stare dropped lower, cascading down her neck, across the bare, wet skin of her chest, to where her hand held the towel in place.

"I should get dressed." It came out as a whisper.

His gaze traveled back up to her collarbone, then anchored to her mouth again. "Probably."

"Well, then . . ." She tried to push past him. He didn't move.

Without a word, he let go of the doorframe and reached around her. His firm chest brushed against her breasts. They tightened and she sucked in a quick breath. But instead of enveloping her in his arms like she'd thought he would do, he snatched the strip-mining T-shirt off the counter and straightened.

"Just not in this." He turned and strolled down the hall, leaving her staring at the lovely way his faded Levi's cupped his firm bottom. Leaving her wanting to feel his touch and taste him again.

Leaving her dripping wet.

# Chapter Eleven

Alone in her bedroom, Miranda dabbed the water off her tender skin and tried to tell herself she did not just want to drop the towel she'd been wrapped in and let Talmadge's hard body rub her dry. She pulled on a pair of old jeans, but when she tried to put on a shirt, it scraped over her arms like broken glass. Finally she gave up and reached for a soft tank top.

Her boots squeaked against the old wood floor as she trudged down the hall and out to the kitchen.

Lloyd ran to her, a new mustache shaved into his snout, and a spiked leather collar around his neck.

"What happened to you, little guy?" Miranda stooped to pick him up, but fire raked over her when his fur brushed against her arm. She flinched.

"I tried to get his dignity back." Talmadge rolled up the cord of the staple gun and set it on the workbench. "Didn't work."

"He looks fine for a toy poodle."

"That's what the groomer said." Talmadge filled a bowl of water and set it next to the small dog bed. "I brought some things over from Bea's for him. Hope you don't mind."

Miranda smiled. An alpha guy like Talmadge putting together the doggy version of a diaper bag for a tiny poodle like it was his newborn baby—who would've thought?

She rubbed the burning sensation on her arm, which sent another shockwave of pain racing through her. She ground her teeth and tried to get comfortable.

Wasn't happening.

"I can help with that."

"With what?" Miranda kept staring at the floor.

"The pain." He grabbed a roll of masking tape from the workbench and pulled out a barstool at the counter, motioning for her to sit. "I'm pretty impressed with your tough way of handling the pain. How long did you work with the insulation?"

She shrugged, and even that hurt. "Close to an hour. Give or take."

"Most men would've been screaming like a little girl after five minutes, much less an hour. Unfortunately, the prolonged exposure probably made the pain much worse." He gave her an approving smile.

That's what she'd been after to begin with—his approval. And that made her both a badass and a dumbass.

He pointed to the stool. "Sit."

It hurt too bad to argue, so she sat.

"It feels like I'm being stabbed with tiny shards of glass."

"That's because you are. Exposing bare skin to fiberglass is a mistake you only make once. Hold this." He held up the jagged end of the tape roll, and Miranda gripped it. He unrolled a strip of tape and broke it with his teeth. "Hot water opens your pores and makes it worse. Cold water tightens the pores and helps work out the tiny pieces of glass." He held up the wide strip of tape. "This will get rid of it completely."

A tiny seed of defeat sprang to life in her soul, and she wasn't sure either one of them was up to the challenge renovating the inn presented.

The way he was babying his shoulder didn't inspire confidence. Plus, she was in a bear of a mood because of the pain. And because she'd acted like a fool and tried to wow him with her self-sufficient, hardworking initiative. And, dammit, because every minute that she was with him seemed to chip away at her resolve to keep it from becoming personal with a man who already had one foot out the door.

"Hold out your arm." With a gentle touch—much more gentle than she'd expected—he smoothed the tape along her forearm.

"Ready?"

Before she nodded, he ripped the tape off, which also tore a small cry from her.

"Sorry, but it's the quickest way to get the glass out. It won't hurt as much on your neck."

"Jeez." Miranda's eyes teared. "Maybe I should bite down on a stick or something."

Talmadge chuckled and kept working the tape, having her help tear off a new strip each time. A few more torturous rips and pulls and her arms were fiberglass free.

"Next time listen to me. I do actually know what I'm doing here." He tossed the used strips of tape into the trash.

She let out a heavy breath that seemed to deflate both her shoulders and her confidence. "I've always taken care of myself. I wanted to do some things for myself instead of sitting around like a powerless girl."

"Woman." He moved to work on her neck. With gentle fingertips under her chin, he tilted her head to one side and exposed the length of her neck. "You're definitely a woman, Miranda." His voice dropped to a throaty rasp, and her insides did a dance.

Yes, she was all grown up. Seven years, three months, and eighteen days ago, he'd helped her take that final step in becoming a woman.

That one magical night during Lorenda's reception had been one of the only times he'd noticed Miranda. But he was definitely noticing now, and her girl parts liked the attention.

She cleared her throat. "Where's my T-shirt?" she asked, as he worked the tape around her neck.

"In the trash Dumpster." His hard chest brushed against her. He was close. So close that the steady rhythm of his breaths caressed over her ears, soothed her aching skin.

No wait. That was the tape, right? The tape took the glass and the pain away. But the tape couldn't have been responsible for the balmy glow that washed through her and made her breasts ache for his touch.

"I spent a lot of money on that shirt," she protested, but the look on his face told her he couldn't care less.

"I'll get you a new one. A better one. From a fancy store."

"This is Red River. I don't wear a lot of fancy clothes."

"Then one of my company shirts." He smiled, smoothing the tape over her neck again. "Unless wearing something of mine is repulsive to you. Then how about I call the Red River Mercantile and you can pick out anything you like."

Repulsive wasn't anywhere close to the feelings that rushed through her every time she saw his name in the news or his company logo on coffee cups and recycled notecards and refillable water bottles scattered around Bea's place. The twinge of excitement that rushed through her every time she thought of their one and only time together . . . *her* one and only time . . . caused her heart to knock against her chest and her pulse to spur into a gallop.

When he was finished, he balled up all the tape and sunk it into the trash with a swoosh. He didn't move away from her, though, and she looked up into his eyes. Even on the tall barstool, he was still more than a head taller than her.

"The truth is, I thought Bea would be around to offer her guidance." The words tumbled out against her will. She shouldn't bring it up. If she let one crack show in the dam of uncertainty and grief that she'd built up since Bea died, her whole world might crumble into a pile of rubble.

His brows came together, and she looked straight ahead at his chest. And *Gawd*, but didn't he make a plain white Fruit of the Loom T-shirt look sexy.

"When Bea suggested I open the inn again, she planned to teach me the ropes. I figured she'd be around for years to lend advice." Tears sprang to Miranda's eyes.

"Bea was a rock for me too." He kept a poker face, but he couldn't hide the grief in his eyes. He bent and placed a hand on the counter on each side of Miranda, framing her in like one of his solid, efficient designs. "But I know she had faith in both of us. So we keep going forward no matter how hard it is. That's how we honor her memory." His eyes slid shut for a beat, several creases forming between his brows like he didn't believe his own words.

When they opened, Miranda found herself biting her lip and staring at his. "This is a bad idea."

"Terrible." He studied her from under thick lashes, his eyes heating to nuclear disaster level.

"I don't . . ." *Just say it!* Tell him you don't sleep around except for that one time. With him. Right before his Barbie girlfriend walked in and reclaimed him. But then she'd have to admit she'd lied about it being a mistake because they'd had too much to drink.

She hadn't had a drop. And she'd never regretted sleeping with him.

But she might regret it now, once he left her brokenhearted.

So she said the only thing that came to mind. The only thing that made sense to her in a world that was spinning off its axis because of his amazing scent and those eyes that made her pulse go thumpity-thump. "You're leaving eventually." Even she could hear the defenselessness in her tone because of her mind telling her, *So what if he's leaving. Enjoy it while it lasts, just like the first time.*

"I am." He didn't deny it. Never had, and she had to admire his honesty.

"Um." Her lips had gone chalky dry from her quick, shallow breaths. She wet them with the tip of her tongue.

His low growl made her pulse shift into high gear, and it drove her restraint right over a cliff. She meant to lean back, but instead she swayed right into him.

After a beat, he placed the edge of an index finger—so powerful yet so gentle—under her chin and angled her face up to meet his. Leaning in, he brushed his nose with hers, then captured her mouth in a kiss.

---

Getting involved with Miranda Cruz was a mistake. Big, big mistake. At the moment, however, exactly why eluded him. Because *holy hell*, she was wearing another one of those skimpy tank tops, and the cold shower made it obvious that she wasn't wearing a bra. Again. The braless tank top streak she was on and the damn dimples overrode every bit of rationale he possessed.

He tried to kiss her as gently as he could, but when her hand slid up his chest, caressed over his neck, and wound into his hair, instinct took over, and the kiss became more urgent. He probed her softness with his searching tongue. Devoured her like a hungry wolf until a sensual sound came from the back of her throat, communicating her approval.

Her tensed posture relaxed, and she molded against him, soft everywhere he was hard. She sank into the kiss, her fingers doing a dance through his hair while the other hand slowly caressed up his arm, then down his chest. Her touch set him on fire.

Common sense told him this was a mistake. He should keep his damned hands to himself. She'd obviously suffered enough because of her mother's notorious romps. This would be history repeating itself, because he'd already started something with Miranda seven years ago that he hadn't been able to finish. He'd do the same now.

But common sense didn't always register in the male brain when a man wanted a particular woman so bad it hurt. Damned if he couldn't stop wondering how holding Miranda Cruz in his arms with her hands and lips turning him on was so wrong, when he'd never felt anything more right.

He pressed in on her, sliding between her legs, nudging them apart.

So this wasn't exactly what he had in mind when it came to keeping his hands to himself.

He tried to pull away, but she tugged him back, fisting his T-shirt into her hands.

He broke the kiss and went to the window to pull the curtains closed. He was right back between Miranda's legs before the warmth of her skin could fade. With a hand on each of her thighs, he flexed his fingers up the length of her legs, wishing the barrier of her jeans were gone. When his fingers wedged between her bottom and the barstool, he slid her forward, pulling her against the evidence of his desire. She squeaked. But instead of pulling away like he expected her to, she laced one of her legs around his and clamped her warm, lush body against him.

*Nice.*

With one hand, he caressed the small of her back through her thin top, then eased his fingertips under it. When his hand connected with bare skin, she shuddered. Her small gasp and tiny moan drove him on. He kneaded up her spine, his other hand finding her breast. He cupped and massaged, and it peaked into his palm, sending flames through him.

He couldn't stand it another second. With little more than a flick of his hand, the top was gone and she stared up at him with eyes the color of bronze all glazed over with lust and desire.

She was even more beautiful than he remembered.

He took in her flaming cheeks, her slender neck, which was just as red, and her full breasts and firm nipples. Then he locked his gaze with hers. The same uncertain look that had filled her eyes seven years ago was back.

"Are you sure?" Was he stupid? She certainly looked sure. Until she didn't.

She hesitated, then nodded.

"Really, really sure?"

"*Talmadge,*" she ground out just like the first time they were together.

He leaned down to capture a pink bud between his teeth and suckled it until she whimpered.

Just as he released it to give the other the same attention, the cell phone in his pocket buzzed. He ignored it and pulled her into his mouth, caressing the taut flesh with his tongue. Her soft skin turned to pebbles under his callused hands.

"We can go to my room." Miranda's words were small gasps. "If we hurry, we'll have time before Langston and Jamie get here."

He straightened and looked down at her dazed expression. "I seem to remember telling you once before that you've got the wrong guy if you expect me to hurry."

She sobered, and her eyes darkened. "Yes, I remember. Quite well." The look on her face told him she remembered much more than that.

Hell.

She had disappeared seven years ago, telling him their one night together had been poor judgment brought on by alcohol and the magical pull of Lorenda's wedding. He tried to lean his forehead against hers, but she turned her head away.

"Miranda—"

His phone buzzed again. He reached into his pocket to turn it off, but Miranda pulled away and grabbed for her top.

"Would you listen to me for a change?" He stood between her and the hall. If he blocked the entrance to her suite, he could keep her from disappearing on him like she did then, because she wasn't likely to go through the front entrance wearing a tank top in frigid temperatures.

With her back to him, she pulled the tank over her head. "There's nothing to say. It was a mistake back then, and it would've been a mistake just now."

Without a glance in his direction, she hurried to the front door. It slammed shut, and Talmadge let out a frustrated growl. "This conversation isn't over," he yelled at the door.

His phone vibrated again.

With a hefty breath, he answered the call. "Hello."

"Talmadge." Larry Jameson, his second in command over the Trinity Falls project, boomed through the line. "Got a minute?"

"Of course." Talmadge rubbed his eyes with a thumb and index finger. "What's the news?" He couldn't keep the weariness from his tone.

When Larry hesitated, Talmadge's chest tightened. "Go ahead, Larry."

"The tribal councils still can't come to an agreement on which nation should have jurisdiction over the site." The burly foreman's voice held a tone of weariness even deeper than Talmadge's from trying to handle the situation in his absence. "We're still at an impasse."

Talmadge almost smirked, because tribal councils could argue over things like this for years. *Impasse* was a polite way of saying *standstill*. A diplomatic way of delivering the news that his life sucked. Hard.

# Chapter Twelve

*Stupid.* Stupid was actually putting it lightly. She couldn't get physically or emotionally involved with Talmadge Oaks. It was a bridge to nowhere that would leave her heart in little pieces strewn from one end of Red River to the other.

Miranda's teeth chattered as she pulled the spare key to her private quarters from under a withered pot of flowers and unlocked the door.

She slammed the door and stomped into the bedroom to look for another shirt. Something that would cover her more than the skimpy tank she'd put on because her skin was on fire. She found an old baggy sweatshirt at the bottom of a drawer and pulled it on. Stood there, pinching the bridge of her nose before going back out to the dining room where she'd have to face Talmadge and lay down some rules. Get him to exercise some willpower, because God Almighty, she obviously had none when it came to him and her.

Whatever. There was no him and her.

Talmadge was in town long enough to rid his conscience of guilt by seeing to Bea's wishes. Asking Talmadge to help with the inn seemed exactly like something Bea would do. Always looking out for Miranda with the best intentions. But fulfilling Bea's request was Talmadge's main concern, not Miranda's future. Thankfully, he'd reminded her of that by bringing up the first time they'd been together. The memory of seeing his flashy girlfriend wrapped around him like shrink-wrap right after he'd been naked with Miranda had hit her like a shock of ice water thrown over hot coals.

He had a life back in Washington. A life he needed . . . no, a life he *wanted* to get back to.

A knock sounded.

"Miranda." The door muffled Talmadge's voice.

Both hands fell to her hips and her head tipped back. With a deep breath, she gathered her nerve and went to the door. She pulled it open with a quick jerk.

"Look, Talmadge . . ."

He leaned against the doorjamb, muscled arms folded across his chest, one knee bent, looking hurt . . . and sexy as hell. Miranda's mouth went dry.

"I'm sorry about bringing up the past. It was bad timing."

"The timing was impeccable." Her fingers tightened around the doorknob. "Why are you even here, Talmadge?"

"I'm here because . . ." His gaze darted away.

"I know you want to honor Bea's wishes, but I told you I can figure something out on my own. You can work on the rec center in a few years when your big project in Washington is done. Bea would understand that you have more important things to do right now."

A muscle in his jaw ticked.

"But you and me . . ." She heaved in a sigh. "Look, I know you're used to girls swarming you because you're kind of famous." Her eyes trailed over his flexed biceps. "And really well formed." One side of his mouth twitched up, and heat flamed up her neck. "But that's beside the point."

She sucked up her resolve. Squared her shoulders.

"You're only here for a short time, and I'm not one of those girls who wants you for your money and your notoriety." Maybe his body. She shook off the thought. "I have to live here after you leave. I have to face the stares and the gossip and the murmurs."

"You're right. But Bea wanted me to do this, so I'm here for the duration. You have my word, I'll be here until the inn is open and the gazebo is finished."

Her hand flexed around the doorknob. She'd heard men make similar promises to her mother, and stupidly, her mother always believed them.

Miranda swore she never would. But the sincerity in Talmadge's silvery-blue eyes made her resolve crumble like a flimsy wooden bridge in an earthquake.

"Even though people are already talking, we have to keep this professional."

"We could tell everyone we're engaged, and then you could dump me," he said, all seriousness.

*Good Lord.*

The man really was crazy. Or stupid. No, no. Talmadge wasn't stupid. *She* was the stupid one for getting herself into this mess. So that just left crazy. Years of loud construction noise had definitely scrambled his brains.

"We are *not* pretending to be engaged. We keep it professional and friendly. Present a united front for Bea and for the festival."

He nodded. "Professional and friendly," he mumbled like he didn't believe a word of it.

And, well. She didn't believe it either. Playing this dangerous game with Talmadge would likely leave her with a trampled heart when he left town for good.

"Let's get back to work then." Talmadge pushed himself off the door. "Oh, Uncle Joe wants us to put in an appearance a week from Saturday at his place. It's a fundraiser for the gazebo so you won't have to depend on the Wilkinsons' money."

"Okay, I'll meet you there."

He turned and strolled down the hall. "I'll pick you up. If we're going to present a united front, we actually have to be seen together acting professional and friendly."

She sputtered.

"Be ready at seven that night," he said over his shoulder.

Miranda wasn't sure how she was going to keep it professional and friendly when she was spending all day, every day with the only man who made her want to give the finger to her reputation and do him every which way she could.

---

Miranda took Talmadge's advice and started to assemble a trustworthy team to help plan the festival. After spending the rest of the week making phone calls to the small group of people that she had let into her inner circle over the years, she walked into the Chamber of Commerce building with enough gooey cinnamon rolls and coffee from the Ostergaards' bakery to feed an army.

If there was one thing she remembered from her high school AP history classes, it was that an army tended to be more loyal if their bellies were full. Not only did she want her soldiers going into battle against Mrs. Wilkinson fully armed and ready to fight, but Miranda wanted to win the war. So she set out the cinnamon rolls and coffee in the conference room and went back for the cranberry-pecan scones—Mrs. Ostergaard's specialty. No one stood a chance against those.

She'd scheduled the first meeting during Talmadge's physical therapy appointment. On purpose. Miranda wanted to establish herself as the commander in chief without her council automatically deferring to him.

Plus, she couldn't think with him in the room, much less plan an attack or lead a charge.

Within fifteen minutes the room was full of chomping, slurping, moaning-at-the-decadent-flavor volunteers.

Miranda went to the whiteboard and plucked the top off of a marker. "Thanks for coming, everyone." Her voice cracked, and she wanted to fan her eyes as she turned and looked at the roomful of helpers. For someone who had felt alone most of her life, she had a lot of friends. Maybe Talmadge was right. Asking for help wasn't always a bad thing.

She wrote out a list on the board. "Here's what we need to accomplish for the festival. Can I get a volunteer to head each category? Everyone else can sign up to work on a task."

Within two minutes each category was filled, and Lorenda furiously scribbled every detail down on a notepad while Miranda wrote the names on the board so everyone could see. It took twenty minutes for Miranda to cover all of the assignments.

"Let's meet weekly for updates. Same time, same place," she told her crew. "I'll bring the refreshments."

As they stood to go, Mrs. Wilkinson walked in with her son, Bart—the Red River elementary school principal—in tow along with the mayor. She didn't bother with a hello before launching her first barrage at Miranda.

"I brought along two respectable people in our community to witness your lack of experience and to ensure that the chairmanship is rightly switched to the better candidate."

"This meeting is for the Hot Rides and Cool Nights Festival. You must be lost." Francine held her travel-trailer-size purse in her lap.

Bart's receding hairline gleamed under the fluorescent lights, and he stared at his shoes. Mayor Schmidt—a tall, seventyish man with a potbelly and a keen eye for local politics—shoved his hands in his pockets.

And wow. Mrs. Wilkinson must donate a lot of money to Mayor Schmidt's campaigns because he looked as hen-pecked as Bart.

Joe spoke up. "Looks to me like Miranda has everything under control."

"Sure does," said Clydelle.

Miranda ignored her quivering stomach and pointed to the whiteboard with an air of confidence. "Everything is well in hand."

Mrs. Wilkinson gave her a calculating smile. "I've got proof that someone of such"—she looked down her nose—"questionable character shouldn't be in charge. Show them, Bart." She elbowed her son in the ribs.

He pulled his phone out and panned the screen around the room so everyone could see.

Miranda darted over to him and snatched the phone. The *Red River Rag* was open with a picture of her wearing the strip-mining T-shirt. It was taken when she had walked out to the Dumpster to throw out the trash.

"How . . . ?" Her words trailed off, because really? Gossip flowed like water in Red River, but this was getting ridiculous in a creepy stalkerish kind of way.

The title read *Betrayal at its worst! Maybe Red River's favorite environmental architect should find another tree to hug. Is this kind of disrespect worth Ms. Cruz wrapping her limbs around his trunk?*

"How indeed?" Mrs. Wilkinson gave Miranda a smug smile. "How do you explain the lewd inference to your behavior?"

"Miranda doesn't have to explain anything to you," Clydelle said. "But Mayor Schmidt and I may have a story or two to tell from way back." She waggled two bushy gray brows at the mayor. "Don't we, Harold?"

A bead of sweat broke out on the mayor's wrinkled forehead. "I think maybe we've misjudged Miss Cruz."

A look of desperation flashed in Mrs. Wilkinson's eyes, and she studied the whiteboard. "I don't see the gazebo on the board. Mr. Oaks rarely came to visit his own grandmother. How can he possibly be trusted with such an important addition to our community when he doesn't live in Red River? He's not even here for the meeting."

"I'm right here." Talmadge walked in with drawings under his arm, his easy saunter exuding the self-assuredness of a leader.

Trying to keep the meeting a secret was probably silly, since this was Red River and everybody already knew what she had for breakfast by now.

"Sorry I'm late." He took the seat closest to Miranda. "I brought preliminary plans for your approval, Madam Chairperson." He gave her a dazzling smile. A real smile that had started to appear more and more since he'd been back in Red River. Not that half-smile that masked some sort of private pain. "I gave Ms. Cruz my word I'd be here until her inn opens." He spoke to Mrs. Wilkinson, but he looked at Miranda. "She has my word I won't leave until the gazebo is finished as well."

She just stared at him, hoping the admiration in her eyes didn't make her look weak.

He gave her an encouraging nod. "I hope they meet your specifications." He said it like she had been the creative force behind his ideas. He placed the drawings on the conference table, and everyone leaned in to have a look. "If I didn't capture your vision for the project, I can make as many changes as you want." He spoke only to her, making sure everyone knew he answered to her and her alone.

Miranda wanted to kiss him. And thread her fingers through his gorgeous sandy hair. And maybe take his shirt off and run her hands all over his chest.

A storm of lust started low in her belly and gathered between her thighs. She crossed her legs and kept a determined and—hopefully—authoritative smile on her face. "Then by all means, Mr. Oaks." That earthy purple color she loved so much flared in his eyes. "Show us what you've got."

———

Sitting at the head of the large oval table, Miranda maintained her composure but not without a sexy flush seeping into her cheeks. The gratitude in her expression, not to mention the craving in her eyes that said she wanted a Talmadge sandwich for lunch, was priceless.

It also made him feel like something he should be scraping off the bottom of his shoe after taking Lloyd for a walk in a dog park. The half-truth he'd told her, leaving out the part about inheriting a truckload of money if he stayed until her inn opened, suddenly became almost as suffocating as the memories of what he'd done to cause his parents' accident. Even if telling her did violate the terms of Bea's will.

He scooted his chair in, spreading out his sketches.

His gaze moved over her pretty face to anchor to those plump lips. Which she pulled between her teeth.

"That doesn't change the fact that Mr. Oaks isn't a true resident of Red River. We should use someone local," Mrs. Wilkinson protested.

"He was raised here," Joe said without looking in Old Lady Wilkinson's direction. "That's good enough."

"I think you'll agree that my design represents Red River beautifully." That was one of his gifts, and the reason he not only excelled at architecture, but eclipsed every architect in the world when it came to environmental designs. He was a master at designing structures that blended with natural landscapes, cultures, and atmospheres.

"My husband and I will fund the project if we find someone else." She sniffed. "And appoint a new chairperson."

"We don't need your money," said Joe. "We'll raise the funds ourselves. I'm having the first fundraiser at my establishment, and I've contacted other local business owners who are on board with raising money."

Mrs. Wilkinson's mouth clamped shut, and her lips thinned.

"I have an idea that might help out with that." Talmadge looked only at Miranda, because how could he not? Her chocolaty eyes got bigger with every thread of help he stitched into her leadership role. "Actually, I got the idea from Miranda." Her eyes widened another notch. "She doesn't waste things." When she smiled, the dimples in her cheeks almost made his heart stop. "I'd like to use as many recycled materials as possible. If we ask people and businesses in town to donate something from their homes, barns, anything really, I can make it work. McCall's Hardware has offered to donate supplies. Anything else we need we can buy with the money we raise. It would be a new structure, but still have a nostalgic meaning for the community. It would be more historic, like the buildings on Main Street."

A ripple of oohs and ahs went around the table.

Miranda leaned over to get a better look at the drawings, and her fresh lemony scent drove him to the edge. When she glanced up, the look of approval in her eyes made his chest expand. The softness in her eyes made him want to snatch her up and kiss her, tell her the truth about his inheritance, and then take her to bed, if she'd have him.

She studied the drawings and placed a slender finger on the top of the gazebo. "That's the weather vane on top of the inn." Her voice had dropped to a whisper.

Talmadge nodded, appreciative and impressed by the fact that she recognized it. "Would you consider donating it? It represents both Bea and you." The two women he cared most about in the world. The thought shook him, and it took a second to catch his breath. "Maybe some of the churches in town, and Uncle Joe, and any number of people could donate something."

"Our church won't donate a thing," Mrs. Wilkinson huffed.

"There's plenty of other churches in town that would be more than happy to donate something," Joe said.

"It could be like paying homage to Red River," Miranda murmured. "Our history. Our culture."

Yes. Exactly. But mostly, a tribute to her, even though no one would ever know. He'd been thinking of her when he designed it. The two skylights were her eyes, and the small river running around the gazebo to converge into a waterfall with a small footbridge over it was her silky hair. The pearl color of the paint was her skin, and the red trim of the eaves and the wood bench inside was the color of her lips.

"Do something," Mrs. Wilkinson hissed at her son and the mayor.

But if anyone in the room had been paying the slightest bit of attention to her before, they had definitely tuned her out completely now. No way would Bart and Mayor Schmidt try to get rid of Talmadge with such a landmark idea, especially since he was offering his services for free.

A glint of something formed in Miranda's eyes. "It's a wonderful idea, Talmadge." Her voice was wistful. "And a beautiful thing to do for the people here."

Talmadge blinked, her words zinging through his creative mind. *Holy shit.* That was it! The answer to Trinity Falls. A gift to the indigenous people. An homage to the native tribes in Washington, with Trinity Falls blending with the natural landscape and flowing *around* the ancient ruins instead of through them.

And he had Miranda to thank for it. He'd stayed in Red River to gain his inheritance by helping save her investment in the inn. Instead, she may have just saved him financially and professionally. If the tribal leaders saw the project as a tribute to all of their people, they might allow Trinity Falls to move forward.

"I'm good with it," said Joe.

"Wait!" Mrs. Wilkinson demanded.

"Let's put it to a vote," Francine said.

Clydelle leaned over and spoke to her sister and her partner in all things mischief. "We don't need to vote. Miranda is the chairperson. Whatever she says goes."

Everyone in the room looked at her, waiting.

She looked around the room, her confidence obviously growing because she sat a little taller. She nodded. "I approve." She pulled her lip between her teeth. She did that a lot. When she was nervous, or unsure, or happy. It played hell with his concentration.

He gathered up the plans and shoved them under his arm. "I'll leave you all to finish up." He needed to get the heck out of there and call his firm back in Washington. If he was lucky, he might be able to salvage *his* professional reputation before it was too late.

# Chapter Thirteen

On Saturday night Miranda propped her feet on her coffee table and flipped through the channels, tired from a long day's work.

She needed a few hours alone. A little time without Talmadge's woodsy scent, incredible mane of hair, and sexy, well-equipped tool belt tempting her to throw her friendly professionalism under the bus and nail him in the biblical sense.

Miranda had never dated because she feared what people might assume. Because of rumors that started small and grew into a cancer that choked the life out of a person before they could stop it. Spending time with Talmadge every day at the inn and every evening working on the gazebo and festival only made her want more of what she couldn't have. The random touches of their hands, brushes of their arms, grazes of their legs, not to mention how she sometimes caught him watching her . . .

A pull started low in her belly.

With so much testosterone flowing off of him that it caused her thighs to clench every time she looked in his direction, she wasn't completely responsible for her actions if those random touches, brushes, and grazes led to him kissing her again. Or if he kept looking at her from under those sleepy, sexy long lashes. He was too damn gorgeous for his own good. Or for Miranda's own good.

She'd done without a man . . . a relationship . . . *sex* for this long, she didn't want to break her record with someone who wasn't in her long-term future. Again. She was already much more dependent on Talmadge than she wanted to be. And she was getting used to his company. Which was bad news. He wouldn't be around forever, and she could stand on her own two feet without a man . . . without Talmadge Oaks.

Her phone range, the custom ringtone blasting out her favorite classic rock song by Bob Seger, "Old Time Rock and Roll." Of all the strange things her mother had tried to instill in her, a love of classic rock and roll was the only thing that seemed to stick. She glanced at the caller ID. Taking a deep breath, she answered.

"Are you ready?" Talmadge asked before she could say hello.

"No." She glanced at the clock on the wall. It said five fifteen. She punched the remote until she found a rerun of one of her favorite reality shows. "Joe's fundraiser doesn't start for almost two hours." She wanted to relax for a few minutes. Kick back and maybe eat a gallon of ice cream.

"It's seven o'clock. We're already late."

She studied the clock on the wall. The second hand didn't move. *Crap.* The batteries had to give out today?

"Open the outside door to your suite. It's locked."

Miranda sat up. "You're here?" She looked down at her faded pink sweatpants and old Three Little Pigs sweatshirt that was two sizes two big and had a bleached Clorox stain on the front. Her hand flew to her hair, still wet from a shower. Greeting Talmadge at the door in worn-out clothes she'd owned since puberty wasn't how she intended to start the night. He was probably used to his dates wearing Prada. Or at least some sort of expensive designer faux leather so no animals had to die.

But Miranda wasn't his date. Maybe her appearance would remind both of them of that. Or maybe it would only make her feel more inadequate.

Her heart rate doubled.

"Glad you keep your door locked, by the way. Bea never did." His voice streaming through the phone startled her.

"I'm not dressed to go out."

"What are you wearing this time? An 'I Club Baby Seals' T-shirt? Come on, open up."

"Go. Away." She didn't try to hide her grating tone. "I'll meet you there."

"Not going away." Talmadge's voice sounded amused. "If you don't open the door, I'll call the sheriff and tell him you had a break-in. You and whatever you're wearing will show up on Tumblr before morning."

Her eyes slid shut. "I'd rather watch reality TV. Alone. I like *Fast N' Loud.*" She got up and went to the door. She threw the deadbolt and slid the chain off its track, tugging the door open at the same moment she realized what she'd just said sounded amazingly sexual. Especially when saying it to an incredibly attractive man who oozed alpha hotness from his very pores.

And oh baby, there he was, lounging against the doorframe like he was as comfortable in his own skin as she was in her faded Three Little Pigs sweatshirt. He wore a white linen dress shirt, the sleeves cuffed up on his forearms. He was the only man she'd ever met who filled out a pair of faded Levi's better than a male fashion model.

His mouth turned up into a cocky smile, and he stared at her with the phone still to his ear.

"I like it fast and loud, too, but not alone." His tone was as smart-ass as his smile.

Miranda's throat closed.

"And if I insist on going separate from you?" she said into the phone, even though they were face-to-face.

His eyes sank to the three small swine stitched across her sweatshirt. "I'll huff and puff and blow your house down."

"I'm hanging up on you." She tapped the End button with exaggerated flare, then turned and walked back into the den.

"Ouch. That hurt. I may not recover."

She ignored him. Until she remembered that the word "Juicy" was scrawled across the seat of her sweatpants. A typical Christmas gift from her mother, which Miranda only wore in the privacy of her own home. When her splayed hand flew to her backside, Talmadge laughed.

Hellfire.

"Can I come in?" he asked with too much confidence. She should say no just on principle.

"Might as well. You're here." She turned to face him with both hands on her hips. He stepped over the threshold. When he turned to shut the door, the sculpted muscles of his forearms shifted and flexed.

Involuntarily, Miranda's tongue darted out to trace her lower lip.

"Uncle Joe is waiting for us. The place is already packed, and a reporter from Red River's real newspaper is going to be there."

"Um, seriously." She fanned a hand over her comfy attire. "I didn't realize how late it was. It's going to take time to get ready, so maybe you should go without me. Tell them I'm sick or something." She couldn't stop her gaze from scanning his entire length.

"It's Joe's, not a state dinner at the White House." He tapped at the screen of his phone and handed it to her.

The *Red River Rag*'s latest post was a picture of her and Talmadge unloading supplies from the back of his truck. Lloyd's head was sticking out of a backpack that Talmadge had modified to carry the little guy around so he wouldn't get stepped on or so they wouldn't have to lock him in the bathroom to keep him out of harm's way. The caption read,

*Red River's newest lovebirds are making a nice little nest together. The inn is transforming before our eyes, and their "baby" is snug as a bug.*

"Wow," Miranda mumbled.

"Scroll down," Talmadge said.

She did and there was another post—she and Talmadge in Brandenburg Park, directing the start of the gazebo. *Red River sweethearts work together to make our little community a sweeter place. Is it too much to hope that they stay together? Or will it turn sour when our favorite architect flies the coop to go northwest for the summer?*

"Oh, for God's sake." Miranda wanted to scream. But it was a fair question. One to which she didn't want to find out the answer. Hence, the friendly professionalism.

Talmadge gently retrieved his phone from her grip with a lazy smile on his lips. "Go get ready. We're going to Joe's together, because it looks like the tide of public opinion is turning in your favor."

---

Shouts of approval rang out when Miranda and Talmadge walked into Joe's an hour later to boost enthusiasm for the festival and gazebo and hopefully jump-start the fundraising efforts. Being the center of attention when everyone thought she and Talmadge were sweethearts made her want to bolt.

Talmadge must have felt her tense. Or maybe he noticed that she held her breath until her lungs wanted to burst. He placed a warm, firm hand to the small of her back and gave her a little nudge. The warm contact made flames shoot all the way to her toes. She should've worn a thinner top, because his touch and the white sweater she had grabbed from her closet in a rush were making her sweat. She faked a bright smile and tried to dazzle the crowd.

Joe's new waitress grabbed two menus. "Y'all follow me. Joe has a table saved for you in the back." With a ballpoint pen tucked behind one ear and enough hairspray on her teased salt-and-pepper hair to hold together a mudslide, she led them through the restaurant.

If Miranda thought Talmadge would move his hand when she started toward their table, she was wrong. To pull away she lengthened her strides. So did he, and his palm stayed flush and oh so electrifying against that intimate spot just above the waistband of her denim miniskirt. Her back brushed his shoulder as he gently guided her forward, staying so close that his musky soap made her mouth water.

"What are you doing?" she whispered.

She tried to focus on the sound of crunching peanut shells under their feet as they followed her replacement past the checkered tables of beaming patrons. But not the peanut shells, or the country-and-western music that played in the background, or the chatter and obnoxious whispers from every table they passed could distract her from the sizzle of electricity that started at her waist where his hand rested and skated up her torso into her tightening nipples.

"Making sure you don't chicken out." He dipped his head and whispered into her ear. "You need to be here tonight. You're their leader until the festival is over whether you know it or not."

"Why would I chicken out?" Sure, she hadn't been able hide the shiver that had started in her legs on the drive over. Come to think of it, she should've worn a longer skirt to hide her knees, which were in a full-blown knocking state by the time they walked through Joe's front door. "Do I look scared?"

"Like you've seen a ghost." He increased the pressure against the small of her back.

Several tables greeted them as they followed the waitress around the wood dance floor and headed to the back of the cavernous room. Miranda waved and smiled and waved and smiled.

"Why? You've known these people for years."

"Some of them don't think too highly of me because of my mother," she said point-blank. "Guilt by association, I guess."

The server stopped at a table along the back wall of Joe's and held out a hand. "Here y'all go. Just for you two lovebirds." She set the menus in the center of the table and darted back to the front where a few more groups had walked in.

"I think you have more support in this town than you realize." Before they sat down, he glanced around the room where just about everyone was watching them. "Look." He nodded to the room of onlookers and turned his gaze back on her. "They don't look like a roomful of haters to me."

"They're staring at you," she said.

"Then it's a good thing you came tonight. When you put on a festival that kicks ass and takes names, they'll wonder why they hadn't given you more credit."

Talmadge guided Miranda into the booth and slid in opposite her.

She squirmed at the stares that kept darting in their direction. And the whispers. The whispers were the hardest to take because of the whispers that had circulated about her mother ever since Miranda was old enough to understand what they were about. They had been humiliating. Cruel even, because some people expected Miranda to be cut from the same rode-hard-and-put-away-wet cloth. And Miranda would rather die a thousand deaths than relive the shame she'd felt from those malicious whispers and stinging stares.

"I'm not used to being the center of attention. It's unnerving." She crossed her legs and waggled her foot.

"Get used to it," Talmadge said. "The *Red River Record* is interviewing you tonight. Their lead reporter has television experience and has connections with a camera crew in Taos, so he's agreed to film the progress of the inn. If we use a local crew, they'll be at our disposal and can document more of the renovations. I've got a syndicated home show lined up to edit the footage and run an episode when we're done." He unfolded a checkered napkin. "I've already informed the show that they can mention my name but you're doing all the talking."

"Wow." Her foot waggling kicked into warp speed. "Do people always jump like that when you snap your fingers?"

He lifted a cocky brow. "In the architectural world, usually." Then uncertainty flashed in his eyes. "Outside of the architectural world, it's another story."

"I don't have any experience with interviews or cameras or microphones. You have to do it."

He shook his head. "No can do. You're the boss. If you want people to take you seriously as a leader with the festival and in the community, this is how you do it."

"By making a fool out of myself for public record? I've already had enough of that from the *Red River Rag*."

"By leading." The corner of his mouth turned up, laughter glinting in his mesmerizing eyes. "You've already got the bossy part down like a champ."

His legs eased around hers, framing her under the table. The fabric of his worn jeans rubbed against her thighs. Her thin leggings did nothing to stop the friction from igniting a slow burn that traveled straight to ground zero.

"Stop bouncing your foot. The whole table is shaking. Being a strong leader doesn't mean you're never scared." He rubbed his inner thighs against hers. "It means you suck it up and do what you have to do even when you're scared."

And that's why he commanded respect just by walking into a room, no matter the crowd. Leadership came naturally to him.

"I'm not like you," she whispered. "I don't know if I can pull this off."

His gaze caressed over her. "Sweetheart, you're far stronger than I am. Bea knew it. I know it. *You* just don't know it yet. I'm staying behind the camera. This is your moment to shine."

Oh.

She stared at him, and her lips parted. She didn't know what to say except, "Let's order."

They both grabbed for the menus, and his hand landed on top of hers. It closed over hers like it was an automatic reflex, and for a second, everyone in the room disappeared except for him and her. And her stupid nipples stood at attention and gave a twenty-one-gun salute.

Maybe she was glad she'd worn a sweater after all. At least it would cover the evidence of how her body responded to him with enough voltage that she might as well have stuck her finger in a light socket.

She tugged her hand free, missing the weight of his. Missing the confidence and security she drew from such a simple thing.

Hating herself for it too.

She'd worked hard to make her own destiny. That path had gained her the self-respect that her mother never had. It had also landed her single and alone and wanting more, the same way her mother always had been.

Go figure.

And for the first time, Miranda's resentment toward her mother eased the slightest bit. Her mom may have gone about trying to find companionship the wrong way, but Miranda was starting to see why she'd wanted it so badly. Being alone was better than being with the wrong person. She glanced at Talmadge, and her breath hitched. But when a person finally realized that the right person might be out there somewhere, being alone sucked.

Trying to refocus, Miranda looked around the room to see if anyone had watched that small moment of accidental handholding. Her thoughts cleared enough to notice that almost everyone wore green T-shirts with Talmadge's company name and logo across the back and printed on the front shoulder.

How cute.

"Have you started a cult or something?" She opened a menu and studied it like she'd never seen it before even though it hadn't changed since she started work there at fifteen.

"Uncle Joe asked me to donate the shirts for tonight's fundraiser. I had my assistant send them from Seattle. It gave her something to do besides spa treatments and knitting at her desk since I'm not there to keep the company wheels turning."

"Your assistant is a she?" Miranda kept studying the menu. Of course his assistant was a she. Women all over the Pacific Northwest probably lined up to do the job for free just to get the chance to look at him. Looking at him was payment enough.

"Jealous?" Talmadge cracked a peanut and popped it into his mouth with a smirk.

*Yes.* "Of course not."

He chomped on the peanut and dug another one out of the tin bucket at the end of the table. "Her name is Ellen."

*Ellen.* Did *Ellen* have long legs, blonde hair, and possibly stand to inherit a hotel chain at some point in her future? Miranda dropped the menu to pick at a callus on her work-worn hands.

"Ellen is almost old enough to be on Social Security. She's also a loyal employee, and I don't have to worry about her wanting our relationship to go beyond professional boundaries."

Oh. "It's none of my business." Miranda picked up her menu again. "You can get back to work in Washington as soon as the inn passes inspection and the gazebo is unveiled at the festival."

She looked up about the time he popped another peanut into his mouth and chewed, slow and languid, his eyes never leaving her mouth.

"I'm sure it will be a relief," she blathered on. "You know . . . the unveiling . . ."

His eyes went all smoky and caressed down her neck to the drooping cowl neckline of her sweater. Flaming heat licked at the exposed skin just above her breasts when his gaze lingered there.

"You can unveil anything, anytime, boss. No argument from me." His voice was low and husky.

Her lips parted, her mouth turning to cotton.

Joe came over to their table and shook Talmadge's hand. "What can I get you two lovebirds? It's on the house."

Miranda's mouth fell open. Seriously? "We're not lovebirds, Joe." And he rarely gave anything away for free.

"Thanks, Uncle Joe. We'll both have a rib eye. Medium well. Your famous coleslaw and two beers. And bring Miranda one of my T-shirts. I promised her one." He shot a cocky smile at her. A sexy-as-hell smile that made her insides melt to liquid.

"Ordering for me isn't exactly letting me lead." She lowered her voice.

"Knowing you and your frugal ways, you would've ordered a side salad instead of a real meal."

Joe shrugged. "He's right, Miranda. You never want to impose."

She exhaled. Loudly. "All right. Since you insist, Joe."

"I'll put that order in." He turned to Talmadge. "But Miranda doesn't drink. Never has. I'll bring water for you, hon," Joe said and disappeared.

Talmadge's expression blanked, and he stared at her. And then the confusion in his stare turned to suspicion as he narrowed those beautiful eyes.

Beads of sweat broke out between her shoulder blades and trickled straight down her spine. Seven years ago she'd told him their two hours of tender, passionate lovemaking were a big mistake because she'd had too much to drink, which had been the first excuse to pop into her stuttering brain after they returned to Lorenda's reception and Momma Long Legs had clamped all four limbs and both Botoxed lips around Talmadge tighter than her tiny designer dress had clung to her size-two figure.

Miranda zeroed in on the menu and refused to look up. Refused to look at Talmadge, because she was afraid of what she'd see. She didn't plan to explain that she'd lied as a desperate attempt to salvage some self-respect and deflect her humiliation that night.

"Miranda." Just one word that said he *expected* an explanation.

"What if I didn't want a rib eye?" Miranda demanded, tossing her menu aside. "Maybe I'm a vegetarian."

*"Miranda,"* he growled.

Her mind zinged to find a way to redirect the conversation. "So what kind of after-school rec center did Bea have in mind?"

A muscle beside his eye twitched. "Stop changing the subject every time the night we spent together comes up."

"Shhh!" she hissed, and the next table looked over with curious expressions.

He leaned in, his teeth clearly gritting together. "It's time we get a few things straight about that night."

"Not now." She leaned in too and dropped her voice. "Not here."

A muscle in his strong jaw tensed. "Fine. But we *will* talk about it later."

Jamie walked up wearing an apron, grabbed an empty chair from the next table, and turned it around to straddle it. His arms propped on the chair back.

"What are you doing here, Jamie?" Miranda nearly choked at the sight of her intelligent little brother wearing one of the aprons that Joe gave to his dishwashers.

"Joe gave me a job here, thanks to your boyfriend." Jamie gave Talmadge a knuckle bump.

Miranda's blood started to sing like a boiling teakettle.

"He's not my boyfriend, and you're too smart to wash dishes." She spoke to Jamie but stared at Talmadge.

"He wanted to work." Talmadge shrugged. "It's an admirable quality, so I helped him get a job."

"Not as a dishwasher," she said through gritted teeth. She'd worked too hard to give Jamie the opportunity she never had. She wasn't about to see it wasted over a sink of soapy water.

"Joe's renting me one of his apartments too." Jamie pointed overhead to the three loft apartments located directly above the bar. "I already moved my clothes, so I'll be out of your hair."

"You're not in my hair, Jamie. You need to stay with me. It'll save money, and you won't have to work." How could he . . . how could *they*? Her anger rising, she leveled a hot glare at one and then the other. She wasn't sure which one she was more pissed at.

Talmadge lowered his voice so only she and Jamie could hear. "Let him be a man and earn his way, Miranda. You know as well as anyone that Joe is a good person to work for."

That was beside the point. She hadn't just been a sister to Jamie. She'd been more like a mother. Jamie should have come to her before making a decision like getting a job washing dishes. Talmadge already had way too much control over Miranda's future. Now he was usurping her authority to control Jamie's too?

Over her dead, sexually frustrated body.

"You look pretty tonight, sis." Jamie tried to lighten the mood by using his I've-screwed-up-so-now-I'm-going-to-suck-up tone.

"Okay, what do you want?" Miranda asked with a raised brow. "Just my approval to work a job so far below your IQ level that it doesn't even register, or is there something else?"

"What? Can't I pay my big sister a compliment?" He feigned insult.

"You're just trying to get on my good side."

"You have a good side?"

Talmadge snorted.

"You two make a cute couple," Jamie said.

"We're not a couple, Jamie, now get lost. We'll talk about you working here in private." She shot a searing glare at Talmadge.

"You look like a couple. Everybody in town thinks so." Jamie drummed the chair back.

And this time, Talmadge didn't try to correct Jamie's misunderstanding of their relationship. Talmadge just crossed his arms over his chest, leaned back casually against the booth seat, and took in the freak show.

"Stop talking, Jamie, before I stab you with my fork," Miranda ground out.

"Okay, okay." Jamie held up both palms. "Jeez, loosen up. Good thing you have a boyfriend now. Maybe you can work off some of that tension and testiness."

A smile slid onto Talmadge's lips, and her ears started to ring.

Miranda picked up her fork and held it like a weapon.

Jamie scooted his chair closer to Talmadge. "I talked to Mom this morning. She mentioned your affair."

*Affair?* The ringing got louder.

"I tried to do damage control, but Mom keeps wailing about how all your troubles are over now that you've found a rich guy."

Miranda's eyes slid shut. When her grip tightened around the fork, Jamie scooted all the way over to Talmadge's side of the table. "Just thought I should warn you. You know how Mom is. Plus, I'm just sayin' that her latest round of rants about you are an improvement."

Miranda pinched the bridge of her nose.

He spoke to Talmadge. "Mom decided Miranda must be a lesbian when she turned twenty-eight and still hadn't shown an interest in any of the men around here."

Something shifted in Talmadge's eyes and they turned a darker shade of blue-gray. Then they caressed over her face.

"I'm going to kill you in your sleep." She gave her little brother a sweet smile.

Jamie returned it with a mischievous look. "Now see, you're proving Mom right. This kind of attitude is why she thinks you can't find a boyfriend." His gaze shifted to Talmadge. "Until now."

"He's not my boyfriend." She tried to keep her voice low and her anger in check. "And I do not need nor do I want a man." Her hand gripped the fork so tight her knuckles turned white.

Jamie nodded toward Miranda but still spoke to Talmadge. "Precisely the reason Mom thought she was a lesbian."

"Go. Away."

Jamie stood. "That's the thanks I get for giving you the heads-up about Mom?"

"I haven't stabbed you yet. That's thanks enough." Then her smile softened at her kid brother and she tugged him down to ruffle his hair. "Okay, *now* go away."

"Hey!" Jamie complained. "I'm not eight."

"See ya around, buddy." Talmadge held up his fists again for another fist bump.

The waitress delivered their drinks. Miranda's was wrong. Before she could ask for water instead of beer, the waitress was flagged by another table that wanted to complain about their food order.

"Jamie's a good kid," Talmadge said.

"Jamie should've come to me. I could've helped him decide what kind of job to get."

"He's old enough to make his own decisions." Talmadge wasn't backing down. "And sometimes a young guy wants advice from another guy." His voice softened and slid over her like the damned butterscotch she loved so much. "That's a good thing, Miranda. It means he's trying to stand on his own two feet, like his big sister. If you keep clipping his wings, he'll never fly."

Well. Dang. Her throat grew all thick as she thought about how good Jamie had turned out in spite of their upbringing. And now he didn't need her much anymore. He wanted guidance from someone else. A man. A strong, successful man like Talmadge.

A man who had swooped into town and managed to strip just about everything from her that mattered. Her independence as a business owner, her independence as a woman, her independence as a mother figure to Jamie.

She fought off the sting in her eyes. Because Talmadge wasn't doing any of those things to hurt her. He was doing them to help. It would be so much easier if she had a reason to hate him. Instead, everything he did stole another piece of her heart until she was afraid there would be none left by the time he left Red River.

"He's a hard worker." Talmadge hesitated, studied her for a second. "Like you."

Her cheeks heated. "When you grow up poor you have two choices. You can either stay poor, or try to work your way out of it."

Talmadge took a pull from his frosty mug. "How come you didn't go to college? You were smart enough. You skipped a grade, right? And you were always on the honor roll."

Miranda blinked. "You remember that?"

"I do."

Talmadge had acted as though she didn't exist in high school. She didn't think he even knew her name back then.

"I did take some business classes." She stopped. Didn't know if she should continue. A scar on the lacquered table became incredibly fascinating.

"So what happened?"

"I quit because I wanted to finish raising Jamie. He needed me."

Talmadge frowned, and Miranda understood why. The pride Bea had carried for her grandson's accomplishments glowed in her aging voice every time she and Miranda spoke. His grandparents probably would've moved heaven and earth to see him finish college.

At that moment, overwhelming loss nearly suffocated Miranda. Her old friend was gone, Talmadge would soon leave, and Jamie was on his way out too.

"Is that why you stayed in Red River?" Talmadge asked.

She nodded, drawing in a weighted breath. "As soon as I could move out on my own I did. No way was I leaving Jamie behind. He was just a kid."

Talmadge's expression blanked.

Miranda doubted he could understand the world she grew up in. Even though his grandparents hadn't been wealthy, they'd done well enough to keep food in the pantry. And Miranda would bet the lights always worked when Talmadge flipped a switch.

"At least here in Red River I had a steady job and an inexpensive apartment over Lorenda's garage. I didn't have legal custody or the money to hire an attorney to try to get it. Staying here was easier. By the time he started college, I'd become friends with Bea and she kept bringing up the inn." Miranda followed a deep scar in the table with her thumbnail. "I figured I had Joe and Lorenda and Lorenda's entire family as friends, so staying in Red River was my best option."

"My father was difficult too." Talmadge's eyes dulled with sadness. "I was lucky to have my grandparents after my parents were killed."

He reached across the table and covered her hand with his. The warmth spread up her arm and wrapped around her heart because it felt so . . . safe.

"I'm sorry you didn't have the same." He caressed the top of her hand with a callused thumb, and the contrast of his roughened fingers against hers made her skin prickle. "But I'm glad you and Bea had each other the last few years. Every week when I called her she'd talk about you. Your friendship meant a lot to her."

Miranda swallowed. Stared down at his large, rugged hand engulfing hers. "She was like a mom to me. Encouraged me to do the things I never thought I could do, like becoming my own boss. Becoming a business owner. I owed her a lot."

"I owe *you*, Miranda. For watching out for Bea the last few years." He stared down at their hands, too. "I should've come home more after my grandfather died. I regret it."

Ah, guilt was a strong motivator. No doubt it was the reason he was still here in Red River helping Miranda. God knew he had more important things to do than stay in this little town that must seem like a joke after the life he'd lived.

He hesitated. "I have other regrets too." His lips parted like he wanted to say something. His expression was troubled. But nothing came out and he kept staring at their hands, caressing the back of hers with his thumb. His muscled thighs slid against hers. His strokes made a quiver start right where they were touching and travel up both legs to settle in between. Finally he nodded. "I want to give something back to Red River that would make Bea proud. Both the inn and the gazebo would've made her happy, I think."

He said it like he meant it from the depths of his soul. But the look on his face wasn't all that convincing. That private pain was back, like he was harboring a Pandora's box of secrets, and no one would ever know why.

# Chapter Fourteen

At the far end of Joe's long bar, Talmadge stood behind Felix Daniels, the reporter from the *Red River Record*, while Miranda fielded questions. Joe's was still packed, but Talmadge and Joe didn't let anyone close enough to hear so Miranda wouldn't feel so scrutinized. The interview was for her sake.

He'd cost his family something precious once, and the memory would haunt him forever. And he'd taken something precious from Miranda seven years ago because he didn't know it was her first time until it was too late, and he'd felt guilty over it for years. He could never repair the damage he'd caused his family. God knows he'd tried through his career. But he could give this small gift to Miranda, have her back while she came into her own as a business owner and a respected leader in the community.

But afterward he had to get her alone and find out why the hell she'd lied to him about drinking all those years ago, and he had to do it without kissing the sense out of her.

He wasn't entirely sure he had enough willpower left to accomplish that, because every time she'd wrapped her lips around her fork, or laughed that deep, sexy laugh when someone stopped by their table to say hi, he'd pictured her naked with nothing on but a dimpled smile. A hole had formed in his chest, because he wondered what it would be like to wake up with her tangled in his sheets every morning. The hole had formed into a crater by the end of their meal because of the warmth and friendliness between her and Joe's patrons—people she'd served since she was fifteen.

Felix, a jovial man with a white Santa Claus beard, pink cheeks, and curly white hair that was stark against a black beret, leaned an elbow against the bar and faced Miranda. He recorded the interview with a thumb hooked underneath one side of his black suspenders.

At first, Miranda's uncertain gaze darted over Felix's shoulder to Talmadge before she answered, and he gave her a subtle nod and warm smile each time. Before the interview started, he'd told her to speak from the heart. He'd learned early in his career that if he spoke about the reasons his environmentally friendly designs meant so much to him, how they would affect a community, the nation, and eventually the world, that true passion would shine through and win the audience. Precisely why he'd gotten quasi-famous. The camera loved him because he was sincere and believed in what he did for a living.

So after the first few questions, she'd sat a little taller, spoke with more confidence, and instead of giving Talmadge an uncertain look like she wanted his approval or encouragement, she'd glanced at him with pride.

"Talmadge, can you join Miranda and tell us about your plans for the gazebo?" Felix asked over his shoulder.

"No, sir." Talmadge crossed his arms over his chest. "The chairperson can answer all of your questions."

She threw an appreciative glance at him, but their gazes locked. He loved the glint of determination that made the amber flecks in her eyes dance every time she looked at him. Every time she smiled his pants grew a little tighter, and his breaths became more labored.

Spending all evening with her in that short skirt, her nice legs and silky leggings brushing against him, and the soft sweater that dipped just enough in front to hint at what he was missing—and the boots. They weren't high-heeled boots that said, "Take me with nothing else on *except* the boots." The heels were low, and the leather was a little scuffed and worn, but in a way that made them look richer with age, simple and elegant, just like her.

Yeah, spending all evening with her dressed like that might have been a tad too ambitious.

Felix asked her another question, and her dimpled smile stole Talmadge's breath as she did exactly what he'd told her to do—she spoke from the heart, *became* the heart of Red River and all that it stood for. She spoke of community, friendship, hardworking folks that a person could count on.

All the things Talmadge had tried to forget. Had left behind. All the things missing in his life.

When the interview was done, Felix clicked off a few pictures of Miranda and Joe together. "This will run in Monday's paper."

"Could you run a story on each fundraiser as they happen?" asked Miranda. "I'll send you our schedule, and I'll be at every one."

Smart. Talmadge smiled. Free public relations and advertising for the project, and it would probably prompt more donations.

Felix scratched his beard and adjusted his beret. "Will do, Miss Miranda."

"Thanks, Felix. You'll be by the inn next week with the camera crew to start filming the renovations?" Talmadge asked.

"Will do that too." They shook hands. Felix gathered up his recorder and camera and lumbered off to find a table.

With the dinner hour over, Joe cranked the C-and-W music and the dance floor filled.

Miranda grabbed her purse and slung it over a shoulder.

Talmadge eased onto the barstool that Felix had just vacated. "You did great. You're a natural."

Her hair was up in one of those knots with just enough messiness to look sexy. Loose pieces framed her face and hung in soft ringlets around her neck. She gave him a smile that slayed him on the spot.

"Thanks. You were right. I thought of what the inn means to me, and Bea, and . . ."

She pulled her lip between her teeth, her gaze gliding over his face. For a second he hoped she was going to say that she thought of what *he* meant to her. The thought surprised him, and he tried to control his quickening breaths.

"And well, I just thought of how lucky I am to have a chance to do something with my life. Not everybody gets a chance like that." Her eyes still wandered over him, landing on his mouth. "Thank you."

He tried not to notice how the weight of the purse made her winter-white sweater dip even further in front. Tried not to notice how sweet the swell of her breasts looked. He'd seen them once, seven years ago. They were spectacular, and he wanted to see them again. Touch them. Taste them.

And for a moment, they just stared at each other. Her plump lips parted. Her cheeks pinked.

His pants got tighter.

"Hey." Cooper Wells and Doc Holloway, Red River's chiropractor and medical doctor, interrupted the moment. "You're looking pretty comfortable with that shoulder," Coop said.

Talmadge nodded. "It's much better. I'm doing the exercises several times a day. Thanks, Coop."

"Great fundraiser," Doc Holloway said to Miranda, then turned to Talmadge. "We're heading over to my place for a guys' poker night while our wives are having a girls' night out." He pointed to a booth against the right wall of Joe's where Angelique, Ella Wells, and Lorenda occupied a booth. "Want to join in?"

"Uh." He'd rather spend time with Miranda, and they still needed to have that talk. "I'm Miranda's ride."

She hopped off the barstool. "Don't miss out on a good poker game on my account." She nodded to the booth where her friends sat. "I'm joining the mommy mafia for some girl time while you no-accounts swill beer, beat your chests, and lose hard-earned money." She slugged Doc Holloway on the shoulder and hurried over to join the ladies, that mouthwatering sashay in her hips.

That was the first time he'd seen her in a skirt except for seven years ago at Lorenda's wedding. A crying-ass shame because those legs were too perfect to hide, and he'd really like to have them wrapped around his waist.

Coop cleared his throat, and Talmadge's gaze left Miranda's silky legs and strutting ass and snapped to the good chiropractor.

"So how 'bout it, Talmadge? You up for some poker?" Coop asked.

He glanced at Miranda. "Maybe some other time, guys. I'm going to hang out here with Uncle Joe and see if I can keep the momentum of the fundraiser going."

And if he was lucky, he might still be able to get Miranda alone to have that talk.

---

Spending time with the girls might help ease the sting of her ebbing willpower. After Talmadge successfully maneuvered her through the obstacle course of leadership roles, project organization, interviews, and renovations, she was having a hard time remembering why she shouldn't climb all over him and enjoy the physical benefits he could offer while he was still in town.

She had to give him credit. Everything he'd done had been calculated and planned to keep up the public illusion that she was in charge. But they both knew the truth. She'd failed at the one thing she needed to do for herself—make the inn a success on her own without depending on a man.

A faster country song kicked up, and flashes of boots, hats, and jeans whirled past as Miranda slid into the booth and sat next to Lorenda.

"We tried to order." Lorenda pointed to the frosty mugs of beer on the table. "But Joe's new waitress messed it up, and she hasn't been back to fix it." Lorenda took a long drink. She was the only one at the table who could have alcohol.

"Seriously." Ella stared at Lorenda's beer with longing. "Who messes up water with a wedge of lemon? Everyone knows Miranda doesn't drink alcohol."

Yes, dammit. Even Talmadge knew, and it was obvious by his earlier expression that he wasn't going to let it go.

"It's a little hard to miss that I'm nursing." Ella pointed to her considerable bustline and absently fingered the ends of her long red hair like she was rethinking the whole nursing thing. "And that Angelique here is expecting."

"What I wouldn't give for a beer right now," Angelique said. "Some ladies'-night-out crowd we are." She rubbed her expanding tummy. "Right now, my idea of letting my hair down and getting wild is watching all three *Hangover* movies back-to-back on DVD."

"At least Bradley Cooper takes his shirt off." Lorenda swilled her beer.

Angelique raised an eyebrow. "Precisely why I watch 'em."

Miranda pointed to both Ella and Angelique. "You two don't have anything to complain about. You've got husbands who look as good as any movie star. I don't."

"That could change," said Ella.

"When you least expect it." Angelique pointed to the bar, and all four of them turned to look.

A thrill coasted through Miranda at the thought of Talmadge changing her world in the marital sense. He'd changed it in every other way, but that way was impossible.

He lounged at the bar, his faded jeans and white linen shirt fitting his purely male build to perfection. Really, the man could make a pair of Dickey coveralls look slick. His canvas hiking boots looked just as natural on him as the expensive Italian shoes he sometimes wore. The way he moved back and forth between the world of a simple, hardworking guy who tromped around jobsites in boots and jeans, and the world of movie stars, architectural magazine cover shoots, and red-carpet fundraisers for his projects with the ease of a chameleon was fascinatingly sexy.

With an easy, hometown boy smile, he propped a foot against the footrest and an elbow on the bar. Joe ambled over and claimed the seat next to Talmadge. Dylan McCoy, Joe's grandson and Talmadge's cousin, slid a beer in front of both of them, then hustled to fill orders behind the bar. Talmadge didn't look around the large, bustling room. He slid one look over his shoulder straight at her, and their gazes locked.

Blood thundered through Miranda's veins.

His mouth didn't curve into a smile, and a mixture of conflicting emotions flashed in his metallic eyes. The connection they had. The familiarity. The distance. The unrequited desire.

"Oh, do him already." Lorenda was obviously drinking the others' share of alcohol. "Or someone else in this town will."

"No!" Angelique hollered. "Doing him might lead to this." She pointed to her growing belly. "And that will lead to labor and delivery." She shuddered. So did Ella and Lorenda.

"*You* do him." Miranda glowered at Lorenda, the only other single gal at the table. "Besides, how do you guys know I haven't already?"

Ella laughed. "Girlfriend, we'd know."

Right. They would. Angelique and Ella's love affairs with their husbands had rocked the sleepy little town of Red River and been fodder for gossip until they both got married and everyone moved on to a new story.

Which, at the moment, was Miranda and Talmadge.

Lorenda dug her smartphone out of her purse and pulled up the *Red River Rag*. She passed it to Miranda. "Have you seen the latest?"

Miranda didn't want to see it.

She didn't.

She pinched the bridge of her nose, then reached for the phone.

Her jaw nearly hit the table. "This was just taken!"

*Our favorite architect makes progress with his latest project, but will he drive the nail home tonight? Miss Cruz is becoming Red River's darling, but if she's going to DATE him while he remodels her inn, she could at least let him stay the night.*

Miranda scrolled to the picture under the caption. Her and Talmadge sitting at a booth just a few minutes ago, gazing into each other's eyes, his hand on hers. Her looking at him like she wanted to eat him for dinner instead of the steak he'd ordered for her.

She tossed the phone back at Lorenda.

"Sweetie." Ella rubbed her engorged breasts as though she were in the privacy of her own home. "They're too hard to resist when they look that good."

Angelique nodded and rubbed her bun in the oven. "Their six-pack abs are a weapon, and they know how to use them to wear us down."

Yes, Talmadge's body was unfair. And uncalled for. "You guys make me feel so much better. I joined you for some moral support." She might just take up drinking after all. If she could ever get the damned waitress's attention. She looked around the room.

"We've been right where you're at, and if his near mythical good looks don't get to you, his charisma will." Angelique flashed a smile and winked. "And it's worth it as long as you don't end up brokenhearted."

And that was exactly why Miranda couldn't let her resistance falter. She was already on the verge of falling so head-over-heels in love with Talmadge that if she actually let it happen, she'd never stop tumbling.

"I can't let it happen." Miranda shook her head. This was her fault for falling into his arms at Bea's wake and then letting him kiss her, not to mention letting him feel up her ass. His lips and his hands were just too hard to resist.

A shiver raced up her spine.

"Then just don't let him take his shirt off in front of you, honey," Ella warned, and Angelique snorted like she knew exactly what Ella meant.

"Come on, Miranda, can't you pull some strings? I need a cranberry juice and something to munch on." Angelique's alpha-female personality was starting to show in her voice because a low growl rumbled through her tone.

Miranda blew out an exasperated breath. "All right." Her tone was just as huffy as the voices of her frustrated friends, who were irritated because they either had joined the ranks of motherhood, or were about to.

"You better hurry. Their hormones are about to mutiny." Lorenda took another swig of beer. "I've been there. Twice. And once the hormones take over, they're not responsible for their actions." She turned glazed eyes on Miranda and tried to focus like she might be seeing double. "Need help?"

"Um, no. I'll take care of it." Miranda started to get up but paused. "I'll drive you home tonight, 'kay?"

Lorenda confiscated Ella's untouched beer. "My brother's picking me up later when he's done with his shift. My parents took the kids to Santa Fe overnight to go to the movies, so I'm living it up with you ladies tonight while I can."

Sliding out of the booth, Miranda smoothed her miniskirt with shaky hands. When Talmadge threw a look over one shoulder and did a double take, his eyes turned smoky. Miranda hardened her nerves.

With each step she took toward the bar, the electrical current swirling around her and Talmadge got stronger. So did the ringing in her ears.

She stepped up to the bar, keeping two empty barstools between her and Talmadge. "Dylan, can we get two cranberry juices for the mommy mafia over there, and I'll take a water with lemon." Talmadge didn't look at her, but she knew he was listening to every word. "They ordered food too. Can you find out what's holding up the order before anarchy breaks out and they start taking hostages?"

Dylan flashed her a grin, the diamond stud in his ear glinting under the dim bar lights. "We miss you here. You're irreplaceable."

Sure. She was the best damn waitress in the Southwest. What a compliment. Someone should give her an award. Maybe a waitress was all she was cut out to be. Why else would she be in this mess, indebted to Talmadge and ready to hump him like a dog in heat if he gave her another one of his lazy smiles?

Still sitting next to Talmadge, Joe leaned back to give her an apologetic look. "Your orders are on the house tonight, Miranda. Sorry for the wait."

Wow. The new server must be really bad if Joe was giving out more free food and drinks.

Dylan filled a mug with ice water, plopped a lemon in it, added a straw, and slid it onto the bar. He dried his hands on a towel. "Have a seat, and I'll see if I can track down your food." He headed toward the kitchen.

Joe pulled his rotund girth off the stool. "I better go see what the problem is." He shook his head, his double chin waggling, and followed Dylan.

Easing onto a stool three down from Talmadge, she squeezed the lemon into the mug and swished it around with the straw.

She pulled her lip between her teeth right about the time Talmadge turned his gaze on her, and it dropped to her mouth. "Do I smell?"

*Heck, yeah. Pretty darn good, actually.* "Beg your pardon?"

"I figured maybe I didn't shower well enough if you're sitting way down there." He got up and came to her. Reclined his long, lean body against the bar and faced her. A beer in one hand, he took a sip and bent one knee so that it rested against hers. "We were getting along so well, and now it's like I have an awful body odor that I'm not aware of." He smiled down at her, that boyish grin growing a little more apparent with every day he stayed in Red River. He set his beer on the bar and traced the water droplets on her glass, his fingertip grazing hers. "It seems we had a misunderstanding seven years ago." He dropped his voice to a whisper. "But we're going to straighten that out. Soon. So stop avoiding it."

She should've let the mommy mafia launch a hostile takeover. Because her pulse kicked, and instead of pulling her hand away from his, she let the current of warm lust seep between them. He reached out and fingered a lock of her hair.

"Another storm must be coming," she blurted, and then wanted to slap herself. "Um, my hair gets a little wild when it's wet."

His pupils expanded to black marbles.

"Moist!" she blurted again.

*Good God.*

"When the humidity rises, my hair gets curlier." She bit her lip again.

"I love your curly hair." His gaze traveled down her length all the way to her boots and up again. "Having fun with your friends?"

"Um." Her throat was as dry as the desert in the middle of summer, and she cleared it. "Yeah. Fun. All the hormones are a little scary actually."

He laughed. Deep. Edgy. Sexy.

"So I have to bring my Jeep in for service on Monday. I might not be at the inn for a few hours." She tried to change the subject.

"If you need to borrow a vehicle, Bea's Subaru just sits in her garage," he said. "I prefer the old truck. Reminds me of home and how much I miss"—his sultry look skimmed over her face—"some things here that I can't have back in Seattle."

Her pulse revved into a low roar like the engine in his old Dodge pickup.

Heads turned in their direction. She and Talmadge being the center of attention should've made her uncomfortable. Instead, Miranda fixated on the way his fingertips kept brushing back and forth against hers. The way his breath whispered across her cheeks when he spoke and made her heart thud against her chest. The way his eyes told her how much he wanted her.

An ache exploded at her center and spread through her until both of her breasts and the spot between her thighs throbbed. She had to remind herself to breathe.

Talmadge's look grew more sultry like he could read her mind. Or her body. Maybe it was that pheromone thing she seemed to have a problem with. Hell's bells, and here she was spewing them around food again.

At this rate, she'd never get through the health department's inspection.

A slow, sultry country-and-western song started up, and more couples took to the dance floor.

"I'd ask you to dance, but I've never been very good at it."

"Me either," she whispered. She should step away. Go back to her table where the mommy mafia would protect her from making a terrible mistake. Where she couldn't breathe in his luxurious scent of timber and masculine soap. Instead, she leaned into him, and before she could get her double-crossing body to obey, she kissed him. In front of the whole damn town.

It was soft and sensual, but his lips moved on hers and he let out a breath like he'd been holding it. Or maybe he was shocked. But his mouth took charge, even though he kept the pressure of his lips gentle against hers. Her lips parted and his tongue slipped in to brush hers.

Miranda sighed against his mouth, and a wave of tension receded like the tide. At that moment not one other person in the world existed, and she rested a hand against his chest. His heart thrummed under her touch.

A throat cleared, cutting through the fog of lust that churned around them. Miranda snapped back to reality and jerked away from Talmadge.

"Uh, sorry. But, uh . . ." Joe's newest waitress stood beside them with two glasses of cranberry juice and a strained expression.

Miranda smoothed her hair and tried to look composed. Wasn't happening.

"Dylan said to bring this to you," the waitress huffed.

Miranda was about to tell her to bring the drinks to Angelique and Ella, but then the poor woman might actually get the tables mixed up during the twenty or so steps it would take to walk the drinks over. Miranda stood. "I'll take them over."

She reached for the drinks, but Clydelle and Francine walked past—Francine's ginormous purse swinging—and bumped into the server. Who proceeded to tip both glasses of cranberry juice over and drench the front of Miranda's white sweater. She gasped as the cold liquid soaked through to the skin.

"Oh, dear," said Clydelle, and leaned on her cane. "Francine, you should really be more careful with that purse."

"What's in that thing anyway?" the waitress asked. "It's as big as a suitcase."

Francine clutched it to her chest.

Talmadge grabbed some napkins and tried to dab at Miranda's chest, which only embarrassed her more because the wet fabric had instantly become transparent. Arms out, jaw gaping, she stared down at the white lace and pale yellow polka dots showing through the soaking wet fabric.

Francine stepped around Clydelle. "Well don't just stand there, Talmadge. Give her your shirt so she can cover up."

"That would be the gentlemanly thing to do," Clydelle agreed.

His lips parted, and his expression blanked.

Miranda panicked. *No! Don't take off the shirt!* She'd be doomed for sure.

Talmadge pulled the shirttail from his jeans and had the buttons undone before Miranda could stop him. He shrugged out of it and draped it over Miranda's front.

The entire room went quiet.

Every woman above the age of twelve stared at Talmadge without a shirt on and all but salivated. Miranda included.

"Glad to see you're staying fit." Clydelle gawked at Talmadge.

"Yessiree," agreed Francine.

Miranda did a double take when Francine gave Clydelle a satisfied look that communicated, "Mission accomplished." *Oh. My. Gawd.* Those two old ladies set him up! To take off his shirt. In a public place.

Miranda wouldn't even have to look at the *Red River Rag* tomorrow. She already knew what would be in it.

She turned to give her table of girlfriends a silent plea for help, but all three of them shook their heads like they had just lost all hope for her. Because like they'd warned her . . .

She looked back at Talmadge's shirtless upper body. The ladies were right on target. His washboard abs, muscled arms, and well-defined chest with a dip in the middle crumbled the last ounce of her willpower.

"Let's get out of here." She grabbed his arm and towed him toward the door.

# Chapter Fifteen

Talmadge let Miranda tug . . . no, *drag* him out of Cotton Eyed Joe's, the
freezing night air stealing his breath. When he offered her his shirt to cover
up the sexy polka-dot bra showing through her drenched white top, he
hadn't thought of the scene it would cause. Or that raw desire would blaze
to life in her eyes and she'd tow him outside for a make-out session. Because
the swirling fog from her heavy breaths and the lusty glaze in her expression
left no doubt in his mind that Miranda wanted to make out. Right now.

And walking down Main Street naked from the waist up wasn't the
least bit awkward.

A chatting couple walked toward them, but their conversation
stopped when they glanced up and saw Talmadge without a shirt. If
Miranda noticed, she didn't show it. She just kept dragging him along,
still clutching his shirt to her front.

"Where are we going?" he clipped out through chattering teeth.

"To your truck." She didn't slow.

Thank God, because he needed to get a jacket.

She threw a look over her shoulder like she was making sure he was getting with her program.

He couldn't hold back a smile. He'd seen the same sexually determined look on her pretty face once before. Seven years ago. And he knew what came with it. Getting naked with her was what he'd fantasized about since he walked out onto the back porch at Bea's wake and found Miranda on all fours, cracking a smile with her backside. Even though it had ended badly once before—he had enough bad juju going on in his life right now, and God knew he didn't want to add Miranda to that list of screwups too—being with her seemed right. He just had to make sure she knew what she was getting into first, before they took off any more of their clothes.

But at the moment he didn't want to be the one to tell her that. Her sweet ass swayed a few steps ahead of him as she pulled him around the corner of Joe's with her fingers threaded in his. Though she was just over five feet tall, her personality was large and in charge at the moment, and Talmadge was enjoying the show.

So was the rest of Red River who happened to be out and about on a Saturday night. A Jeep lumbered past and honked. Talmadge waved. Miranda didn't seem to care.

Instead she headed straight to Talmadge's truck in the parking lot behind Joe's. She stopped at the driver's door, clamping his shirt to her soaking chest, and held out her hand. "Keys."

He smiled down at her. Even though he was freezing, she was adorable as hell like this. "It's not locked."

"Oh." She whirled and jerked the door open. Leaned way inside the truck and rummaged around for his jacket.

Talmadge took in the view. *Sweet.* Her denim miniskirt rode up, and through the skintight leggings, the nice curve of the bottom of her cheeks greeted him. Miranda wasn't the vegan-skinny type. She had nice full hips and a round ass that was perfectly shaped. Shapely legs disappeared into the boots just below the knees. And when she turned around with his jacket, her nice rack was apparently ready and waiting for him because she'd lowered his shirt and two proud nipples strained through the wet fabric of her clinging top.

"Put this on." She shoved his jacket at him.

As soon as he had it on, she launched herself at him like she had to have him right that instant. In the parking lot.

Her full breasts pressed against his bare chest. She felt so good wrapped around him that his arms instinctively closed around her waist and smoothed up her back. One hand threaded into her hair, and he tugged her in so that she stood in between his wide stance. He stared at those lips, the ones he'd been fantasizing about all night, and took her mouth with such force it nearly bowled him over. She whimpered when his hand slid south and found the hem of her miniskirt, then slid up the soft, silky leggings to cup her ass—the other thing he'd been fantasizing about all night—and she shuddered, making those magnificent breasts with their rock-hard nipples brush against his bare skin.

He let out a tortured moan, and his kiss grew more urgent, drawing another whimper from deep inside her.

He wanted to bend her over the seat of his truck, hike up her skirt, and give her a whole lot more to moan about, but it was for her own good that they stop, so he broke the kiss and nipped at her lower lip. By the look on her face and her aggressiveness, if he didn't stop it, they *would* end up doing it right there in his grandpa's old truck, and it would be all over the Internet before they could get their clothes back on.

And she'd hate him. And she'd hate herself. But worst of all, her reputation would be forever ruined in this town because of him. The gossip would follow her around for the rest of her life, like it had her mother.

She angled her head toward her shoulder to study him, and one of her hands still fisted the shirt he'd given her at the bar. He guessed he didn't look too convincing about wanting to stop, because she went up on her tiptoes and pulled him into another hot, wet kiss, her hand roaming under his jacket against his bare skin. Damn, he didn't want it to end. He wanted what she was trying to give him. But not at the price it would cost her.

He broke the kiss and pulled back to look at her. Lips swollen from their kiss, eyes glazed with lust. Ah, hell. "Miranda, this is a mistake." The misty fog of their heavy breaths spiraled into the air.

Had he lost his mind?

Her lusty expression turned to hurt. "I depend on you for everything. Every single part of my life is in your hands. I'm even ready to get it on with you in the parking lot. And now that I'm willing, you're pushing me away." She tried to push out of his arms, but he wouldn't let her go. "At least you were man enough to reject me before we had sex."

"Miranda, you'll regret it by morning. I don't want to sleep with you and then have to leave you."

Something kicked inside his gut. Leaving her was the last thing he wanted, but that's pretty much what he'd done the first time, and it was likely what he'd have to do this time.

Her lips parted for a second like she was stunned. Her hand, still fisting his shirt, pressed to her chest. She tried to pull out of his embrace again, but he was not going to let her go like this. Not again.

She huffed out a hollow laugh. "I'll regret it, Talmadge? Or you'll regret it?"

"That's not what I meant. We could work something ou—"

"You know what? You're right. I would regret it."

"Can I finish a damn sentence, please?"

For once, she seemed to acquiesce.

With the pad of his thumb, he traced her bottom lip. "I want you, Miranda. I won't lie." And he did. He wanted her so damn much it hurt to look at her. Plus he wasn't crazy, or dead, or gay. She was a great catch. "But not like this. If we ever sleep together again . . ." *If?* He was surprised he'd managed to keep his dick in his pants around Miranda this long. "We're going to spend all night together . . ." He gave her a soft, sweet kiss. "We're going to wake up together."

She drew in a breath and held it.

"And I'm going to spend hours . . . days, showing you how much I really do want you. Because that's what you deserve."

He placed a finger under her chin and lifted her gaze to his. And hell, he didn't mean to make her cry, but a tear spilled over and ran down her soft cheeks. He pulled her into his arms and caressed the back of her head.

"What can I do?" Besides take her home where they could have some privacy, make love to her, and kiss all of her tears and worries away.

Her crying got harder. "That's the problem. You want to help me with everything." She hiccupped against his chest.

Okay. Helping was what he did best. And that was a bad thing? "I know your situation with the inn is difficult." He could relate, because his situation sucked balls.

"Not the inn." She hiccupped again. "Well sort of the inn, I mean"—hiccup—"*you* at the inn, and now the gazebo, and Jamie looks up to you and doesn't need me anymore, and the way you look at me, and the sound of your voice that makes me want to call you in the middle of the night and have phone sex." Hiccup.

His hand stilled against the back of her head. "I should've been calling you every night." He couldn't keep the amusement from his voice. "I've never had phone sex."

She gripped his shirt, which she still held in her hand, and gave his chest a soft thump. "Neither have I." Hiccup. "That's my point. I think of doing a lot of things with you that I've never done with anyone else." That elicited a sniffle and two hiccups. "It's just too hard to keep being with you all the time when I really can't *be* with you. Not for long, anyway." Another hiccup. A cute, sweet one that tore at his heart. "And then after you look at my mouth like I'm dessert, you push me away and tell me it's a mistake."

Double hiccup.

He caressed the space between her shoulder blades and waited to make sure she was finished. When she sniffed but didn't keep talking, he pulled back. "Feel better now?"

She shook her head, and her hands eased up his chest, her killer body rubbing up against his.

"Why did you pick me?" What the hell? He might as well take the plunge while she was clinging to him and acting so vulnerable.

She seemed to stop breathing, and for a moment, the swirls of fog came only from him.

With a gentle finger under her chin, he tilted her face up. "Seven years ago. You obviously weren't drunk, like you said. So why did you pick me to be your first? And don't change the subject this time." His tone had an edge to it as he whispered into her hair.

She clung to his jacket and quietly breathed against his chest like she was afraid to tell him the truth.

He'd walked away from her once without making her listen to him. Actually, she'd pushed him away, and he'd let her. He wasn't going to make that mistake again. "Bridget and I weren't together when I made love to you. I'd made that clear, but she showed up after finagling my whereabouts out of my assistant. I wanted to spend time with *you* that night, but then you said it was a mistake because you'd had too much to drink, so I left you alone."

Miranda stared up at him, her plump lips parted. "Oh," she finally whispered.

"Why me? I want to know. I've wondered for seven long years, and I'm not leaving you tonight . . ." He stumbled. *I'm not leaving you.* That's the part that sounded so right, even if it wasn't. "Until I know the truth."

Another tear fell, and she swiped at it. Drew in a breath like she was about to confess the secrets of the universe. "Because you were leaving to go back to Seattle, and I figured it would stay a secret. I didn't want it to get around because I didn't want the same reputation that my mom has."

That wasn't the answer he was hoping for. He actually wasn't sure what he'd wanted to hear. He pulled back to look at her.

She closed her eyes tight, like she was gathering courage. Like there was something more she wanted to say. Her lashes fluttered up, and she stared him straight in the eye. "If I had a do-over, I'd pick you all over again."

She pulled her bottom lip between her teeth.

"If you think that's going to push me away, you obviously don't know how fucking sexy it is." He brushed his mouth across hers to get another taste of her, and nipped at the same spot she'd just been nibbling on.

"Bridget not being your girlfriend, and me not letting you explain," she whispered, her voice small and desperate, "didn't matter then any more than it matters now, Talmadge. Your life isn't here, but mine is. You're right, sleeping together would be a mistake that we both might regret."

He exhaled. Hard.

He couldn't argue with her logic. Even though the bulge in his pants was trying desperately to do so. Yeah, that bulge that didn't want to admit how starting a physical relationship with Miranda would catapult him to number one on the Top Ten List of Worst Assholes Ever. Unfortunately, he already deserved to be on it, because he'd lied to her about his grandmother's will. Yep, he was at the top of that list, along with a crooked contractor who would steal a woman's life savings.

"I'm invested here and I'm in too deep with the inn. The inn is my only chance to be something more than Red River's star waitress." She said it with sarcasm. "And it all depends on you, if the renovations don't break me first." Another tear fell.

"You know I'm not going to repossess the place. It's yours," he said.

"That's even worse. I won't take your charity, and don't you dare pity me. If I can't pay my own way, then it's not worth it."

Talmadge scrubbed a hand over his face. "That pride of yours is going to ruin you. I get it that you want to earn your own way and not be like your mother. But this is different." He waggled a finger between them. "We're different."

"If I can't make this place work, then I'm giving it back to you, Talmadge. You can keep it, you can sell it, you can dismantle it piece by piece and move it to Washington if you want." Her voice seemed desperate. Hopeless. And it stabbed at Talmadge's chest. "I'll accept your help with the renovations because I have little choice, but I won't let you give me anything."

"Bea obviously wanted you to have it, Miranda. The inn was a part of my grandparents, a part of me, but I don't want it back. I can't run an inn from Washington." If he had to sell the place to someone who had no connection to his grandparents, someone with no appreciation for the place it once was . . . well, he didn't think he *could*. Miranda was the only person who seemed right to own it . . . the only person who fit there. "The inn would be nothing to me except a sentimental memory."

Several creases formed between her beautiful brown eyes, and her shoulders sagged. "That's the difference between you and me. It's *everything* to me. And Bea knew that."

And that was the reason the money he stood to gain from this whole venture was prickling his conscience more and more with each passing day. In the beginning, it was business—renovate the inn that his grandmother had already sold to Miranda, then collect his inheritance. Clean and easy.

He ran a hand through his hair.

Not so clean and definitely not easy anymore. It was all muddied up now, and somehow, his priorities had become entangled and entwined until he didn't know what was more important—Miranda and the inn or his life back in Washington.

Actually, he did know. He just didn't know what to do about it. "Why not accept Bea's gift from me? It would've meant so much to her." It would mean a lot to him too, and give him some peace of mind after he went back to Washington.

Miranda scoffed. "You really didn't know her at all, did you?"

His head snapped back at the insult. "Excuse me?" Of course he knew his own grandmother. A hell of a lot better than Miranda did.

Miranda swiped at another tear.

"When I turned down her generous offer, she understood it was because I needed to gain the confidence that only comes from a person working hard and earning what they have. The inn will either be a success or a failure because of me alone. And if it fails, it'll be *my* failure. Not because of my mother. Not because of gossip. And damn sure not because of a man."

She pushed out of his arms and backed away.

Damn but he didn't want to let her go. Being with Miranda here in Red River was the *only* thing in his life right now that felt safe and right. He couldn't help the pull of desire every time he saw her, heard her purring voice, breathed in her flowery shampoo every morning when he walked into the inn. Fending off the squeeze in his chest when she worked alongside him, putting forth more effort than any construction worker he'd known, was getting harder with each passing day.

"I'm walking home." She held his shirt to her chest. "Alone."

He shouldn't let her. But somehow he didn't think him "letting" her do anything was an option. "Call when you get there? Just so I know you're safe."

She didn't answer. Just bit her lip and looked up at the stars blanketing the clear night sky.

Talmadge shook his head. He respected Miranda's work ethic, but there was a good work ethic and then there was foolishness. "At least tell me what I can do to help you besides the renovations because I don't know." Dammit, he'd never figure women out. At least not this woman. But all she had to do was ask and he'd try to give her the moon. He'd do anything she wanted, except the one thing that was beyond his control.

"Don't want me." Her voice shook.

He let out a deep, dismal sigh.

*He was so screwed.* Because that was the one thing beyond his control.

# Chapter Sixteen

"Dammit." Miranda realized her purse was still inside the bar as she walked up to the outside entrance of her suite.

No way was she going back to Joe's to face the snickers and stares because she'd acted like a cat in heat in front of the entire town. Because *daayum*, when Talmadge had taken off his shirt, she'd lost all reasonable thought and dragged him outside with the full intention of getting it on in his truck. She would've if he hadn't been smart enough to stop it.

One of her friends would realize she wasn't coming back and grab her purse.

It took some time to find the hidden key in the pitch dark. She felt under a clay pot, hoping something furry didn't greet her with fangs. Where was her mother when she needed her set of unique skills? Boyfriend number six hundred and sixty-six had done hard time for breaking and entering. Before he hit the road in the middle of the night with their only television, stereo, and the game system Miranda had worked all summer to buy from a friend, he'd taught her mom how to pick locks.

Two more pots, one slimy unknown creature slithering across her hand, and several *oh shit*s later, Miranda found the key and let herself in.

The first thing she did was strip out of her wet clothes and into a cozy robe. Shuffling down the hall to the main kitchen, she grabbed an entire carton of Ben and Jerry's from the freezer and plodded into the great room, where she plopped down on the antique sofa in front of the fireplace.

She tore off the lid and dove in with the biggest spoon she could find. The place was coming together. She looked around as she munched her comfort food. The insulation was finished and so was the drywall. The bathrooms were almost done, and new kitchen cabinets and countertops would go in soon. They'd even started hanging new wallpaper.

She swallowed and shoveled in another bite.

Wallpaper was outdated, but she wanted to keep the same historic feel. The mahogany molding that trimmed the arched doorways and rimmed the walls where they met the ceiling looked tired and worn, but a fresh coat of varnish would make it look bright with character again.

The roofing supplies she could probably cover with what was left in her bank account. The outside of the inn still needed to be scraped and painted, and she hadn't bought the paint yet. The plumbing and electrical might also be a problem. Maybe she could find someone to do it on credit until the inn opened, because she wasn't about to ask anyone to do the work for free.

Sounded like a solid plan.

And then Talmadge could go. Of course he still hadn't discussed how he planned for them to pull off building a rec center, but maybe he intended to come back to Red River more frequently to see that project through.

A seed of hope sprouted in her heart, but she plucked it right out by the root. Didn't matter how many times he came back to Red River. He wouldn't stay. And she wasn't leaving. Not when she was so close to her dream. And especially not for a man who hadn't offered her anything beyond a guarantee that her inn would pass inspection and the gazebo would be ready for the festival before he left town.

Her eyes slid shut in appreciation as the generous mouthful of butter pecan slid down her throat.

Thanks to Talmadge, most everyone in town was behind her, except the Wilkinsons and their pew-warming band of friends. Even so, she was tired of trying to prove herself. What had it gotten her? She was closing in on thirty years old and had already walked Red River's chalk line so tight that it would probably keep her single for the rest of her life. Or, at the very least, extremely sexually frustrated.

Sadly, she'd throw all of her hard work and clean living away to be with Talmadge if it wouldn't mean getting her heart trampled on like a stampede of cattle going to slaughter. She sensed the danger the same way those poor cattle did.

Owning a business in Red River was risky. Heck, as much as she loved it here, life in this little town was risky.

A thought zinged to life and took shape in her mind. She couldn't stop the broad smile that spread across her lips.

Why not have a little fun now? By herself, since she was likely to be alone most of her life anyway. Unless by some miracle another straight, single guy who wasn't secretly a serial killer moved to town. And yeah, she wouldn't hold her breath on that one.

Miranda jumped from the couch, darted toward her rooms, dropping the ice cream in the kitchen as she scurried past, and emerged a minute later with an iPod, a speaker dock, a hairbrush, and wearing a pair of socks and Talmadge's white dress shirt, which simmered against her skin because of his woodsy, musky scent.

The only thing she'd gleaned from her mother's years of hanging out in honky-tonks and biker bars—a taste for old rock and roll—often came in handy when she needed to cheer herself up.

She shuffled through her iPod until she got to one of her favorite retro songs and popped the device into the speaker dock. With a flip of both wrists, she flicked the collar of Talmadge's shirt up. The front flapped open, revealing her matching yellow polka-dot and lace bra and panties. She turned the speaker volume to the highest level and hit Play, then ran into the hall.

When Bob Seger banged out the first chords of "Old Time Rock and Roll" on the piano, Miranda took the hairbrush firmly in hand.

*This inn was a risky business indeed.* And Cruz *was* her last name, even if it was spelled a little different.

With a running start, she slid into the arched doorway between the dining room and parlor. And then good ol' Bobby started hammering at his keyboard while belting out something about old records and being by himself.

Miranda spun around and danced to the music, mouthing the words into her hairbrush while Mr. Seger's whiskey voice and piano skills filled the inn. She danced over to the fireplace and planted her feet firmly apart while Bobby scorned discos, and she tossed the brush to the side and grabbed the poker.

With a shimmy that would've made Tom Cruise proud, she jumped onto the couch and bent her knees, playing the air guitar like she was channeling Eddie Van Halen. Bobby's fans cheered through the speaker, and Miranda decided to go for it. She jumped off the sofa and did the half splits in the air. When she landed and twisted to the music, her soul definitely felt more soothed than it had in the parking lot at Joe's with a half-naked man pushing her away.

*Pfft.* Who needed a man when she had Bobby?

She wiggled her butt to the music and moonwalked backward, the socks making her slide across the wood floor like it was glass.

Someone clapped once. Then twice. Then again. And it wasn't one of good ol' Bobby's fans on the recording.

Miranda spun around, and the poker clattered to the floor.

Talmadge's long, hard body lounged against the arched doorframe, her purse dangling from one of his hands. A wide, dazzling smile graced his perfect face and made his eyes twinkle.

*Oh. My. God.* He'd just witnessed her doing something no one else had ever seen. Except Jamie. And he was still blackmailing her with it, the little ratfink sibling that he was.

"What are you doing here?" she yelled, her heart and her pride dropping to her toes.

The song lilted to its inevitable end, and they stood in silence staring at each other. Him smiling like the smart-ass he was. Her probably looking as horrified as she felt. And as ridiculous.

He held up her purse. "You forgot this."

"You should've called!" She pressed her fingers to her eyes for a second.

"I tried." Talmadge pulled his cell out of his back pocket and dialed a number. Her purse started to vibrate and Bob Seger began wailing the same tune from the depths of her handbag.

Miranda closed her eyes, cursing her mother for the years she'd spent playing old rock albums. Why not Brahms or "The Wheels on the Bus" like any normal mother would do?

"Then you should've knocked. Or buzzed. Or something! You're breaking and entering." Her mother would really love Talmadge.

"Tried that too. The music was so loud you probably didn't hear it, and I thought something might be wrong because, well, the music was so loud." He tried to give her a deadpan expression, but the twinkle in his eyes still made him look like a smart-ass.

His gaze turned all smoky as it took a nice long trip down the front of her open shirt, lingered on her panties, and then caressed back up to her mouth.

She pulled the shirt closed at her breasts.

"You're wearing my shirt." His voice was gravelly.

"I'll give it back. Let me go change," she whispered. Unfortunately, he was between her and her room. She had no choice but to walk past him.

His eyes smoothed along her bare legs as she approached. When she tried to step around him, his arm snaked around her middle to stop her. "Keep it. It looks better on you than it does on me." He licked his lips, and an electric shock gripped her below the belly button. He tugged her gently until her front grazed his. And holy lip-smacking moly, no switch in the world could turn off the electrical current that jolted through every nerve ending in her body when she felt the firmness under the front of his jeans.

"Talmadge, you can't keep doing this to me." Her tone wasn't desperate. It was disheartened and unsated. Okay, maybe just a tad desperate. "You show up every seven years or so—"

"I've been back a few times more than that, Miranda. You avoided me."

"You lure me in with your killer smile—"

"I've never killed anyone, not with a smile or anything else." The corner of his mouth quirked up.

"You flirt just enough to get me to fall for you—"

His smile widened. "You've fallen for me?"

"Can I finish, please?" Huh. That sounded vaguely familiar. No idea why. At least none that she would admit to at this moment in time.

The sensual purr of his voice smoothed down her neck and pulled at her nipples. "Not until you hear me out." He settled against the wall and dropped her purse to pull her closer. "I've never regretted being with you seven years ago. My only regret was not seeing where it might lead."

She started to speak up, but he put a finger to her lips and tutted. "I should've come back for you."

She pulled her lip between her teeth, and his eyes turned almost purple with lust.

None of that changed the fact that Talmadge had gone back to his life in Washington then, and he had to do the same now.

"But—"

"Uh-uh." He shushed her again. "You've never been like your mother, which is why I didn't want to get it on in my grandfather's beat-up truck behind Joe's. I wouldn't do that to you, Miranda. Especially not with the *Red River Rag* stalking us."

"Oh, Talmadge." She leaned her forehead against his chest. "It's just that you smell so good, and I love the way you look at me with those sleepy eyes and long lashes, and I've been letting myself get drawn in by your sexy smile and your brilliant plan and your skilled lips and your big hammer . . ."

He laughed, his hand sliding down her back to her ass.

Her cheeks turned so hot, she let go of her shirt and put both hands over her cheeks to cool them. He took full advantage and slipped one hand inside the gaping shirt. It brushed across her stomach and settled around her hip. Every inch of her skin from burning cheeks to curling toes exploded into tingling pebbles.

His other hand slipped inside the shirt and slid over her ribcage. Brilliant move.

Her girly parts burst into flames.

He did it again, and her eyes slid shut. When a soft gasp escaped through her lips, he pulled her into him and buried his face in her hair. And oh good God in heaven, the man was rock hard. All over. But especially where it counted most.

She shouldn't. It might be too late to save her reputation after the near X-rated show she'd started in Joe's and almost finished in the parking lot, but it wasn't too late to save her heart.

Or was it?

"I want something with you, Miranda. I don't know how or what right now. I just know that you're important to me." He whispered against her ear and slipped his fingers under the elastic of her panties.

Oh good Lord, she'd agree to just about anything with him touching her and whispering such delicious words in her ear. Was he asking her for something more permanent? Something with a future?

"I . . . I . . . don't know, Talmadge," she all but whimpered. His sweet words were too vague, and she'd seen her mother stake too much on vague promises.

He pulled her earlobe between his teeth and worked it with his tongue. Sank his hand all the way inside her panties to cup her ass and press her flush against his magnificent package.

She almost orgasmed right there.

She needed to think this through. But thinking was a little difficult at the moment with his tongue and lips and hands and package making her brain malfunction like she'd been sniffing one of the cans of varnish sitting on the back porch.

He brushed her hair back and suckled kisses down her neck to her shoulder, hitting that perfect spot where they connected. His callused fingers massaged the tender skin at the small of her back. "We'll figure something out." His warm, wet breath made a shudder race through her.

"What I said earlier, about picking you because you wouldn't tell anybody, that wasn't the only reason. I wanted you to be my first because you're the only man I've ever . . ."

A strange thud beat against her chest. For a second she wanted to say he was the only man she'd ever loved.

The purple in his eyes flared, and he seemed to hold his breath.

"Why me, Miranda?" He sank his teeth gently into the soft flesh of her neck with just the slightest pressure. Her mind blanked, and her knees turned soft.

The full force of her weight was completely in his hands and against his hard body.

"Hmm?" she asked, her head tilting back to give his hungry mouth a better taste.

He pulled his hand from her backside and found the spot between her thighs that was screaming for his attention. The silk material between his fingers and her flesh created just enough friction to drive her to the brink. He increased the pressure with each stroke, and she angled her knee out to give him better access. He suckled the nook of her neck where his teeth had just been. "Why not someone else? Tell me."

She sobered. Drew back just enough so that their noses brushed and their heartbeats mingled. Her head tilted back, she stared deep into his silver-blue eyes, the color and the emotion there mesmerizing her into a near-trance.

She gave him a deep, soft kiss. One that she hoped communicated every bit of emotion she was feeling right then. Then she said, "Because you were the guy who would never expect me to *get it on* in your truck, even when I wanted to."

On her tippy toes, she pressed her lips to his again, giving him more of the tenderness that she felt all the way to her soul.

---

Miranda's sweet kiss against his hungry mouth communicated a clear message. She was his. And he wasn't going to let her go again. He engulfed her in his arms, molding her softness against him. It was time to finish what they'd started seven years ago. What they'd been circling around since he'd been back in Red River.

Even with him leaning against the doorframe, he was still a head taller than her, so he dipped his knees to trail greedy kisses across her cheek to her ear. Her breath whispered across his neck and made his skin prickle with need. The warmth of her leaning against him flooded through his limbs and made his pulse sing like Bob Seger.

At the thought of her performance, a smile started on his lips, encircled his heart, and spread all the way to his . . .

She pressed her hips into his, and the heat in that particular area turned to a raging storm of desire. He caressed one palm down her back and over her bottom to cradle the soft flesh in the palm of his hand. The soft, feminine contours of her full breasts pressed into his chest, her thighs brushed against his, the length of her pulsing body molded and melted into his, and a deep, satisfied sigh escaped him as she settled into his embrace.

He took her mouth with his. Gentle, but firm enough to control the kiss.

Jesus, even her lips were a perfect contrast to his. Their plump softness, a wicked pleasure like the feel of expensive and forbidden animal fur against bare skin.

Delicious and decadent.

With a flick of his tongue against her lips, they parted for him. He slipped through to find hers.

Her hands slipped inside his jacket and glided over his bare flesh. Ah, the spoils of giving the lady his shirt. Her hands weren't as soft as most women he knew, because Miranda was used to manual labor, but still softer than his. They slid over his torso, leaving a trail of blazing desire in their wake. His muscles twitched and hardened as she explored his chest and then dropped her hands to his stomach and waist, like she was committing every inch to memory.

Like it would never happen again, so she wanted to make the most of it while she could.

His heart squeezed, and he deepened the kiss. Threaded his fingers into her hair and cradled her against him to show her this wasn't just casual sex for him. It meant something. It meant more than she could probably imagine.

Her mouth against his, their bodies flush, it was so sensual, so luxurious that he didn't want it to end. He ran his hand up her length and felt a shiver of delight pass through her. He smiled against her mouth and framed her face with both hands to kiss her as deeply and affectionately as he knew how.

She whimpered out her approval and slid a foot up the side of his leg.

He broke the kiss. "Damn, woman. Do you know what you do to me?"

She pressed a soft kiss to his neck and nuzzled her nose just below his ear. "Let's go to my room."

He shook his head. "No."

She tensed and pulled back to look at him, her expression communicating her fear of rejection.

He ran gentle fingertips across the line of her silky smooth jaw to soothe her doubts. He wasn't sure if he succeeded, but the delicate feel of her against his fingertips sure as hell soothed him. "We're going to the honeymoon suite."

Her features relaxed, and a stir of sexual energy seemed to surge through her and jump from her pulsing body into his. With a swift movement, he ran both hands down her arms to her ass and lifted her off the ground.

She squeaked and laced her arms around his neck.

"Put your legs around me," he said and pushed off the doorframe to straighten.

Both of her ankles clamped to his backside. He carried her up the stairs. Tried to consume her with a kiss so hot and searing that the spot between her legs pulsed against his belly just above his jeans, and he wanted to be inside her so badly it hurt. A minor problem, because he was about to shuck his pants and make love to her all night. Maybe let her sleep for a few hours, then wake her up just before dawn to do the same thing all over again.

The crazy thing about making love to a woman who had just finished playing the air guitar was that he wanted it to be just as fast and just as furious as her performance.

He doubted he'd ever again see anything cuter or sexier than Miranda sailing through the air in the half-splits with a poker in her hands. But no. The same woman who'd entertained him with a moonwalk dressed in nothing but a bra that didn't quite match the panties because of the red cranberry stain, a pair of socks scrunched at the ankles, and his shirt, unbuttoned and flapping as she'd gyrated around the room, had also confessed why she'd allowed him to be her first lover.

After such a bold unveiling of her heart, he didn't want this time to be just a tumble in the sack or a quickie against the wall. Not that he would mind that in the future. But not tonight. Tonight was the beginning of something new with Miranda. They could work something out. What, he wasn't exactly sure yet.

He took the stairs as fast as his legs would carry both of them. The sweet scent of her—subtle perfume mixed with a remnant of cranberry—the way she melted into him with such intimate ease, the feel of her thundering heart beating in rhythm with his, he wasn't sure if he'd ever be able to let her go. And why should he?

Why *would* he?

They reached the second-floor landing, the old wood creaking. He had every loose board on that staircase memorized from his childhood, and he remembered every step of the same journey he'd taken up those stairs with Miranda seven years ago. He turned left toward the honeymoon suite. The one night they'd shared together was the best of his life. She hadn't warned him that it was her first time, and the shock that had rippled through him when he realized had made him freeze up for a moment. What happened afterward when they went back to the reception had turned the evening into a nightmare.

Not tonight.

Tonight was all for her. And there would be many more nights just like this if he had anything to say about it. Unfortunately, she had a habit of not letting him finish whatever he was trying to say. But maybe after tonight, he could change that.

———————

Miranda slid down Talmadge's hard body until her toes touched the floor, and she tilted her head back to stare up into his metallic blue eyes. A chill of anticipation coursed through her and she shivered. And not just a little shiver. It was more like an earthquake.

He stared back, those unique eyes glazed with lust. For her. This time it wasn't just her throwing herself at him.

She was about to do this. With Talmadge Oaks. Again. Her long sex sabbatical had made her as nutty as a pecan orchard, because she was scared. She hadn't done this in . . . well, seven years. Seven years, three months, and twenty-nine days.

He laid another panty-dropping kiss on her. The man's lips were pure genius. His hands weren't bad either because they were currently slipping inside her panties and flexing into her flesh. Caressing and massaging until she moaned.

He bent to suckle her neck, smiling against her prickling skin.

A whole different kind of fear seized her, and she pushed at his chest. "Um, I don't have any protection. I mean . . . I don't usually . . ."

He shut her up with a kiss. This one wasn't just a panty-dropper. It melted her yellow polka dots right off. Gripping her shirt . . . well, his shirt . . . with his fists, he pulled her into him.

He released her mouth, giving her nose a teasing graze with his. "I've got it covered."

"Oh." Of course he did. He probably needed to be prepared. Often. Unlike her.

And then his lips brushed across hers and her insides went all soft and gooey right along with her knees. He slid a strong arm around her waist to steady her as another brush with his lips coaxed her mouth open. Her eyes fluttered shut when he feathered tender kisses down her neck. The touch of his lips against her skin was so sweet, so deep with emotion, so generously loving that Miranda didn't think her heart could contain another ounce of emotion for this man.

Her eyes flew open, and she stared at the old brass light fixture overhead that hung in shadowy darkness. He trailed kisses up to her ear and suckled her earlobe. She swallowed.

She loved him. She was in love with Talmadge Oaks and had been for seven years, three months, and twenty-nine days. And if she didn't know better she'd think that he loved her too, by the way he was showing it with his gentle hands and generous mouth.

Of course she didn't have anyone else to compare it to, so what did she know?

"You're thinking too much." Talmadge's voice was hoarse with desire, and his words whispered across her ear, sending a shiver lancing all the way through her. Even her scalp prickled. He backed her toward the antique four-poster bed. "I can almost hear the wheels turning inside that stubborn head of yours."

She stopped his advance and stared up at him with an eyebrow firmly raised. "Did you just insult my head?"

He ignored her and tugged on her ear with his teeth.

She cleared her throat.

Both of his hands threaded into her hair and he cradled her head in his large palms. "It wasn't an insult, but you're the stubbornest woman I know." His mouth found hers and issued a languid, lush kiss. "You're also one of the smartest." Another slow, sweet kiss. "And definitely the most beautiful."

"Oh. Okay then," she panted out.

When his mouth found hers again, she kissed him back with the same careful ease, matching the rhythm of his mouth and his tongue to perfection. It was so precious, so pure, so utterly delicious that Miranda's world tilted off balance. With his hands still anchored in her hair, he leaned her head a bit to one side and angled his mouth fully against hers, deepening the kiss to mind-melting intensity.

Her hands slid under his jacket and found his contoured chest. His muscles jumped and twitched under her touch, and his smooth but hard flesh heated as she explored the hills and valleys of his perfectly formed body.

Good God, he was perfect. So perfect it was almost painful.

A heavy sigh of pleasure skipped through her lips, and his hold on her tightened. So did the pressure of his mouth on hers. And he took his sweet time exploring her mouth with his tongue and her body with his hands. Like a blueprint that he was trying to read. Trying to understand and discover where all the most sensitive spots were so he could pay careful attention to those before moving on to others.

Miranda smoothed both hands up his chest and over his shoulders so the jacket eased backward. He let it slip to the floor, and then he did the same to her.

"I like you in my shirt. It's sexy as hell." He eased her backward until the bed came up against the back of her thighs. The wood planks in that particular spot creaked under their feet, scraping and squeaking with the slightest shift of their weight.

"You wearing no shirt at all is sexy as hell." She reached for the top of his jeans and unbuttoned them.

He chuckled at her brazen honesty. When her fingers grasped the zipper, his hand covered hers and stopped the movement.

"I'm staying the night this time." He gave her an earnest stare.

She inhaled deeply and held it for a second before releasing the air from her lungs. "Okay."

Most of Red River already thought they were sleeping together or hoped they would soon. She'd even heard rumors on a pool. So far Al the plumber was expected to win. And she couldn't believe she was thinking this, but if anyone had anything nasty to say about Talmadge spending the night . . . well, they could bite her. Being with him, waking up with him just seemed perfect and natural. And right.

He released her hand and eased a bra strap off one of her shoulders. "And we're not going to be weird about this tomorrow, like we were after the first time." He bent his head to place a kiss where the bra strap had just been, and she shuddered with delight. He smiled against her shoulder.

"Okay. No weird stuff." Her voice wobbled as much as her knees. Damn straight they wouldn't be weird about it, especially if he planned to keep touching her like that.

He straightened and slid the other strap down her arm.

Another wet, warm kiss landed where the second strap had sat, and he nipped at her shoulder with his teeth.

*Good God.*

"And you're not going to tell me this was a mistake, like last time," he murmured against her shoulder, then started to trail kisses across her chest.

"Um, I'm thinking that was because of Bridget." She swallowed when his lips grazed across her nipple through the thin fabric of her bra. "Or a full moon. Or a spike in hormones because we were at a wedding." His lips closed around the aching bud. "No, it was definitely Bridget." He pulled the cup of her bra down, and his teeth tugged at the peak, to punish her. "*Oh,*" she rasped out.

He smothered her sensual cry in a fierce kiss. When he released her mouth he nipped at her bottom lip. "Because another one-night stand between us just doesn't work for me."

Her insides went nuclear.

"Whatever you want, Talmadge," she panted out. Her hands found his luxurious hair, and she pulled his mouth back to hers.

She had no idea how either of them got completely naked. His mouth and his touch consumed her, and he laid her back on the bed. She should've still been nervous. Terrified, even. Because it had been so long, and she didn't have that much experience. But his touch was so gentle and attentive that all her nervous energy channeled into desire for him.

With a dreamy kiss, he eased her back. The mattress dipped under his weight as he followed her, settling next to her on his side. Without breaking that sweet kiss, he threaded his fingers into hers and pressed their hands into the soft quilt.

"I wasn't sure how to please you last time," he said while showering butterfly kisses down her neck. His hot breath whispered against the moistness of his kisses, and she shivered with delight.

"You did just fine." Her voice went all croaky. Real good, because it was so sexy to sound like a frog at a time like this. She swallowed.

"Just fine wasn't good enough." He kissed behind her ear. "It was your first time, and I wasn't sure how to handle that."

*He* wasn't sure? He had seemed pretty sure to her. Much more so than she had.

"So I get a do-over tonight." He feathered more hot, wet kisses down her chest and took an aching nipple into his mouth, suckling.

She arched into him and gasped.

He let out a quiet, satisfied chuckle against her skin, then worked the tight bud with his tongue.

"You don't need a do-over," she panted out. "It was wonderful. The best." *The only.*

"We need to raise the bar, then." He kissed his way to her other breast and took it between his teeth, nipping and sucking it into a throbbing peak. "It's been seven years since we've been together. I want to make sure it was worth the wait." He circled the bud with the tip of his tongue, and she bucked.

One hand still pinned to the bed, she used the other to run splayed fingers through his luxurious hair. A tear sprang from her eye before she could beat it back and trickled down the side of her cheek. She *had* been waiting for him all those years. She just hadn't realized it. "I never wanted anyone else, Talmadge. You're the only one."

His head popped up, and she swiped at a tear. He stared down at her. Released her hand and smoothed a strand of hair away from her face. "That was your only time?"

She swallowed. Placed the palm of her hand over his as he cradled her cheek. She nodded. Moonlight streamed through the lace curtains to cast a glow on his handsome face.

His eyes were soft and sure as he gazed down at her. "Then we have some catching up to do." A gentle smile curved his lips, and gently, he kissed her tears away.

She sighed.

With that, he dipped his head to trail kisses back down to her breasts, and he proved to her why once just wasn't enough.

His mouth scorched a trail down her stomach to her belly button, where he circled with his tongue and nipped with his teeth. He pressed a soft, wet kiss to the inside of her thigh. When his mouth moved to the edge of her curls, a pang of fear welled inside of her. She gripped his shoulders.

"*Talmadge.*" Her voice was a desperate whisper.

"It's okay." He lifted his head and murmured against the super sensitive skin below her belly button. "Promise." He blazed a trail of scorching heat over to her hip, then down the crease where her thigh connected. Gently, softly, he nudged her thighs farther apart.

Her lungs locked.

With exquisite tenderness, his magnificent tongue delved between her folds and found her center.

She cried out and arched against his mouth, her hands fisting his hair.

"Do you want me to stop?" he whispered against the swollen nub that pulsed and ached for his thrilling touch.

"Dear God, no," she managed to breathe out.

"Good." He pressed a kiss against her throbbing flesh.

He loved her like that until her mind blurred with ecstasy. When she thought it couldn't get any better, he slipped two fingers inside her, and she exploded around him. A climax crashed into her so fierce, so fast that she thought she would break apart.

Talmadge kissed his way back up her length, stopping to give attention to each straining breast. He placed a kiss in between. "Your heart is beating so fast." He kissed the spot over her heart again.

Of course it was. The sensations rippling through her made her heart knock against her chest like a drum. Running both hands up his chest, she placed one palm over his heart. "So is yours."

"That's because I love touching you." He was almost as breathless as her. "I love looking at you, especially like this."

Within seconds he had protection on, and his weight swept over her again. He pressed his hips into hers, and it stole her breath. Pulsing against her, his erection nudged at her entrance. Her fingertips curled into his broad shoulders as her insides tightened again with anticipation. She locked her ankles around his waist and pressed him farther into her. Another wave of heat ignited deep inside her, and she strained her hips toward him.

"Slow," he said. "We have all night. I don't hurry, remember?"

She let out a strained laugh. "I do, in fact, remember. Every detail." She rose to kiss the crook of his neck, and he hissed out something that sounded like a curse but dripped with pleasure. Since he seemed to like that so much, she closed her lips over his neck and suckled, gently at first, then with more pressure, flicking her tongue over his cleanly shaved skin.

His breathing got heavier.

With both hands she traced down his powerful arms, then over his ribcage and up his back. His muscles danced under her fingertips, his flesh heating everywhere she touched. He circled his hips and nudged in a little farther, moving slowly in and out without fully penetrating her depths. Rhythmically, he teased and taunted, her insides turning to a fiery liquid.

She smoothed her palms down his back, over his butt, and pulled him into her.

Apparently, no restraint left—thank all the saints—he went for the gold, burying himself deep inside her. He let out a groan of pleasure. Her quivering flesh closed around his incredible erection, and she tried to stifle a scream. Did no good. His name tumbled out, and she clamped her shaking legs tighter around him.

"Jesus, you feel so damn good," he said through clenched teeth as he throbbed inside of her. When he opened his eyes, his beautiful gaze shimmered down at her, and her heart expanded just a little bit more with love.

He rolled his hips into hers, each stroke causing her insides to coil and tighten. Pleasure licked over every molecule of her body. Her eyes shut, head turned to one side, he plunged into her over and over until another orgasm overtook her, and she cried out his name again.

He gave in to it a moment after she did, whispering her name into her hair.

His weight bearing down on her, pressing her firmly into the old mattress was utterly exquisite, and she wound her arms and legs around him as tightly as she could. She wanted to stay there forever, enjoying his touch, his scent, his heart beating against hers. They lay there entwined for what seemed an eternity. Their heartbeats swirled and churned together until they became one.

And Miranda knew she was lost. If Talmadge left . . . *when* Talmadge left, her heart would break, just as surely as the sun would rise tomorrow bringing her another day closer to having to say good-bye.

# Chapter Seventeen

The soft, worn quilt against Talmadge's bare skin felt nice. Like a dream. The image of a beautiful brunette shuddering with pleasure underneath him was more like a fantasy. He bundled deeper into the covers and threw an arm across Miranda's waist.

Except she wasn't there.

His eyes popped open to the soft blush of dawn cascading through the lace curtains, and he sat up.

The spot next to him was empty, the pillow still indented with Miranda's silhouette. The ivory sheets hinted at the distinct angles and planes of her body, her soft curves and the perfect shape he had spent most of the night exploring.

Best night he could remember in the last seven years.

He rubbed the sleep from his eyes.

What time was it? And why did she ditch him without waking him up? He slid out of bed and grabbed his pants.

A ripple of tension zinged through his chest. He really hoped it wasn't buyer's remorse on her part, like she'd had seven years ago. He wasn't going to be her one-night stand again.

Hell no. That just wouldn't work for him this time.

He hadn't slept so soundly in weeks. Not since the Trinity Falls debacle. Of course, not a lot of sleeping had happened until well into the night. He wasn't complaining, because he was pretty sure he'd used quite a bit more finesse with Miranda than he had seven years ago. The way she'd responded to him, murmuring his name with every orgasm, had made him want to keep pleasing her. After every climax, she'd wrapped herself around him like she was hanging on for dear life, until finally they settled into the cozy covers with her cheek against his shoulder and their legs tangled. They'd fallen asleep with him running his fingers through her hair until it fanned out on the pillow. She'd caressed his chest with her fingertips, the softness of her touch lulling him into a deep, dreamy sleep.

It made him want to spend every night doing the same.

He pulled his jeans on and looked around for a shirt. He couldn't help a smile that reached all the way to his soul when an image of Miranda wearing it popped into his mind.

Barefoot, he padded down the creaking stairs, and a sense of home filled him. He had never felt completely at home in Red River since his parents died, because of the shameful secret he kept buried deep inside. So he'd blazed a trail out of there as soon as he could, accepting a scholarship to a university as far away as possible. When he'd come back to visit, the memories started to choke the life out of him after a few days.

During the past few weeks with Miranda, the memories of the past hadn't felt so suffocating. And he wasn't exactly revving his engine to get back to Washington the way he should be. Spending time with Miranda had also softened the blow of losing Bea.

His hand slid down the slick banister as he took each step slowly, remembering the exact spot that made each one creak and groan under his weight. It had been a game he played as a kid when his grandparents still ran the inn.

Thanks to Miranda for inspiring a possible solution to Trinity Falls, he'd spent the last several evenings drawing up a proposal, complete with a PowerPoint presentation that he'd pitched to his investors via video conference. Luckily Ellen had put down her knitting needles long enough to organize it. The investors seemed to like it and promised a decision within the week. If they were willing to keep their money and their support behind Trinity Falls, the next step would be pitching it to the tribal councils.

Finally some good news. Maybe his luck was going to change. Now all he had to do was finish the inn, build Red River a gazebo, finish rehabbing his arm, figure out how to break the whole truth about Bea's will to Miranda without her kicking his sorry ass to the curb, and figure out a way to keep Miranda in his life.

Sure, no problem. He doubted Houdini had pulled off more impossible stunts.

After last night, he needed to come clean and tell Miranda about his inheritance. It wasn't important to him anymore—not as important as her, but she deserved to know the truth about the way he'd twisted the facts regarding the rec center so she'd let him help with the renovations and he could claim the money Bea left him.

He rubbed the stubble on his jaw.

One thing at a time. He hit the landing and took a step back to look in the antique oval mirror and run a hand through his bedhead. He leaned in to get a closer look at his neck. A broad smile cracked his face wide open, and he rubbed the round, cherry-red blotch where Miranda's mouth had left her stamp of approval for last night's activities.

Her marking him made his chest swell. It was like she was saying, "You're mine," and that's what he wanted—to belong to her.

The rich aroma of coffee told him where he might find the culprit responsible for his hickey, so he walked through the great room. Sure enough, Miranda was in the kitchen, the coffeepot gurgling. He rounded the bar and got a full view of her wearing exactly what she'd been wearing last night. Her back to him, she bent to get a dishcloth out of a bottom drawer. And sweet Jesus, no she wasn't wearing exactly the same thing. His white shirt, yes, minus the bra and panties.

He growled, which caused her to spin around and press up against the counter.

Her hand went to her heart.

"I didn't mean to scare you." He shuffled over to her, the old flooring cold against his feet. He placed both hands on the counter, framing her in. "Hi."

"Hi." A soft pink glow spread over her creamy cheeks, down her neck, and disappeared beneath his shirt, which, unfortunately, was buttoned this time. "Aren't you cold?" Palms flat against his shoulders, she smoothed them over his chest.

The nip that settled over the Red River Valley every night year-round still hung in the air, but he had barely thought of it. Thoughts of Miranda not being in bed next to him when he woke up had crowded out any concern over the cold. Thoughts of how she'd rotated her hips while riding him last night kind of distracted him from the temperature too.

He leaned down, still framing her, so they were eye level and nose-to-nose. He breathed her in, the scent of coffee and vanilla making him want to taste her. "I was counting on you keeping me warm this morning."

A shy smile formed on her mouth, and she pulled in her bottom lip. He growled again. "Plus, you've got my shirt."

"I can give it back," she whispered. "Right now." Color bloomed on her neck and chest, the soft skin between her breasts visible just above the buttoned shirt.

"Not necessary." He angled his chin up so she could see her handiwork. "I'm going to have to wear turtlenecks for a few days."

She blushed, but the amber flecks in her eyes ignited into lust.

"But you can still take off the shirt," he said.

To hell with the fresh gurgling pot of coffee, because she laid a sultry kiss on him that had him wrapping her up in his arms. Her hands wandered over his chest, slow and easy, across his shoulders, and into his hair like she wanted to hold him there.

He planned to stay right there, too.

His hands did some wandering too. Down her back, over the dip of her waist, then they found the hem of his shirt. And, thank you God, she really was commando underneath.

Her sigh morphed into a heavy gasp for air as his hands found that sweet spot that had made her scream his name several times last night. So he wedged his thigh between her legs and spread them for better access. Sure enough, a few circles with his thumb, a deeper, hotter kiss, and a hand cupping one full, perky breast and she was murmuring his name all over again.

She squeaked when he lifted her onto the counter. "I may never get this place to pass inspection if the health department finds out about this." She smiled at him. Reached for the front of his jeans and had him in her hand with that sexy smile still on her lips.

That smile turned to another gasp when he inserted his hands between the cold counter and her hot ass and pulled her to the edge in one swift motion. "I know a thing or two about dealing with inspectors." He pulled something from his back pocket and had it on in a blink of her sleepy eyes. He slid all the way into her with one bold stroke, and as if his fantasies hadn't already been fulfilled the past twenty-four hours, she screamed his name, her fingers digging into his shoulders.

He leaned his forehead against hers, letting both of them adjust to how completely he filled her. How perfectly she fit around him. The only woman he'd ever been with who made him feel whole again.

Her wet flesh was already quivering around his cock, so he hooked an arm under one of her knees. "Lean back with your hands behind you." She did, and he ground into her, hard and fast until neither of them could breathe and he never wanted to leave that spot or leave her again.

She moved her hips in rhythm with his, reaching to meet him as best she could. Her head fell back and that beautiful head of flowing black locks tumbled over her shoulders and swayed behind her. Eyes closed, a smile curved onto her lips, and the glow of heated skin and rushing desire spread over her.

"Jesus, you look so good."

Her eyes fluttered open and locked with his. And his heart nearly stopped, because she looked at him with so much love in her gaze that he didn't deserve. He slowed his strokes.

Her leg clamped around his butt. "Don't stop."

Accommodating guy that he was, he obliged by grasping her hip with his free hand, lifting the leg that was draped over the crook of his elbow, and drove into her as fast and deep as he could.

The sexy moans, parted lips, and tightly closed eyes told him the storm was building inside of her. His teeth clenched, he tried to hold on to his own sanity until she lost hers. And sure enough, a little rotation of his hips as he buried himself in her over and over, and a shimmy overtook her and she cried out, "Yes!"

That pushed him over the edge, and he buried his face in her hair to breathe her in. She threaded her arms around his neck, and he did the same around her waist. And there they sat for what seemed like hours, because it was just so damn amazing and so damn right.

"I made you some coffee," she whispered against his neck.

He laughed.

"Let's have a cup," he said, trailing kisses up her neck to her ear. "In bed." He suckled her earlobe. "Maybe get some breakfast at the

Gold Miner's Café later this morning." His warm breaths against her ear caused her to shiver. "Then go back to bed."

She laughed. "Aren't we going to work today?"

He lifted her off the counter and set her down. "Nope. It's Sunday." He smacked her on the bottom. "We'll pick Lloyd up too. He's been alone all night."

And the thought of him and her and Bea's prissy little dog together right here in Red River eased the weight of regret that had always settled over him when he came back to town. It also caused his mind to reel because he wasn't sure he could make it all work.

Trying to maneuver his life so that he could have it all might just leave him with nothing.

# Chapter Eighteen

"I did him," Miranda said two days later, slumped in the chair across from Lorenda's desk at Brooks Real Estate. Actually Talmadge had been the one doing *her*. Several times. All of which were quite phenomenal.

"Did what to who?" Lorenda's printer spit out listings for a client, and she stapled and organized them in the order she planned to show them. Miranda had watched her BFF's routine a thousand times.

"Talmadge. I *did* him." Miranda widened her eyes in a you-know-what-I-mean gesture. "Didn't you see the latest *Red River Rag*? Everyone in town knows he's been staying nights at my place."

Lorenda froze, papers in hand. "You slept with Talmadge? Why on earth would you do that?"

"You told me to!" Miranda threw an arm over her eyes.

"I was drinking," said Lorenda, kind of defensive. "You know I don't spend much time away from the kids, and I didn't want to waste perfectly good beer." She let the listings fall to the desk. "I didn't think you'd actually do it."

Miranda pulled the *Red River Rag* up on her phone and handed it to Lorenda.

A picture of Talmadge carrying her purse into the inn was first. Then a close-up, obviously taken with a zoom lens, of Miranda and him leaving the inn the next morning. His bedhead said, "I stayed the night," and his glaring hickey said, "And hell yes, I got laid." The caption underneath read, *What we've suspected all along is finally official! Red River's darling has DESIGNS on our favorite architect. But if he built it, did she come?*

Lorenda grabbed the phone and ogled it. "On the bright side, you're now labeled the town *darling*."

"There is that," Miranda snarked. "It's much better than being labeled the town slut."

"No one in this town has ever seen you that way. You're just sensitive because of your mom."

"If Mrs. Wilkinson had her way, I'd have a scarlet letter tattooed on my forehead."

"Mrs. Wilkinson's a bitter old woman. My parents joined a different church years ago because of that old bat. Maybe she's jealous because her husband's never given her an orgasm."

Miranda moaned from under her arm like a wounded animal that had been hit by a car.

"So are you guys together"—Lorenda chose her words carefully, her leather executive chair creaking as she shifted—"long term? Because, sweetie, you're not the sleep-around kind of gal, and he's not the stick-around kind of guy. He can't stay forever."

And that was just the point. He wasn't in Red River helping her with the inn because he was madly in love with her. He was here to fulfill some sense of obligation to his grandmother. Maybe he didn't want a one-night stand this time, but at most, they were a short-term fling.

"Together, yes." In many different positions. "For how long, who knows?" She flung her arms over the sides of the armchair.

Lorenda gave her the same look she gave her two boys when they'd done something stupid and she wanted an explanation. "And why are you *together* with a man who's going to leave you?"

Because it typically worked better if a girl was actually *together* with the man she was in love with. "Well. He distracted me with his lips and naked muscled chest. You and the rest of the mommy mafia warned me about the chest." She stared at the ceiling. "And his eyes turned this incredible shade of purple when he watched me play my air guitar routine in nothing but a bra, panties, and his dress shirt."

Lorenda's jaw fell open.

"You know I adore purple, right? And it was like I was in this weird trance when he had his lips and his hands all over me. And then I gave him a hickey, and it's all your fault for telling me to do him, which was clearly the worst advice ever. What kind of best friend are you, anyway?"

Miranda lifted her head off the back of the chair to find Lorenda's eyes dilated and her mouth still agape.

"You have an air guitar routine? How could I not know this?"

Miranda huffed. "It's a long story."

Lorenda laced her fingers and leaned forward. "I'm just worried about you. Starting a sexual relationship can cloud a girl's judgment." Her eyes turned sad, and it plucked at Miranda's heart. She was the only person who knew Lorenda's secret and what a lonely, rocky road she'd traveled with her late husband. "Once you take the first couple steps through that door, it's hard to close. It's like a gushing faucet that can't be shut off."

Precisely the problem. Miranda didn't want to shut it off. She wanted to keep the water running hot and steamy. But that would require Talmadge staying in Red River, which was impossible.

"So what am I going to do now?"

"I can see why he was impossible to resist." Lorenda leaned back in her chair and gave the ceiling a dreamy stare. "I mean, come on, he's gorgeous. And very nice. Talmadge is a great guy, actually."

"Not helping," Miranda growled.

Lorenda stopped gazing at the ceiling like she was longing for a prince charming to come along for her. "Um, sorry." She swiveled back and forth in her chair. "You must really care about him, because I've never seen you take a chance like this before."

Miranda choked back a sob. She'd been able to let him go seven years ago because he hadn't really been hers. But now they were *together*. Like *together*, together. And she didn't know if she could survive him leaving again.

"Oh, sweetie," Lorenda said like Miranda was one of her kids and had just skinned a knee. "It's obvious by the way Talmadge looks at you that he has feelings for you. Maybe you two can work something out."

The only solution Miranda could see was Talmadge leaving, and her staying to pick up the pieces of her shattered life.

---

Miranda smoothed wallpaper onto the walls going up the stairs just the way Talmadge had shown her while he went to Coop's office for more treatment, and she found herself singing. She brushed the damp walls, getting out every bubble, and trotted a few steps up with a bounce in her step and a smile on her face. That bounce and smile hadn't left her in two solid weeks because of how fast the inn was coming along and the festival was coming together.

The great sex hadn't hurt either.

Life was good. Maybe it was waking up with the most gorgeous man on the planet wrapped around her every morning. Or the way he touched her so inappropriately when no one was around to see, even with all her clothes on. Or the way he smiled and winked at her when people *were* around and touching was off limits.

It was so good that she had barely noticed Jamie's absence. How could she with Talmadge filling her bed, filling her thoughts, and filling her body? Heat flashed through her. Talmadge had become her whole world.

And that scared the living hell out of her. It was exactly what her mother had allowed time after time. It was exactly what Miranda had tried to avoid her entire adult life.

Her cell rang, Darth Vader's heavy breathing—the ringtone reserved especially for her mother—rasping through the inn like a disturbing porn flick.

She took a break to answer. "Hi, Mom."

"Hi, sugar." Her mother's scratchy voice came through the line.

Hellfire. What did she want this time?

"I've been following the stories about you and Bea's grandson. New picture of you two every day."

Every day? The last one she'd seen was two weeks ago, taken after he spent the night for the first time. "I don't keep up." Probably because of all the sex they'd been having. She choked and cleared her throat.

"Since he's rich, do you really need to keep going with this pipe dream of yours?" Her mom sucked in an audible drag from a cigarette and blew it out. "It will just suck up all your money if it hasn't already. And then you'll be worse off than you were before."

True. But too late.

Another drag. "Maybe Talmadge could give you the money back, now that you two got a thing goin' on."

Well put. She and Talmadge did have a *thing* going on. And she wasn't sure what else to call it. She was afraid to even discuss it with him. He'd tried, but she managed to change the subject every time. How could it end any other way but bad? The inn and the gazebo were almost done. After that, he wasn't staying, and she couldn't go.

She loved Talmadge. And she was pretty sure he loved her. He hadn't said it, but she felt it every time he touched her, made love to her, and even when he looked at her.

But love wasn't always enough.

"I'm not giving up the inn, Mom," Miranda said. "And I'm not letting Talmadge give it to me either."

Her mother sighed. "You've always been so determined, Miranda. I wish I was more like you."

"You could be, Mom. It's not too late."

Her mom blew out another drag. "I hope it works out for you, sugar. I really do. I don't want to see you end up broke, crying, and pathetic like me," her mother said, being honest for the first time that Miranda could remember.

"Then do something to help yourself, Mom. Help your situation. And for God's sake, set a better example for Jamie."

Her mom went quiet. "I don't know where you got your strength, but you didn't get it from me."

Miranda pinched the corners of her eyes.

Unfortunately, at least some of what her mother said made sense. Miranda was quite sure she'd end up pathetically crying over Talmadge Oaks sooner or later.

---

Talmadge rolled his shoulder in its socket as he left Coop's office to head to Bea's for more clothes. "Almost good as new," he said to Lloyd, whose poufy head stuck out from the makeshift puppy backpack Talmadge had created. He rarely went anywhere without the little guy anymore.

Lloyd barked at him.

Talmadge made his way across the street to his truck, drawing the warming mountain air into his lungs. Since he'd been back in Red River, he'd somehow acquired several new projects. Miranda's inn, the gazebo, a fake rec center—which he still hadn't manned up and told Miranda the truth about because, hell, he couldn't bring himself to watch the joy on her face, the skip in her step, and those amazing dimples disappear. It was almost like having a career right here in Red River.

Besides the volunteer work he was doing, the good ol' hardworking proprietors of Red River's historic district had approached him about renovating their buildings to make them more energy efficient without disrupting the historic preservation of the structures. And since Red River was growing, the Red River Independent School District had called him to consult on a new high school and update the stadium with solar lighting and artificial turf to preserve water.

He'd had to regretfully turn down the paying jobs since he wouldn't be in Red River long enough to see them through.

At Bea's he flipped on his laptop to check e-mails and froze.

The home page of his browser was set to the local news in Seattle, and Trinity Falls was headlining. He clicked on the link. The damn nervy reporter had obviously been desperate enough to dig for a real story. The article talked about Trinity Falls, a good idea in theory that had turned into an environmental nightmare. A blemish on the country's most beautiful natural landscape. And who was at fault, but one of the most acclaimed green architects in the world. A crusader for sustainable living who had a wall full of awards in his field was going to single handedly blight out several miles of nature because of his folly. And where was he, the reporter demanded to know. On sabbatical, nowhere to be found, not answering his messages, and unwilling to take responsibility.

Talmadge could imagine the protestors picketing outside his firm in Seattle and chaining themselves to trees around Trinity Falls. His investors pulling out to point the finger at him, because someone had to take the fall. And it was sure to be him.

He dialed Larry Jameson's number.

"Yeah, I've seen it," Larry said without a greeting. "What do you want me to do, boss?"

"Get Ellen on the phone. Have her schedule an emergency video conference with the investors. We need to get the tribal councils on board with my plan."

"Will do, boss."

They clicked off, and he sent Miranda a text that he would be late. Instantly, a response dinged back. K. Got a quick meeting with planning committee. Last-minute details. I'll bring you a gooey cinnamon roll from the O's bakery if you'll make it worth my while ;)

He smiled. Texted back. Bring 2 and I'll make sure you have enough Os to last a year.

Her response was a blushing smiley face.

Twenty minutes later he was live-streaming a business meeting with a multitude of people, all of whom stood to lose a fortune if Trinity Falls went down the toilet.

"Any news from the tribal councils?" Talmadge asked.

"None, but it would help if you were here to meet with them in person."

True. But he'd given Miranda his word that he wouldn't leave before the inn and gazebo were finished.

"I'll schedule a video conference with them as well," Talmadge assured his investors.

"Not a good idea. The tribes like to do things old-school. When are you coming back to Washington?"

Good question. One he didn't want to answer.

When he hesitated, one of his investors spoke up. "Look, Talmadge, we know you needed some time to deal with your family matters." He shifted in his chair, his head bobbing all over the laptop screen. "But we need you to come back here and make this work."

Another one of the investors intervened. "We've been discussing this, and we're willing to stay in." He hesitated, tapped a pencil against his desk. "If you'll get back here to speak to the councils yourself. We feel it's the best way to move the project forward."

Talmadge resisted the urge to rake a hand over his face. That probably wouldn't inspire much confidence in the men holding the purse strings at the other end of the Internet connection.

"When do you want me to meet with the council leaders?" he asked.

"This Friday. Be here, or we're pulling out of Trinity Falls completely."

That was the day before the festival. And before the inn would open, unless he could rush the inspections. But inspectors didn't like to be rushed, especially in small towns where things tended to move at a snail's pace. That would give him no other option but to break his promise to Miranda.

He had no choice, though. It might be possible to fly to Seattle the day before the festival, do the presentation, and fly back to finish the inn. It wouldn't be a total breach of his promise, but he'd still miss the festival. Still, the festival wasn't nearly as important as Trinity Falls, and surely Miranda would understand that.

"I'll be there." He had to be. He couldn't leave an entire town half-built and uninhabitable after disrupting so much of the ecosystem. It went against every principle his profession stood for. "But keep this quiet until the day of the presentation."

First he had to tell Miranda the truth. His conscience wouldn't let him *not* tell her. He'd known what a worthless shit he really was since he caused his parents' death. By some miracle, no one else had seemed to figure it out. Once he told Miranda the truth about Bea's will, she'd know how far out of her league he really was, and she may not want him anymore.

Which was the same reason he'd hidden the truth from his grandparents.

# Chapter Nineteen

An hour later, Talmadge was back at the inn on all fours laying new kitchen tile when Langston walked in. Yellow paint was splattered all over him, goggles shoved on top of his head, and a painter's mask hung around his neck. Sitting in his doggie bed, Lloyd sported a sweater with a skull and crossbones on the back. He yipped at Langston, then resumed watching Talmadge work.

"What's up?" Talmadge said without looking up. His latest problem, the one that involved breaking his promise to Miranda by leaving Red River before the inn and gazebo were officially done, ground on his nerves.

"Your cousins stopped by. They're yelling for me and Jamie to take off our shirts." He poured coffee into his thermal cup. "It's a good time for a coffee break."

Ah, Clydelle and Francine, no doubt. "You threw Jamie to the wolves, in other words." Talmadge hammered in another spacer and placed the level on a new square of tile.

Langston shrugged. "It's a tough world out there. The kid has to learn to sink or swim."

Talmadge smiled but couldn't bring himself to laugh. He had too much on his mind to find anything funny.

Langston picked up the bouquet of lavender and yellow flowers Talmadge had gotten on the way back to the inn. "For me?" He sniffed the flowers and laid them back on the counter. "You shouldn't have."

Talmadge shot him a go-to-hell look.

"So you and Miranda." Langston sipped his coffee, leaning against the counter.

An involuntary twitch started in Talmadge's jaw. "What about it?" He hammered in another spacer.

"She lives here and you don't." Langston hooked a thumb into the pocket of his jeans.

"Your point being?" Talmadge still hadn't looked up. He couldn't, because he knew Langston was looking out for Miranda, his friend since childhood.

He shrugged. "Just curious. She's like family. So are you." Another slurp of coffee. "I wondered how it was going to shake out."

Hell if Talmadge knew. He'd been wondering that himself nonstop since they started sleeping together. He wanted her to come to Seattle with him, because he couldn't stay here. Sure, he could find plenty of work. He always did. The casinos and movie studios going up around the state were tempting, and he'd considered submitting bids. He'd been approached with enough work right here in Red River to last a long while. Not the massive, high-profile projects he was used to. But massive and high-profile wasn't exactly working out for him lately. The projects here were smaller, more manageable, and meant something to the people who were trying to do something to preserve their little piece of the world.

Talmadge liked how that made him feel inside. That's how he'd started out in his specialized field, until his career snowballed and it became more about celebrities and fundraisers and hotel owners who were going green for PR reasons. But he had too many loose ends back in Washington to walk away now. And Miranda had the inn to think about. So he hadn't known exactly how to bridge the gap between Red River and Washington, and every time he brought it up, she shut him down.

He hammered the spacer too hard, and the tile chipped.

"Whoa," Langston said. "Didn't mean to strike a nerve."

"Don't you have painting to do?" Talmadge grabbed a tool from his belt to pry up the broken tile. "Or are you going to pussy out and make the kid do it all?"

"You mean the painting I'm doing for free on my days off? When I'm not saving lives, rescuing lost hikers from the wilderness, and life-flighting critical patients to the city?" Langston laughed over the rim of his cup. "Is that the painting you're talking about?"

"You're an asshole, you know that?" Talmadge sat back on his boots.

Langston laughed harder. "I do know that. But I'm a good friend who doesn't want to see either of you get hurt. Especially since you're both looking so happy."

Talmadge rested a hand against his thigh. "You're giving me advice? How long did your longest relationship last?"

Something flashed in Langston's eyes, and he stared down at his mug. "You'd be surprised."

Talmadge lifted a brow. "Is there something I don't know?" He moved the broken tile aside and pulled a new one from the box.

"Yup." Langston straightened to head back outside. He stopped and stared down at Lloyd, who'd rolled onto his back and stared at Talmadge upside down, legs limp and hanging open. Langston's forehead crinkled. "Uh, have you thought of getting your dog neutered, Tal? Because I gotta say, that's disturbing."

For being such a little dog, Lloyd was pretty well endowed. Talmadge shook his head and eyed the level to make sure the bubble was dead center. "The fluffy haircut has already stolen too much of his manhood. No way am I taking the rest."

Langston laughed and went back outside.

Talmadge stared at Lloyd. If he didn't figure out a way to make this situation *shake out*, as Langston had so eloquently put it, Talmadge would likely be the one getting neutered.

———

Miranda drove back to the inn after the planning committee meeting, gooey cinnamon rolls in the passenger seat.

The festival was almost ready. A dry run was scheduled so there would be time to make last-minute changes if needed.

Maybe it was time to let Talmadge finish that discussion he'd been trying to have with her. She'd been too scared to talk about it. Too scared the dream they'd been living would end.

Every part of her life was invested in Talmadge.

Miranda sighed. Including her heart. One hundred and fifty percent of it.

As she turned off Main Street toward the inn, Clydelle and Francine meandered down the lane, Clydelle with her cane and Francine with that ginormous purse of hers hiked on one shoulder. Miranda slowed to a stop and rolled down the window.

"What are you young ladies doing so far out of your way on foot?"

Clydelle lifted her cane at Miranda, waving her off. "We're getting exercise. Doc Holloway's orders. The young men working on your inn weren't very hospitable."

Miranda's brow wrinkled.

Clydelle waved her cane again. "That handsome paramedic even went inside until we left."

"That's because you offered to stuff a twenty into his waistband if he took off his shirt." Francine rolled her eyes. "The view was just fine with their shirts still on." She leaned toward the Jeep window and whispered. "They're painting. On ladders."

Miranda couldn't stop a frown. Painting the outside of the inn? She hadn't bought the paint yet.

Francine kept talking. "Their butts jiggle when they move the paint sprayer back and forth." She shot a disgusted look at her sister. "Until she went and ruined it."

"I would've gone as high as a fifty," Clydelle huffed.

"If we get to heaven, I'm telling Mamma on you," said Francine.

"You do that." Clydelle repositioned her weight against the cane. "Who do you think taught me to watch the firemen when they're washing the truck on a hot summer day? She used to bring them sweet iced tea after they were good and wet all over."

Okay. Too much information.

"You ladies need a ride back?" She sized up Francine's purse. What on earth did she carry in that thing? "That purse looks kind of heavy. Maybe I should drive you home."

Francine clutched the bag like it contained a treasure. "We can walk. The senior center van is waiting for us in front of Joe's."

"Well, don't do anything I wouldn't do." Miranda smiled at them.

"Dear, we'd love to do what you've been doing." Clydelle waggled her bushy eyebrows.

Miranda drew in a pained breath, because really, talking about sex with those two old women was just wrong. On so many levels. "Have a nice day, then." She rolled up the window and started moving again.

Since the warming temperatures had melted a lot of snow on the slopes, the lifts had shut down for the season. The afternoon sky was crystal clear against the small amount of snow that still capped the mountaintops as she pulled her Jeep into the parking lot beside the inn. She lurched to a stop.

She leaned over the steering wheel to look up at Jamie and Langston on ladders spraying pale yellow paint onto the outside of the inn.

Where'd they get the paint? And why was it yellow? She'd planned to paint it blue. Besides, she didn't have the money to buy paint. The inside of the inn was almost finished, and so was her savings. There wasn't much left for the outside until she could open to paying customers.

She hopped out of the Jeep and hurried over to them. Shielding her eyes from the sun, she yelled up at Jamie and Langston. "Where'd the paint come from? That isn't the color I picked." Although, she had to admit, it was a really nice shade of buttercup yellow. Soothing and peaceful and quaint. Just the look she wanted for the inn. The same warm, inviting look she'd thought a dusty blue would create.

Jamie and Langston both pointed behind her, neither lowering their masks. Instead they kept the paint guns spraying the pretty yellow paint onto the siding.

"We're not expecting another storm for at least a week." She whirled to find Talmadge behind her, holding a color chart and some printouts in one hand, the other hand behind his back. "I thought we could get started on the exterior and make good use of the weather."

"I told you I can't take your money, Talmadge." Bad enough she was taking his help free of charge. And all the sex he could give her while he was still in town.

Her heart thumped against her chest.

"You can pay me back if you want. This color with black and white trim will look soft in the sunlight and bright when it's overcast. We can paint over it if you don't like it, but I wanted you to see the front side of the inn first before you decide."

Oh. Well. Okay.

It *was* beautiful. Even more so than the dusty blue she had imagined. "It's really pretty."

"And these are for you." He pulled out a bouquet of fresh yellow roses that matched the color of the paint he'd picked. Small lavender mountain asters—the same color his eyes turned when he wanted her— filled the spaces between each rose.

"Thank you," she whispered.

He laced an arm around her waist and pulled her against his chest. A very broad chest. And firm. Yes, it was really firm. She'd explored it quite thoroughly, and firm was the best description she could think of. Except maybe tasty.

No, tasty wasn't the right word. Delicious. His chest and neck and mouth were delicious, like expensive chocolate, and she'd tried to devour him many times with her lips and tongue. Hence the hickey that had faded and was only slightly still visible.

Her mouth watered just thinking about the taste of him. "They're pretty too." Her voice sounded all croaky again. *Real nice. And attractive.*

His head dipped and he kissed her.

"Get a room," Jamie called down.

"Some of us have work to do. We don't need the distraction," Langston yelled too.

"Our gossip stalker is probably photographing us as we speak." She picked at a petal.

"Then let's go inside where they can't see us."

Yes, his eyes definitely matched the mountain asters when they were filled with lust. Her girl parts screamed for more purple.

"Your flowers need water." His gravelly voice told her he wasn't just talking about the flowers in her hand.

She pulled in a lip. "I think I have a vase inside."

He led her up the steps without another word. Inside, Talmadge closed the front door and turned the key in the lock until it clicked.

He took slow steps toward her. When he reached her, he brushed her nose with his. "I was thinking you could come visit me in Seattle."

Her chest tightened, and she measured her words. "We'll see."

He pulled her closer. "That sounds . . . noncommittal."

She fisted his shirt in her hands and stared at his chest. How could their future sound any other way? "It's just that I have a business to run here, and I mean, really, it's not like you were here all that often before, so what reason is there for you to come back now? Sure, visiting you in

Seattle would be fun, but you'll be busy, being all successful, and I'll be busy with the inn, and I have to build clientele the first few years while you're saving the world, and then I'll keep wondering how long before I hear from you, and I'll miss you, and you won't miss me because, well, you'll have lots of other options—"

He pulled her into a kiss so deep, so sexy that she couldn't think straight. And what was it she'd been saying about businesses to run and some such?

When he trailed kisses down her neck she panted out, "You're developing a bad habit of not letting me finish."

"I learned it from you." He kept the trail of blazing hot kisses going. "We need to talk soon," he murmured between suckles and licks. "About . . . that rec center." He seemed to tense. "And about us." His voice went a little hard. "And other things." Then he resumed more nips and kisses along her jaw.

Dang, she didn't want to hear it yet if it was bad news. Which it almost surely was. The inn and gazebo were near completion, the inspections were lined up, the festival was this weekend, and Felix had been over several times with a camera crew to film footage of the renovations, which Talmadge planned to forward to the producer of a home show when the inn was finished. He'd made her be the spokesperson, walking Felix through the inn to showcase the remodel. It would put the spotlight on her instead of him and garner vacation business in the process.

Brilliant.

And almost over.

He shifted and closed the small space between them. Just his closeness muddled her senses and scrambled her thoughts. He smoothed the back of his fingers across her cheek. Heat rushed through her veins to pool low in her belly.

And yes! The purple of his irises deepened.

"I don't want to talk, Talmadge. Not right now." Maybe never if it meant she didn't have to hear him say it was over.

"I lose sight of everything when I'm with you, Miranda." His heavy breaths washed over her skin.

"Me too." There went that croaking sound again. "I mean, we both probably need to refocus, and—"

And then his lips were on hers, masterfully shutting her the hell up. She couldn't really complain because his technique was so good. His taste wasn't at all bad either. Neither were his roughened hands finding their way inside her jacket to her sweater, then caressing up her back and around to her breasts.

A purr of approval and appreciation escaped from somewhere deep inside her and he deepened the kiss. Tugged her close and dropped a hand way south of the border, pulling her against his granite body. So hard. So hot.

*So mine.*

She slid her arms around his neck, and one set of fingers speared into his hair. Good God she loved his hair. It was so thick and soft and perfect and who cared about talking at the moment? A thick fog of lust swirled inside her brain, pushing every sensible thought out about paint colors and reputations and different states and indefinite separations because of work. There was nothing more important right now than him and her and this wonderful, dangerous, unstoppable chemistry that churned the air around them and made her palms all sweaty and her ears ring.

An urgent need thrummed through her. A need to have him. A need to forget even just for a little while that their futures weren't on the same path.

He eased her back toward the staircase.

"Langston and Jamie are here." She broke the kiss, her voice all breathy, only to reclaim his mouth again with a desperation that made him chuckle.

He nuzzled her neck, still moving to the stairs in small, easy steps. "They're busy. I told them to go to Joe's when they're ready for a break. It's on me. Neither one of them will turn down a free meal."

Clever man.

When his heated breaths whispered across her ear, a shudder of pleasure so violent it could probably register on the Richter scale lanced through her. He let out a low, husky laugh and pulled her earlobe between his teeth to nibble.

Her head tilted back, giving him better access, which he took full advantage of. "*Ah*," she gasped out, the sound coupled with a moan when his mouth found the sensitive skin where her neck met her shoulder. "Let's go to my suite." Her words came as quick pants. "It's more private."

"Good idea." He changed course and backed her toward the hallway. "Because if you moan like that again, I'll have to have you right here against the wall."

*Good Lord.* Talmadge doing her like that was the most exciting thing she'd ever heard.

She grabbed a fistful of his shirt and towed him into her suite, slammed the door, and jumped on him in the den before he could protest. Not that she thought he would.

With a desperation she'd never felt before, she yanked his black knit shirt up, but he flinched at the pain. "Oh, sorry!" She tried to back away, but he grabbed her around the waist.

"Don't be. It's much better. Only hurts when I raise it over my head at a certain angle." He tugged her against him again. "Stay right there." His gaze locked with hers, he reached behind his neck and drew the shirt over his head, one-handed, then pulled it off.

She let her gaze wander over his broad, bare chest. His skin under her fingertips caused a shudder to roll through her. Flattening her palms against him, she ran both hands over the silky skin that covered the hardened muscles underneath. He eased a hand behind her neck and pulled her in until his mouth hovered just above hers. His breath was warm against her cheeks, his hunger apparent in his darkening eyes, and Miranda's need spiked.

"Kiss me," she said in a frustrated whisper against his mouth. He did. His mouth consuming her.

At that moment she was so glad Talmadge had been her one and only. It was right. And so true.

She trailed hot, urgent kisses down his neck and across his chest. He sucked in a breath and held it. When she placed her lips in the valley between his pecs, he growled. A flood of satisfaction shimmied through her.

With the tip of her tongue she traced a line to one of his nipples and nipped. He hissed and threaded a hand into her hair.

"Do you want me to stop?" she asked and nipped at the pebbled circle again.

"Hell no." He ground out his words.

She covered the peak with her mouth and suckled.

His other hand slid under her sweater and found her aching breast. "*Fuck.*"

"Okay." She giggled. "Just hot, hard sex."

"Jesus, Miranda." His hand still fisted into her long hair, he pulled her mouth to his and kissed her hard, his breaths fast and shallow.

One of her hands slid down his ripped torso to the front of his jeans. She swallowed hard, and her breathing grew shaky. When his kiss grew almost punishing with desire, her courage swelled. Her hand glided over the rough denim fabric of his jeans, and she cupped him in her hand and massaged.

Lord, but he was huge. And he was all hers, at least for now. He'd promised to stay until the inn was open and the gazebo was done, so she planned to make the best of it while it lasted. Then maybe the demands of running a business would fill the void. Or at least keep her mind off of loving a man who lived somewhere distant.

When she slid a warm palm down his length and up again, he growled. He inserted his fingers into her waistband and unbuttoned her jeans with a flick of his thumb. The zipper whizzed as it went down.

She kicked her shoes off and grabbed his hand, backing toward her bedroom.

He shook his head, a piercing gleam shimmering in his eyes. He tugged her against him again. "There's a difference between making love and hot, hard sex." He kissed her, angling her head with his heated palm at the back of her neck. "I promise you'll like both." He slid both palms around to her lower back, wedged his fingers under her jeans and panties, and guided them down.

Miranda shuddered, her heart thundering against the inside of her ribs. "How do you know I'll like both?" She kicked out of her jeans and pushed them aside with a toe.

He smiled down at her, a languid, playful grin on his lush mouth. "Because you're going to tell me what you like and don't like."

The spot between her thighs turned to fire.

He eased a thigh between her legs, and the rough fabric of his jeans rubbed against her already wet center. He hooked one hand behind her knee and pulled her leg up over his muscled thigh. Miranda's eyes flew wide and she looked up into his lust-glazed eyes. Desire blazed like an inferno in the purplish irises. His husky gaze licked over her flesh, down her neck, then anchored to her lips as his other hand found the tender contours between her thighs.

He smoothed two fingertips along her folds, tremors rippling through her as his work-roughened touch grazed over her heated flesh.

"Baby, you're so wet already." His voice was an urgent whisper, and he brushed his lips across hers. He slid the tips of two fingers inside her.

Her head tilted back at the mind-altering ecstasy of his touch.

"You seem to like that," he whispered against her neck. "But I want to hear you say it."

"Yes," she panted out. "I like it."

"And how about this?" He buried both fingers inside her.

The heat at her center exploded into a fireball that singed every nerve ending in her body. She cried out and arched into him, clinging to the last threads of control. He smiled against her neck again. "Is that a yes?"

"*Yes!*" Good God, yes.

"And this?" When his fingers left her, she groaned her disapproval.

"No? Then let's try this." He buried his fingers in her again and worked his palm against her pulsing nub.

Her knees gave way.

He caught her. "Hold on to me," he whispered against her ear. She did, and he withdrew and slid into her again. "Do you know how fucking gorgeous you are?"

Her eyes opened, and she took him in. His chiseled jaw, his strong neck, his arched golden brows, and his extraordinary eyes that changed colors to communicate his mood. Which at the moment said he was ravenously hungry for sex. Hot and hard sex.

Fine by her.

"Keep looking at me." His gaze held her prisoner. Held her completely mesmerized. "Do you know how fucking insane you drive me every time I see you?" Another thrust of his fingers made her moan as a shiver raced over her and covered her skin with little bumps of pleasure. A sinful smile curved onto his exquisite mouth, and he repeated that wonderful motion again, making sure his palm worked its magic against her clit.

Miranda's brain went fuzzy. Him dropping the f-bomb while doing that very thing to her with his talented fingers was so sexy she was about to—

"*Talmadge!*" she gasped as he buried his fingers deep inside her again and twitched them to massage the deepest part of her. Her nails dug into his shoulders, and she splintered into tiny pieces as a fierce orgasm washed over his fingers.

"Yes, baby." His lips hovered a breath away from hers. "That's it. I can feel you throbbing around me." His thrusts slowed to gentle caresses, prolonging her orgasm. Kneading every ounce of it out of her. "You like that."

It wasn't a question. Clearly she did. But she gave a frantic nod anyway and swallowed. As the convulsions around his fingers ebbed, he withdrew, and Miranda melted against him.

He shook his head. "We're not done yet." It was a promise. She loved his promises, because he always kept them.

"Let's . . . let's go to my bedroom."

"No." He picked her up and set her against the wall, pinning her there. Then he reached into his back pocket and pulled out his wallet, retrieving a foil square. He handed the condom to her before tossing his wallet onto the sofa. "You put it on."

"What?" She couldn't possibly . . .

"You wanted to know the difference between making love and fast, hard sex." He held the square out to her. "Put it on for me." The roughness of his voice made her insides tighten again.

Without taking her eyes off of his, she took the square and raised it to her lips. Lust set his irises ablaze, and a long breath threaded through his tempting lips to smooth across her neck.

A sharp rip sounded as she tore the square open with her teeth.

She gulped most of the oxygen out of the room.

He chuckled. "If you don't like this . . . *method*, we can make love." He brushed a kiss across her lips. "You turn me on no matter what."

She pushed against his chest just enough for him to stop kissing her, and gave him a wicked smile. It was now or never. She wasn't going to have too many more chances to experience this kind of sexual pleasure because Talmadge wouldn't be around forever. She lowered her feet to the ground and unbuttoned his jeans, pushing them down over his narrow hips. And discovered he was commando.

Her gaze flew to his, and he arched a silky brow.

Placing the condom over his generous flesh, she drew up her courage and rolled it on with long, slow strokes.

His eyes slid shut. "Damn, Miranda." His voice was husky, and his body quivered with strained self-control.

No matter how many times she'd seen him naked, *Gawd* he looked good. Mouthwatering, lip-smacking, thigh-clenching good.

"Does that mean you like it?" she asked, trying to sound coy and flirtatious. She did have the man's family jewels in her hands.

Instead of answering, he gave her a hard kiss. One that had her girl parts coiling even tighter. So she stroked along his length one more time.

He growled in response. Then braced one hand under her ass and the other against the wall next to her head. He dipped his knees and came up inside her with one thrust.

She cried out and wrapped her legs and arms around him tighter. Her head fell back heavy against the wall, and her eyes shut.

"Open your eyes and look at me," Talmadge commanded.

She did, and he pinned her gaze with his. A gaze that promised exquisite pleasures and wild, wicked sensations. No, this wasn't the same as making love. It was raw desire. Unbridled passion. Hot and hard sex. She saw it in his lusty stare just as much as she felt it in her quivering body.

But she also saw something else that matched the deep well of emotion that was building in her heart for him. He cared about her. Maybe they could find a way . . .

She swallowed. "You know, taking orders from you has gotten infinitely more enjoyable than it was at first," she panted out.

His mouth came down on hers, and she couldn't think beyond what was happening right then. He thrust inside of her hard and fast, the pictures on the walls banging with each unyielding stroke. And all the while, he stared down into her eyes like he could see into her soul.

Her body responded to him, molding and unfurling around him until she was on the brink again. He must have seen it in her eyes, because he buried his face in her hair and said her name.

*"Miranda."* It came out like a whisper, each syllable entwined with emotion, and he kept driving into her.

It pushed her over the edge into oblivion, and she fell into the abyss with a shout of pleasure. He followed her, pulsing inside of her.

He kept her pinned against the wall for what seemed a long time. Their hearts beat against each other, their breathing slowly returning to a normal rhythm. The sheer, raw desire that had just swirled around them threaded through every muscle in her body, making her limp and satisfied. It was potent and powerful, and Miranda would never forget it. She melded with him and wrapped her arms around his head.

With tenderness that didn't match the sex they'd just experienced, his lips feathered up her neck to her mouth and he gave her a soft, affectionate kiss.

"See the difference?" he asked, then gave her another lazy kiss.

"Oh, yeah." Her voice was raspy like she'd just run a marathon. "I can see how both methods serve a valuable purpose."

He chuckled.

"I didn't even get all my clothes off." She looked down at her rumpled top, now damp from working up a passionate sweat.

"Uh-huh." He nipped at her bottom lip, then slid out of her.

She gasped, already missing the sensation of him being inside of her.

"That's the point. It's unpredictable and you just go with it." He lowered her to the ground.

She tried to push him away so she could get to her pants, but he held her in place. "I'm game to try the other method." Naughtiness gleamed in his eyes. "So you can compare."

She pulled a lip between her teeth, which made desire flare in his eyes again. "I'm in."

With a dip of his head in agreement, he had her top and bra off in a nanosecond and swooped her into his arms, carrying her to the bedroom.

She rested her cheek against his shoulder and breathed his manly scent in—soap mingled with the dewy sweat he'd just worked up. A scent she had gotten used to.

A scent she wanted to enjoy forever.

# Chapter Twenty

Miranda stood on the announcer's stand at the edge of Brandenburg Park for the festival run-through and tried not to think about the inspectors who were at the inn at that very moment deciding if she could finally launch her dream and fly. She also tried hard not to think about the conversation Talmadge kept trying to have with her. She could guess what was coming. Knew he was either going to end it or suggest a long-distance relationship that wouldn't last, because how could it?

She ran a finger down the list of parade entries on her clipboard.

Less than most years, but enough to put on a decent parade.

Every restaurant, café, ice cream shop, and bakery in Red River was busy decorating booths along the edges of the park. Artists from all over the Southwest would display and sell their work. Several wineries and breweries around the state had reserved booths and were getting their spaces ready.

Up and down Main Street red-white-and-blue pleated flags were going up, windows were being spit-shined, and shop owners were gearing up for the influx of vacationers who would flood in for the festival that kicked off the summer tourist season.

For the kids, Miranda had lined up face-painters, a caricaturist, and even Pebbles the Clown who was driving in from Albuquerque to make animal shapes out of balloons. She shivered, hoping that wasn't a mistake. Because, let's face it, clowns could be creepy.

Best of all, the gorgeous man on the other side of the park, a fluffy poodle strapped to his back, was putting the finishing touches on the gazebo the town had worked so hard to raise money for him to build. And he was hers. For a little while longer. He promised even the landscaping around it would be complete by festival day, so he hadn't looked up from his work all afternoon. She'd stolen looks at him every chance she got, though. Especially when he bent over.

She'd done it. She'd organized the best damn Hot Rides and Cool Nights Festival yet. Without the almighty Mrs. Wilkinson's help.

And speak of the she-devil, here she came, marching toward the announcer's stand with a sour look on her face. Her cross bounced more than usual today. Miranda looked heavenward and sent up an apology for Mrs. Wilkinson's poor example. Just in case. Because Miranda was pretty sure the cross was a disguise to distract from her forked tail.

Clydelle and Francine, who shared a sixth sense as big as their attitude, hurried across the street on a collision course with Mrs. Wilkinson. Clydelle's cane steadily thumped against the pavement, and Francine's purse steadily thumped against her leg.

"*You* have a problem," Mrs. Wilkinson spat.

Yes, Miranda's biggest problem was standing in front of her wearing her Sunday best, even though it was a weekday. "What would that be, Mrs. Wilkinson?" Miranda did her best to sound civil.

"*You* don't have enough entries for the parade." Old Lady Wilkinson let loose the first sincere smile Miranda had yet to see on her bitter, pinched face.

Miranda held up the clipboard. "I have them right here."

"Count them." Mrs. Wilkinson tapped her foot.

An uneasiness settled in the pit of Miranda's stomach. She counted the entries one more time. "Sixteen."

"The festival bylaws say there has to be at least twenty." Old Lady Wilkinson crossed her arms.

*There were bylaws?* News to Miranda.

"And you just happened to forget to mention the bylaws?" Clydelle accused. "You've been in charge of the festival for years, and no one else has a copy, I'm guessing."

Mrs. Wilkinson ignored this. "Twenty is the minimum by the day of the festival."

Before Miranda could ask "Or what?" Mrs. Wilkinson gushed the answer. "Or you have to cancel the whole thing. Instead of cavorting around in public like a hussy, maybe you should've researched the rules." Mrs. Wilkinson turned on her heel and marched off.

Francine made a gesture with her bony finger at Mrs. Wilkinson's back.

"Now, ladies." Miranda tapped her clipboard, fighting off the urge to use some sign language of her own. "No need to give her more ammunition. I'll fix this." Even if it was the last thing she did in this town.

"Darn right, we'll fix it." Clydelle waved her infamous cane in the air. "Count us in for the parade. We'll get the senior center's van to drive us, and we'll decorate it up real nice."

Miranda wasn't sure if that was a good thing or not. These two characters might end up driving down Main Street with a float carrying the Chippendale dancers, but she'd chance it if it meant not having to cancel the festival.

Miranda narrowed her eyes as the wicked witch of the Southwest stomped down the street. Miranda hadn't come this far to fail now. The whole town was behind her for the first time in her life. Or at least that's how it felt. She'd *earned* their respect, and she wasn't going to give up easily.

She pulled her phone from her back pocket and dialed her mom's number. *Come on, Mom. Come through for me just this once.*

---

Talmadge found himself whistling as he directed his crew of volunteers to paint the gazebo and finish shingling the roof.

*Hell.* He didn't whistle. But life was good here in Red River with Miranda. He glanced over his shoulder and smiled as she walked toward him. If she got much hotter his work goggles might fog up. Rounded hips sashaying, wavy hair bouncing around her shoulders as the sun glinted off of it, lips parting into a knowing little smile when her gaze caught his, the dimples that appeared on each cheek when her lips curved up. All of it, the entire package that she'd kept wrapped up tight and had saved all these years for only him . . .

Stunning. Scrumptious. Sexy as hell.

That was the problem. He cared about her so much that he'd been selfish and hadn't wanted to jeopardize their bond, their connection. But he couldn't stay quiet any longer. Tonight he was going to tell Miranda everything when they were done with the long day's work and alone. And to hell with his inheritance. He really was going to forfeit it for a rec center here in Red River, regardless of what happened with Trinity Falls. Then his lie would become the truth, albeit after the fact. But he still planned on telling Miranda everything, because she deserved to know.

He swiped at a bead of sweat on his forehead as she approached. But then she didn't just approach. She walked right up to him, leaving no space between them.

"Hi," she said, with a sultry look and sexy tone.

"Hi yourself. How's it going?"

A glimmer of worry raced across her face, but then it was gone. "Nothing I can't handle." She was somehow different than she'd been several weeks ago. Oh, Talmadge had always seen her strength. How could he not? But now she saw it too. He was proud of her and what she'd accomplished in such a short amount of time. More importantly, she was obviously proud of herself.

"I checked on the inspections a little while ago. Seems to be going well," he told her.

"Thank you." The amber flecks in her eyes glowed.

"Are you ready for the festival?" he asked. A gentle breeze blew a lock of wavy hair across her face, and he tucked it behind her ear.

"Ready," she said with confidence.

"Felix is coming by the inn again tomorrow to film the last of the renovations, and the home show is going to call you to set up a date to film the rest after you open." He adjusted the straps of Lloyd's carrier on his shoulders.

"Thank you again." Her gaze fell.

"You're the one knocking them dead in front of the camera. I just made a few calls."

"Why didn't the home show film the whole thing?" Her brow wrinkled.

Because he needed to keep his presence in Red River low-profile and out of the news until he could get back to Washington in a few days. Another little detail he had to disclose tonight. "On sabbatical to rehabilitate his injured arm" was the only comment his firm would make to the reporter sniffing around. If his investors knew he'd been renovating an inn and building a gazebo in New Mexico, they'd be pissed, especially after that reporter ran a story about him neglecting the very thing he was trying to prevent—an environmental catastrophe.

He smiled down at her. It took a hell of a lot of willpower not to kiss the heck out of her right there in broad daylight. "I'll tell you all about it tonight. When we talk."

Her smile faded.

He took in the flurry of activity going on around them as he spoke. "I'm a patient man, Miranda. I've been waiting to talk to you about some important things." He hadn't really put up much of a fight when she kept shutting him down. "But it's time. You might not like what I've got to say, but we're going to talk. Tonight."

She pursed her lips, trying to hide her emotions, and the faintest hint of her dimples appeared. That was nearly his undoing. He'd give anything to make this right.

She cleared her throat. "I've arranged an interview with the *Record*."

Good. That would give her another opportunity to showcase her intelligence. Her skills. Her worth in the community that had been overlooked for far too long until now.

"You're doing this one, Talmadge." The happiness in her eyes returned, setting his heart on fire. "The planning committee and the city council have decided to award you the key to the city during the festival celebrations." Her smile widened.

His didn't. He'd managed to keep what a shit he really was a secret for years. Buried the truth about his parents and pretended to be the good boy who would make his grandparents proud. Hell, that's why he'd devoted his career to environmentally conscious building projects. It was a way of doing penance, giving something back because he'd so selfishly taken so much.

He had an office full of awards back in Seattle, all to recognize his accomplishments for blazing the trail in sustainable designs and environmentally friendly building. HGTV practically stalked him to do one feature segment after another.

But the key to the city? In Red River, where he'd hurt—was still hurting—the people he loved most? Even though they didn't know it, his conscience had limits, and he'd reached them.

"Who made that absurd decision?" His voice was harsher than he'd intended.

Miranda's eyes widened. "I . . . I told the planning committee your plan to build a community rec center in Bea's honor."

Did she mean the rec center he'd twisted the truth about to get what he needed from her? Yeah. That was probably the one she was talking about.

"Why would you do that?" His volume and tone were close to a bellow.

"It's a great thing you're doing for Red River," she said. "We want to recognize it."

Talmadge shook his head. "No."

Miranda's face blanked, communicating her confusion. She meant it as an honor. A show of gratitude. But he couldn't accept it.

"Find someone else to give it to." He pointed to Miranda. "You deserve it. I don't."

Before she could respond, he turned and trudged to his truck. It was time to man up. First, he'd pick up some flowers and spend some time at the cemetery. Then he'd finally tell Miranda what a selfish asshole he was.

So much for life being good. His life was shit right now, no matter which state he was in. And it was about to get even worse when Miranda heard him out tonight.

━━━━

Miranda shoved her clipboard at Lorenda, who was hanging a Brooks Real Estate banner in a booth. "You're in charge."

"What? Wait!" Lorenda yelled after Miranda as she hurried to her Jeep.

"Just follow the schedule, and you'll be fine," she hollered over her shoulder. "I'll be back soon."

As she approached the Red River Market, Talmadge's truck jetted out of the parking lot and headed west, tires squealing. He sped up, which left her trailing behind at a distance. And damn well confused.

So like her entire history with Talmadge.

She followed him along Highway 38. His driver's side window was rolled down, and one elbow jutted out. His thick hair fluttered in the breeze. After a few miles, he turned left without a blinker and entered the Red River Valley Cemetery.

Sorrow tugged at her heart. She'd been so caught up in her own problems she hadn't considered that Talmadge hadn't fully mourned Bea's loss. The grief he'd kept bottled up since Bea's funeral might be ready to blow like a cork.

She pulled to a stop on the far side of the cemetery and blinked. He wasn't standing over Bea's grave. He placed a fresh bouquet of flowers in front of two headstones that stood side by side about fifty feet from where they'd laid Bea to rest.

Miranda killed the engine and watched Talmadge. His lips moved, hands were shoved in his pockets.

And then he rubbed his eyes under his sunglasses.

Miranda's heart stuttered.

She got out of the Jeep and walked up behind him. When Lloyd saw Miranda, he yapped through the driver's window of Talmadge's truck. Talmadge didn't turn, just stood in silence as he stared at the headstones with the names Pamela and Gerald Oaks carved into the fine granite, an angel on one and two interlocking hearts on the other.

His mom and dad. The dates of their deaths were identical.

She slid both arms around his torso, locking her hands in front, and leaned her cheek against his arm. His quick, shallow breaths told her how upset he was. A gentle breeze kicked up, rustling the evergreens like a soft, sad song that whispered across the acres of marked graves.

"Would you rather be alone?"

His strong hand clamped over hers. Another vehicle motored into the cemetery and parked on the other side of a crop of evergreens, still offering them some privacy.

"It's my fault." He reached back with his other hand and brushed her thigh with his fingertips.

"What's your fault?" Miranda asked.

"My mom and dad." His voice cracked. "I killed them."

"Talmadge . . . that can't be true." Miranda smoothed a hand up his back.

He nodded. "I did. The accident was my fault."

From behind, Miranda slid a hand inside his coat and gently placed a hand over his heart where it drummed against her open palm. "What happened?"

"I was young but big and tall for my age. All the makings of a pro athlete, Dad thought. He demanded that I win at everything. Second place was for losers."

The pain of those memories threaded through his words.

"He drank a lot. If I didn't win, he'd go into a tirade." His fingers slid under his polarized sunglasses to massage his eyes.

He went quiet like he was remembering.

Miranda could sense what was coming, and it broke her heart. She snuggled her cheek against his shoulder and held him close. "I'm listening," she whispered against his shoulder.

Talmadge's voice grew shaky. "I was just so damn sick of his ranting and him pushing me."

Miranda closed her eyes, her cheek still flush against his back, which rose and fell in sharp succession.

"What happened?" she asked.

"I was playing little league baseball. I struck out and lost the game." His hand tightened over hers. "My dad went insane. It was so bad that my grandparents insisted I ride home with them. They took me for ice cream. I suspect to give my dad time to cool off before they brought me home. My parents never made it."

His voice broke and he heaved in a breath.

"Oh, babe," Miranda whispered. She moved to stand in front of him and lifted a hand to caress his cheek. "You can't possibly blame yourself. It wasn't your fault."

"*It was.*" His voice was desperate, and he pulled her against him, burying his face in her hair. "I struck out on purpose. I wanted to lose the game to get back at my dad."

And for the first time, Miranda understood the quiet, private pain Talmadge had carried around in his expression. Why his smile never fully formed when they were teenagers. She had thought he took his grandparents' love and the pride Bea carried for him for granted, and that's why he didn't come back to Red River much. She'd thought he had it easy growing up.

She'd been wrong.

"You were just a kid, sweetheart." Miranda tried to soothe him. Tried to take the pain and the guilt he'd obviously been carrying around for years. "There's not a kid on this earth who hasn't done something similar at least once."

Talmadge straightened, and his voice went steely. "I doubt their childishness caused their parents' deaths." He hesitated like he wanted to say something else, a silent, painful plea in his eyes. "And the worst part is . . ." He stumbled over the words. "I didn't miss them. My mom wasn't much of a mom, because she was so preoccupied with trying to keep my dad happy. My grandparents were so good to me that I was relieved when I went to live with them. They grieved for their son, and I didn't." He blew out a choked laugh. "How messed up is that?"

"It sounds to me like you did grieve."

He looked away, but she framed his face with her hands and turned his gaze back to hers. "You grieved for the kind of parents your mom and dad should've been. I know what that's like."

"I'm not the person you think I am, Miranda. I'm not what anyone thinks I am." That sad, lost look of private pain was back in his eyes.

"Don't say that, Talmadge. I . . ." She swallowed. "I love you."

The plea in his gaze turned to sorrow. "Don't." He shook his head. "I can't accept the key to the city. It's the one award my conscience could never live with, because I don't deserve it. Not here in Red River."

He turned to walk away.

"Talmadge, wait!" Miranda hurried after him and grabbed his arm.

He whirled on her. "It's the reason I rarely came back to visit. Too many bad memories. When I was here for more than a few days, they started to suffocate me."

What he said next made her heart drop to her feet and tears threaten.

He ran his fingers through his hair. "I twisted the truth about Bea's will. At least some of it." His jaw turned to granite. "The money she left wasn't for a rec center. The only way I could inherit it was if I stayed to help you open the inn."

He'd lied, in other words. "You . . ." She didn't hear him right. "You used me for money?" Oh God. She'd become her mother. Maybe she'd taken a different path to get there, but she was there nonetheless. She'd staked everything on a man—her dream, her reputation, her savings. And yes, her heart. And that man had just driven a stake right through it.

"I lied. I'm sorry. I wish I hadn't."

His eyes said he was sorry, but so what? She'd accepted his help with the renovations out of respect for Bea. She'd agreed to his help with the gazebo because his idea was so brilliant. And he'd been dishonest. Made her feel like he wanted to be there helping her . . . for her. But it was all for money.

She'd been played like a song during the dance hour at Cotton Eyed Joe's, and she'd danced to Talmadge's tune.

"I wanted to tell you. I tried several times." He took a step toward her.

She took a step back. "But you didn't."

He looked away as if to say, *You got me there*. "Bea loved you. She wanted you to be a success. I figured it would be a win-win for both of us."

"You knew how hard it was for me to accept your help. For me to depend on you. And you slept with me under false pretenses."

"It wasn't false—"

"I mean it's my own fault." She blew out a gust of laugher that rang hollow. "I knew better, and I let it happen anyway." The sting of tears welled up in her eyes. She was all used up and felt empty, like she had nothing left to give.

She took another step back.

"Don't go." Talmadge held out a hand. "Not yet. I do plan to donate the money for a rec center. Trinity Falls might pan out after all, and I won't need the money anymore."

Her jaw fell open. "Gee, Talmadge. I feel so much better now." The sting of tears turned to a burn.

He pinched the bridge of his nose. "Everything I say to you comes out wrong."

"Well, maybe that's because everything you say is a lie."

He shook his head. "No, it's not. You said you love me, so let's work this out. I made a mistake. One I regret wholeheartedly. I don't want it to end like this. I care too much about you." He closed the distance between them in two long strides and ran a hand down her arm.

She jerked it away. "I've seen how you care about people. I was the one sitting with your lonely grandmother while you were off playing big boy Legos with movie stars and rich hotel chain owners." Not to mention their daughters.

That hit home, because he flinched.

"Well, guess what?" She took several steps back. "I've got a life to live, Talmadge. And I've earned the right to live it. Without anyone else's approval." She swallowed, because suddenly it felt like her world was caving in. She wasn't going to let it. "And without you. You've fulfilled your commitment. The inspections should be complete by now. The gazebo is all but done. You can go back to your life and take your money with you."

Miranda wished she could say "no hard feelings," but that would've been the biggest lie of all.

# Chapter Twenty-One

When Talmadge finished giving his crew of volunteers the final instructions for the gazebo and went back to the inn, Miranda had locked him out, removed the hidden key from out front, and given Jamie and Langston instructions to not let him in no matter what.

"Dude, give her some time to cool off," Langston said. "She was crying pretty hard."

The look of admiration Jamie usually gave him was gone, and Talmadge couldn't blame him.

Talmadge stared at the inn, looked up at the window of the honeymoon suite. Finally he nodded. "Call me if she's not okay."

"She's already not okay." Jamie gave Talmadge an angry look.

"Then will you call me if she needs anything?" Talmadge scrubbed a hand over his face, happy that Jamie wasn't a big kid. If he had been, Talmadge's ass would've already been kicked halfway to Seattle. And Talmadge wouldn't have tried to stop him.

He went back to Bea's, and after leaving about a thousand messages on Miranda's cell, he sat in front of his laptop to check e-mails. His inbox was flooded. His investors wanted to know when he was arriving, because the tribal meeting was in a few days.

Going back for that meeting would mean breaking his promise to Miranda to stay until the gazebo was unveiled, the festival was over, and the inn was open for business. Even if she never wanted to see him again, he never left his projects unfinished, which was one of the reasons he wanted to get back to Trinity Falls, because it sure as hell wasn't about his fortune anymore. It was about his commitment.

*Screw the money.*

The only thing he wanted was Miranda in his life, because she *was* his life. Unfortunately, she may not want him to be part of her life anymore.

He picked up his phone and dialed Angelique's number.

"Law offices." Her voice commanded strength. He marveled at how that same strength had started to resonate in Miranda's voice lately as she'd grown into the woman she was always meant to be.

"It's Talmadge Oaks."

"Talmadge. How are you?"

"Listen, I'm not going to be able to fulfill the terms of Bea's will."

She went silent for a beat. "I thought the inn was almost finished."

"It is." He left it at that.

Two silent beats this time. "You do realize this means the money will revert to the next beneficiary, which is the city of Red River."

"I do know that. For a rec center. Frankly, I can't think of a better use for it." Tension released from his chest as he said it, because he knew it was right. "I've broken the terms of Bea's will. I told Miranda about the money, so it's done."

"Okay then. The money will go into a trust until the city can start the center. These things take time. There are bids and designs and approvals and permits before they can even break ground. You better than anyone know the drill."

He sure did.

After they hung up, he made his travel arrangements and went to pack his suitcase.

Several more unreturned phone calls and unanswered knocks on the inn's door later, Talmadge sat in a back booth at Joe's. Uncle Joe had asked him to come by for dinner for a chat with him and Sheriff Lawson.

Huh.

This couldn't be good. The last time Uncle Joe and Sheriff Lawson had wanted a *chat* with him was so the sheriff could question Talmadge after Cotton Eyed Joe's old building had burned to the ground, the night he'd graduated from high school, and suspicion fell on one of his high school buddies.

Talmadge couldn't eat. He pushed the food around on his plate without taking a bite.

A booming voice sounded at the front of the restaurant, and Talmadge glanced over his shoulder. Joe greeted Sheriff Lawson with a handshake and a bear hug. Funny to watch two large, intimidating men hug each other. It's what Talmadge had always loved about his uncle. His heart was as big as his girth, and he wasn't afraid to show it. Same as Bea. And that made Talmadge's heart ache all the more, because he'd run from Red River and his problems. Repaid his grandparents' love and support by running away instead of standing fast and being there for them the way they'd been there for him.

Joe pointed in Talmadge's direction, and the two formidable figures lumbered over. Joe had an iPad in his hand. Talmadge's stomach did a flip, instinct gnawing at his insides.

"Talmadge." Sheriff Lawson greeted him and slid into the opposite seat. Uncle Joe took the seat next to Talmadge, and he scooted against the wall. The two boxed him in.

"What's this about?" Talmadge blurted. He was already under enough pressure with the mess back in Washington, and because Miranda had made it clear she didn't want him around anymore. Might as well get this over with as quickly as possible, because he couldn't take much more.

"Have you seen the latest post in that smut column?" Uncle Joe said.

Talmadge shook his head. "I've had a lot going on. Haven't kept up with the rumor mill."

Uncle Joe flipped the cover off his iPad and brought up the *Red River Rag*. He laid it in front of Talmadge. "I'd know that spot in the cemetery in any picture. You were at your momma and daddy's grave."

Talmadge's brows drew together. Why was visiting his parents' grave important enough to call a meeting with the sheriff? His irritation level spiked. His parents weren't a topic he liked to discuss with anyone, and today the subject had already run its course.

"You know your grandma and I were close. She was like a second mom to me," Joe said. "Just like she was to you."

Talmadge scrubbed a hand over his jaw. "Look, this subject doesn't make me feel all warm and fuzzy, so can we get to the point?"

"Bea told me that she suspected you blamed yourself for your parents' accident."

Talmadge's spine went stiff. How did she know? He'd never admitted it to anyone. "Why did she think that?"

Joe gave his head a shake, a smile of admiration on his lips. "She was one sharp cookie and good at reading people. I guess she had her reasons."

"When your uncle here saw this picture"—Sheriff Lawson pointed to the iPad—"he asked me to speak to you." The sheriff lowered his voice so no one could hear. "Son, I'm about to tell you something that we've managed to keep a secret since the accident. I've always followed the letter of the law, but I made an exception for Bea and your uncle that one time."

"Get to it, gentlemen." Talmadge's voice had dropped to a low simmer.

Sheriff Lawson looked around like he was afraid someone else might hear. Then he leaned in. "Your dad had five times the legal amount of alcohol in his system when the accident happened."

Talmadge was stunned. He'd known his dad drank too much, but he had no idea his dad was that drunk the day he and his mom died. Since the day it happened, Talmadge thought the accident was because his dad was angry over Talmadge striking out and losing the game.

Joe scratched his temple and shook his head. "Bea had nightmares for years about you being in the car with them that day."

"She did?" Talmadge never knew. But that was Bea, always trying to protect him.

"Yep, she did. And she was always torn about telling you the truth about your dad's alcohol level. She wasn't sure if it would alleviate your misplaced guilt, or make you more resentful toward him."

"When I saw the photo," Joe said, "I knew it was time for you to know the truth."

Talmadge leaned back against the booth with a thud. He'd carried the burden of the accident on his shoulders long enough. The painfulness of the memories had eased since he'd been spending so much time with Miranda, but all of a sudden, being back in Red River didn't seem in the least bit suffocating anymore.

Too bad he still had to leave. He would fly to Seattle, make the pitch, and hop the next plane back to New Mexico.

But not before beating down Miranda's door and begging her to forgive him first.

---

Miranda waited down the street until Talmadge's truck pulled away. Then she parked behind Al's Plumbing and Septic Removal and walked to Joe's to meet Lorenda for dinner, and hopefully get her mind off Talmadge for a while. Jamie walked past with a tray of food and winked at her. "Lorenda's in the back corner."

Before Miranda could ask him why he was waiting tables instead of washing dishes, a table of patrons called her name. Then another. Everyone at Joe's congratulated her on the festival, said they couldn't wait, told her she was doing a great job, they were proud of her, she was going to be a fine business owner. They didn't just look at her as the best damn waitress in town. Respect showed in their expressions and their greetings and their handshakes.

And no matter how much her heart ached because of Talmadge's betrayal, Miranda knew she'd be just fine on her own. Somehow. Sure, her heart thudded in a sick rhythm because of losing the man she'd loved for seven years. Seven years, four months, and eighteen days. But she'd move on. Move forward.

Even if she doubted she'd ever love anyone as much as she loved Talmadge. And she'd never settle for less.

"Hey, girlfriend," Lorenda said as Miranda slid into the opposite side of the booth. Her BFF tried to sound cheery. "Everything set and ready?"

"Sure." Miranda wrinkled her nose. "Ready." Except her heart was going to explode all over Joe's.

Lorenda handed over her phone, the *Red River Rag* pulled up on the screen.

*Is it over for Red River's favorite lovebirds? Or does their relationship have one foot in the grave? Arguing in a cemetery can't be a good sign.* Under the caption was a picture of Miranda backing away from Talmadge, his parents' grave markers in the background.

"I only read this thing for laughs, but is there any truth to this?" Lorenda asked.

Of course it was over. How could it be anything *but* over? "So over."

"Are you okay?" Lorenda gave her an affectionate smile.

"Do I look okay?" Miranda raised a brow.

"Actually, you do. That's what has me worried. My guess is you're putting on a brave front, but inside you're not as okay as you want everyone to think."

Lorenda knew her so well.

Jamie came over and pulled out a pen and paper. "I'm your waiter. I got a promotion from washing dishes, so the tips will help with tuition next fall." He smiled at her, proud of himself. It gave her heart a little tug, and she realized how she'd been hanging on, not wanting him to face the painfulness of real life the way she had. But he wanted to grow up, and she needed to let him.

"Congratulations, little bro."

Lorenda ordered, then Miranda rattled off an order a mile long.

"Stress eating?" Jamie teased her.

"Yep," she said. "And don't pretend to write all that down. I know you have a memory like an elephant."

He flashed a brilliant smile at her. "I can remember every order in the room. Just like you." He slapped the order pad against his palm. "The pen and paper is just for show. I'll get your drinks." He walked to the bar, but not without taking orders from two more tables without writing a single thing down.

Clydelle and Francine waddled over. Clydelle leaned on her cane. "Instead of sittin' around here, you should be huntin' down your man," she said to Miranda. "He needs a shoulder to lean on right now."

*He* needs a shoulder? With her phone under the table so Clydelle and Francine couldn't see it, Miranda typed a text message to Lorenda.

Plz make it stop.

When Lorenda's phone dinged, she read the text and gave Miranda a helpless look.

Francine clutched her enormous purse that looked as though she carried half of Fort Knox in it. "Maybe gussy yourself up. Wear something sexy to cheer him up. Used to work for my Henry until . . ." Francine blushed through the layers of wrinkles. "Well, Henry died with nothing but his boots and a smile on. He might've lived a few more years if I hadn't ordered that new outfit from Frederick's."

Was it Miranda's imagination or did an eighty-five-year-old woman just tell her that her elderly husband died because of kinky sex?

She fired another message off to Lorenda.

    I'll give you a kidney if you make it stop.

Lorenda read the text and snorted, then cleared her throat and smiled up at the two old women. They eyed Lorenda and Miranda suspiciously.

"We're just saying," Clydelle said, "that man of yours is a hunk." She looked off into space as though she were fantasizing.

Miranda shot a glare at her BFF. Lorenda chuckled, eased her phone under the table, and sent her a text.

    Every gal for herself.

Miranda narrowed her eyes at Lorenda, who smirked, clearly enjoying the show.

"Don't let go of him so easy," Francine said. "Try more makeup, and maybe order something from Frederick's, only stay away from the pasties and anything in black leather." She tapped her chin. "You never know if there might be a genetic heart problem that runs in the family." She shook her head thoughtfully.

"Um, okay. Thanks for the tip." Under the table she fired off another text to Lorenda.

```
Can we go home now so I can cry?
```

"You're welcome." Clydelle looked completely satisfied with herself until she turned a scolding tone on Lorenda. "When are you gonna find a man? You're too pretty to sit around this town growing old alone. What's wrong with you? You got a third nipple or something?"

Lorenda sputtered, and Miranda typed another text.

```
I could've gone my whole life without hearing
about your third nipple.
```

Lorenda tried to keep a pleasant look on her beet-red face while she glanced at her phone under the table and typed back.

```
I do not have a third nipple!!!!!!!
```

Miranda typed back while Clydelle and Francine gave Lorenda pointers on how to snag a man.

```
Now you do.
```

The way gossip flowed in this town, by tomorrow Lorenda would have to strip naked in the town square to prove that she didn't.

Lorenda said something incoherent to Clydelle while typing at the same time.

```
Help!!!!!
```

Miranda smirked and typed.

```
What happened to every gal for herself?
You're on your own. I'm going to the john.
```

Miranda slid from her seat, ignoring Lorenda's explosive glare. But before she could excuse herself, Clydelle's cane slipped, and she tumbled into Francine, whose purse flew out of her hand, the contents scattering across the floor at Miranda's feet.

The four of them froze, because one of the items protruding from Francine's purse was the tip of a very large, very heavy telephoto lens.

Miranda's head shot up, eyes narrowing at Francine. "It's *you*."

"You two should be ashamed," said Lorenda.

At least Francine looked contrite. "I admit to nothing."

"Really?" Miranda's hands went to her hips. "Then how about I announce this little discovery to everyone here?"

"I like to take wildlife photographs," Francine said.

"And I like to write about them," Clydelle countered.

"So you took the pictures," Lorenda said to Francine before turning her glare on Clydelle, "and you wrote the posts."

Miranda stooped to stuff the evidence back into Francine's purse along with a tube of lipstick, a bottle of geriatric vitamins, and a . . . *bottle of lubricant?* She almost threw up in her mouth.

She stood and handed the purse back to Francine. "If you don't shut that blog down immediately, I'm going to tell everyone in this town what you've done, and you'll never get a ride in the senior center van again."

"Dear, the senior center van driver showed us how to use Tumblr." Clydelle looked proud of herself.

"Then I'll tell the fire department to wash the truck during your weekly pinochle game so you can't watch. Especially on a hot day." Miranda put both hands on her hips.

Both of the old ladies gasped.

"We were just trying to get you and Talmadge together," Clydelle said. "You should be thanking us."

Right. Because that worked out so well.

"And you were going to be our next project," Francine said to Lorenda. "We were waiting for the right man to come along."

"Oh no." Lorenda shook her head. "I'm no one's project. I've got two boys to raise, and that's not exactly a hunk magnet."

Both old ladies harrumphed.

"I mean it, ladies," Miranda warned. "Your Tumblr days are over. Are we clear?"

Clydelle and Francine both hesitated until Miranda put two fingers in between her lips like she was going to whistle to get everyone's attention and make an announcement.

"Oh, all right," both old women huffed at the same time.

"But our matchmaking is better than online dating," Clydelle said. "The men only want a booty call. Trust us, we know."

Both Miranda and Lorenda's jaws fell open.

"They're dishonest on their profiles, the pictures they send of their junk aren't usually real, and when they get what they want, they disappear," said Francine.

And well, Miranda couldn't argue with that, because they had a point. But pictures of their junk? Miranda's hand covered her mouth, and she fought off a gag.

"All we're saying is, that hunk of a man we spent so much time throwing in your direction is about to leave town, and you need to do something to stop him," said Clydelle.

Miranda let her brows snap together. "What are you talking about?"

Clydelle leaned on her cane. "A few minutes ago a story broke in Seattle." She puffed up like she was proud of herself. "I've been monitoring the news up there since Talmadge was one of my matchmaking persons of interest."

Miranda crossed both arms over her chest and leveled a stare at Clydelle.

Clydelle cleared her throat. "Well, anyway, this reporter . . . I think her name is Fran . . . no, Faye . . ."

"Frankie," Francine interjected. "Frankie Burns." She gave Miranda an I'm-so-pleased-with-myself look. "I remember because her first name is so close to mine."

"Who cares what her name is!" Miranda couldn't take it anymore.

Francine gave her an offended scoff. "No need to get testy, dear."

"You two are the ones sneaking around, taking pictures through windows, and invading my privacy." She put her fingers in her mouth again and let a sharp whistle rip through the room. Everyone in Joe's turned to them. Lowering her voice, she gave Clydelle and Francine a thin smile. "Tell me now, or I'm outing you both."

"Okay," Clydelle hissed.

Miranda looked around the cavernous room. "Just wanted to let you all know the dancing will start soon."

Everyone nodded a thanks and went back to their meals.

Miranda tapped her foot.

"Well, Talmadge has to be back in Seattle right away to present his Trinity Falls plan to the tribal councils up there. It's such a big deal, some national stations are even picking up the story."

So he was leaving. Before the gazebo was unveiled and the inn was open. The inspector wouldn't hand down his verdict for several days, but maybe just having the inspections completed was enough to get his money.

Breaking his promise and leaving now that he'd gotten what he wanted shouldn't surprise her. She'd seen it a million times while her mother played musical boyfriends.

And even though Miranda knew she'd get through it, it didn't stop the room from spinning. It didn't stop her world from tilting, like it would never be set right. And it didn't stop her heart from completely shattering into so many pieces that it could never be fully put back together again.

# Chapter Twenty-Two

Well, hell. Manning up was proving to be much more difficult than Talmadge thought it would be. He drove to the inn after leaving Joe's, but Miranda wasn't there. He tried Lorenda's, but no luck. Jamie wouldn't answer his phone. No big surprise. Langston was working a shift on the helo and wouldn't be off for a few more hours.

He drove past Joe's to look for Miranda's Jeep and even pulled through the back parking lot, but nothing. So he went to Bea's and walked Lloyd. Then sat down on the sofa for a few minutes with Lloyd curled in his lap. "Sorry, dude." He scratched Lloyd's head. "I screwed up."

Lloyd let out a sleepy sigh.

Talmadge leaned his head back against the sofa and closed his weary eyes. Saying he'd screwed up with Miranda was like saying Lloyd wasn't prissy. Talmadge was tired. So damn tired that he wanted to fall asleep right there on Bea's sofa with Lloyd and stay there for a month.

Or forever.

The thought startled him.

Forever in Red River sounded right. A hell of a lot more right than going back to Washington. But it only seemed right if Miranda was with him, as in with him forever.

A call came in on his phone, and Ellen's number popped up. He answered it. "It's after hours. Shouldn't you be knitting?"

"Nah," she said. "I do enough of that *during* office hours."

He laughed.

"Glad to hear you'll be back in Washington to do the presentation."

Wait. He hadn't told anyone he was coming back to Seattle specifically because he wanted to keep it quiet. He'd hurt Miranda enough. He wanted to tell her in person. If he could ever find her.

"How did you know about my travel plans?"

"Um, it's all over the news. Your stalker-reporter broke the story today. The investors made a public announcement that you've come up with a brilliant plan to save Trinity Falls and preserve the ruins at the same time."

*Shit.* His damn investors were so busy trying to get their names in the papers that they'd done exactly what he'd asked them not to do.

"Does this mean we'll have actual work to do around here again?" Ellen said.

Talmadge wasn't sure what it meant. He didn't see himself living in Washington anymore. He couldn't see himself living in Red River unless Miranda was part of his life. And since he was pretty sure the temperature in hell hadn't dropped below freezing, he wasn't going to count on Miranda forgiving him, whether he manned up or not.

"I haven't figured everything out yet," Talmadge said.

"Anything you want done around here before your big return to the real world?" Ellen asked. "Because the knit-and-purl thing is getting boring. If you don't give me some real work soon, I'll have to take up origami. Or underwater basket weaving."

"There is something you can do," Talmadge said, changing the subject. "Have a shuttle ready to take me back to the airport as soon as the presentation is over and get me a ticket on the next flight back to New Mexico. I've got some unfinished business here that's more important than Trinity Falls."

"You got it, boss, but I didn't think there was anything more important to you than Trinity Falls."

He wouldn't have thought so either just six weeks ago.

Another call beeped in. Maybe it was Miranda. "Gotta go," he said to Ellen and answered the other call without looking at the number.

"Talmadge, it's Larry. Looks like that reporter has snooped around enough to find out what you've been doing back in your hometown. She's about to write up another story about your little projects in Red River while Trinity Falls has been sitting here neglected."

*Shit.*

"The investors are going nuts," Larry said. "Get back here on the double."

He pulled in a breath. "Okay. Let me change my ticket."

"No need. The investors have a chartered plane waiting for you at the commuter airport in Taos. If you're not on it in two hours, they're pulling out."

So Talmadge was gone. And she hadn't heard a word from him since they left the cemetery.

Okay, so that wasn't totally true. He'd left plenty of messages, none of which she'd bothered to listen to, because she didn't want to hear any of his excuses. By the time she was fifteen, she'd heard them all from her mother's boyfriends.

To give her mom some credit, she might have finally grown up. She'd stopped by the inn yesterday to show off both Ted and the wedding ring he'd given her when they'd gotten married two days ago. They'd called in some favors at the biker bar where they'd met and had another entry for the parade. And what do you know, but Ted had found gainful employment at a lumberyard, moved them into a better house, and even offered to help with Miranda's renovations. Nice as that was, Miranda declined. She'd accepted enough help from men for one lifetime. But she was happy for her mom, because Ted actually seemed like a nice, sincere guy.

Then again, what would Miranda know about sincere guys?

Taking a rare break from her responsibilities, she slept in that morning. By eleven thirty she was still in her pajamas, relaxing on the sofa. She punched the button on the television remote and hugged a box of chocolates to her chest like it was her lifeline.

Did people really need to go on a talk show to figure out who the baby's daddy was? She stuffed another chocolate truffle into her mouth.

Someone knocked on the door.

Maybe if she ignored it, they'd go away. She swallowed a mouthful of chocolate and popped in another. Mmm. She closed her eyes and savored the rich flavor.

The knock escalated to a bang.

*Still ignoring it.* Even with her mom and Ted's entry, she was still two entries short. Before she went to the last committee meeting she wanted a few more hours to herself to process the failure. Or another bag of chocolate. Whichever came first. Whoever was at the door could bite her.

How silly had she been, letting herself get in so deep with Talmadge? Yet she couldn't give up on life either, just because a man had walked out on her. Her entire life had been about survival. She'd survive this too. How, she wasn't sure yet. That's what she had to figure out.

Plus, she was kinda liking the pity-party she was throwing for herself. So who the hell was trying to interrupt it?

She jumped when Lorenda's voice yelled through the door "Open up!"

With a huff, Miranda threw off the crocheted blanket and stomped to the door. She flicked the latch and opened it. "I'm not home," she said to the mommy mafia standing there to greet her.

"We brought more comfort food." Ella held up a bag from the market, Ben and Jerry's showing through the plastic bag.

She waved them in and plopped back on the sofa.

Ella opened the pints of ice cream, pulled out four plastic spoons, and distributed the precious remedy that could heal just about anything. Except a broken heart.

They took seats around her like the mother hens they were. "So how are you?" Angelique asked, licking her spoon.

"Well, let's see." Miranda tapped a finger to her chin. "I've been sleeping with someone who lied to me, left town, and broke his promise. My savings are gone, and the inspectors still haven't given my inn a certificate to open." A sting started behind her eyes. "Oh, and I forgot that I've got to show up to the most important community event of the year and probably cancel it because there's not enough parade entries to satisfy the stupid bylaws that no one even knew existed."

She threw her arms wide and pasted on a dazzling smile. "I'd say my life is pretty grand." She dove into her pint again. "You guys are jealous. Admit it."

Lorenda's eyes dropped to a spot on Miranda's chest, and she looked down too. A chocolate stain soaked into her pajama shirt along with cherry soda. Lorenda gave her a sympathetic smile, and they all shoveled in another bite of B & J. "You guys are real friends, you know. You let me feel sorry for myself, and you're even joining in."

"We've all been there," Lorenda said, and the rest of the mommy mafia nodded, chirping agreement while they sucked down ice cream.

"I'll buy the chocolate until you feel better," said Ella.

"I'll provide the ice cream." Angelique held up her spoon.

"And I'll take you shopping for new jeans, if yours don't fit by the time you're over him," Lorenda offered.

"Deal, because I'm broke." Miranda dug out another mouthful of ice cream. "Unless I open soon, I'll have to ask Joe for my old job back." Considering Joe's staffing problems, the whole town would probably love it if she went back to being the best damn waitress in town. Yay for her. She was so proud.

"Even though Talmadge lied to you," Angelique said as she swallowed and leaned back in one of Bea's old recliners, "at least he gave up his inheritance willingly by telling you about Bea's terms in the end."

Miranda stilled, the wad of ice cream freezing her tongue. "Beg your pardon?" She stared at Angelique.

Angelique's eyes rounded, like she'd just made a mistake. "I thought you knew," she said with a mouthful of Cherry Garcia. Which came out more like, "I aught oo noo." She swallowed. "Talmadge said he told you."

Miranda sat up. "Told me what exactly?" At the cemetery he said he could inherit the money once the inn opened. "Are you saying that he couldn't inherit unless he kept the money a secret?"

"Um," she said, and gave her an oh-shit look. "It's confidential. I only mentioned it because I thought Talmadge had filled you in."

Apparently, he hadn't filled her in on everything. And she wanted answers. She stared down Angelique. No easy task since Angelique was the most alpha female on the planet. But Angelique caved, probably because she'd had her trials and tribulations too, until she and Doc Holloway finally worked things out.

"Look, I can't tell you everything. It's unethical," Angelique said. "Maybe he did lie to you. He's human, and he made a mistake." She set her ice cream on the coffee table and laced her fingers. "All I can say is that he was in a tough spot because of Bea's will." Angelique gave her a sly smile, her killer instincts shining through. "So make a donation to the Drill Baby Drill movement in his name if you want to get back at him, but at least hear him out."

There was just one problem with Angelique's grand relationship advice. Talmadge had still left and broken his promise.

"And don't forget, you still have a festival to put on. You can't let Old Lady Wilkinson win," Lorenda said. "Langston's trying to switch shifts with another flight medic so he can enter his Mustang into the parade."

Langston's car, her mom's biker friends, plus the senior center van— those would all help. But she was still one entry short.

She sat there for a second, torn between wanting to hole up in isolation for the next decade and wanting to show everyone, including Talmadge Oaks, that she might get knocked down, but she'd always get up again.

So she made a decision, set her ice cream on the coffee table. And she got up.

# Chapter Twenty-Three

Miranda stood at the base of the announcer's stand a few minutes before the parade was supposed to start. The park was teeming, and Main Street was already lined four-deep on both sides for the parade. And seeing as how Mrs. Wilkinson had been accommodating enough to finally produce the bylaws and prove that twenty parade entries was indeed the magic number, the mayor and Mrs. Wilkinson's son had blocked Main Street with their cars to stop the parade from starting until the final count was in. Unfortunately, Miranda was still one entry short.

She tapped her pen against the clipboard in her hand.

She sighed. She'd failed as a leader in the community and at having her dream, because the inspectors still hadn't given their approval, and that wasn't a good sign. Joe said it didn't usually take that long. And if the inspectors wanted changes to the inn before they'd let her open for business, she was out of luck and out of money.

Worst of all, she'd failed at love.

She'd finally listened to Talmadge's messages, all of them saying he was sorry and promising he'd be back to talk to her face-to-face. Well, to heck with his promises. He'd already broken two very important ones. His track record on keeping promises already sucked, so she hadn't answered any of his one million and one calls, texts, or messages. She had enough problems here to deal with at the moment.

A crew set up amplifiers and musical equipment inside the finished gazebo where Joe had arranged for a band to play. They worked behind a canopy that covered the gazebo from public view, so it would be a big reveal to the whole town at once.

She checked her phone to see if anyone had texted in a new entry. But no, nothing. Her heart sank.

As if on cue, Mrs. Wilkinson strutted across the park and stood in front of Miranda. Joe must've seen her coming because he started in their direction.

"So how many entries do you have for the parade?" Mrs. Wilkinson gave her a grand smile, knowing she'd won the war.

Miranda's tapping got louder. "Nineteen," she ground out.

"Still not enough," said Mrs. Wilkinson triumphantly. "Do you want to make the announcement that the festival is canceled or should I?"

Joe walked up, his cell to his ear. "I have another entry." He held the phone away to speak. "Just getting the word now."

Mrs. Wilkinson's face soured like spoiled milk.

"Who?" Miranda held her pen ready to scribble the name at the bottom of the list.

"Who should I say is entering?" Joe said to the caller. He listened, then ended the call. "Bob. He's entering a classic car, model unspecified. He's en route, so he said to put him last in the lineup." Joe turned to Mrs. Wilkinson. "So I guess the show goes on. Why don't you go find a place to stand?"

"She's still a hussy!" Mrs. Wilkinson wagged her finger at Miranda.

"Look," Miranda said. "I don't know what I've done to make you dislike me so much, but there's enough room in this town for both of us. I'm not leaving, no matter how hard you make it for me, so we might as well find a way to get along."

Mrs. Wilkinson pursed her lips.

Miranda dug deep and tried to be the leader Bea would've wanted. "During the parade I plan to announce Red River's gratitude for all you do in the community." Miranda motioned to a roped-off area to the side of the announcer's stand. "I'd be honored if you'd sit in the spectators' box for our special guests."

She waited for Mrs. Wilkinson's answer. It took a lot of courage to forgive someone who had hurt you, but an invisible load seemed to lift from Miranda's shoulders. Then she thought of Talmadge, and it shook her. Because she loved him, and unconditional love meant forgiving people when they made a mistake. He'd done so much to help her, and yes, it was crummy that he had lied. But he had tried to make it right. Except for the leaving and breaking promises part.

"Well," Mrs. Wilkinson sniffed. "If you insist."

Joe gave Miranda a respectful nod and escorted Mrs. Wilkinson over to the box.

Miranda sagged against the announcer's stand. Now if she could just get through this day without crying into the microphone, she just might make it.

Because the one person she wanted to be here the most was absent. She drew in a deep, cleansing breath and stared up at the blue sky and the mountains, still tinged with snow at the top, but with the lush greenness of early summer foliage washing down the slopes. So perfect. So gorgeous. Like a painting, not like something you'd see in real life.

She loved this town. And she loved Talmadge. If she could forgive Mrs. Wilkinson, then why couldn't she have found it in her heart to listen to Talmadge before he left?

The cars, trucks, motorcycles, and floats lined up and waiting as far as Miranda could see down Main Street started to honk.

"You ready to get started?" Joe said.

She nodded, climbed the stand, and put on the microphone headset.

"Um." Her voice rang out over the crowd. Oh. Okay. That was really loud. "Welcome to this year's Hot Rides and Cool Nights Festival."

The crowd cheered.

When she thanked Mrs. Wilkinson a few jeers rang out, so she quickly moved on and announced the first parade entry. The quicker the parade was over, the sooner the festival could get underway, and Miranda could make a much overdue call to Seattle.

So what if Talmadge got two speeding tickets trying to get to Red River in time for the festival? When he flew into the commuter airport in Taos with Lloyd and the rental car agency didn't have any cars left, he thought he might have to hitch a ride all the way to Red River. He finally flagged down a gangbanger with a bandana tied around his head and a tattoo down his arm that said, "Be my bitch for twenty-five to life," and exchanged his credit card cash advance limit for the kid's low-riding, tricked out car that bounced to the rap tune "One Minute Man."

Whatever worked. He was back in New Mexico and on his way to the woman he couldn't live without. Now if he could just get there before the festival started so he wouldn't break his promise, maybe she'd listen and give him another chance.

And Rome was built in a day.

He shook off the odds of all those things happening.

He sniffed under one arm. Of course he was kind of rank now, seeing as how the car only had a *two/eighty* air conditioner—so he rolled down *two* windows and did *eighty*. Which the county sheriffs hadn't seemed to appreciate.

A 1960-ish step-side truck with an open bed full of cow manure passed, blowing a layer of it into his window. Talmadge gagged. Lloyd hid his nose under both paws. He swiped specks of cow dung from his face.

"Come on, Lloyd. We can do this." He reached over and gave the dog a scratch. Lloyd barked.

He couldn't lose someone else he loved. He'd lost his parents and his grandparents while hiding behind shame and regret, which had driven him to go out and try to save the world. He couldn't lose Miranda too. Because she *was* his world.

He just hoped he wasn't too late.

---

Miranda's face hurt from the fake smile she kept on her lips as she announced the tenth entry in the parade lineup. Standing on the podium, she had what she'd wanted for so long. Respectability in the community. At least that's what she'd thought she wanted.

Turned out she'd been wrong. She wanted Talmadge, and this whole ordeal had taught her not to care too much about what people thought. They could take her the way she was or not at all.

Ten more to go and she could call him. She'd listened to his recorded apologies—all of them—but she had a lot of apologizing to do herself. All he'd done was try to help her. Try to love her. And she'd been so selfish that she couldn't even accept his apology. Or the fact that he'd made a human mistake. She still didn't like the broken promises part, but he had problems too. Problems just as big as hers back in Washington. And she hadn't been too sympathetic to that.

What if he didn't come back, because she hadn't given him a reason to?

As the senior center's van rolled forward, filled with a load of silver-haired women dressed in red hats and purple boas, Miranda smiled. Before the next float was up, she said to the crowd, "When the parade is over, folks, don't miss out on the vendors set up here in the park." She flipped a page on her clipboard. "Cotton Eyed Joe's has arranged live music in the gazebo, which we'll unveil and dedicate while you all enjoy food and spirits from our local restaurants." She waved a hand across the rows of booths behind her.

The band of bikers dressed in leather jackets and bandanas roared down Main Street, her mother and Ted in the lead. Her mom waved. So did Miranda, and a flash of wetness sprang to her eyes. Her mom had finally come through.

And check. Another person Miranda could forgive. Just like that. So much easier than she'd thought.

A few more entries rolled by, and finally Miranda could see the end of the line down Main Street. She lifted her hand to shield her eyes from the sun. She didn't recognize the last car in line, the mystery entry. She squinted to see. And . . . every few minutes it . . . bounced.

Entries eighteen and nineteen rolled by, and then the last entry was up.

"Next we have . . ." She looked at her clipboard. "Bob."

The low-riding car at the end of the line bounced again, lime green no less, and it rolled forward. A message was scrawled across the front windshield in shoe polish that said, "I love you."

A head dipped, and she caught a glimpse of a chiseled jawline and sandy blond hair, and then the driver leaned into the passenger seat to look up at her through the window with silvery-blue eyes. And her mind blanked.

"Tal . . . Talmadge?" she whispered into the microphone.

He nodded up at her and waited.

Her brain and her heart stuttered just like her words. "*Talmadge*, what are you doing?"

His lips moved, but she couldn't hear what he said. Lloyd's head popped up, and he barked at Miranda. The thing Miranda wasn't sure could really be called a car stopped rolling, and Talmadge got out. He was at the base of the podium in a few long strides. "I came back, because I didn't want to break my promise. I damn near had to jump out of a plane to get here, but I'm here."

The breath Miranda sucked in echoed through the amplifier. She blinked back tears.

He came around the back of the podium and climbed the stairs. She tried to calm her racing heart, but it only galloped harder with each step that brought him closer.

"It wasn't just about the money." He kept climbing. "It started that way, but then we built something together. And not just the inn or this gazebo." He motioned behind him to the canopies and tarps. "We built *us*." He reached the top and stood there staring at her. Looking uneasy and uncertain. And so damn sexy that she wanted to run to him.

"I'm sorry I didn't listen when you tried to talk to me." And she was. "I was afraid of it being over between us." She closed her eyes for a second, then looked up at him. "And I was afraid of it not being over, because of how much I depended on you."

"I don't have much to offer you anymore, Miranda." He closed the small distance between them. Didn't touch her, but his closeness wrapped and coiled around her, and something started to unfurl low in her belly. And also in her heart.

"I sold my share in Trinity Falls for a fraction of what it's worth so I could come back here and start over, and Bea's money *is* going to build a rec center." His hair was windblown, face dirty, sleeves rolled up, and his shirt was unbuttoned a little too low in the front because he was sweaty. Her head tilted as her eyes took a trip over the gleaming beads of perspiration on his chest.

"I don't care about your money. I never have." Her voice rolled over the hushed crowd.

"I know." He reached up and brushed a lock of hair off of her face. "That's one of the things Bea loved about you. She obviously saw the woman you were growing into, and she wanted me to finish what she'd started. I think that's why she set her will up the way she did." His gaze raked over Miranda's face. "I resented it when I found out about the terms, but then I realized she wanted me to come home to my roots." He dipped his head to brush her nose with his. "Come home to you." His thumb grazed across her cheek.

A wave of *aww*s zipped down Main Street.

"Tell me the rest about Bea's will." She had to know. Everything this time. And she wanted to know that he could tell her the truth.

He looked at the sky for a second. "The terms and the money were to be kept a secret." He ran his hand down Miranda's arm, and a zing of desire threaded through her. "At first I couldn't figure out why. But now I realize she didn't want me to miss out on the best thing that could ever happen to me—a future with you." He caressed up her arm again, and the rest of her body took notice. "If she'd lived longer than it took you to finish the inn, she probably would've kept changing her will with new ways to throw us together." He chuckled. His lips were just a breath away from hers. "I love you."

Her eyes stung. "I've loved you for seven years."

"Then give me the chance to love you for a lifetime." He smoothed a finger across her cheek. "Marry me."

Her eyes closed against his touch.

This time the *aww*s were like a tidal wave rippling through the crowd. His words also rippled through Miranda's heart, and she stepped into his arms.

Clydelle had somehow appeared at the bottom of the podium next to Joe, and she tapped it with her cane. "Say yes, dear, or I'll take him up on that offer."

A smile spread across her face so big her cheeks hurt, and she nodded. "Yes."

"Um." He gently tugged the headset off of her head. "I'd like to kiss you without the sound echoing across the state."

He did kiss her, long and deep and so, so sweet. And all Miranda could think about was spending the rest of her life drowning in Talmadge's beautiful eyes and his lovely smile.

When they came up for air, she sniffed the air. What was that smell?

"Uh, sorry. Lloyd and I had an unfortunate run-in with some cow manure."

Miranda laughed. "I'm glad you didn't let that stop you."

Lloyd barked again from the passenger seat.

Talmadge's embrace tightened around her. "Uncle Joe, did you get that surprise taken care of for me?"

"Sure did." Joe took off his cowboy hat and waved toward the gazebo.

Someone pulled a cord, collapsing the tarps that had been blocking the gazebo. The band took their places and struck up a tune.

Miranda's hand flew to her mouth as they started to play "Old Time Rock and Roll."

"I still have to fly back to Trinity Falls once in a while as a consultant." He looked down at her. "It was the only way I could get the investors to buy me out and the tribal councils to sign off."

She threaded her arms around his neck. "I don't care, as long as you always come back to me."

He kissed her then. Soft and gentle. And then he said, "Always." He nipped at her lip. "I promise."

# Chapter Twenty-Four

"What can I do to help?" Miranda asked the mommy mafia. She straightened the framed certificate of business hanging on the wall in the inn's newly remodeled kitchen and smoothed the skirt of Bea's antique wedding dress, which had been altered to perfection. When Talmadge found it in Bea's attic nicely boxed and preserved, Miranda hadn't thought twice about wearing it.

"It's your wedding day," Lorenda said, refilling the punch bowl. "Enjoy it."

"You'll be working plenty next week, when you open for business." Ella hurried past into the dining room where she placed elegant paper napkins on the table around Joe's catered spread of food—his wedding gift to her and Talmadge.

"Yep," Angelique agreed and arranged cups around the punch bowl. "I looked at the website Jamie designed. You're already booked solid through the summer, so my obnoxious Italian relatives are coming into town for Thanksgiving instead and have rented the entire place out."

Yes, the home show episode Talmadge arranged had the reservations flooding in.

"My obnoxious Texan family has dibs on Christmas." Ella laughed.

Miranda sniffed the flowery scent of her bouquet of yellow roses as she searched the reception crowd for Talmadge. He stood at the stone fireplace, chatting with Jamie, who'd been his best man when they exchanged vows under the gazebo an hour ago. They both looked so handsome in their tuxedos, and Miranda's eyes grew a little wet.

The key to the city hung just over Talmadge's head on the mantle, Beatrice Oaks's name engraved on it. With a hand in one pocket and his tux jacket hanging open, he leaned an elbow on the mantle. He looked just as handsome, just as sexy, just as enticing as he had seven years ago at a different wedding wearing a tux. She'd picked him that night, and today he was finally hers. A good thing, since she'd been his from that night on and always would be.

As if he sensed her staring at him, his gaze found her, and he smiled. Big. Bright. Beautiful. And her heart expanded.

She loved that full-on smile. It touched her soul like nothing else she'd ever experienced.

She made her way through the crowd, with a lot of congratulations along the way, and a big hug from her mom and Ted. Finally Miranda reached Talmadge. He pulled her into the crook of his arm and smiled down at her with those beautiful blue eyes.

"Hi," he whispered.

"Hi," she whispered back.

Jamie rolled his eyes. "Get a room, you two."

Oh, she planned for them to get a room as soon as the reception was over. The honeymoon suite, in fact. The very reason she'd chosen to delay the grand opening of the inn, fondly named the Bea in the Bonnet Inn, another week. She wanted her and Talmadge to have the place to themselves, because . . . well, they were going to make good use of *every* room before they both had to start back to work.

"Do I know you?" She gave her little brother a curious look.

"Yeah." He unknotted his tie and let it hang loose. "I'm the one who sucks all the money out of your bank account for tuition." He looked into the dining room. "Speaking of, I'm only here for the free food." He walked off.

Talmadge laced both arms around her waist and pulled her into an embrace. "You are so beautiful today. I wish Bea could see you in her dress."

Miranda wished Bea could too.

"You ready for the rest of our lives?" he asked.

Bea had told Miranda to reach for the stars, and she'd managed to catch a few. Her dream of being her own boss, her dream of being a respected leader in the community, her dream of Talmadge loving her as much as she loved him. Tears welled in her eyes. "It's all so new, so different." So unexpected, and so very, very wonderful. "I feel like I'm jumping off a cliff. In a good way, but still plunging over this unknown mountain and you've agreed to follow me over." Talmadge had stayed in Red River, starting a small green architectural firm in one of the office spaces in Red River's historic business district, where he planned to focus on smaller jobs and stay close to home. He already had the Red River Independent School District and the owners of the historic buildings on Main Street lined up as clients. But he'd moved back for her too, so she wouldn't have to leave her dream.

He laughed and nuzzled her neck. "Well, someone has to bring the parachutes."

She laughed. "Where's Lloyd?"

He yipped when Miranda said his name, and Talmadge moved a step. Lloyd sat on the hearth in a small bed with rails that boxed him in. Talmadge shrugged. "I built this contraption because I don't want him to get stepped on, and I can't carry him around all the time. He's getting kind of spoiled."

She slid a hand inside Talmadge's jacket and smoothed her fingers over his chest. Purple flared in his eyes.

Clydelle and Francine walked over, interrupting Miranda and Talmadge's silent, sensual communication.

"What are you two going to do for entertainment now that the *Red River Rag* has disappeared?" Talmadge teased. Miranda had filled him in on who was responsible for the blog.

"I'm starting a strip pinochle night at the senior center. Co-ed, of course." Francine waggled her brows, and come to think of it, her purse looked substantially lighter. When Talmadge frowned, she said, "Don't judge me." They lumbered off to cause trouble with Langston and a few young members of the Red River Fire Department.

"So can we sneak upstairs soon?" She batted her eyes at him. "I have something I want to show you."

That purple in his eyes was back, and her heart skipped.

"Give me a hint?"

She toyed with a button on his shirt. "Since you seemed to like seeing my panties so much that day out on the porch, I got a special pair for today." She smiled up at him, loving the lust that blazed in his eyes just for her. She looked around to make sure no one was close enough to hear. "I'm wearing a white, lacy thong." His eyes dilated. "And a matching bustier."

"You're the best wife ever," he growled against her ear, and her insides coiled. Then he looked deep into her eyes, and the love she saw there stole her breath. "I'll love you forever, no matter what life brings. I promise." He brushed her lips with his.

She nodded, her heart so full, so content, that she thought it might burst. "Just keep smiling. That's all I need."

*The End*

# $\mathcal{A}$cknowledgments

I am indebted to Ted Grumblatt for giving me insight into green architecture and for coming up with the solution to Trinity Falls. It was brilliant.

A huge thank-you goes out to Katy Pierce, Fritz Davis, Ron Weathers, Steve Heglund, and the entire town of Red River, New Mexico. While the characters and establishments are formed solely from my imagination, the real people and places of Red River are wonderful.

I am ever grateful to my BFF and partner in crime, Kim Rasmussen. Without her, I wouldn't have nearly as much funny material to write about.

A big thank-you goes to my critique partner, Shelly Chalmers, for helping to breathe life into my stories. I'm so fortunate to know you.

And last but certainly not least, my deepest gratitude to my editors, Kelli Martin and Maria Gomez of Montlake Romance at Amazon Publishing, and Melody Guy, the entire Montlake team, and my agent, Jill Marsal of the Marsal Lyon Literary Agency. You guys are simply maaaaarvelous!

# About the Author

Photo © 2014 Frank Frost Photography

Shelly Alexander is the author of *It's In His Heart* and *It's In His Touch*, part of the Red River Valley series. A 2014 Golden Heart finalist, she grew up traveling the world, earned a bachelor's degree in marketing, and worked in the business world for twenty-five years. With four older brothers, she watched every *Star Trek* episode ever made, joined the softball team instead of ballet class, and played with G.I. Joes while the Barbie Corvette stayed tucked in her closet. When she had three sons of her own, she decided to escape her male-dominated world by reading romance novels and has been hooked ever since. Now, she spends her days writing steamy contemporary romances while tending to an obstinate English bulldog named Lola.

# WITHDRAWN